Not Quite Human

E.E. Warren

Cover Art elements: Canva, VectorStock and Adobe Firefly
Design by Ellie Warren

TABLE OF CONTENTS:

	Prologue	Pg 1
1	What Hides in Shadows	Pg 3
2	Ancient History, Modern Rules	Pg 15
3	Preparing for Life After Death	Pg 25
4	Ancient Beginnings	Pg 33
5	London Calling	Pg 45
6	Of Etiquette and Politics	Pg 53
7	Welcome	Pg 63
8	The Unexpected	Pg 95
9	Betrayed	Pg 125
10	Betrayed Again	Pg 149
11	Tangled Web of Deception	Pg 161
12	Reality Check	Pg 183
13	Fateful Moments	Pg 217
14	Sweet Revenge	Pg 267
15	Bad News	Pg 285
16	A Season in Hell	Pg 327
17	Coming Storm	Pg 365
18	Dead Men, Walking	Pg 407
	Dedications	Pg 447
	Note to the Reader	Pg 449
	Other Books by E.E. Warren	Pg 451
	About the Author	Pg 453

PROLOGUE

Look around you.

Look really closely. Stare a little, even.

Humans have a funny tendency to look away; to not see things that either make them uncomfortable or make little sense. The only things that truly see everything about humanity without looking away are cameras...and vampires.

I said vampires. They don't call themselves that, of course. They are known amongst themselves as the Virehnai.

It's just as well people don't notice when they are around, because if they did, they would be scared shitless. It's not really that there are that many; there are considerably more humans than there are Virehnai. It's that they're...different, in a palpable way if you chance to spend time with one for longer than a few moments.. Much in the way that gazelles get a sense whenever cheetahs are near, we get a sense when Virehnai are near. The only real difference is that a gazelle knows a cheetah is a cheetah, and they do their very best to get the hell out of the way before they become cheetah chow.

Unfortunately for humans, we can look a Virehnai right in the face, get a seriously uncomfortable feeling - and not know why. We see them, and they look like us - only prettier; somehow more - vital. We see them, and despite looking completely human, there's a niggly little feeling that crawls up our spines telling us that we aren't completely - safe. Only we don't know what exactly to call the feeling. The one certainty is that we wouldn't think of labeling them a vampire, and we wouldn't know to call them Virehnai.

The Virehnai prefer it that way. Vampires don't exist, right?

Right???

1

WHAT HIDES IN SHADOWS

Elaina Jacoby rode the elevator up to her floor and her suite of apartments. Her family's company owned this building, along with eight other properties. The building is considered 'mixed use,' as it has offices on the lower fifteen floors, with the upper floors reserved for apartments. Elaina started her ride with several professional types, but at the last stop, she put in her key that allowed her access to the upper floors. She was expecting a guest tonight; her co-worker, good friend, and now tutor, Amalie Bisset. It was going to be a fun evening with a friend, and some pizza, along with some studying. The evening may sound like a normal evening, but the subjects she's studying with Amalie are anything but. She's taking lessons on becoming a Virehnai. In her own mind, she's been humorously referring to them as 'vampire lessons;' The Virehnai don't call themselves that and would probably not think her joke funny. Her friend Amalie looks like she's in college, maybe twenty years old, and Elaina is thirty-two. Elaina looks older, but you'd be wrong. Dead wrong. Amalie is one hundred and thirty-two years old, and not exactly human. In eight weeks, Elaina will join her, and become Virehnai, as well. As deals go, it's a big one.

Elaina, despite having known many Virehnai her entire life, never once expected that she would become one. Her brother was still sore about not getting picked, but she understood why her father, Walter Jacoby, the current Jacoby in Jacoby, Lightner and VanEtters, wanted it for her. Elaina, being made Virehnai and ascending, was her family's chance to sit at 'the big table;' to be players in the game instead of merely trusted underlings. Not that Elaina's dad's not perfectly happy as an underling - it's gotten him everything he ever wanted or desired, and provided for generations of his family into the future. But as is the case, while he never desired to be a Virehn for himself, he wanted it for one of his children. He and his family were wealthy–but not Virehnai-wealthy.

Elaina's great-grandfather immigrated to this country in 1874. Stories abound on her family's 'rags to riches' origins from Italy, and how her family was self-made, and came here with little more than the clothes on their backs, and within fifty years, built a thriving law firm. It's true to a point; but there's so much more that never made it into the newspapers and never will. That her great-grandfather, grandfather and father all shared a secret partner, for instance. A patron. A Virehnai named Michel Robichaux. Like her grandfather and father, she had known Michel all her life. She called him Uncle Michel, and he's always referred to her as his 'niece,' out of simple fondness. He told her to never change that, even after she becomes Virehnai. He liked it. He told her when you've been alive as long as he has, family and connections seem to mean more. It overjoyed him that his newest child would not only share bonds of blood, but actual familial-style love.

Once on her floor, and inside her apartments, Elaina walked through quickly, dropping items and clothing as she went to her bedroom and finally finished undressing. She wanted a hot shower and pizza after a long day at work, and an hour at the gym. She's been upping the amount of exercise she's been getting, because she's been eating literally everything she loves, knowing that soon she'll be consuming blood instead. That was some of what she and Amalie covered first. Blood will be the only nutritious food source that her body could handle once she's Virehnai. If she were at a function and the act of 'not eating' would 'out' her, she can have something small and nibble at it, but it WILL make her sick later.

"Define sick." Elaina asked. Best to know your limits, right?

Amalie looked at her that day and shook her head. "Heads and tails. It's NOT pleasant, but everybody does it at least once.

Remember; I warned you…heads and tails. I reserve the right to tell you 'I told you so,' and laugh my ass off at you."

"What about alcohol?"

"Only in tiny amounts, and to fit in. It won't give you a buzz anymore. Drink enough, and you're right back to 'heads and tails.'"

"Really???!"

"Really."

Knowing that; knowing that all her favorites were soon going to be–literally–off the table, she's been enjoying all her favorites. Pizza? Bring it on! A Philly cheese steak, in all its messy goodness? Oh, hells yes! A huge steak, and fries with gravy? Pass the gravy! New York Super Fudge Chunk Ice Cream? Oh yeah!

Elaina's been exercising like a fiend to counter her nightly dinner forays since she learned about her upcoming 'food allergies.' Learning that she was going to be made Virehnai was a surprise but not unwelcome at all. Who wouldn't like the idea of not getting older? She was ambivalent about the idea of consuming blood. Mentally, Elaina keeps comparing, from a human perspective of course, the satisfaction gained from imbibing a bag of blood, vs, say…downing a cheesesteak sub with all the fixings from Olde City in Midtown. There was no comparison!

The sheer amount of what she needed to learn before she's made Virehnai was overwhelming, and Amalie kept drilling that fact into her head. From what she has seen, and even knows firsthand, they have lots of niggly little rules, and they're always worried about observing the niceties; etiquette matters. Elaina always knew that and grew up with it; she never realized how many weird little rules there were and how much she DIDN'T know until she started coving it with Amalie.

One of those things she'd learned recently was something you'd have thought she'd known…but she didn't. One night while she was chowing down on 'House Special Lo Mein,' Amalie was going to drink a glass of blood and brought one with her. Elaina watched, fascinated. Normally, Virehnai don't eat in front of humans; they consider it an 'etiquette' thing. That much, she knew. Amalie warmed her meal up to the proper temperature and then took a knife and cut the bag open, pouring it into one of Elaina's coffee mugs. Amalie knew she was being watched. That was part of the reason she was openly eating in front of Elaina. She would need to know this herself. The question Elaina asked actually made her laugh.

"I notice you used a knife to open the bag. Couldn't you just rip it open with your teeth?"

"I could, but it would be messy, and the bloodstains would be a bitch to get out of this shirt. I LIKE this shirt…." They both laughed. Amalie continued, more seriously. "That would be a breach of etiquette. Sometimes you use your teeth, and sometimes you don't." Elaina's brows wrinkled in confusion.

"The only acceptable time any Virehn uses their teeth is when they're feeding directly from a human; for a Sulahnai," she waggled her coffee cup of blood, "that would likely be during sex."

"Oh…." 'Whoopsie…my bad,' she thought to herself.

"No matter what faction you belong to, feeding directly is quite…intimate."

"I wondered why Michel used that sharp-ass knife at my succession ceremony instead of just biting himself."

Amalie broke out into hysterical giggles. When Elaina looked at her like, "I don't get the joke," she only shook her head and laughed harder. Once she stopped, she looked at Elaina.

"Okay, so during your succession ceremony, what impact do you think it would have had if Michel had dropped trou, and did a suggestive 'helicopter' dance with his junk?"

Elaina's mouth dropped open, and her eyes opened wide. "What???" That was an image she didn't need in her head! Elaina's reaction made Amalie double over with laughter.

Once she stopped laughing, Amalie tried to explain. "Yup. Michel whipping out his fangs at an event or in public would've had the same impact on another Virehn as it would if you were at a human party or out in public, and some guy exposed himself to all the guests, or you went topless."

It was just one more of those things that she needed to learn. She thought she knew SO much about the Virehnai, having grown up around them...but the more she learned, the more she discovered she didn't know. She was trying to take that in stride, assuming if she made a mistake, they would correct her; much in the way you corrected a young child. Her father and her brothers kept reminding her she would join the ranks of apex predators, and needed to remember that, and act accordingly. Apparently, her brothers didn't believe she could be an apex predator. She understood that it's high stakes, even if her brothers Doug and Rob think she's dense and doesn't get it. Elaina doesn't want to go down in flames because she made mistakes and end up taking generations of her family's good name with her...but she doesn't want to be an asshole, either.

Generations of her family were known as Raal'virehn–bloodsworn–in their case, to the Robichaux clan. Her brother, Doug, was bloodsworn, too. Being bloodsworn is a position of trust. She never thought she would be anything other than oth'kaar–oathsworn–simply because she was the youngest of four children. It surprised her and everyone else to learn that she would become Virehnai. Normally, such an honor wouldn't have been given to her, as her brothers kept reminding.

Once in the shower, Elaina's busy day melted away. Her shower had ten heads, and it was easily one of the favorite things in her suite. She had her music going, all ten shower heads pointed at her, and was oblivious to anything else except enjoying the experience. Eventually, she tapped at the programming display on the wall and shut down the various sprays one by one. The music was the last to go. Elaina toweled off, threw a towel around her hair, and put on her robe as she headed to her bedroom. While she dried herself, mentally she chose a simple pair of nicely cut cotton trousers in olive green and a blouse in a geometric pattern in shades of olive green and burgundy that would complement her dark chestnut colored hair. She had an hour to get ready, to eat, and then Amalie would drop by for her 'lessons.' It would be a fun night in... or that was the plan.

Elaina rounded the corner out of the bathroom into her bedroom to find two strange men already there: one man was lounging on her bed with his hands behind his head in a 'devil may care' sort of way, the other was standing by her window, armed with a gun, aimed squarely at her.

Unfortunately for Elaina, there was an attacker she didn't see, as strong arms grabbed her from behind. Somewhere in the fray, she lost her towel and her robe. Elaina was naked, wet and angry, and fighting like a wildcat. One of them punched her and knocked her out, and stretched her out on the bed, facedown. Another pulled out a small gun-like instrument and put it against the back of her leg in the crease between her leg and her butt cheek and pulled the trigger. One RFID tracking chip, in. Mission accomplished.

The men then staged a faux tableau: they used a couple of her own bras to tie her hands to the headboard, and Elaina woke up to being fondled, and fought again, kicking at them. As she worked her way free, the men left in a hurry. The man who hired them needed an RFID tracking chip in her and he wanted her to feel unsafe…but did not want Elaina harmed. He also didn't want those he hired to get caught. He told them he paid them extra, because if caught, they would be on their own; it would also prompt uncomfortable questions that would be best avoided.

Elaina got herself untied, put her robe back on, and called 911, which took her to the VarenCorp dispatch. She was so angry; she fought off tears. While she was on the phone in her bedroom reporting her break in and assault, Amalie arrived, only to discover Elaina's apartment door unlocked. She could hear her speaking and went looking for her. Amalie heard what had happened as she listened to Elaina explaining her situation to the VarenCorp 911 operator. VarenCorp had their own private system and used bloodsworn and oathsworn off-duty and retired NYPD to staff it. While she waited for them to arrive, Elaina called her father to let him know, and Amalie called Michel to tell him what had transpired, as well.

Before long, Elaina's spacious suite of rooms seemed quite crowded compared to normal. Two officers were dusting it for prints and searching for any traces of the men who invaded her home, and a nice plainclothes detective who identified himself as Patrick Hall carefully interviewed her about every little detail of what transpired. Elaina went over her timeline with him: coming home from work, and then the gym, both of which were in the building; taking a shower and then walking into her bedroom to find them. She provided him with descriptions of the three men, along with what happened to her when she woke up. The detectives' questions seemed endless, and some of them, she expected.

"Ms. Jacoby, did you know the men who attacked you?"

"No."

"You said the man standing by the window was armed?"

"Yes, sir."

9

"Do you know what kind of gun?"

"Other than scary, not a clue." He chuckled.

"Have you ever seen any of them before?"

"Not that I'm aware of. No one looked familiar."

"Who has knowledge of or access to your schedule?"

Elaina thought for a moment and began rattling off a list. "My mom and dad, my brothers and sister, Uncle Michel, Amalie, and most of the folks who work for Jacoby, Lightner and VanEtters." Detective Hall nodded. "So...lots of people."

"Exactly."

"Are you currently dating anyone?"

Elaina shook her head. "No. I'm not seeing anyone right now."

"Do you have any ex-boyfriends with axes to grind?"

"Not that I'm aware of. I've never had a relationship that ended badly enough that something like tonight would happen."

"You had plans for this evening?" The officer glanced around while they stood in her living room.

"Yes, sir. Dinner in with my friend Amalie Bisset." A female plainclothes detective that identified herself as Irene Martin approached them and asked if she could ask her some other questions, privately, related to her attack. Elaina went with the detective out to the kitchen–the only place people weren't, to ask those other questions.

"I'm so sorry for what happened to you tonight. I'm also sorry it took me a bit to get here. They called me in, since your attack had a sexual component to it, and they thought to send a woman to discuss it with you."

"Thank you for coming; sorry you got called in."

"It's no problem." Detective Martin paused, changing gears. "Can you describe for me what they did to you; what do you remember about it?"

Elaina took a deep breath. She'd be repeating herself multiple times that night, apparently. "I left work at around 5:15; I worked out in the gym for another hour. Both are right downstairs on 16. By the time I got up here, I was alone in the elevator; To go above the 15th floor to the residential floors, you need a key. My apartment was locked when I got home; I didn't see or hear anyone else when I let myself in. Nothing seemed out of order. For all I know, they could've been there all along; I was oblivious. I got in the shower; maybe they came in while I was showering, since I had my music going. Once I finished up there, I got ready to spend the evening with my friend Amalie. I put my robe on after I got out of the shower, and when I walked into my bedroom, there was a man laying on my bed, and there was another standing next to the window, who had a gun. I didn't know there was a third man waiting behind me. He grabbed me, and in the struggle, I lost my robe. One of them hit me and knocked me out." She pointed to the rapidly expanding bruise on the side of her face near her eye socket. "I woke up tied to my headboard with a couple of my bras, and they were fondling me."

"Did they rape you?" Detective Martin asked.

"No, I don't think so." Elaina ran her hand through her hair. What a day.

"You should probably go to the hospital to be checked out, to rule it out, as a precaution," the detective told her.

She sighed and looked at the police officer. "I don't really want to, but okay."

Her father Walt, her Uncle Michel, and their gaggle of assistants along with a police officer and building security were still in her living room, chatting in a corner, and they looked up at her when she emerged from the kitchen with the female detective, and approached them.

"So you know, as a precaution, I'm going to the hospital in a few minutes to get checked out." Even as Elaina was apprising her dad and Uncle Michel, Amalie joined them; Detective Hall interviewed her about what she heard or if she saw any of the men, as well as the state of both Elaina and her apartment when she arrived, including the unlocked door.

The police officer turned to Elaina. "The bloodsworn officers here, including myself, have training in forensics; we're going over your apartment for any evidence. One of us is already coordinating with building security to get the footage from the cameras in the elevator. They have that car out of service at the moment until someone can dust it for fingerprints." He looked at Elaina's father, Walt. "There's a list of people who have keys allowing them into the residential portion?"

"That's correct. The building manager keeps that; the only people that have keys are residents. Those residents are primarily company employees, along with a few retirees. Amalie has a key because Elaina arranged for her to get one."

"So, potentially, anyone who lives in here could've either requested a key for a friend, or lost a key and needed a replacement?"

Walt nodded after thinking about it. "Yes. The building manager maintains a list of key requests, lost keys, and authorized visitors for each suite. The only other people who would have access are the building maintenance folks. They have master keys, and they don't keep them; they're strictly controlled. We know who has each set, and they have to be returned at the end of their shift."

"Thank you, Mr. Jacoby. Those lists should help narrow down a list of suspects."

Elaina looked at the officer. "Thank you." She turned to her father and Uncle Michel. "I'll see you later; I should go to the hospital if I'm going to. I want to get it over with."

"Want me to go with you?" Amalie asked.

"You don't mind?"

"I offered, didn't I?"

"Thanks."

Her father looked at her. "Would you like me to go with you?"

"No, that's okay, Papa. I'll be fine." She told him.

Michel looked at her. "At least let one of my drivers take you." As she and Amalie gathered up their purses and jackets, he added, "They're going to be working here for some time yet; I don't know how you feel about spending the night here after what happened, but would you like to spend the night in one of the guest suites at the main building downtown?"

"I'd appreciate that." Elaina told him.

Walt looked at his daughter. "I'll have your room re-keyed as soon as the officers are done."

"Thanks, Papa."

As they left, she could hear her dad and Uncle Michel continuing their discussion regarding the fact that someone could've gotten into her apartment at all. Everyone who worked for the law firm, or any of their other businesses, as well as all the people who either lived in the building, or did maintenance, staffed the gym, or worked in the coffee shop downstairs in the lobby all had access cards, and were trusted and vetted; it was a secure building. Someone who shouldn't have had a key did, which meant someone they trusted betrayed them.

The female detective met Elaina and Amalie at the hospital, where Elaina was examined to see if they had raped her.

It was a relief finding out they didn't, but she still couldn't shake the feeling of violation. Aside from the serious case of the creepies it gave her, the worst things she suffered were several bruises from the struggle, along with the bruise by her eye socket where one of them clocked her; all of which were now documented for posterity.

Amalie texted the driver that they were ready, and he met them at the front entrance. The two women gratefully climbed into the back of Michel's limo, as they headed to the main Robichaux complex in lower Manhattan. The complex comprised two buildings that sat side by side. One was all businesses from their group of allied families. Jacoby, Lightner and VanEtters was one of several, as well as a satellite office of VarenCorp provided as a convenience, plus Shadow Dance Holdings, the real estate company owned by Michel, and RAIC–Richmond Atlantic Investment Group owned jointly by Clan Robichaux as a way of maximizing their already considerable wealth.

The other building was purely residential, and it's where Amalie lived, where the guest suites were located, and soon, Elaina would move there herself. Its residents were mostly Virehnai, with a light sprinkling of allied trusted humans that worked in that location, along with a few other Virehnai who merely rented from Shadow Dance. Tonight, she would enjoy the comfort of one of the guest suites. She watched the city whizz by, as she and Amalie discussed whether they would continue training as planned, or just kick back and watch a movie. It'd been a hell of a night. The only thing Elaina knew for sure: her evening better include pizza!

2

ANCIENT HISTORY, MODERN RULES

After they arrived at the residential building downtown, and Elaina got settled into her suite for the evening, the women sat down in Elaina's suite for the first time since everything transpired, completely alone. Elaina slumped down in her chair, and Amalie sat beside her friend, silently. Normally not an emotional, teary person, tonight Elaina's emotions were right up front and center. Even as she relaxed and let her guard down, along with a long breath, tears welled in her eyes.

"Could what happened to me tonight have happened to you, as Virehn?" Elaina asked Amalie.

"No...and maybe." Amalie responded. Elaina looked at her friend sideways, waiting for an explanation.

"Well," Amalie began, "it shouldn't...but it could. Virehnai have excellent reflexes, and as one, you might've been able to defend yourself better against the intruders. We have excellent senses, so you might have smelled them, or heard them, alerting you to their presence and allowing you to be ready to fight them; either before you walked in if they were already there, or alerting you to their approach; either way, it would've destroyed their element of surprise. Our reflexes and senses are one of our greatest assets."

Elaina was watching her teacher intently. "How could it still have happened, though?"

"High emotion. Distraction. Loss of focus. For instance, sex. Virehnai aren't immune to that. Sex is sex, and many a Virehn met his or her end while..." she paused, "uh...otherwise engaged."

"What a way to go, though. Out in a blaze of glory..." They both giggled for the first time that night.

"Another way is death. Particularly if you're witnessing the death of someone you care about, like I cared about Johannes. While you have your attention focused on what you're seeing, and maybe feeling, too, another can use it against you. Grief is also a distraction. The day I found out Johannes died? During the times before the Compact, someone who might've wanted me out of the way could've used my grief against me and killed me while I was crying my eyes out. In fact, that exact scenario happened many times before: a rival would kill someone you love as a distraction, and then they would ambush you in your grief. Before the Compact, it kept people extremely cautious about being mated to someone, particularly declaring it openly in the Khes'tara Kharvirehn - for that exact reason. Your love could be a liability. A thousand years ago, the Khes'tara Kharvirehn ceremony was quite a declaration. Today, it's more like a human wedding, and it happens regularly." Elaina knew of them but didn't realize the ceremony used to have such dire implications.

"Anything that takes your attention and places it elsewhere, whether it's an event happening around you, or your own emotions inside you...if it's a distraction, it can get you dead. It's sad; by the time your senses finally get your attention, it's too late and you've given away your natural advantage, and...potentially your immortality."

Elaina nodded. It made sense. Amalie continued her lesson, since there were no further questions.

"Most of this, you know, on some level; you've known Virehnai your entire life. The difference is, your knowledge is from the vantage of being human, not Virehnai. While we are hard to kill, never forget, we can be killed. Distraction and particularly treachery, especially in combination, once made up the number one way a Virehn could die. The oldest among us in the old days before the Compact only attained a great age because they remained vigilant. Most of them, you would've described by today's standards as hermits. They trusted NO ONE. Each and every person you trusted was a liability. It kept your circle small."

"Is that why Papa and Uncle Michel were so disturbed that someone betrayed us?"

"It is. Every human that goes in and out of that building has been vetted at the very least; most are bloodsworn or oathsworn, and we know their families too; sometimes generations of them. Michel was there when the Compact came into being. He remembers the Third and Fourth Virehnai wars firsthand and remembers the way it used to be. He would take that betrayal seriously."

When Elaina didn't comment, Amalie went on. "Back before the Compact, every Virehn protected themselves, and protected wherever they lived. They had to, because if they didn't, they could end up dead. The ONLY reason you see so many old Virehnai around TODAY is because of the Compact, which expressly forbids Virehnai from killing one another. Those of us who die in modern times die mostly of accidents that are deemed 'incompatible with life.'" Amalie paused for a moment, sighing sadly. "Distraction often causes accidents. Guard against it. My best advice to you once you ascend is to stay focused and remain present in every moment; there's safety in being present, and mindful."

"So there's no threat of that kind of treachery anymore?" Elaina asked.

"Treachery is uncommon, but not impossible. The only way treachery occurs now is if you use a human to do your dirty work for you. Even at that, there's a lot involved in it; by the Compact, treacherous actions against other Virehn can't be...direct. It's difficult to work around the Compact, but we have known it to happen. That's part of the reason World War I almost became the Fifth Virehnai War." Amalie looked so sad as she was explaining this whole topic. Elaina understood. The Virehn she was succeeding was Amalie's sire and lover, Johannes; Uncle Michel's son. She'd known Johannes all her life and counted him as a friend. He and Amalie had been in a relationship and would've been mated to one another next summer. Before his recent death, Amalie told her all about her plans. There would've been multiple ceremonies and celebrations, all from different traditions. There was going to be a civil ceremony at the Courthouse that would fulfill the modern day paperwork and necessities; there would be the Virehnai ceremony up in the Hall called the Khes'tara Kharvirehn, or 'the becoming of shared blood,' and finally, there would be a private service in a little church in France where she and Johannes were baptized centuries apart. Amalie asked her to be one of her bridesmaids in the church ceremony in France, and she'd been looking forward to it.

"You've been together since 1926. Why didn't you do any of this sooner?" Elaina asked her once, as they were discussing plans. "We're not in any hurry." After Johannes died, Amalie told her sadly, through a round of tears, that they thought they had loads of time. They should've had centuries; the time they thought they had, unfortunately, they didn't, much like humans often find out themselves.

"Let's see what you remember from last week. I just mentioned The Compact. What do you remember about it?"

"The Compact," Elaina explained, "is what keeps the peace between the two factions of Virehnai, the Draz'kul and the Sulahnai, and it has for nearly a thousand years. It came into being after the Fourth Virehnai War."

"And what prompted the Fourth War?"

"Tensions between the Draz'kul and the Sulahnai, over groups of humans that they were both bloodsworn and oathsworn to. Besides that, there was lots of politics at play, including a war between the Holy Roman Empire and the Ottoman Empire. Several of the bloodsworn and oathsworn humans on both sides of the conflict were royalty. It divided their loyalties between their

Virehnai blood bonds, as well as family relationships and political considerations that were all inter-mixed. Ultimately, they couldn't resolve their differences, and it became one of the bloodiest conflicts in Virehnai history, and most of what humans think they know about us comes from this period in history."

"Correct." Amalie nodded, happy that Elaina was taking what she needed to learn seriously. Still…it'd been a strange evening.

"Should I continue on for a bit, or do you want to watch a movie instead, considering how the evening began?"

"Split decision, maybe? Study for a little while longer, and then get comfy and watch something funny? The chances that I'm going to work tomorrow at this point are nil. It's a hell of a way to get a day off, but…I'll take it." Elaina picked up her phone from the coffee table. "Before we do anything else, I want pizza. How about we go until the pizza gets here?" She tapped on her phone for a minute, and ordered a pizza from Joe's, and then let the concierge in the lobby know she had a pizza on the way. The building was secure; they would never let a pizza delivery person in, so it meant she'd have to run downstairs to get it…but it would be worth every single step for every single bite.

Amalie laughed. "Are you all good now?"

Elaina sat up a little straighter and made a face. "I am."

"May I continue?"

"Please, do."

"Last week, we covered The Compact. Today, we'll touch on the origin of factions. As a human, it's merely a history lesson. On the day you ascend, you will see this through blood and understand. You will truly understand the meanings of the phrase 'Virehn zuth akret.'"

Elaina learned from Amalie that it meant "blood never forgets.' She'd said it to Uncle Michel a couple of hours before that succession ceremony that changed her life trajectory forever. She didn't exactly understand what she said then, but she did now. Elaina understood it was more than simple 'condolences,' such as a human would say to another human. It was a reminder that though Johannes was no longer physically with them, he literally lived on and would be remembered within their blood's memory–personally and collectively. Amalie paused for a moment and then continued.

"Every Virehnai alive descends from one of four people, known as the First Flames. The First Flames were two brothers and their mates: Khnurn, and his mate Renenet; and Zuberi, a priest of Ptah, along with his mate Sati. They are the basis for our divisions, as well as our family clans."

"Which one does Clan Robichaux come from?" Elaina asked.

"We descend from the priest, Zuberi. Today, you learned that. After you ascend, you will know it, because you will have seen his face, and felt his flame as you ascend." Elaina cocked her head to the side but didn't interrupt.

"You know that Clan Robichaux is Sulahnai?" Amalie asked.

Elaina nodded, "yes."

"At first, all Virehnai were Draz'kul, and hunted for their food; not everyone enjoyed hunting humans. The humans also noticed us. As the number of Virehnai grew, the more dangerous it became; we stood out too much. Too many of us in one place causes problems, not only because of limited resources, but because we attract attention: being pale in desert areas and not aging makes us stand out; the more of us there are, the more we collectively stand out. That attention is dangerous, then as now, although it was considerably more dangerous back then."

"Because of the potential for discovery, our ancestors divided into clans and moved. Some stayed in Egypt, others moved to

Sumeria, some went to the Indus Valley. That is called the 'first diaspora.' The clan that moved to Sumeria split into two after a woman named Sulana and several other individuals formed ties with humans, trading food for protection. Sulana didn't want her to hunt her friends and neighbors and instead sought a balance with them. Their agreements formed the first blood oaths. In exchange for a steady, voluntary blood supply, Sulana and her children promised to keep her family, friends and neighbors safe from aggressors, human...or otherwise."

"Over time, Virehn from other clans and locales joined with Sulana's clan; they chose 'arrangements' over hunting. That is when the factions truly began. It caused a rift, as Sulana permitted others to swear an oath and join with them. Eventually, they called themselves 'Sulahnai,' which means Children of Sulana. This is when the other clans opposing the Sulahnai began calling themselves the Draz'kul. In the old language, it means 'disciplined hunter.' Anyone NOT Sulahnai hunted their prey - humans–and kept to the shadows, trying not to attract attention. The first Virehnai war was fought in Sumeria, because of the Sulahnai's blood oaths."

"There were four Virehnai wars. You've studied the Fourth Virehnai war because it led directly to the Compact. You remember that the Fourth Virehnai war took place during an ongoing human war?"

Elaina nodded. "Uh huh."

"If you remember nothing else, remember that there is a Virehnai component to every major war the humans have ever had. The ones that were numbered became watershed moments we remember eras by; this is because the scope of the battle was large enough that great numbers of Virehnai were involved–either dying or being made - right there on the battlefields. Michel is one of those. His sire made him Virehn on a battlefield north of Athens during the human Peloponnesian War, which is our Second Virehnai War. Howard, too."

"Wow. I knew they were old, but I didn't realize."

"Neither of them talk about it much. Michel, especially; he loved his human wife and children, and after he became Virehnai, his sire told him to forget them. 'Go on with your life and let them get on with theirs.'"

"That's…horrible."

"Different times, different ways of dealing with longevity, I suppose."

"I suppose…"

Amalie paused for a moment, collecting her thoughts.

"You know Michel is old. Did you know he was there when the Compact was cast? It was formed as an act of magic. There were three Virehnai blood witches remaining; for a change, they weren't being used as a weapon. Instead, they were called upon to create something that would protect us and keep us from self-annihilation. The Compact they cast guaranteed a Virehnai couldn't kill another Virehnai without their own life being forfeit."

"So…wait. Back up for a minute." Elaina said, and Amalie stopped. "Witches really exist? Witches that had…power? Power enough to control the Virehnai?"

"Oh,…..yes."

"I'm sorry, all I have to equate it to are some girls I went to high school and college with. They always smelled like weird incense, dressed like gypsies or goths, cosplaying being Stevie Nicks or Wednesday Addams…"

Amalie chuckled. "When you ascend, you'll see. The magic's real, alright. The magic that worked almost 600 years ago was strong enough THEN that if you violate the Compact, it can KILL you today. Remember that. EVERYTHING about the Virehnai–from our very existence, which started out as a spell, to the Compact – also a spell - is because of and underpinned by magic, still."

"I didn't realize."

"As a human, I wouldn't expect you to. Unless you've overheard us talking about it, why would you? Never forget: the Compact covers every Virehn, and the magic enforcing it passes through our blood. Today, it keeps the peace between the factions as they meant it to, and in fact, its helped narrow the divide between the factions. Today, via VarenCorp, the factions work together regularly to keep all Virehnai not only safe, but secret."

"During your succession ceremony in the Hall, you remember there was an 'honored elder' named Carolyn?"

Elaina nodded yes.

"Carolyn's the CEO of the NY Office of VarenCorp. You've worked with VarenCorp before; we deal with them regularly at the firm, and your father's other businesses, along with Michel's and Howard's businesses do, too. That's why. They're an international corporation, with offices in major cities wherever Virehnai live near one another. They own international hotel chains and are behind several international banks and chemical companies worldwide and also specialize in logistics and material handling."

"Those are their 'human facing' businesses; they're so much more than that. VarenCorp forms what passes for our government, separate and apart from the human governments we deal with. Those hotels, banks and the logistics company are a cover for us, and humans will never realize the true nature of VarenCorp, even if they dig and discover how many companies it includes. That kind of anonymity allows us to not only move goods, but people. It enables them to protect our own, wherever they are. Worldwide, there are around two hundred and eighty thousand Virehnai living in plain sight, against billions of humans. When there was a higher ratio of Virehnai to humans in proximity, bad things had a tendency to happen. Keeping the numbers around where they are keeps us all safely off the radar."

"How do they keep the factions from causing wars now?"

"Because of the Compact, and VarenCorp, they don't worry about it like they used to. Particularly among younger Virehnai, faction barely matters. It's simply a feeding preference." It got silent for a minute, and then Amalie spoke up.

"Did you know that once, Michel was Draz'kul?"

"No. Why did he change faction?"

"Somewhere around the 1870s, around a century after his sire died, Michel switched sides and joined with the Sulahnai. In 1884, he moved from France to New York and set up a new life and a new identity. He contacted the other Sulahnai in the area and declared his intentions and took oaths. Several of his clan, including Howard, followed him to New York and formed their own clan…which was less regulated back then. This is where we come full circle, to the part you already know: not long after Michel moved to New York, he set up a company, and made a blood pact with a man named Howard Pancioni, who because of anti-Italian sentiments, changed his name to…"

"Howard Jacoby. Great Grandpa."

"Yup."

Elaina's phone buzzed. She looked at it. "Pizza's here!"

3

PREPARING FOR LIFE AFTER DEATH

While the attack on Elaina was frightening, she was busy; busier than she'd ever been, it seemed. Her 'transition date' was rapidly approaching, and it wasn't merely her physical existence that would be changing.

It felt like her whole life was flipping upside down. Thank goodness she had Amalie to guide her through everything!

Because they knew she was going to be transitioning, Amalie took her to the New York office of VarenCorp. It was required; it was the equivalent of immigrating to a different country. VarenCorp assigned her a 'case worker,' and she and Amalie were there to fill out paperwork that helped VarenCorp keep track of all Virehnai 'under their care.' It blew her mind when her caseworker, a Virehn named Sam Roth, tapped for a few moments on a keyboard, and there she was! VarenCorp had a dossier on HER…even as a human!

"Oh, my gosh! I'm in your database!"

"Of course you are. Everyone who's oathsworn or bloodsworn is in our central database. We keep comprehensive files on every Virehn, as well; We know their sire, along with their faction, and if it changed; what their human name was, what all of their aliases have been since, where they've lived, their involvement in the wars if they're old enough, and who their offspring are…..and if they've caused trouble in their past that we've had to deal with, in terms of human governance. We don't believe in surprises."

The file he brought up showed everything about her: her entire family history, her blood type, along with the date she became oth'kaan; her work history, along with a copy of her badge was there, as well her address, and even her bank information! She watched as he placed an addendum on her file, at the top, above everything else: a transition date; who the Vel'sheth was that would guide the transition; Michel's name was added as her sire, which then automatically populated clan and lineage information. He turned to her. "You've already had your succession ceremony, if I understand correctly?"

"Yes." He checked a box and went on.

"From what I can see here, it looks as if you'll be moving into the main residential building downtown soon. Is that correct?"

"Yes."

"Want to know what your suite number will be?"

"Sure, why not?"

It was on the 12th floor and was suite 1207.

Yesterday's visit to VarenCorp was…surreal. Sam went over so much. If she moved abroad, she needed to contact VarenCorp, so they could arrange it for her. They would act as her agent to get whatever governmental permissions or visas she needed. Whether she traveled or moved abroad, if she booked through VarenCorp Hospitality, they would send her info to the closest VarenCorp offices to where she was going, where they acted much like an embassy; if she needed anything at all, including help, they would provide it. She would receive an email before traveling with a temporary case officer abroad, and all of their contact information. If she was traveling to a city where there was a VarenCorp hotel, she would stay there on a secure floor. Elaina was told that because Michel was Sulahnai, she would initially be listed as Sulahnai as well. If after ascension, she decided she wanted to be Draz'kul instead, all she needed to do was shoot them an email and let them know; her file would be updated, and they would put her in contact with someone who would instruct her on any further actions she needed to take. It was a lot of information in one day.

Elaina had no clue prior to yesterday that any of this even existed. When Amalie told her they acted as a government, she was surprised–but the reality of that didn't set in until she sat there with her caseworker.

She dealt with VarenCorp before, in limited ways through her father's firm, but this was well beyond anything she expected. It was all there, in plain sight. She only needed to know how to see it, before she actually COULD. Elaina remembered seeing an illustration as a child that it reminded her of. While that type of illustration takes various forms, the one that she remembered vividly looked like a meadow. If you knew 'how' to see it–meaning someone pointed out the hidden picture within, or you stared at it long enough -you saw the face of the devil staring back. Once you saw the devil hidden amid the meadow, you could never unsee it.

Elaina had a realization: VarenCorp was the same way. There was the forward-facing corporation, which was exactly like any other large corporation - which was the picture they showed to the world. Then, there was the VarenCorp that kept tabs on all the lives of the Virehnai worldwide and functioned like a de facto governmental agency. It was all but invisible as it pulled strings and ran things in the background. You would never see that part, much like the devil staring out of that meadow picture – unless you knew to look for it. Once you knew it was there, that was all you saw.

Once she finished with her caseworker, she reported to VarenCorp's medical suite, where two things happened: she got a pre-transition physical and then had a conversation with the doctor that she never expected to have…on egg preservation. Imagine it! The doctor talked her into harvesting her eggs.

"Why would I want to do that?" Elaina asked the lady.

"Once you transition, you won't be having any children naturally. Because you KNOW you're transitioning, I'd recommend you have your eggs harvested because it preserves that option for you to have children later. Think of it this way: what if you someday regret that you didn't have any human children? It doesn't matter to some women; to others, it does. How you feel today is fine, but what if you change your mind later? If you don't save them now, you won't have that option. Occasionally, when a couple goes through Khes'tara Khar'virehn, they want human children. I tell men the same thing about preserving their sperm. You never know."

She knew she wouldn't be able to carry them herself, but the doctor informed her of the listings of bloodsworn surrogates available through VarenCorp that could carry her future children for her. Elaina had no clue that existed. If she had her own human children to pass on wealth to, she could. It would probably send her brother Doug into a full-blown panic attack, thinking that someone other than him might benefit from her being a Virehn. It might be worth it for that alone.

While they were at VarenCorp's NY office, she stopped in to see their museum. Because the Virehnai were so secretive, it never occurred to her that there might be a museum. As soon as she realized there was one, she wanted to go! Elaina was a museum geek, so the visit turned out to be the highlight of her trip to VarenCorp. Elaina found it riveting. Ordinarily, she wouldn't be allowed entry, as it was off limits to humans, but her transition date allowed her entry.

There were many displays. One that particularly drew her attention were the displays on the First Flames, and then the Compact. Elaina was glad then that Amalie had taken the time to explain some of the history to her. It was because of her lessons that she knew about what she was looking at and could understand any of what she saw. Amalie told her again that once she ascended, she would see and understand what she saw today in a completely different way.

One thing Elaina saw that really struck her was an exhibit on their beginnings, in the spell gone awry. As part of an art project in Switzerland over a hundred years ago, four Virehn artists got together, and each painted the First Flame within their ancestry. The result was four pictures, as remembered from their blood; one of each ancestor. There was also a picture of a long-forgotten tomb that their spell occurred in. She could see that the Hall was modeled in small part or at least inspired by it. In a case sitting before these images was a replica of the spelled knife that created them. It started out as a simple Egyptian hunting knife and became SO much more. The sign labeling the display said its name: 'Zar'kanet ai Virehnai,' meaning "The blade that made Virehnai", or more poetically, "The Blade of Becoming." The rune on the handle was what Amalie called "the rune of becoming."

"That's amazing," Elaina said, trying to pronounce the name. Amalie chuckled when she butchered it, then added, "There's another name for that blade that you'll never see listed in a display. Many people call it 'Ash'kulat.' That means "witch fang." Most Virehnai have a healthy fear of magic. Much as that knife made them, it also brought the Compact into existence, too." Amalie gestured toward it. "You should see the way they protect the actual knife in Zurich. On one hand, they want to show it in the museum, and have our people freely see it - but on the other, the display case needs to be indestructible! The priests had to hide that puppy for a few centuries, particularly around the time of the French Revolution. They were afraid someone would get it into their head to destroy it, hoping that its destruction would end the Compact; there's always been a subtle fear that if someone destroyed the knife, it might end us. They don't know, and they don't aim to find out."

There were also displays on each of the four Virehnai wars; there was an amazing mosaic map of the ancient world that showed the locations of the earliest strongholds, brought about as migrations needed to occur. A rune represented each city's name. There were no boundaries shown; simply topography. It was beautiful. There were displays showing Egypt; Drawings of a temple, currently buried, and 'undiscovered,' outside of Memphis. It was round, and it too looked remarkably like the Hall. Amalie told her there was a distinct prohibition on looking for the temple, or the cave they cast the original spell in. Since Virehnai money bankrolls many colleges with archaeology programs, digs to that area rarely get funding.

Taking up an entire wall was a timeline of history: human vs. Virehnai history. Elaina also found the exhibit with books on loan from the Swiss HQ in Zurich fascinating. There were several Virehnai who chronicled their lives, giving true accounts of history (instead of whitewashed or altered versions.) Elaina hadn't doubted it before, but the timeline on the wall illustrated beautifully that history is truly written by the victors, even if the victors were on the wrong side of history. It was a fun afternoon.

Every place that she and Amalie visited, she mentally called 'field trips,' just like when she was in school. There was so much that she never knew, or even suspected, and going to places was like a little bonus. Elaina liked her job, but she was paid to take these field trips. Win-win!

One place she visited, she was excited to go to: back to the Hall, this time, to meet with the Vel'sheth. He would instruct her on what she should expect and also do a deep dive into history. Even Amalie was looking forward to it.

Vel'sheth Reman had an office at the back of the Hall. It wasn't large, and it was crowded with books in a multitude of languages. Vel'sheth Reman looked like he was in his late 40s, but his vibe was 'old man.' His hair was salt and pepper gray. Normally during events at the Hall, he wore red robes, which was how he appeared at her succession ceremony, which was also Johannes' memorial. Today, if she saw him on the street, she might have passed him by, not recognizing him, thinking he was a priest. He dressed simply in black pants and a shirt and wore a clerical collar. It was one of those things that helped him blend in, in plain sight. A human seeing him out on the street would make assumptions, and never question him because of that cleric's collar, and do it with a nod and a smile. His red robe hung on a hook on the wall beside them in his small, crowded office.

He brought Elaina and Amalie there to talk. "This is one of my favorite parts of my job." He joked with them that every truly old Virehn had a little 'history teacher' in them for good or for bad, so they should be prepared.

Reman told them, "To the ancient Egyptians, the afterlife was every bit as real as their daily life. Their goal was to reach it and be comfortable. Have either of you heard of the term 'Heka' before?" Amalie nodded yes, and Elaina said 'no.'

"Heka is magic. For a soul to make it to the afterlife, ancient Egyptians expected they would need magical spells. The soul's final trip was dangerous; perilous. Without Heka, they would never have made it. Everything the Egyptians did had a magical component, with the goal of getting into the afterlife. Mummification was more than mere body preservation; it was a spell. Priests carefully wrapped the deceased in linen, including amulets with spells on the back, meant to help souls past the demons that would prey on the souls making the trip. Back then, you must remember, everything that was written was a spell. Finally, once the soul of the deceased made it past the demons, it would face a trial by the Judges of the Underworld. With the aid of magic and planning, they would make it past judgment. What form did the judgment take? The goddess Ma'at would weigh your heart against a feather. If your heart weighed more than the feather, a creature referred to as Ammit would eat your soul. If you know anything about Christianity, you might know Ammit as 'The Hellmouth' or equate him with that. Regardless of what he's called, if the soul made it past the judgement, they became an 'akh' - a transfigured spirit, and were infused with 'akhw' - a potent magic that could aid any of your relatives that were still living. So let's put all this into perspective." Reman said.

"Then, even as now, people were worried that when they died, it would be the end. They feared nothingness would greet them. Some days, weeks, and years went better than others. Life in ancient Egypt was hard. People suffered mishaps and issues in their lives, much as they do now - and regularly sought help from their departed ancestors, hoping against hope that there was something beyond.

They hoped their departed loved ones, now surrounded by plenty and no longer suffering from hardships, could aid them in this life."

"Human nature has changed little, if at all. Then, as now, there are people who play by the rules, and people who don't. There is always someone looking for a way to cheat the system or try to arrange situations for their own benefit. The Four Flames, much as they created us, were attempting such a thing when the spell they did went wrong."

"They were trying to cheat the system?" Elaina shook her head. "They did that?"

Reman nodded his head. "They did. Much as we revere them as our first ancestors, we always remember that they were fallible individuals who, having lived normal lives, did something that resulted in something quite unforeseen and unanticipated. They could never have foreseen the world we inhabit now." He paused for a minute and was happy that he had receptive students sitting before him. Some people in the last century weren't as appreciative of the history. Michel was right. This one would make a good Virehn. "Did Amalie tell you the story of how our people began?"

"She went over it, along with the Compact's beginnings." Reman looked at Amalie and nodded. "Good."

Amalie looked at him. "I went over it, but I didn't go in depth. She may have gotten more from the Beginnings display in the Museum at VarenCorp yesterday."

"I see." Reman looked over to Elaina. "May I tell you a story about   the   First   Flames?"

4

ANCIENT BEGINNINGS

"Before I start, Reman paused, "Do you know what a Vel'sheth is, and does? I mentioned that this is the favorite part of my job...and it is...but it occurred to me you might not have learned about the Vel'sheth yet."

"No, Amalie and I haven't gone over that yet."

"The Vel'sheth are priests; the rememberers. We are the ones who remind the Virehnai who we are, and where we came from...along with providing continuity from one age to the next."

Elaina looked at him sideways, her eyebrow questioning. "Amalie told me the meanings of 'Virehn zuth akret.' If the 'blood never forgets,' why does the Virehnai need someone to remind them of where they came from?"

He chuckled, "I was told you were bright. To answer your question, yes...our blood remembers. It remembers everything within our own clan, bloodline, and lineage. Soon, you will have these memories dwelling within your blood as well. But there were four flames. Most of us only remember what is in our own blood, which came through our own sire and from our lineage. As a Vel'sheth, I am a keeper of all the histories, regardless of lineage. After I became Virehn, I realized I wanted to be Vel'sheth, a rememberer. As part of the ceremony where I became Vel'sheth, I had to partake of blood from other lineages. It's also my job to interface with the entity; the egregore known as Varet'Sul'Akha, the one that enforces the Compact, and because of that, I carry within the memory of all the First Flames." When there were no further questions, he told them a tale.

"The very first of us, known as the "First Flames," died to this life and rose to another in the year 2830 BCE, in the ancient Egyptian city of Memphis, when it was called Hut-Ka-Ptah. The city worshipped the god Ptah, and the goddess Neith. Ptah was the god of artisans and craftworkers; Neith was a mother goddess and seen as the great weaver of time."

"Khnurn was a merchant who had many contacts. He sold items the local artisans made to visiting traders, while buying the visitors' goods from faraway places and selling them locally. He had a good life and was wealthy. His brother Zuberi was a priest of Ptah, and a scribe."

"Khnurn had a concern, which lurked in the back of his mind, which he discussed with Zuberi. What good was all your wealth if you couldn't use it to have better lives and more power than everyone else? He had a fair amount of wealth and power he had amassed. Did he want to spend eternity keeping company with Pharaohs and Gods, or did he want to be forced to spend it with people he saw as riff raff; people who had nothing, and spent their whole lives toiling so they could finally live better in the afterlife?"

"These thoughts kept Khnurn up at night, as he tried to figure out a way that he could have not just life in the afterlife, but true wealth and power there. He didn't want to share it with people whose newfound abundance, to his mind…still represented poverty. He didn't socialize with those people in this life; it was one thing to sell to them; but why would he want to spend eternity with them? He wanted what he felt he was entitled to; what befitted his elevated station in society that his wealth brought."

"Khnurn and Zuberi discussed it at length, and the two of them hatched a plan with their wives and included several people of their acquaintance who they'd talked their plan up to. As a priest familiar with magic, it fell to Zuberi to create the spell that would accomplish their aim. He'd spent several days in a cave, apart from others, seeking the blessing and direction of the gods. He only brought with him water, his scribe kit, and a simple hunting knife. How the spell and the design he used came about, felt like divine providence and the active blessing of the Gods. He had sat here in that cave, and the spell and a design, full of power, had come unbidden to him…as a complete ritual, in an instant. He saw it in his mind; he knew how to use the spell and the design even as he saw it."

"He carved the design into the handle of the hunting knife he had with him and drew the hieroglyphs onto the blade. He also chiseled them into the wall. At the moment he saw the design and the spell, Zuberi also knew they would complete the spell here, in the cave. He stood back, looked at his work chiseled roughly into the wall, and was satisfied that he'd captured what he had seen. It would be an intense and difficult magical rite that, if successful, would allow them all to skip the normal process surrounding death. Instead, they would become transfigured spirits, a cross between human and god, with great magical power like the gods they served, and they would be as gods in this life. Even more, the journey to the afterlife, when death finally came for them, would be simpler, and they would merely transfigure into it, and go wherever the gods themselves dwelled, avoiding judgment and Ammit."

"The day came when they were ready. It would happen at the full moon, as the first blush of pinks and orange crested the horizon, kissing the landscape as the new day began. The surrounding cliffs and the cave they were in had a natural light and beauty that stood starkly in contrast to the magic they were about to perform. They each used the hunting knife Zuberi gave them, inscribed with hieroglyphs and the design carved into the handle to cut their wrists deeply, and bled into a chalice marked with spells, hieroglyphs, and their names. The others who joined them in the cave comprised three other priests and a priestess, who had no clue that their lives - both current and eternal - were about to be forfeit as a sacrifice when they shed their blood in the same way and into the chalice. Once they had all bled into it, Zuberi, in his priestly role, cast the spell, and a red mist formed above the chalice, as they watched, rapt. Each took the chalice and repeated the words that Zuberi spoke and drank deeply of the blood it contained."

"Shortly, all of them were gagging, gasping for air, clawing at their throats, panicking and afraid. Zuberi's last thought was, 'This wasn't supposed to happen!' The last thing any of them remembered was slipping into darkness as they died."

"Later that evening, as the moon rose, four of the eight who'd assembled that morning awoke: Khnurn and Zuberi, and their respective wives, Renenet, and Sati. They awoke to the overstimulation of their senses, all heightened to the point of madness, and a burning thirst that the water they brought wouldn't slake. Thus began their new lives as something 'other' than what they previously had been."

Elaina held up a finger. "I'm sorry to interrupt, but I have a question."

Reman nodded to her to continue. "I know Amalie told me that when I awake after being made Virehn, that my senses will be heightened; she told me that when she awoke, everything seemed so noisy. What you described sounds way worse than waking up to lots of extra noise and being especially hungry. And they were in a cave...so how noisy could it have been?"

"It likely was worse. We know now what happens when we make another. They didn't, and they were completely unprepared for what they faced. It was entirely unexpected. As the progenitors of our line, they learned everything 'the hard way.' You won't encounter the difficulties they did. When you awake, your clan has taken care to limit the noise and light you're exposed to. You will awaken hungry; it won't be unbearable. Your first blood consumed will be Michel's. After you ascend, we'll give you something more to eat."
"Good to know."

Amalie stifled a chuckle. When Reman looked sideways at her, with an eyebrow cocked, she said out loud what she was thinking, looking at Elaina. "It won't be a cheeseburger and fries, or a loaded pizza."

Reman laughed. "You really will crave blood, even if as a human you can't imagine it now." He looked at them. "May I continue?" They nodded yes.

"Our first ancestors were alive, but not. They weren't exactly human anymore, but they weren't gods either. They had a form of life but quickly learned that death would not come easily. They discovered being outside in daylight in the desert was horribly uncomfortable. The desert sun caused their pale skin to burn easily, and the burns were incredibly painful, and took longer to heal than it had as a human. Eating food was possible, but only in small amounts, and it didn't satisfy their hunger in the least; if anything, it made their hunger worse and made them ill. The only thing that thoroughly satisfied the hunger that consumed them was blood. Initially, they hunted jackals at night in the desert, but the sweetest, most satisfying blood was human."

"The differences between the First Flames and those around them quickly became plain. They were considerably paler than everyone because of what they now were. They could go outdoors, but they never tanned, and it stood in stark contrast. When they went outside, they covered up as much as they could. Covering up as they did helped on two fronts; not only did it help keep their paler skin from burning, but it helped hide how pale they were from everyone else, to minimize differences. This was around the time they referred to themselves as 'The Virehnai,' and became more insular. At first, they maintained friendships and their normal lives, but as time passed, it became dangerous. They ceased any friendships they had with humans, because they didn't age as the humans did, and it became increasingly obvious. It put them in danger. Only a very few humans were permitted into their circle. If they broke trust with the Virehnai who trusted them, the price was death."

"Keeping a low profile became more and more important the longer they stayed in Hut-Ka-Ptah. Most people were uncomfortable around them, anyway. The Virehnai were...simply put...different. Their energy felt different. They looked different. The differences made them stand out, as well as made them dangerous."

"Most of what the First Flames wanted out of life, they now had: long life, wealth, power and connections. While most people were uncomfortable around them, some, strangely enough, were unexpectedly drawn to them. Several, despite discomfort, saw the quality of their lives, and asked to become like them."

Reman stopped, as he could see Elaina struggling with something. "What?"

"Do people still do that? Approach one of us, seeing that we're 'different,' and then ask to join us?"

"Yes. It doesn't happen much, though. The way the world is today, we blend in much better. Technology helps us hide. Humanity's own proclivities to group with others like themselves keep them together, and don't make them suspicious when we do likewise. Being overly pale doesn't 'out' you like it used to. Not dying during a plague doesn't 'out' you. The further you go back in time, the easier it is to play 'spot the Virehn.' In Egypt, so far back in our past, there were far fewer people, no technology, and you relied on your neighbors considerably more than we do now. Being pale while living in a desert was so different that we stood out more."

"Did they actually make new Virehn when someone asked? How did they decide who would and wouldn't become a Virehn? I know there's a process for deciding who will and won't ascend now."

"Until the humans' "World War I," there wasn't a process, so much as it depended on someone in a clan deciding that a human would make a good fit. Sometimes they were right and sometimes they weren't. When they weren't right about a person, usually it became a problem. Luckily, after the Compact, the egregore sorted the problems out." Reman paused for a moment, then continued, "To answer your question, though - Initially, our First Flames weren't sure how to make another Virehn."

"They weren't?" Elaina asked.

"The First Flames didn't come with an instruction manual. They had to figure it all out on their own."

Both women giggled.

"The first time one of their friends asked to join them, Zuberi's only thought was to go back to the cave where they themselves began, and to repeat the spell that went so wrong."

"If the spell went wrong, why would Zuberi assume it would go wrong again in the same way?"

"He didn't; it was just the only idea he had. It didn't matter anyway; the spell didn't work. Not only didn't it work, but that time, something ghoulish appeared, and attempted to inhabit the dead body of the friend he tried to change. It terrified him and Khnurn both, and they had a difficult time killing it. What happened in that cave when they returned disturbed them enough that he and Khnurn and their wives quickly sealed up 'The Cave of Making' forever. He didn't want another to summon such evil, ever."

"Zuberi realized, belatedly, and totally by accident, that their blood, which set them apart in the first place, is what would also create more like themselves. Sati nearly drained someone, almost killing them. They didn't need to carry more dead humans out into the desert, leaving them for the animals to maul. As an experiment, Zuberi cut his own wrist and fed some of it to the human Sati almost killed before they expired. He appeared to die anyway. Thinking it failed, they carried the body out into the desert...only to see the person alive later. It worked. The only thing necessary to create another Virehn was a willing person - who was brave enough to allow themselves to mostly bleed out and consume Virehnai blood...which kills them the rest of the way. Later, they would rise as something only described as 'not dead.' Not exactly alive; but not dead. Not exactly human anymore, either."

Reman looked at her, to see how Elaina would react to the graphic, accurate depiction of being made. She blinked, but that was about it. Mentally, Reman chuckled to himself. "Let's see how she is in two weeks." He went on.

"Now that they knew how to add to their numbers, they added several people almost immediately. For over a hundred years, they kept the numbers small. Those living in and around Hut-Ka-Ptah were in danger of the appetites of the Virehnai, and as a group, they worked hard to keep a low profile, hunting animals more than humans. They still hunted humans; they used extreme care. There were persistent rumors of monsters that would stalk you after dark. Killing people for their blood attracts attention if you're unlucky and pick the wrong people. As their numbers grew, tensions within their group rose as well." He looked at Elaina. "Amalie went over the wars with you, correct?"

Elaina nodded her head, yes.

"Good, that's good." His eyebrows went up. He rubbed his hands together vigorously, chuckled wickedly, and grinned. "Pop quiz! Let's see what you remember. Didn't know there'd be a test, did you?"

Both women laughed; Elaina more hesitantly than Amalie, now that she was on the spot!

"What were the causes of the First Virehnai war?" Reman looked at Elaina, waiting.

She took a deep breath before answering. "It's okay," he told her, waving his hands. "I'm not grading you. I was teasing, more than anything else."

"Good to know," Elaina told him, breathing a sigh of relief. "Differences in feeding caused the first Virehnai war. The Draz'kul hunt, and the Sulahnai form blood bonds with humans for their food in exchange for protection. When the Draz'kul fed from humans bound to the Sulahnai, it widened the rift between the two factions.

When the humans living in the two Sumerian cities later went to war, the Sulahnai did too, because of their blood bonds with the humans."

"Precisely. Now, what about the Second Virehnai War?"

"Fighting broke out between the humans in Sparta and Athens. There were Draz'kul and Sulahnai in both cities. They tried successfully for some time to stay out of it, remembering the causes of the war in Sumeria. If I understand the downfall for this war correctly, there were too many Virehnai in both cities; there were more than was 'safe,' and many of them were recent, new?"

Reman nodded at Elaina, and she continued to answer him. "Unfortunately, when someone becomes a Virehn, it doesn't change their beliefs, or their allegiances to families or causes. As Athens began losing, the Virehnai living in Athens defended them. The Virehnai living in Sparta fought back in kind, and they found themselves at war again."

"Correct. Your Uncle Michel and his brother Howard were both made Virehnai by Diotimus Artimidorus after the battle of Amphipora, and for the record, all three fought on the side of Athens." He asked Elaina, "Now, what of the Third War?"

"The Third Virehnai war started in the year 238, as part of 'The Crisis of the Third Century.'" Elaina laughed. "What a dumb name for a war. The Virehnai who took part in the siege of Aquileia didn't even realize it was the first skirmish in the Third Virehnai War; by that time, there were always Virehnai fighting one another, whether it was because of treachery or somebody taking offense. Besides that, when Amalie was explaining it, it sounded like all the conflicts going on drew Virehnai to the battlefields like hanging up a 'free buffet' sign draws humans."

Her description made Reman stifle a laugh. "This time, it wasn't alliances with humans at fault. The Roman empire's problems were destabilizing everything, including the Virehnai living in their lands. The Roman empire was too big and stretched out; there wasn't consistent leadership, and they were fighting too many enemies and battles at once. Those battles were being taken advantage of by the Virehnai clans as well. It might've ended with that, except that it became a faction war. Someone assassinated one of the last remaining original children of the First Flames. The guilty person was Draz'kul, and the Virehn who died was Sulahnai. The elders tried to calm everyone, but it didn't work. The human war lasted for 100 years; the Virehnai component was almost that long, but not quite."

"And the Fourth War?"

Elaina stopped to think for a minute. They'd just gone over this several nights before. It was complicated. She answered hesitantly. "We just covered this. There were multiple Virehnai clans involved, that were primarily Draz'kul, but one of them was Sulahnai. The downfall came about because of blood bonds and oaths between humans and their Virehnai patrons, as well as the Virehnai and the humans both getting involved in human politics. The Virehnai made bonds and alliances with humans that put the humans at a loss?"

"What do you mean by at a loss?" Reman asked Elaina. She thought to herself, 'I guess we're going for bonus points...'
She replied, "The humans they formed bonds with were royalty, who already had bonds, oaths and allegiances in place based on loyalty, relationships and marriages; once the additional blood bonds and oaths they formed with the Virehnai were added to what already existed, it didn't work. It put humans into situations where they had to make nearly impossible choices; many went back on their oaths and allegiances to humans and Virehnai patrons multiple times. They were trying to keep all of their oaths and alliances, even when they were at odds. It didn't work, and left scores of humans dead, along with a great number of Virehnai. There were enough people suddenly aware of the Virehnai, dead or alive, that it drew attention to us and nearly outed us. The Compact came about as a result and was an answer to what happened in the Fourth War." When he remained quiet for a few moments, Elaina looked at him expectantly.

"I was alive when the Compact came into force." Reman said quietly.

"You were? You were there?"

"I was alive, and experienced it, but I wasn't in Romania. I had only been a Virehn for a year or two. I was crossing a room at my house in Susa, which was in Persia back then; it's Iran now. I didn't know then what happened; only that something did, and it changed things. I found out much later that what I felt was the Compact being cast."

"You could feel it that strongly?"

He nodded his head slowly and answered yes. "It uses ancient, very strong magic."

"I'm still getting used to the idea that magic exists, and that there are witches. It's strange for me to imagine them in a modern, tech-driven world."

He laughed. "I can understand that. You will know with a certainty in about two weeks' time, though. You won't doubt anymore. Michel was there when the Compact was cast. As they say, 'The blood remembers.' His blood will be your blood." His face took on a more somber expression. "Technology may have changed the world we interact with, but it hasn't ever, and truly won't ever, change human nature. Or Virehnai nature, for that matter. Did you know that there was almost a fifth war?"

"No." Elaina gave Reman a questioning look.

"There was," he told her. "It was all the same people and players as the Fourth War but removed by several centuries. And if you look closely enough, you'll discover many of the same players in the Third War, as well. They had all the same loyalties, all the same problems, were still fighting over the same patches of land, and intermarriage and family feuds still complicated it. It is true; there is nothing new under the sun."

Elaina looked confused, because she wasn't connecting the dots he was leaving for her. "You would likely know what could have been our fifth war as your World War I." He sighed. "It is what it is. Never forget…we were all as human," he pointed at Elaina, "as you are right now. Well….at least for the next two weeks, anyway."

5

LONDON CALLING

The CEO of the London office of VarenCorp sat at his desk, going through his email. David Lambert was old as Virehnai go; he became a Virehn immediately after the Second Virehnai War. It happened in Gaul, in the city of Massilia, now known as Marseilles in the year 398 BCE. He fought in the Third Virehnai War; that's how he met Michel Robichaux and his sire.

Once, David, Michel and Howard, along with Michel and Howard's sire, Diotimus Artimidorus, were all good friends. They weren't from the same clan, but that wasn't mattering as much, the further they went from the beginnings of their people. All were Draz'kul; they hunted together, fought together. They stayed close like that all the way up through the end of the French Revolution.

The French Revolution had been costly to him; it hadn't been another named Virehnai war, but David still lost many a good friend because of it. Most of the good friends he lost had to do with losing their heads–literally, including several of his clan siblings, along with Vibia Sabina and Artimidorus. Two of his losses, though, simply walked out of his life: Michel and Howard. It felt like a slap in the face; an affront. They had all been Draz'kul, and close. Within a hundred years after Artimidorus died, Michel decided he was now Sulahnai and moved to New York. Howard, ever following on Michel's coattails, went to New York soon after. Maybe Michel thought he'd change his mind and follow, too; as far as David was concerned, it'd be a cold day in hell before he changed allegiances. He never understood what caused Michel to do it. Instead of moving around like they used to, Michel put down roots - set up a life, and an identity. He visited the Sulahnai in the area and made known his intent to change allegiances. Several of his children followed him to New York, along with a bunch of Howard's children, too. Soon after, they set up a company and hired a bunch of humans. Among them was Howard Pancioni, and soon Michel had a blood arrangement with him. They supposedly were great friends, though how a Virehn can truly be friends with their food, David couldn't understand.

Michel tried explaining, although to David, it sounded…hollow. Michel told him he'd lost too many people; it seemed like so much babbling to David, particularly since he didn't seem so broken up about the death of his sire. The way David looked at it, anyone who didn't want to be in his life didn't need to stay there. Michel exited, as did Howard. Good riddance, David thought. Who needs them?

Fast forward to the modern day. When he became the CEO of the London Office of VarenCorp, he now crossed paths with them occasionally. They kept their distance from one another. His youngest daughter, Jodi, laughingly told him he and Michel were 'frenemies.' Once she explained the concept, he had to agree. Whenever they were physically in contact, they were friendly, albeit in a standoffish way. Any communication between them was polite, civil, and open–exactly how executives should communicate with one another. He had to admit he still held a bit of a grudge against them but couldn't fault their behavior toward him. David kept his behavior and communications likewise.

Three months ago, something changed, and it pissed David off to no end. It wasn't business. It was personal. It pissed him off enough to do something about it.

What changed? Someone hacked his private businesses in some very weird ways. The first time it happened, he thought nothing of it. In this modern day and age, it was almost the cost of doing business. That whole concept of 'shit happens.' There would always be unscrupulous people, and if you ever caught up with them, it was damned hard to make any charges stick, especially if you're in one country and the hackers are in another. You almost needed to have a forensic accountant in your back pocket. The second time he got hacked, he was angry—especially as it involved properties. The third time came right on the heels of the second. At his company, Equinox Holdings, they found proof of hacking; the metadata, which are like digital fingerprints, implied that someone in Robichaux's camp did it. When they looked deeper, they found many irregularities. That only made David angrier.

There was money being siphoned in small amounts from many accounts that amounted to millions of dollars. There were several properties that Equinox held solely as investments where property titles were hacked and changed. They were now in the name of a company called "SanguineHoldings.com, Inc." When they searched the company, it was like a Russian nesting doll with one company owning another, ad infinitum. He had yet to determine who owned the company "SanguineHoldings.com." The only thing he knew was his companies didn't legally own certain properties anymore. SanguineHoldings hadn't sold them; they weren't doing anything with them – they simply transferred the ownership to the holding company. Who does that?

One of his oathsworn employees discovered the link to Robichaux. He volunteered to kick around in the technical details, and said, "Does the name Robichaux mean anything to you?" That's when he realized the scope of his problem. Equinox's IT guy, working with the bloodsworn forensic accountant they hired, later found metadata clearly implicating Clan Robichaux in the thefts. His employee had been right. It left him gobsmacked, as well as disappointed and angry. Why? Why now? What prompted such an action? The only thing he could think of was a recent judgment that went against Robichaux's company, determined by the VarenCorp Council; The Council is five randomly picked Virehnai, who are asked to judge on a docket of assembled cases on a monthly basis. The cases are ones that are strictly between Virehn, so they stay in their own orbit instead of involving the human legal system. It's the VarenCorp version of 'jury duty.'

Lambert was picked and served. One of the legal matters they asked him to weigh in on was Robichaux's case. Usually, whoever is the oldest Virehnai serving chairs the Council, to guarantee both fairness, and to serve as a tiebreaker. The ability to be impartial and have no relation to the cases is a requirement. As David had no relation to the case, he didn't recuse himself. Maybe Michel thought he intentionally swayed the outcome. Michel would've seen his name on the judgment, and as the oldest Virehn on the Council this go-round, all the paperwork would've reflected that he not only served, but that he chaired it, and his vote broke a tie against Michel. Some days you win, some days you don't. That day Michel lost.

But to steal money and properties from him in response? It seemed…petty. It was overkill. Even estranged from Michel, he'd thought better of him than that. The only one he knew of in Michel's orbit that had the chops and bonafides to accomplish that kind of hacking was Michel's son Johannes. David saw it as flaunting the Compact; the difference is that nobody died because of the hacking. Technology, computer fraud and hacking were some of the modern ways you could screw another Virehn over, without drawing the attention and the wrath of the egregore - and it made David blazingly angry. 'Steal my money? Steal my property? Game on, bitch.'

He decided that as payback, he would respond in kind, so he began siphoning off money from Shadow Dance Holdings two months ago. He thought about doing it from Robichaux's investment firm, RAIC: Richmond Atlantic Investment Corporation. That was the investment group that funded his whole clan. He went with siphoning from Shadow Dance because it was personally owned by Michel. The response? Another property's title was stolen. It infuriated him. Which is why a little over a month ago, David came to a rather extreme decision for this day and age: Michel would forfeit someone. It wouldn't be easy to do, but it wasn't impossible, either. It was more a matter of finding the right people. He didn't realize how close at hand they were. He was acting out of anger but felt he was within his right. Financial terrorism was the modern-day equivalent, he felt, of yesterday's treachery. He was successful in his aim but now was overly cautious. On reflection a couple of weeks later, he was questioning whether he'd gone too far with his revenge. It was making him nervous and afraid of discovery.

David had been watching his emails and quietly checking databases to see if he was clear of suspicion. He saw when the death certificate for John came through. He died in a gruesome multi-car accident on I-95 between Newark and Manhattan that left him decapitated. Invariably, the internal VarenCorp death certificate stated the means of death as "accidental decapitation; incompatible with life."

David read it with a certain amount of relief and then shrugged his shoulders. Maybe it was wrong, but that's what Michel deserved for fucking with his businesses, property and his money. He was still watching for any updates, and who John's successor would be. So far, there were no updates. He was safe. The 'accident' appeared to everyone to be a legitimate accident. There are lots of accidents on that stretch of I-95. With as many people passing through that are unsure of where they're headed, or what lane they need to be in…it wasn't unusual. Nor was it especially hard to hire someone to cause an accident. The woman driving the minivan had stage four ovarian cancer, and an extremely poor prognosis. In exchange for a very generous sum of money placed into a trust fund for her two children, she simultaneously ensured their futures, and saved herself and them from the sad, long death that awaited her. An accident was considerably faster than dragging her family through death by cancer. That John Robichaux was decapitated? That…? That was a pure stroke of luck, and he saw it as a sign that things would go his way. That day, he'd had another person on standby, discreetly following the woman's minivan…a 'concerned bystander' who would attempt to render aid…the 'aid' that involved gasoline and John's car being torched. Fire is incompatible with life, too. Because John was decapitated, the man didn't need to do anything; David paid him anyway for his time. My stroke of luck is his stroke of luck, too. Bonus. He would've stopped there, except…his forensics guy found more signs of mischief, including thefts of money, which added up. All the mischief STILL led back to Robichaux's camp. WTF.

Two and a half weeks ago, he was waiting to see who would replace John. He hoped it would be someone useful to him. Like clockwork, he saw the succession forms in the database. "Elaina Jacoby."

Elaina was the youngest daughter of one of the wealthiest families in New York, long tied to the Robichaux family. Her immigrant great grandfather Howard Pancioni changed his name to Jacoby to help hide his Italian ancestry in a time when being Italian in New York was difficult, and went to work for Michel, becoming bloodsworn to him, starting a dynasty. Michel was taken to task several times for being close friends with Howard's son, HJ. So much of all the information about their family was a total sham. The Jacoby family's public story is "Immigrant comes to America with nothing and creates an empire." HJ was the step and fetch-it guy for a Virehn, who was smart enough to parlay his association and friendship into wealth and businesses. All wealthy families come with a certain amount of drama, posturing, and politics, and the current Jacoby's wouldn't be any different. Having Walt Jacoby's youngest ascend was completely unexpected, however. From what he heard through the grapevine, he was replacing his oldest and best-loved son with a human he truly cared for, ignoring the politics that came along with wealth and power. How touching. He quietly did a bit of research into Elaina and decided that she might be useful after all. David had been incredibly lucky thus far.

He came to this conclusion after sitting with several of his own children as they had dinner together, draining the two unconscious men who lay on the conference room table before them.

As news spread about the demise of John Robichaux, he felt he needed to act sooner than later, and his children agreed, particularly after they found new signs of financial mischief. It had just been an idea, but an employee…made known his desire to be useful, and willingness to help.

David Lambert and his most trusted children decided the soon-to-be newest Robichaux child should have an RFID tracking chip in her. Getting it there would accomplish two ends: first, with her in

Michel's 'inner circle' it would give him a strategic opportunity to know where she was should he…need it…in the future, and second, he wanted her to feel unsafe…because if Michel truly loved the woman, her lack of safety would get under his skin.

The employee who wanted to be useful, a man named Carlos, claimed to know sketchy people who could get into the midtown Robichaux building and even access the residential portion of it. That would accomplish his aims. He warned Carlos that he was paying him double BECAUSE if he or any of those 'sketchy people' were caught, he would deny all knowledge of them or the task, and they would be on their own. Carlos seemed fine with that and took it in stride. He wasn't bloodsworn, only oathsworn. David also made sure Carlos knew he didn't want Elaina to be physically harmed. He didn't want to risk being subject to the Compact's egregore. He saw this as a way of finding out what ELSE Michel was up to. David remembered all too well the days of treachery before the Compact, and knew Michel would, too. David ramped up security and precautions around his businesses and person, just in case.

David hated to think that way, but he had no other way he could think about it after turning it over and over in his mind. Once, he and Robichaux had been good friends. Both had misgivings about the Compact, but accepted it, knowing there needed to be an end to the wars that threatened their existence in multiple ways. David Lambert had little use for Michel anymore…not since he'd abandoned the Draz'kul.

6

OF ETIQUETTE AND POLITICS

As Elaina came into her last two weeks as a human, she was busy. She had a to-do list that only seemed to grow. Elaina received her key to her new suite at the primary Virehnai building downtown; as her case officer had told her, it was suite 1207. Elaina was mostly packed. She'd got a friendly email reminding her that movers would arrive in the middle of next week to move all her furniture and whatever boxes she wanted them to move for her, and that those things needed to be ready. They were. Elaina decided that there were some things that she would move herself. As she perused the email, it looked like her first night in the new building would be next Thursday.

Aside from moving, tomorrow she will have her first 'official' meeting with Uncle Michel. Official, meaning they would have 'lunch.' She was going to have a pecan encrusted chicken and cranberry salad, and he would have a glass of O Negative. Much like when Amalie ate in front of her, this was another etiquette situation where Uncle Michel would eat in front of her.

What made it official was that he was supposed to be 'officially' letting her know that when she received his blood and ascended, that she would be subject to the Compact. It was another VarenCorp 'box' to check off; Elaina already knew. She'd already gone over the Compact with Amalie, and with the Val'sheth, Reman. However, because not every clan was as efficient, they still had to go through the motions and check off the requisite boxes. Aside from meeting with Uncle Michel, she also had a lunch meeting with her father scheduled on Friday to discuss wills and succession, and there would also be a celebration dinner at her parents' home the night before the ritual. Her mom had already checked with her to see what she wanted her last meal to be, before she…well…died the next day. Elaina decided she wanted Fettucine Alfredo. That alone prompted odd discussions. Her mom wanted to cook homemade, her dad wanted to celebrate out, and her brothers were only going because their father would give them grief if they didn't. Unlike her parents and sister, they weren't celebrating her good fortune.

What capped off how surreal everything felt? She got an email from Reman, the Vel'sheth. It was nice, truthfully. He was double-checking with her to make sure she wasn't freaking out about the process of being made Virehn as the date approached and also suggested spiritually aligned things she could do to make her transition to Virehn more meaningful. His suggestions were thoughtful, and she contemplated doing some of them. He'd suggested going to visit her grandparents graves, and telling them about her decision as if they could hear her; writing herself a letter as a human that she would tuck away and open when she was older and possibly facing the loss of someone as Amalie lost Johannes, and finally, suggested that she get absolutely wrecked on her favorite alcohol, since it won't have any effect soon. Reman also recommended watching a sunset on a beach and picking up a shell or a trinket to remind her of the moment. He also asked if she wanted a blessing before going into the ceremony, which she ultimately declined. It had the desired effect, though, and left her thoughtful.

Elaina wasn't scared of dying…exactly. Amalie unofficially sat down with her the other day and spelled out the death process in gory detail. She herself didn't remember being made; Johannes turned her while she was sick, unconscious, and near death. There was no consent involved, other than him checking with her family members before he did it. Amalie only remembered waking up, and the assault on her senses more than anything else. Since Johannes made her, she'd been to two makings; there was a little light she could shed on the process. Elaina could tell she was trying to prepare her without scaring the absolute shit out of her. "Both times," Amalie told her, "The people being turned started out fine; they were calm and quiet–at least until they hit a certain point. There's a place where your innate human desire to survive shows up. One was a woman; she was so frightened she cried through parts of it until she lost consciousness. The man…he didn't cry, but I've seen no one look more frightened, with wide-eyed panic in my life."

"Great to know. Check. Make sure I go to the bathroom first, so I don't publicly pee myself out of total fear."

Amalie burst out laughing. "Oh, my God! You're going to make me laugh during the ceremony, thinking of that." She tried to shake the notion away. "Don't elaborate on that; if I laugh, it'll be all your fault…"

That's where Elaina's psyche was tonight, and what she was squaring with. She was alive as a human today, and her calendar was getting full of things she either needed to do or wanted to do to prepare for NOT being human. As the next twelve days counted down, it was counting down to a liminal moment that most humans never face that wasn't in their realm of experience; when she would cease to be human and become something…other.

Truthfully, it felt like walking up to an enormous precipice, and contemplating leaping off of it. As she readied for bed, she realized she truly had no clue what she was getting into. Elaina only knew she trusted her father and Uncle Michel and had to believe that if she was going to do the equivalent of jumping off of a cliff, that she would land on her feet and they would be there for her.

The next day, she had her meeting with Michel. She came up to the elevator, exiting at the penthouse level. "Hi Emily," she said, greeting Uncle Michel's executive assistant. She was petite, with blond hair and green eyes. From what Amalie told her; she was about 320 years old. Not bad, since she didn't look a day over 28.

"Hi Elaina. He'll be ready for you soon. He wasn't expecting the meeting he's in. Go ahead and have a seat."

Elaina only waited about ten minutes. The door to Michel's office opened, and Uncle Michel walked with his visitor to Emily's desk. "Thanks, Bobby. I appreciate the update." That's when he noticed Elaina was sitting there waiting for him. Michel smiled when he saw her.

Bobby glanced at Elaina and smiled at her. "Hello."

"Bobby, let me introduce Elaina Jacoby. She'll be transitioning soon; she's succeeding Johannes." Michel turned back to Elaina, "Elaina, this is Bobby Davidov, of Clan Sabin."

He held out his hand, and they shook hands. "Elaina, nice to meet you."

"Likewise, sir."

Bobby turned to Michel, and they shook hands, too. "See ya later, Michel." Bobby turned, and went to the elevator, and Michel turned to Elaina, gestured to his office, and said "Shall we?"

Elaina sat in the cushy leather chair across from Michel's desk. He chuckled. "I'm supposed to talk to you about the Compact, but I know Amalie's already gone over it. So what would you like to talk about?"

"I still wouldn't mind talking about the Compact. Amalie told me you were there when it came into existence?"

He nodded. "I was."

"What was that like?"

"Remember; the Fourth Virehnai War had ended recently. I fought in it; so did Howard. Many Virehnai died, whether in actual battle or through some form of treachery. There were lots of battlefield transitions. All the sides had witches; most of those were turned against their will, and they were forced into terrorizing their opposition. There were so many of us stretched between Bosnia to Bulgaria that we were truly in danger of being discovered."

"After all that, one of the very best and brightest of us was able to facilitate a large-scale meeting to broker a peace. Her plan: to have some of the ill-used witches create a spell that would keep us from killing one another. Some people were…hesitant to agree. To be really honest, I was hesitant, too; so was my sire, Diotimus."

"What made you so hesitant?" Elaina asked.

"That after having the witches fighting against us, we'd now be trusting them to cast a spell that bound us all. You'd be hard pressed to find a Virehnai blood witch these days, but if you show me one, I'll show you someone not trusted by most of the Virehnai around them…" He took a sip of his lunch. "That we all agreed, and they cast the spell at all tells you everything you need to know about how destructive the Fourth War was. We were THAT close to discovery." He gestured with his thumb and forefinger, nearly touching, showing the narrowest of margins. "That was not only because of our numbers of living and dead but also by nobility who knew of us that were notoriously capricious, along with the Holy Roman Empire, and even the Church. We were ultimately less afraid of the witches than we were about being outed; particularly by royalty or the church."

"So fear was the primary reason everyone agreed to it?

"Fear, and the hope of peace. Ultimately, we were talked into it. Once the spell was cast, and the Compact went into force, the numbers of people dying because of treachery dropped to zero. Worked like a charm. Back when I was made, the very oldest of us only made it to old age by trusting no one, and all but becoming hermits. Even now, Ari, the head of VarenCorp never travels, and stays sequestered at his compound in Zurich. I can count the people he sees physically on one hand."

"Why?" Elaina had a puzzled expression. "Doesn't the Compact keep him safe? That's what it's supposed to do…"

"Well, yes…and no. Look at it from Ari's point of view. In theory, no one will risk killing him because to kill him means the killer's own life would be forfeit. But when you've lived as long as Ari has… Let's just say that Ari wasn't the nicest person before the Compact was signed, and his major concern before agreeing to it was to make sure that the Compact wouldn't count his past actions against him…because if it did, it would kill him outright. To this day, Ari stays put in Zurich and limits physical access to his person because he doesn't trust that someone won't 'take one for the team,' and off him out of simple revenge."

"Wow." Elaina contemplated it, then asked, "How does somebody like that end up in charge? I thought the Virehnai were supposed to be smarter than that."

Michel laughed. "How do they ever, human or Virehnai?" He paused. "Power. Money. Connections. In Ari's case, he owned an inn. It was a crossroads of society, and served everyone from humans on pilgrimages, Crusaders and Knights Templar fighting in the Holy Land or leading knights to it for the church, to both Draz'kul and Sulahnai. In fact, that was how VarenCorp got its start. He made it known that any Virehnai that needed help could find it there, as long as they treated everyone with respect, didn't hunt while on his property, and kept a low profile when among humans staying there." Michel harrumphed. "VarenCorp didn't hire him…he invented VarenCorp." Michel paused, while he took another sip. "One reason he's STILL in charge is because the thing he was always best at, aside from hospitality, was information. One well-placed word from Ari could make you rich, get you dead…or be used against you. VarenCorp has an intelligence arm that rivals the CIA."

"Wow. Actually, that doesn't surprise me; I get it now. My case officer brought up my files, and it surprised me to see so much of my information in there. Now I know why." She shrugged her shoulders. "Amalie never told me any of that about VarenCorp. Until now, I only knew the CEO was named Ari Cottrell. I didn't know that he created it…or that it could give the CIA competition, though it makes sense." Michel nodded and smiled.

"It's known as VarenCorp today; it wasn't originally called that, though. The name change and restructuring didn't happen until 1924. Originally, the Draz'kul traditionally ran inns and hotels. The Sulahnai were merchant bankers…and that's mostly still the case. Beyond that, both groups had advocates as well; called lawyers, and law firms today. The precursor to VarenCorp, 'The Velascar Company,' had its' beginnings in 1539, in Zurich, which drew most aspects of all of them under one umbrella, not only serving us all, but tying the Virehnai together as a group, and giving us more structure. The Velascar Company was Ari's brainchild, and because of his dealings with both Draz'kul and Sulahnai, he had buy in from both groups and made many people – including himself – insanely wealthy." Michel paused as Elaina connected dots in her head. He could see it on her face even as she did.

"It also brings up the current Virehnai political hot potato, too. You should probably know about it, because I'm sure eventually, you'll hear someone talking."

As Michel stopped to gather his thoughts, Elaina took a couple of bites of her salad. "We who were there when the Compact came into being knew what a toll the war had taken, and exactly what was at risk. Everyone knew they were deciding on behalf of everyone; even if they weren't at the meeting. Some of the newer Virehnai…question…our decision. I think honestly, most of us want the Compact to stay exactly as it is. It…works. Those who criticize it complain that it serves those of us who are older, claiming that it allows us to have what amounts to a stranglehold on everyone else; 'it gives us too much power,' they say. To a degree, they might have a point; particularly if they're talking about Ari. I can tell you: if it weren't for the Compact, I would never have made it to the age I am. Someone, somewhere, would've done me wrong."

"Those who criticize the Compact fall into two camps. The first group believes the world is a different place than it used to be, and we should 'get rid of the Compact' entirely."

"That explains something," Elaina said. "When we went to the museum at VarenCorp, Amalie was telling me the real knife in

Zurich is in an indestructible display case, in case someone gets the brilliant idea to destroy it."

"She's right. That's exactly the reason the Knife of Becoming is so protected. There are some who think if they could get rid of the so-called 'Witchfang,' it might get rid of the Compact. Others…are a bit more hesitant. Even if they think destroying it would get rid of the Compact, they question if destroying it would it get rid of the Virehnai, too? Would we all go 'poof'! and disappear? Who knows? No one wants to find out." They both laughed.

"The second group…" Michel shook his head, "They see someone like Ari Cottrell, and get angry."

"Because he's old? Or because he has dirt on everyone?"

"Yes." He chuckled, and bobbed his head around, like 'Duh.'

"Recently, Ari talked about 'retiring;' letting someone 'younger' take over."

"That would be good, right?"

"It sounds good in theory. It would, if he were talking about someone unrelated to him taking the reins. Unfortunately, he's talking about his son Tim, taking over…and Tim's closer to my age. VarenCorp would stay with Ari's family, instead of allowing the rest of us to have more of a say; the person in charge would still be someone who's considerably older than most. Despite trying to tell him, Ari isn't listening to anyone else's opinions or thoughts. That doesn't sit well with a lot of folks. That's one way we SHOULD change with the times. Is Ari our CEO? Our king? A dictator? With VarenCorp, some think there's not much difference, whatever the title Ari chooses for himself. If the company that governs us is a family possession, it leaves us little recourse if we don't like the way things are going."

Michel paused. "If you thought you were joining a democracy…uh, no." He shook his head. "As a human, you still have more say in your life than we do. I've always felt that most of the time, younger folks, when they complain, are speaking out of jealousy. Everything is relative, I suppose. I don't know of any impoverished Virehnai…but I guarantee you that as an older Virehn, the substance and means at my disposal is more than what most have access to. That's one reason why most clans, including ours, set up Clan-owned businesses and investments that benefit the entire Clan. It helps spread the wealth, even to the surrounding humans. The bonus checks you get quarterly through the firm are part of that effort. Aside from that, every Virehn gets a generous check monthly; you will too. Nobody around us is hurting, no matter how jealous individuals may get."

"I didn't realize."

"Most of the humans have no reason to question it or ask. The Virehnai, though? Quite a few don't like the way VarenCorp is structured and will openly vent about it. That's…normal. There's a smaller subset of that second group that is considerably smaller, and extremely secretive. That's…not normal. They're off the radar and tend not to play by the rules. They use tech. They use people as proxies to do their dirty work. They do whatever they must. Those Virehn differ from most, because they don't merely want some change; they want to see the status quo come crashing down. When I say crashing down, I mean VarenCorp as an entity, Ari as a person, and the Compact in its entirety. What makes them really dangerous is that they don't stop there. They want to be public; to out us. All of us, whether we, individually or corporately, would choose to be outed or not."

Elaina's eyes widened. "Why would they do that? Wouldn't that put targets on everyone's backs?"

"It could. They want every Virehnai-owned business openly revealed as Virehnai. They want our whole society to be revealed to the world. They believe it would be a win-win proposition for the Virehnai regardless. Either the humans accept us – which they believe will happen, based on nothing more than humanity's love of stereotypical 'vampires' as they've been depicted; or…if humanity decides the Virehnai, once we reveal ourselves, are too scary to continue to live, we would simply rise up, quickly dominate humanity, and take charge."

"We would become humanity's overlords, or something like that?

"That's accurate." Michel shook his head. "Usually, from what I've seen in my long life, the people who want to be in charge the absolute worst are the ones least suited mentally and emotionally to be allowed to do it."

Lunch wrapped up after that. It was an interesting conversation, but it couldn't help but make her think about what her future as a Virehn held.

7

WELCOME

Two days and counting.

There would be ritual and ceremony. As Amalie had schooled her, the Virehnai liked to remember the niceties. She also reminded her, "The ritual, where you die, makes you immortal. The ceremony where you drink Michel's blood first is where you ascend."

It was a long-held belief among the Virehnai that they weren't soulless. How could they be? In Egypt, they had a ka and a ba. When a Virehnai died, they believed their soul would be reincarnated into a newly born human being, giving them another chance at life as a mortal. That made some Virehnai happy, while others preferred the life they led.

Midweek, Elaina officially met with her father and his personal attorney, to write her will. More than anything, this was an 'escape hatch,' so to speak. That way, if she decided in the future that she needed to change her look, and her identity, and the personage everyone knows as "Elaina Jacoby" officially gets 'knocked off,' she'll be leaving her worldly goods to herself, along with her family. It also covers her assets in the off chance that like Johannes, she were to physically die. She had to laugh. Uncle Michel was officially "Michel Francoise Robichaux, the Fourth." He'd been leaving his money and wealth to himself for quite some time, as had Uncle Howard.

The other notable thing Elaina did midweek was arrange an outing. Specifically, she took Reman's advice; She got together with Mia Lightner, Mia's cousin Michael Ratner, her own elder sister Janet, and their cousin Amy Haussman. All of them played together as children, though Janet and Amy, despite being oathsworn, lived separate lives away from the Virehnai. They went to a club in lower Manhattan with a rooftop lounge; good music, good food…and an excellent view of the city. They had dinner, enjoyed each other and the music, and afterwards, they all went back to Elaina's, checking out her new place downtown.

She used her keycard to get them all in and up to her suite.

"Nice digs," Michael commented.

"Thanks. Excuse the boxes…As you can see, I'm still unpacking."

They sat and drank, and would be chauffeured home, for sure. Elaina got plastered. When Janet commented on her state…not that Janet was far behind her…Elaina made them all laugh. "The Vel'sheth… Reman? He TOLD me to do this. He told me, 'Go get drunk.'"

They howled with laughter. "Why?" Janet snorted. "That's like a…a…priest telling you to get drunk!"

Elaina nearly fell off the edge of the sofa laughing as she answered. "It's because in another two days, alcohol will NEVER have this effect on me again." They had a good laugh. Why not? It's rare to hear of a priest telling a parishioner to get wrecked.

"Are you scared?" Janet asked her, after the laughter died down.
"Nope." She shook her head no. "I'm more afraid that it'll hurt, or that I'll embarrass myself or Papa."

"How could you embarrass yourself?" Michael asked her.

She told them the story Amalie told her, about the one lady who cried and the man that had a panic attack…and then that she didn't want to pee herself, which made them all laugh. It was funny, sure, but they were all mostly plastered, so it seemed twice as funny.

64

"Really?" He asked her, more seriously. "Howard told me I was on a short list; that I've "impressed" everyone," he said, making air quotes. "If I mind my p's and q's, it could be me next time. It seems like a lot to deal with, to be contemplating…like…your death, and navigating through all of that, plus worrying about doing something embarrassing at the same time."

Mia looked at him. "Wow. If Howard told you that, you're a shoo-in for the next go-round."

Janet giggled uncontrollably, and they all looked at her. They weren't sure if it was that she thought it was funny, or if it was just that she was wasted….or both.

"What?" Michael asked. "I think I'd be a good Virehn."

"You would, Michael. I was imagining how butthurt Doug would be when you DO."

They all broke out into laughter then, but after it died down, Elaina got more serious.

"When I met with Papa the other day about my will, Papa warned me to stay out of Doug and Rob's way for a while. He apologized for them. He said both of them approached him, lobbying to succeed Johannes. Papa said after I got named, they both acted like spoiled 10-year-olds. He told me basically to 'take the high road,' and if they won't be nice to me, or happy for me, at least avoid them."

"You know, that kind of sucks that your old man had to tell you that." Michael commented, as he finished another beer.

Elaina shrugged her shoulders. "It is. But he followed it up with a really epic speech about how it's all about family. He said if by keeping my distance, I can keep Doug and Rob from saying anything now they can't take back later, it will strengthen us as a family someday down the road."

"Papa said that?" Janet asked.

"Yeah, he did."

They all lifted their glasses and toasted Walt. "Walt Jacoby; smart man."

The evening before her ceremony, she went out to dinner with her family at Osteria Barocca, their favorite restaurant in Little Italy. Her great grandfather had lived in Little Italy after he immigrated here, but before he met Uncle Michel. Whenever generations of her family had something to celebrate, they ended up in Little Italy. She had the restaurant's Fettucine Alfredo that featured their handmade noodles, and a rich, yummy parmesan sauce, along with a couple of glasses of limoncello. For dessert, she had some of the raspberry panna cotta that was the evening's special. It doesn't get much better than THAT for a last meal as a human.

The next night, Elaina would partake in the Ritual of Becoming, and the day after, the Ceremony of Ascension. During the ritual, Elaina's human life would end. Only Virehnai could attend the Ritual. An exception was made for Elaina's father. No other humans would be present; if Walt Jacoby hadn't been Elaina's father and bloodsworn both, he wouldn't be in attendance, either. It comes back to the prohibition on drinking in front of humans.

In the Ascension Ceremony the next day, Elaina would stand before her "uncle" Michel, and swear fealty to him, and then would solemnly acknowledge that she was bound by the Compact, as was every Virehnai. The magic of the Compact came along with the blood Elaina would receive at the Ritual of Becoming from Michel, and accepting it was more a detail than anything else, but it was a necessary detail. The members of Robichaux's clan, friends and allies from other clans, representatives from VarenCorp, along with several trusted human friends, would also be present, including Elaina's mom and dad, and her brothers and sister. The Ascension Ceremony was one of the few exceptions to 'no drinking in front of humans.' It was a small amount. There would be a party after the Ascension Ceremony was complete.

The evening of her Ritual of Becoming came. Elaina dressed in simple black linen pants and a white t-shirt. She took a small sip from a bottle of water beside her. "Don't forget to bow towards Reman first, then Michel." Amalie told her. They were sitting in one of the small antechambers that sat next to the Hall from the vestibule. All the Virehnai were assembled, and when they were ready for her, someone would fetch her and Amalie.

In the Hall, Michel addressed his clan, and Walt. "While it's always sad when we lose someone, gaining new members is a happy occasion. It helps lessen the sting of loss."

"Most of you here know Elaina, at least in passing; some of you, like myself, have known her all her life. I remember holding her the first day Walt brought her home from the hospital. It's been a joy to watch her grow into the woman she's become. I've been proud to be her 'Uncle Michel' her whole life, and I've even made her promise to still call me that." He paused for a minute. "I can't imagine a better person to join us. She will be an asset to our clan, and I'm looking forward to seeing the Virehn she will become. I've loved her as my 'niece' her whole life; I'm delighted that she will now be my child."

"Walt? Will you please join me here?" Walt walked up beside his friend. Michel put a hand over his heart. "I'm thankful you've let me be such a part of Elaina's life. Thank you for sharing her with me. I've always loved being her 'Uncle,'" as he did air quotes. "Once she's Virehnai, I'll love her as a daughter, as well. I solemnly promise you that I'll take care of her as you would. From now on," he told Walt, "Not only will you have the Robichaux clan watching over your family, one of your own will watch over them, too." Michel paused. "Walt, will you escort Elaina and Amalie in to join us?"

Elaina heard a soft knock at the door, and it opened, and her father's head poked in. "It's time." As she stood, he opened the door wider, opened his arms wide, and gave his youngest daughter a long hug. "I'm so proud of you, sweetheart. Your Mama and I love you."

"I love you, too, Papa."

They moved toward the double doors with the frosted glass that led to the Hall. There was a symbol etched into the glass. She always imagined it meant something mystical and deep. It was both the sigil and the proper name for the Hall that took the place of a word in old Virehnai: "Tual'Sa'virehn." It meant "Hall of the Bloodbound."

It was odd. She'd been through these doors a handful of times; the thought occurred to her that this was the last time she would pass beyond them as a human. There was a granite wall, with an inscription carved into it, in multiple languages, like a Rosetta stone. She'd asked Reman about it in passing while he was giving her and Amalie their history lesson, as another VarenCorp box got checked off. It contained Egyptian hieroglyphs; the writing she'd thought was runic was actually proto-Arabic. There was also cuneiform, Sanskrit, and Greek. Thanks to Reman, she now knew each line said "We are the Virehnai" in each language. There had been major diasporas of Virehnai to all these places in their history; it was one more way of remembering what came before.

The wall, though beautiful, wasn't solely decorative. It actually helped to preserve the ancient feel of the space once inside the Hall. It blocked participants from seeing the modern double doors. It forced anyone passing through the double doors from the vestibule to turn either to the left or right forming a small hallway. Once beyond the hallway, there was the hall: a round space that Elaina could only ever describe as ancient-looking, with the feel of a church. There was a stone dais in the center, lit from above, with low lighting around the room. Whenever Elaina entered the Hall, it felt to her as if she were traveling through time and ended up in the ancient past. Amalie lead the way down the hallway, with Elaina behind her, and Walt bringing up the rear. She turned into the round space, where everyone waited for her.

Tonight, the dais in the center was covered with a red drape. There were candles on tall stands at either end. Michel and Reman stood behind the dais as they approached. Amalie stopped, knowing where she was supposed to wait. Walt and Elaina continued forward. Elaina acknowledged the priest, and then turned to Michel and acknowledged him, as he winked at her so quickly that she almost wondered if she saw it. Reman gestured toward the dais. She turned and hugged Papa one last time. "I love you, Papa." Walt smiled at her. "I love you, too, baby girl."

Elaina approached the dais and sat on the edge, swinging her legs up and lying upon it as gracefully as she could muster, trying not to take the red drape with her.

Michel moved to stand off to one side, behind Elaina's head; his hand rested on her shoulder. Walt joined them at the dais, stood by her other shoulder. Reman came to stand next to Michel, looked down at Elaina, and asked, for all to hear: "You wish to become Virehnai?

"Yes," she answered.

Reman then looked over to Michel. "You wish to claim this mortal being, and remake her as Virehnai, for the good of your clan?"

Michel answered, "It is." He squeezed her shoulder reassuringly.

The priest looked at Elaina, at Walt, and then finally at Michel. He nodded at them, and then slowly turned to all those assembled. "As it is spoken, so shall it be."

The priest came around to the front of the dais, beside Walt, saying: "From the first drop, we become. With the last, we rise. What is mortal will die. Whoever drinks will live. The Virehnai remain after all else turns to dust and blows away." The words, although spoken in English, were merely a newer translation of something ancient. When Reman finished speaking, all who were gathered responded with their expected reply:

"Ashera Virehnai. Zharath ka'velis."

The words were in Ancient Virehn and when translated, meant, "We are of the blood. The sacred fire remains unbroken." It was referencing her succession ceremony, where they ceremonially snuffed Johannes' flame and lit hers. The promise of the flame lit that evening would be fulfilled tonight.

"Viren Zuth Akret," the priest said, and all present repeated it. "Blood never forgets."

The priest came close; It was then that the knife he held caught the light and flashed in the candlelight. He cut quickly. The bite of the blade into Elaina's left wrist, though she knew it was coming, was still a surprise, and she gasped a little. Her blood flowed freely from the cut, and a basin was placed beneath to catch it; they wasted none. This blood would be given to all those Virehnai gathered who would be her clan. They would drink from the basin, and from their new sister Elaina, as they celebrated her last moments as a human. Her father and Michel moved closer to her as the priest moved to her right side and cut the other wrist.

Elaina lay there quietly; she knew what her body would do. While most of her lessons with Amalie had been on the history of how the Virehnai began, and about the wars, the Compact and when and how it came into being – she had prepared her on what to expect at this rite. Amalie had warned her. Mentally, she was checking off all the stages as she passed through them. The priest would cut her wrists, and she would feel a bit of pain; Amalie told her it would soon fade away. In fact, it already had. There was only a dull throbbing that remained.

She knew as she bled out, she would eventually lose consciousness as she progressed into physical shock and her organs failed. Amalie told her, "Never forget: to become Virehnai is to die to your human life. Some of the stages you pass through before that happens will feel scary."

This is the point Amalie told her about the lady crying, and the man panicking during the ritual as they bled out. The only thing that made her worry is whether she would do likewise – or worse, do something that would end up embarrassing her, her family, or Uncle Michel.

"Remember that even though you may feel frightened or feel a sense of impending doom as your body passes through those stages that you will rise as Virehnai, but before you drink and live…you bleed and your physical body will die."

"That makes it sound so scary." Elaina remembered whining to Amalie.

Amalie didn't shrink away from the truth. "It IS. It should be. When you have nearly bled out, Michel will feed you his own blood – and his blood will kill you the rest of the way…but then, you'll rise, even as the First Flames did. After that, you'll be one of us. You'll be my clan sister forever."

Laying there on the dais, Elaina felt her heart beating faster and faster, and she was growing sleepy. She knew that her body was dying; there was no tap dancing around it; it really felt like doom, descending. Amalie had told her correctly. The process, while peaceful, had some frightening elements. She did her best to remain calm, although at several points, she shook and broke into a cold sweat. Papa and Michel stayed by her side, each with a hand reassuringly on her shoulder. She could see Amalie there, too, as well as any other number of Virehnai she had known or seen all her life. The love she felt both for them and from them helped to counter the fear she felt as she began drifting off into oblivion.

As Elaina reached a critical point where most of her blood was gone and she was unconscious, Michel sensed the erratic and considerably slower beating of her heart, and knew it was time. He used the same knife that took Elaina's life to cut his own wrist and give her life anew. Blood flowed, and he placed his copiously bleeding wrist carefully at her lips, and it flowed into her mouth. As Michel's blood pooled inside her mouth, the soft tissue lining the inside of her mouth, permeable with numerous blood vessels, began absorbing the blood.

The magic inherent in Michel's blood found a home in Elaina's as blood and magic spread throughout her body and began changing it; sustaining it. After a few minutes passed, Michel removed his wrist from her mouth and stepped back.

Reman stood at the foot of the dais, by Elaina's feet, as she hung somewhere in limbo between life and death. "It is done. Sanghir ka'zharath velai'thuun." It meant 'Blood and flame, bound, becoming.'

The assembled Virehnai all said as one, "Virehn Setha."

"Blood is Life."

Thump.............Thump..............Thump.

Gradually, something in the back of Elaina's brain was picking up what sounded like a steady drumbeat. She opened her eyes, and it seemed almost too bright. Amalie sat beside her, and as Elaina stirred, she sat her book on the table.

The room Elaina was resting in was known as a transition room. It had better soundproofing; the lighting was muted. In times past, a new Virehn's first awakening was...rough. Too bright, too harsh, too loud, too much going on and wanting their attention. This little thing: muting all the noise into something more bearable - they could do.

"Hey, sleepyhead." Amalie said, quietly.

"Hi."

Amalie giggled. "I get to be the welcome wagon…! Welcome to Clan Robichaux. How do you feel?"

Elaina sat up too fast.

"Reflexes, check." Elaina sighed, and even her own voice sounded loud to her. "Everything seems especially loud, and especially bright…but you told me that would happen." She sat for a minute, taking stock. "I mostly feel okay. My whole midsection feels like it's trying to cramp up."

Amalie nodded. "That's normal."

"Normal? That's normal?"

"Uh-huh. It's called hunger. Get used to that feeling. It'll be especially strong this time, because you haven't ascended yet. In these 'oh so modern' times, you're lucky. You'll get blood soon. The First Flames weren't that lucky. Never let yourself feel hungrier than you do now, or you may go hunger-blind and kill someone."

A soft rapping sounded at the door, and then it opened to reveal Michel poking his head in. "Good, you're awake…right on schedule. How are you feeling?"

"Like everything's too loud, too bright, and Amalie tells me the cramps I feel are hunger."

"Your brain and eyes will adjust to the light fairly quickly. The sound will take a little longer. Hunger? We can take care of that right now."

Amalie stood and held out a hand to Elaina. "Get up slowly unless you want to faceplant and make me laugh at you." Elaina took her friend's hand, and despite Amalie's warning, STILL stood up too fast. She didn't faceplant...but could've. Her first steps were almost experimental. Her reflexes were sharper now; like, knife edge sharp. Her senses were too. If she quieted her mind, she could hear her own heartbeat...along with Amalie's and Michel's. When she went through the door, suddenly she could hear what sounded like a symphony of heartbeats, going various speeds.

They walked with her very slowly, tentatively; giving her senses that much more time to acclimate. The lights out here were much brighter than the room she woke up in. The walk down the little hallway seemed slow, but the extra few minutes took the sharp edges off of her senses. By the time they reached the Hall, and passed through the doors, the light was mostly bearable; hearing all the heartbeats was still weird, but not as distracting. The one thing the hallway hadn't prepared her for was her sense of smell, which was also sharper. The humans either smelled faintly of body odor: dirty socks and lingering farts- or like they bathed in perfume trying to cover their smell up. Weirdest still, she could pick out some scents individually: laundry detergent, fabric softener, deodorant, bubble gum, along with a symphony of perfumes and aftershaves that blended into a department store perfume counter's nightmare – all with a chemical bottom note.

Michel went to stand by Reman, as Amalie continued past, and joined the rest of the group nearby.

Elaina stopped to stand in front of Reman, and Michel, facing them as Amalie had instructed. They both smiled at her.

Reman began speaking.

"Elaina Jacoby, your human life is past, and you are literally dead to it. You have received a gift of life, as passed from sire to child for millennia, which is right, and proper, and as it should be. It came about by an act of magic, and what is about to happen is no less an act of magic. That magic lives in the blood we carry within us."

"Tonight, you stand before us as one of us. You will ascend. You will receive your first blood as a Virehnai from your sire, and the magic within his blood will claim you, and bind you both to him, and to the Compact. You will see how Michel has lived his life; you will see his sire, and you will see all your ancestors back to the First Flame from whose blood you carry. Their flames now burn within you, along with Michel's flame...and your own."

"All that remains is that you swear fealty to your sire and the Compact within his blood, and drink of him. Do you do this freely and of your own accord?"

"I do."

"Then, Elaina, make your oath," Reman said. His words reverberated throughout the room.

"I, Elaina Maria Jacoby, swear obeisance to my sire, Michel Robichaux, today and always."

Michel stepped forward and smiled at Elaina. "I accept your oath and obeisance." He took the dagger from Reman that made her the night before; cutting his wrist, he bled into a chalice and handed it to Elaina.

Elaina took it and drank from her sire. It tasted coppery; a little peppery, even. The consistency was unlike anything she'd drank before. For a minute, she felt nothing different. She'd heard Amalie tell her that the magic came along with the Ritual of Becoming, when you became Virehn. The first blood you drank at the Ascension Ceremony after becoming Virehn acted as a fuse to the magic within, to set it on fire. Even as Elaina thought to herself, "Is this it?," the first individuals to call themselves Virehnai reached forward into the future through Michel's blood using magic as a conduit, and claimed Elaina as their own, and her mind...exploded in light, sound, color and emotion.

No matter how much Amalie tried to school her about what was going to happen, and how it would feel, there was nothing that could ever have prepared Elaina for the rush of images and feelings she both saw and felt. It was like watching movies whizz by at 10x their normal speed as she tried to keep up with what she was seeing. The emotions that came flooding along with it were consuming, random and sped along and were equally hard to register before they too moved along…. The visuals and feelings, when combined, felt like a ride in an amusement park.

There were things she saw that were imprinted on her mind. She saw a woman with dark curls that was always laughing, named Kaleena, and two little girls: one older with light brown hair, named Katya, and a younger one with dark hair, Niómë. There was an outpouring of love, followed by intense sadness and regret. There was a rough-looking soldier with a crooked nose and an easy smile; the name that came to mind was Diotimus Artimidorus. She could see Diotimus, Michel, and Howard with a man with blondish brown hair. They called him Davidek. The other man that was with them was dark-haired and seemed so serious; they called him Sasho. Elaina could see they were close friends.

Next, Elaina saw a castle; it felt like hope and doom, mixed: salvation with a side of ruination. There was a beautiful, cultured woman who wore a crown standing among a large crowd, and the crowd hung on her every word. The name that leapt to mind was Vibia. Then, she saw rolling hills and countryside, and a very different, less cultured and wealthy but still beautiful woman with light brown hair, and homespun clothing. Even as she felt how much Michel loved her, she knew the woman's name: Aibhilin (Ave-leen), and almost immediately felt the deepest sadness and regret she'd ever experienced. It was like a gut punch. She saw wars, random people he knew and the faces of random humans that he'd fed from; most of them frightened, and then she saw Diotimus Artimidorus' sire: a woman named Anthea, of the city of Athens. She saw Anthea's sire, a man named Hadi, from the port town of Ugarit, in Northern Syria. Hadi was short, barrel chested and was probably the hairiest man Elaina had ever seen; He spent most of his life fighting others, and he spent a great deal of it involved in treachery. Elaina could feel Anthea's utter revulsion for the man. She saw Hadi's sire next: a man named Zaya from the city of

Ninevah. Zaya had beautiful eyes. The man that sired Zaya was Hurin from Lagash. He felt…argumentative. Dissatisfied. Hurrin's father, their Clan's ancestral sire, was Zuberi.

While Amalie had taught Elaina that Clan Robichaux's ancestral sire descended from the First Flame Zuberi, and she knew that fact going into ascension…it was completely different knowing in a scholastic way than feeling a sire/child connection TO him. She could see him wearing his priestly robes in a dimly lit temple. He had removed his shoes; this temple was holy. She could feel the coolness of the stone on his feet, in stark contrast to the warmth of the surrounding air. He closed his eyes, smiling, lost in the worship of Ptah.

The rush of imagery stopped so suddenly it was disorienting; like the feeling of riding a roller coaster that brakes to a sudden stop…but everything still feels like it's moving. Michel put out his hand to steady her. It was about that time she noticed that the cramps in her stomach had ceased. Thank goodness.

"Who is my sire?" Michel asked her.

"Diotimus Artimidorus."

"Who was his sire?"

"Anthea, of Athens."

"And Anthea's sire?"

"Hadi the Syrian."

"Who was Hadi's sire?"

"Zaya of Ninevah."

"Zaya's sire?"

"Hurin from Lagash."

"And who was Hurin's sire?"

"Zuberi of Hut-Ka-Ptah."

Michel nodded. "Very good," he said, and smiled at his newest child. "What did the blood show you? What stood out for you, outside of the lineage?"

"I saw a really beautiful woman, wearing a crown in what looked like a castle, surrounded by people; I saw a woman named Aibhilin that you loved and, I think, mourned; I saw a lady named Kaleena, and two little girls named Katya, and Niómë. I also saw you, along with Uncle Howard, your sire Diotimus, and two other people; a man named Davidek with sandy colored hair, and a serious one with dark hair you called Sasho."

What nobody told Elaina about…kind of like that surprise test question which ends up on an exam, and was asked merely to see how the tested person would react to it…is that what a new Virehn sees during their 'first blood' of Ascension is often a prophecy for their upcoming Virehn life. What a new Virehn sees, aside from the unbroken line of sires they descend from ancestrally is usually significant. The parts of Michel's blood that reached out to Elaina; what she saw, what she felt – likely would have some bearing on her, or have meaning to her. More than anything, it gives a sire insight into his newest child.

That his newest child - which he had long equated mentally to his human daughter, Niómë, dead for millennia - had seen that very daughter through his blood, surprised Michel. He'd told no one but Howard that he saw Elaina in that way. He never mentioned Niómë to Elaina, ever.

Also, it didn't surprise him in the least that she'd seen Dio, or Howard. But to see Davidek? He was now known as David Lambert, the CEO of VarenCorp London. Why would she see Sasho? Sasho was his long-dead brother, Aleksandr Philipou. Why would she see either of them, of all people? That boggled his mind. He thought it odd that she would see Vibia, and the making of the Compact, though maybe it shouldn't. Amalie told him she'd had a good many questions about it – and even about the fact that he had been there when it came into being. He knew it to be true, because they discussed it. Time would ultimately reveal the meanings.

Reman turned to everyone, and smiled, inviting Elaina to turn as well, and face everyone. "May I present our newest sister, Elaina Maria Jacoby."

There was a party following, at a ballroom down by Battery Park; it was mostly for the humans. Many of the Virehnai of Clan Robichaux attended, at least for a time. By the time most of the Virehnai had left, only Elaina, Amalie, Howard, and Michel remained. They stayed the longest, and Elaina left when Uncle Michel did. He cautioned her earlier that she needed to avoid too much stimulation while her system was still getting used to heightened senses; she followed his suggestion. That was one reason the food didn't come out for the humans until the new guest of honor and most of the Virehnai left. If the smell of fabric softener, body odor and too many kinds of competing perfumes were rough, the smell of cooked food was worse in many respects. When she asked Amalie about it weeks ago, she told her that the beef from her favorite steak subs and burgers would now smell...dead. Like death smells. Even though the hors'd'oevres hadn't come out yet, she could still smell them a bit. "Damn." Elaina thought. Amalie, unfortunately, was right.

"I'm sorry, Amalie."

"For what?" Amalie looked at Elaina quizzically.

"All those times I ate cheeseburgers, steak subs and pizza in front of you. Why didn't you TELL me? You never told me how bad it would smell to you!" Amalie started laughing.

"Apology accepted. And I didn't tell you because you were enjoying them. Why kill that for you?"

Elaina nodded. "Thanks. At least the smell takes some of the sting out of not being able to have any of those. There's no way I want to eat that stuff if it smells that...unappetizing."

The way these parties were handled proved that more than anything, they were for the living members of the newest Virehn to celebrate their family's good fortune; the Jacoby family was no different. It might as well have been a family reunion. Besides Elaina's own immediate family attending, she had other family she didn't see nearly as often there as well. Bloodsworn and oathsworn family members from both her mother's and father's sides were there...including the oldest members of their family, her grandfather's twin sisters, 96 years old, and everyone, including Elaina, wanted pictures with them. They didn't come out much anymore – but for such a momentous occasion for their family, they did.

One thing that made Elaina especially happy was the chance to sit down and catch up with two of her cousins, Carly and Joanna. The last time Elaina saw them was when Joanna graduated from college. While they sat there at the table talking a mile a minute, Uncle Howard came over to chat; he hadn't seen Carly or Joanna since Elaina's college graduation. Howard had known all three women from birth. "What are you doing these days?" he asked them. "I'm working as a dental hygienist," Joanna told him. Carly looked over at him. "I got laid off two weeks ago; I was working as an accountant, but one of the owners embezzled money from the firm, and they had to let a bunch of us go."

"That's terrible. If you'd like to come work for me, I know we've got a couple of openings at Vespera Solutions."

"Really, Uncle Howard?" Carly asked, excited. Howard nodded, and she jumped up from where she sat and gave him a hug. "Thank you!"

He pulled a card from his wallet and handed it to her. "Call my secretary, Gracie, and set up an appointment. We'll talk."

Jeff and Amalie walked up to them. Moments later, Jeff and Howard were waved over to another table, and Amalie stayed. "What did I miss?" she asked Carly.

Carly, still standing, leaned down, hugging Elaina's shoulders, and then looked back up at Amalie, and giggled. "I came for the food, and I got a job," she teased. "Looks like I'm going to be working for Uncle Howard."

Amalie looked at Carly. "Congratulations," she said, even as Elaina laughed. "I'm glad I could provide a networking opportunity." "Congratulations again, Elaina. I'm excited for you, too." She glanced around, spotting her mom across the room, talking to Elaina's dad. "While I'm up, I'm going to tell Mom. She'll want to thank Uncle Howard."

Not everyone attending was happy to be there, however. Elaina's brother Doug was there because if he wasn't, his father would be angry with him. Rob was there mostly for the same reason; his absence would make more of a statement than his attendance. The whole party left a bad taste in his mouth. He knew how Doug actually felt; he saw his brother's attempts at schmoozing with his father and trying to make nice with Elaina and the Virehnai in attendance as desperate, and pathetic. He watched Doug go up and hug Elaina and make a public show to congratulate her and Michel. Doug could pretend if he wanted to, but he wasn't. When his cousin Carly got all excited about being offered a job by Howard, her laughter and happiness felt like sharp blades, especially as Elaina was laughing with her, and hugged her.

Rob looked around and became annoyed. He saw his father with his younger sister Peggy talking to Howard, as Aunt Peggy fawned all over Howard, kissing his ass for hiring her daughter. That was the final straw, for Rob. Right after that, he left early; well before the bulk of the Virehnai started leaving.

When Doug texted him and asked about him why he left so early, he tersely replied "I came, I saw, I fulfilled my family duty."

Doug texted back, "You'll never be more than oathsworn with an attitude like that."

Rob read it and shook his head, deleting it. "Thanks for the vote of confidence, bro. Fuck you, too."

Elaina's days settled quickly into a routine.

Elaina and Amalie spent more time at the gym…particularly that first day after the party. She was working on her reflexes mostly, and learning what her new, improved body could do. After that first day, which was more extensive, she began working out for an hour after work every day. Amalie told her that her first six months, she NEEDED to do that daily. While she may be Virehn right away, some things would continue to improve; her senses, her reflexes and her appearance.

The physical side of things wasn't the only thing that changed. Since she was now living in the residential building in lower Manhattan, she switched jobs within the law firm and now worked in the corporate building next door. The office she transferred to specialized in contract law as it pertained to real estate, run by Uncle Howard's son, Jeff Garvin, who was her new boss. She would also work alongside her friend Michael Ratner, who was bloodsworn to Jeff. Her new office mates welcomed her by decorating her desk (and even the door to her new suite) with baby items, since she was a mere baby compared to them.) It was all done in good fun. She was happy to land there with them.

Elaina spent most of her time with Amalie, who was still teaching her. Amalie told her while she was human that some lessons she'd either have to go over again, or couldn't teach her until she, too, was Virehn. Elaina got that now, realizing she still had much to learn.

The first thing Amalie tackled was eating. She'd seen her and Michel eat. Now, she had to feed, too. "As a young Virehn, you'll probably be hungry more often."

"How often should I eat, then?"

"Whenever you're hungry. Some Virehnai only take blood every other day; others can go longer." Amalie paused. "Remember those stomach cramps? Those are your friend, particularly now. When you notice cramps, you'll want to eat; when you feel them. It's kind of like all the human diet advice; don't eat unless or until you're hungry. Let your body be your guide. Remember, I told you that your body would continue to improve, and that's why you should work out daily? That's one reason a newbie needs more blood." Elaina was sitting on Amalie's sofa in her apartment and had brought her mug with her.

Elaina stared down into the mug pensively. "It IS satisfying…oddly enough. But it still lacks the fun of eating a messy cheeseburger. In THAT, it'll never compare."

"You think not?" Amalie laughed.

"No." Elaina was adamant. Amalie laughed more.

"WHAT? What's so funny?"

"Wait until you do a horizontal mambo with someone, and you share blood. That's the one exception to the 'don't eat if you're not hungry' rule. Ooohweee, it's messy as all hell; your sheets will look like an autopsy afterwards – and fair warning, the stains might or might not come out – but I'll one up that cheeseburger with hot messy Virehnai sex ANY day."

Amalie's laughter rang out again as she took in Elaina's expression as she contemplated the picture she'd just painted for her mentally. Elaina's eyes were deer-in-the-headlights wide as her imagination took hold, and she was hanging on to her mug of A positive with both hands like she'd drop it.

"The expression on your face is priceless…"

Amalie picked up her own mug, and drank once her laughter subsided, and Elaina had put down her own, for safety's sake. She didn't want to spill blood on Amalie's sofa. "I'm so glad you're a Virehn now," she told Elaina. "I loved you as a human, but we can share so much more now….it feels like having a sister again. One that won't age."

Amalie got a faraway look on her face, seeing something in her mind's eye from a time long past. "I loved my family; I was close to my sisters, but our paths diverged. They were human; I was Virehn. They aged; I didn't. They had lots of children; I couldn't. It didn't stop me from loving all of my nieces and nephews, and their children, too. I never, ever stopped loving any of them. I'm still in contact with my family living in Concarneau. My sisters, brothers and I always had our roots in common, along with family time we shared before I ascended. The further we got from the day I ascended, the less we had in common. I miss that. It was as if I…lost them while they were still alive. By the time my brothers and sisters physically passed away, while it was painful to lose them? It was merely a…period, at the end of a sentence that seemed too short. In truth, I started slowly losing them the day Johannes turned me. I didn't know that, then. I do now."

Elaina hugged Amalie. She knew where her mind was going, even as a couple of rogue pink tears formed, which is what prompted the hug. Amalie had lost her family once, and then Johannes became her family. She thought she'd spend the rest of her years with him…and then she lost him, too.

After the moment passed, Amalie sniffled. "Do yourself a favor. Be close with your human family now…because what happened to me, familywise, will happen to you, too. The better the memories with them you have…when the time comes when your paths diverge? It'll make it easier to bear."

"Thanks. I'll try to remember that. I'll do fine with Janet. Well, you know that. She's a sweetie. You should see Sophie and Hayden! They're growing like little weeds." Elaina smiled, thinking about her nieces. "My brothers? Maybe things'll get better after a while. Right now, they're still pissed I got picked…although I have to admit, Doug was being nice at the party. He congratulated me and hugged me, and Papa wasn't even around to see it." She giggled, and it trailed off and turned flat.

It was Elaina's turn to be sad. Her brothers had always been a bit…dismissive of her, but at least she used to feel like they had her back; she was never entirely sure if they dismissed her because she was the youngest, or if it was a sense of superiority on their part. She didn't know. Once, they were protective of her. That time passed the day they chose her to succeed Johannes. She wasn't sure where she truly stood anymore with either of them. "Papa told me to mostly keep out of their way for now, so they won't say anything that they can't take back later. He basically said it was on me to make sure they take the high road, because at the moment, they're acting like spoiled brats." Elaina sighed and shrugged her shoulders. "I can keep out of their way to keep the peace, and I'll be here when they finally decide to remove their heads from their arses."

"Michel made a wise choice choosing you, I think. But…I'm biased." Amalie sighed. "Sorry I ended up getting my sad on you. We need to change things up and change the vibe."

Amalie suddenly sat up straighter and looked at her watch. "Wanna go out?"

"Huh?" Elaina looked at her watch. "It's 10:30 at night."

Amalie snorted. "You don't really sleep anymore. Does it matter?"

"You have a point. I guess it doesn't. What is there to do this late, anyway?"

"All kinds of stuff. Did you know you can take a ferry ride late at night? Or walk across the Brooklyn Bridge? Both are fun, and the city's beautiful at night. You always enjoyed taking pictures. Why stop now?" Amalie paused. "Oh! I know something you'll adore! Clans Robichaux and Westcott are both major donors to the Metropolitan Museum of Art; I mean, it figures, right? It's preserving both artifacts and history. They host a private evening for each clan."

"Oooh, now you're talking! I want to do that! I never knew that happened…"

"The Met has always had 'after hours' things going on, but once a year for both clans, they'll open up the Museum to us beyond their 'after hours' hours. It's one of those subtle-but-not-so-subtle perks that comes with money. When you sponsor things, run things, and throw money into projects…the people who are grateful for that money often let you…bend the rules a bit. In our case…that's a good thing. Plus, I'm sure they don't realize that a person currently on their board of directors is Virehn."

"For reals? I'd like THAT job." Elaina mused. "Those nights where it's open only to us sounds like it would be…awesome, actually. I'll bet Uncle Michel and Uncle Howard see things they probably remember; maybe even recognize…"

Amalie nodded. "They do. Michel and Howard are a blast to do that with. It's Virehn only, which is why you wouldn't have heard about it. They can give the artifacts displayed a perspective that most would never see—not even with a docent all but holding your hand all the way through. Reman's pretty interesting to hear, too. When he told us that most really old Virehnai are half history teacher? He wasn't kidding. Plus, Virehn zuth akret; there will be things you will look at in a museum now, and it'll be like every exhibit is an interactive exhibit. Say you went to the Egyptian exhibit; if you quiet your mind, your blood will remember what you see and feed you information about it that someone in your bloodline knew, but you didn't."

Elaina's jaw dropped, imagining. "I want to do THAT."

Amalie chuckled, watching Elaina's growing excitement. "I know you do. We can go to the Met whenever you want to; we don't have to wait until nighttime, or when they have a Virehn-only night. The beauty of those "Virehn-only" nights is that we can TALK about what we see openly to each other. And someone who has firsthand knowledge can and will expound on it. You'll realize in short order that history isn't always what they have recorded in the books. Truth gets bent, spindled and mutilated to suit political whims. It's been going on…forever."

Elaina looked at her watch. "They aren't open now."

Amalie shook her head no but smiled. "What I had in mind for tonight is a club. It's Virehnai only. Live music on a small stage inside; a rooftop lounge to view the city by….It'll give you a completely different view of our world that's been off-limits to you until now. Call it another lesson, on 'exploring your new horizons.'"

"That sounds…cool, actually. I didn't realize there were Virehnai-only clubs."

"It is cool. There's about five or six clubs between the New York/New Jersey area. The one I have in mind is called Sanguinarium Obscura. It's got an interesting vibe. It's somewhere between…dark and dangerous, and mystical. There are lots of quiet places to sit, talk and disappear. Or you can sit around at the tables in front of the stage because you're likely to hear amazing, amazing music. You wouldn't realize, but many Virehnai are accomplished musicians; it's a treat to hear them play music from many styles and eras. The Sanguinarium features different eras of music depending on the night, and it's not unusual for someone to just grab an instrument and jump up on stage and improvise. You name the style; you can probably hear it there."

"I'm in. Let me go up and get dressed. Meet you back down here in fifteen?"

"Yup. See you in a couple."

Fifteen minutes later, both women were ready, and Amalie called down to the building concierge and asked for transportation to the Sanguinarium Obscura. Once the car arrived, the ride took twenty minutes; traffic was relatively light. Elaina's excitement was palpable as they drove there and got closer.

"Most people don't know, but there are at least two major mainstream musicians that are oathsworn. They're the ONLY exceptions to the Sanguinarium's 'no humans' rule. One of them is…sort of…local. He's oathsworn to Clan Sabin; he was originally from Jersey. The other is English and used to be a teacher. Both of them have standing invites; Whenever either of them are in town, sometimes if they get a chance, they'll come in and do a show for us, or better still, they'll play along with some of our musicians. It's incredible. I haven't been that lucky yet, but Jeff has. Ask him sometime. He'll tell you."

They got out of the car. There were no visible signs; nothing indicating a club anywhere. Elaina followed Amalie down an alley. Several feet into it, a metal flight of steps with multiple levels led up to a rusty door. Most humans would see it and ignore it, thinking it was an emergency exit; a fire escape. The man sitting at the top, on the railing was Virehn. He looked bored. As they reached him on the landing, Amalie tapped the solid gold necklace she wore, which functioned as her key. "Good evening. She's my +1. This is her first time here." He nodded at them and opened the door. "Ladies, welcome. Enjoy."

They could hear the sounds of a guitar coming from somewhere as they walked down a long, dimly lit hallway that barely had room for two to pass one another. As Amalie opened the door, a man waited for them to enter, even as he scooted around them, leaving.

Going through the door, they were now standing in the back of the room. Turning to their right, the space was deceptively large; the stage was directly ahead. It was dark, with a combination of recessed lighting and wrought iron lanterns that would've felt at home in a gothic church. There were numerous tables of varying sizes dotted around, and there were many Virehnai seated randomly at them, listening. The man currently on the stage, illuminated by the spotlight, was playing a song Elaina didn't recognize, other than it was classical guitar, really intricate and challenging, and his fingers were fairly flying on the strings. Partially enclosed booths ran along the wall on the right side of the room, with a few along the back of the room, where they'd come in. Some booths had deep red velvet curtains that hid what? Dark obsessions, darker deeds? Anything could go on in the privacy of those booths. Elaina thought to herself, 'I guess that's the point.'

There was artwork everywhere. Most dominant in the room was a mixed-media mural behind the man playing. It was striking; startling, even. It was a Virehn, emerging from out of darkness…his fangs bared, with what looked like blood dripping from them, down his chin. Veins of red stood out from his neck, his face, his arms…which were outstretched, reminiscent of Christ. This image, however? Between the Virehn emerging from blackness, his fangs and blood, mixed with shards of steel and shards of glass, carried a different message entirely. It let you know the sort of welcome you would receive: the fangy kind…that might fuck you, kill you, or, if you were lucky, transform you, allowing you to survive the encounter. The sign above the stage said "Sanguinarium Obscura."

Elaina looked around in wonder. The whole room was painted a very dark red that was nearly black. There were disturbing–yet beautiful–paintings on all the walls. Several looked as if they were in the style of…Caravaggio? She was trying desperately to remember her art history classes in college that she took for the credits only, and she wasn't sure if she was remembering the artists correctly. The painting closest to her was darkly reminiscent of St. Francis of Assisi in Ecstasy–except the angel was dark with smeared blood on his face and chin, and blood covered the figure lying in ecstasy.

There was a painting like Medusa; the face was both haunting and wore a horrified, surprised expression. It was a head only, dripping blood from where it had been severed. The snakes coming out of the head all had vampire fangs, which were dripping blood and looking back at him. It was titled "Treachery Revealed." Some of the artwork seemed to delve into the contrast between light and dark. A portrait next to the St. Francis painting had a Jekyll and Hyde vibe to it. The artist painted one side in light, with lots of outlines drawn, and hair lights. A sharp cut diagonally through the face separated the light side from the dark side; that side was entirely dark, in shadow and out of focus, with no edges discernable and curious smudges that weren't blurry that read as blood. All the art was like that.

"I thought Virehn weren't supposed to show their fangs in public?" Elaina leaned over and asked Amalie.

"That's what makes this place so edgy. What's on the walls is almost Virehnai porn. This place throws etiquette to the wind, at least as far as what's on the walls. If anyone's planning on using their fangs, though, that's what those curtained booths are for. Otherwise, they'll pitch you out, and if you're lucky, you won't get pitched off the landing. They'll let you walk out."

"Wow."

Amalie picked a table, and they both sat down while they listened to the man's set as it finished out.

The next people that went up on stage played two blues songs; the man singing said the first one was 'Cross Road Blues,' and the second was 'Born Under a Bad Sign.' It was probably the best blues she'd ever heard.

"So, wanna join?"

"I do."

"Let's go take care of that, then." There was a bar-like area where, if you found yourself in need of blood, you could get it. The Virehn behind it was petite and looked like she was about twenty, with a halo of short blond curly hair, and green eyes. "Hi Brioni," she told the woman. "Hi Amalia. Whatcha need?" She said, looking at Elaina.

"This is my newest clan sister, Elaina Jacoby. Her sire's Michel."

"Oh.... You're the one that just ascended. I heard about that. Welcome."

"What do I need to do to join?" Elaina asked.

Brioni got a devilish smile on her face, and reached under the counter, and pulled out a scary, nasty old looking knife that aside from being dull and rusty, looked as if they had never cleaned it once in its ancient life. "Show me your arm," Brioni said, and at Elaina's look, broke into hysterical laughter that had a beautifully musical sound to it. "Your face...priceless....." was all she could gasp out until she finished laughing, and Amalie and others near the bar witnessing it got in on it, also.

"That NEVER stops being funny." Brioni told her. She reached again under the counter, and pulled out her cellphone, equipped with a card reader, and a deep red velvet box, which she sat in front of Elaina. Brioni opened the box to reveal a gold necklace just like Amalie's. "Either I need a credit card, or if you prefer, I can bill Clan Robichaux, and they'll extract it from your next payment."

Elaina looked at Amalie. "Which should I do?"

"Bill the Clan. That's the best way."

Brioni brought up a page on her phone, and started asking questions, some of which Amalie ended up answering, like the VarenCorp number that was assigned to her suite, which was registered to her through her clan. Once she paid for it, Elaina removed it from the box, and clipped it on along with her pearls from Uncle Michel.

When they left the 'bar' area, Amalie asked her if she wanted to go upstairs. "Sure." Elaina followed Amalie back the way they came but realized between two of the booths in the back was another curtain against the wall. Go through the curtains, and there's steps leading up, as narrow as the hallway coming in had been. Both women had to stand to one side as a man and a woman passed them by while they were going upstairs. Emerging on the roof, it was breathtaking. They had a view of Central Park, and the city surrounding. It was beautiful. Amalie stood there, lost in thought, and then turned to Elaina, a devilish look on her face.

"I know what we need to do."

"What?"

"See that rooftop pool over there?"

"Yeah. What about it?"

"Wanna go skinny dipping? Johannes and I did that before. It's...exhilarating, between breaking in, and being naked in public..."

"What?"

Amalie giggled. "Come on. It'll be fun."

"But anyone up here could see us..."

"That's kind of the point. Anyone in any of these buildings could be watching us. Anyone could watch us break in, get naked

92

and swim. Some of them are pervy enough to be watching with a telescope, for that exact reason. The best thing? Not a single person watching would know we're Virehnai. They just see naked people, and get off on it, if they see us at all."

Elaina learned something that night. Quite a few things, actually.

…Amalie had a freak side that she never knew about…but would probably come to appreciate.

…Breaking into that pool wasn't all that hard, and the water felt delightful against her extraordinarily sensitive skin; it felt like kisses all over her body as they splashed and the water moved. Amalie hadn't warned her about that.

…and maybe–just maybe–Elaina might've discovered this night that she had her own freak side: there was something about standing there totally naked when she got out of the pool, water dripping all over, and feeling the sensations from the water trickling down her body leaving her in a puddle, as gravity pulled on her, going from buoyant to weighted… The sensation gravity gave her was near to ecstasy. Between that, and realizing that there might be people watching her while she felt this way…and maybe desiring her…or fantasizing…? Elaina realized right then and there that she'd probably had one of the most erotic evenings of her life…ever. And all she did was go for a swim in the nude. If the rest of her Virehnai life were like this or better?

Wow.

8

THE UNEXPECTED

The evening started out peacefully enough.

Elaina transferred offices and now worked in the same building in lower Manhattan that Amalie did; it was like the old days when she was a college intern; this time, it came with more responsibilities, but a better paycheck. The plan for the evening was that Elaina was supposed to work in the gym with Amalie after work so she could get a better handle on her reflexes; which were considerably better than they had been as a human, and even after a week, her reflexes had improved. She'd only come close to faceplanting once or twice; Amalie assured her that the rapid improvement would continue.

Around lunchtime, her dad, whose office was mid-town. called and asked her if she could stop by for a few minutes later that afternoon for a meeting with him and the man who would take over the project she'd been working on to get them up to speed on it. Two days earlier, the building manager contacted her, asking her to drop the keys to her old suite off. If she had to meet with her father, Elaina figured she'd cancel on Amalie and the gym, drop off the keys, and then meet with Papa, and Darius. When she told Amalie, her reaction was to laugh. "You think you'll get out of the gym that easily? I'll go with you, and we'll go to the mid-town facility... I'll just get an earlier start to my workout than you will, that's all."

Elaina laughed. "Fine with me."

Using their IDs at the entrance, she stopped at the security office on the first floor where the building manager, Evan, usually was. She didn't know the man sitting behind the desk today. "Hi. I'm Elaina Jacoby. Evan called and asked me to turn in the keys to my suite. Can I leave them with you?" The man smiled at her and said, "I'm new. Let me check what Evan wants to do first." He picked up a walkie-talkie and called out to Evan on the radio. "What's your 20? Ms. Jacoby's here to return her keys. Can I take it, or is there a procedure?"

She heard Evan's familiar voice from the man's radio. "I'm up on 24. Can you get her to meet me in her old suite? A fellow doing prep found a small box of stuff that got left; I can make sure she gets it directly, and she can give me her keys, too."

"Will do." he replied, and then the man looked at Elaina and Amalie. "He'll meet you on nineteen."

The mid-town building had 37 floors. Everything above the fifteenth was residential, and aside from generously sized suites, the 16th floor also held residential amenities: a gym that was the equal of any paid facility that included two oathsworn trainers that offered occasional classes; a party room with a commercial kitchen in it, and even a small private theater where they held occasional meetings, and even weekly movie nights for residents.

The two women got into the elevator. Elaina hit the button for 19 to meet with Evan, and afterward, would head back down to talk to Papa. Amalie was going to the gym, so she pushed the button for 16. The door began closing; just before it closed, they saw a hand stick through. A man outside called out, "Hold the door..." As Elaina, closest to the buttons, was looking for and then pressing the 'open door' button, the person got on, and the door closed.

Once the door closed, that's when all hell broke loose, and the day ceased being anything vaguely resembling peaceful.

Elaina looked up from the elevator buttons to apologize; she and the man locked eyes for a hot second and they instantly recognized one another. The last time Elaina saw him, the man lay on her bed with his arms behind his head on the day of her attack. Before either could say anything, the man panicked, and proceeded to physically attack Elaina, who hadn't been Virehnai for a whole week yet. The man easily knocked Elaina off balance, ramming her into the elevator control panel; she accidentally hit the stop button. As the elevator lurched to a sudden halt, the alarm began going off.

Amalie responded automatically, launching into a physical barrage against the man. She had no clue who he was; and had never seen him before. There had been no time for Elaina to let her know that this was one of the three men that previously attacked her. The only thing Amalie knew was that he was attacking Elaina. Amalie's hits were effective, and the man lurched off balance for a moment. They stared at each other for the briefest of moments, before they resumed their attack on the other in the enclosed space.

As the man's rage and ire turned toward Amalie, ready to rend her limb from limb, Amalie struck him with what she thought would be a killing blow. As that blow physically made contact with him, he bared his teeth at her; Amalie saw the man's fangs then, her eyes widening in fear and surprise. He crumpled to the ground, as if he was in slow motion, and someone pulled his power plug. Amalie, to Elaina's horror, did the same; Her last words came out with her final breath, a whispered, "…didn't know…" just before she hit the ground, also dead.

Elaina stood there in shock. Everything happened so quickly. She was still stunned at being knocked so hard against the wall of the elevator. That elevator wall now holding her up. Elaina was aghast at what played out before her eyes, her friend now dead, along with her attacker. The elevator alarm bell was so loud, so shrill, it felt like it was bouncing around in her head, causing physical pain. She was trying to make sense of what was before her: he was human the last time she encountered him. Amalie was simply reacting. Elaina had no chance to explain who the man was.

As part of her 'lessons,' Amalie told her all about what happened with 'death by Compact.' What happened looked and sounded like Amalie described. Everything happened so quickly, charged with so much adrenaline that Elaina had no clue that he was Virehn; he was human when she saw him last. And poor Amalie! All she knew was that he was attacking. The lack of time between instinct and action cost both Amalie and her attacker their lives. It horrified Elaina, watching her friend die in front of her. As Elaina realizing that Amalie died protecting her, Elaina hit the button to release the elevator. She sank to the floor beside Amalie, in horror. Crying, running on what felt like her last functioning braincells, Elaina, hands trembling, called Michel, trying to get something aside from ragged crying out. Michel could barely understand her; he only knew something was wrong, and it filled him with foreboding. When the elevator came to rest on 16 and the doors opened, building security was waiting. They found Elaina sobbing bloody tears on the floor of the elevator as she cradled her dead friend in her arms, and another lay beside her.

Several things happened in quick succession. When Michel received Elaina's call, she was crying so hard that he couldn't tell what she was saying. She was a very grounded person, so hearing her so…freaked out…which sent a shiver up his spine. Michel hung up; his next call was to Walt - to either let him know there was a problem or find out what or even where the problem was. As Michel was describing the call he'd just received from Elaina to Walt, building security, after seeing the horrible tableau in the elevator – put the entire building on lockdown. Little red lights in the hallway and the elevators and public areas/offices began flashing erratically; they warned the building occupants to stay wherever they were until they stopped flashing.

"Michel; hold on," he interrupted, "I don't know if it's related, but something's going on. The whole building just went on lockdown."

"On my way." Michel said, hanging up. Before Walt could call anyone to find out what was happening, his secretary, Dolores, opened the door and one of Evan's security crew came through; though trained to respond to emergencies, you could clearly see something rattled him. "We've got a problem, Mr. Jacoby." He took a deep breath. "It's your daughter."

Walt took off up the stairs one flight, and came out of the stairwell, located across from the elevator bank where Amalie originally planned to get off and head to the gym. Walt Jacoby opened the stairwell door on the landing for 16…and stopped in horror. In the elevator across from him, he saw his daughter crying uncontrollably, cradling a dead Amalie in her arms, with a dead man lying on the floor of the elevator car alongside them. "What the actual fuck?" Walt exclaimed.

One of the Virehn standing nearby stopped Walt from rushing in. Walt tried to shake him off to get to his daughter, but the Virehn (who had been in the gym) shook him a bit to get his attention. "Sir!" Walt turned angrily. The man told him, "She's newly made, sir, and it looks like she's in shock. Don't go in there. Wait for Michel; he's her sire. I called him as soon as I saw her like that. He's aware. The Vel'sheth is on his way as well. It'll be alright. We'll figure out what happened there, Mr. Jacoby." Walt was frustrated and wanted to help his daughter. He kept looking back and forth between the Virehn who was still lightly restraining him and his daughter. "Really, sir." The man told him, trying to be calming and sympathetic to his fear. "She could hurt you and not realize it's even you she's hurting. Whatever happened in there, she's got enough to deal with aside from accidentally hurting you, too."

"Elaina, honey…?" He called out. Elaina didn't even look up at him. She was someplace else entirely.

Michel got there as quickly as he could, and the building manager put the other elevator car back into service for him. As the doors opened, he saw several people standing in a group that included Walt. They were all staring into the other elevator car. Walt looked completely distraught. Michel came out and turned to face the car that Elaina was in, and his heart sunk at the sight that greeted him. Greg Roundtree, the Virehn who called to update him, was correct on all counts. Unfortunately, Elaina was in shock; beyond that, Amalie was dead, and there was a dead Virehn he didn't know in the car with them.

"Elaina?" Michel called her name, but she didn't look up. "We're here, Elaina. You aren't alone." He walked over to Walt, who was standing next to Greg. He looked like a mess, seeing his youngest child like that. Michel put his hand on his friend's shoulder. "It'll be okay, Walt. You'll see. She'll be okay. She's in shock. Reman's coming."

"What will Reman do for her we can't?"

"If Elaina were human right now, someone would talk her down and give her a sedative to calm her. Unfortunately, most of what's created for humans doesn't work on Virehnai. Our biochemistry is changed enough by being turned that any of them are useless. We have something that works; its medical trade name is Veltharinex these days, but it's ancient. It was used for shock and trauma for centuries; particularly around deaths and battle fatigue. It's a blood-based opiate derivative, but when combined with an herb we call thornsap, the alkaloids in the thornsap bind themselves to the opiates and allow it to work. Reman keeps some for emergency use."

Reman got there about ten minutes after Michel did, and when he got off the elevator, two others got off with him: a plainclothes detective, and a police officer, both bloodsworn. The detective was the same one who'd been called to the building the night Elaina was attacked the first time. Security called when they realized there were deaths involved; the two men shared the elevator with Reman, and he did them the favor of letting them know what they were walking into on their way up. The detective remembered Elaina. "You know the drill, Reman. Touch nothing if you can help it." Reman nodded at the detective. He walked over to Michel, and a very anxious Walt.

"Elaina will be fine, Walt. Right now, stay back, and leave her to Michel and I." Reman looked around at the dozen people gathered, who were watching the drama playing out before them. He said to them in a low tone, "If you aren't immediate family or police, I'd like to take this moment to ask you to depart quietly and keep

Elaina in your thoughts this evening." As everyone moved away, Reman turned to Michel. "Shall we?"

"Please."

They approached the elevator car quietly, making no quick moves. Both called Elaina's name gently. They were trying to be calm, reassuring, and, above all else, quiet. Being newly turned, she was dealing with shock and sensory overload, caused by the mental and emotional trauma that came with the attack and seeing her friend die. People in Elaina's state reacted in one of two ways. Either their body shut down functions and reactions to a minimal state to protect itself, or…they turned into a walking grief-bomb with a side of predator: similar to the human fight-or-flight response, but considerably worse. Based on the fact she wasn't answering them, they assumed she wouldn't fight them.

Detective Hall and the officer stood by the car, watching to make sure they wouldn't disturb any evidence while they waited. They were used to it; in a normal human vs. human crime, officers and a Crime Scene Unit would've responded. VarenCorp had its own 911 dispatch that ran parallel to the public system. The folks that responded to VarenCorp 911 calls are actual cops and detectives that are bloodsworn or oathsworn and off duty. Whenever bad things happened between Virehn, which wasn't often - wherever possible, the bloodsworn officers and detectives currently assigned to various precincts were the first line of defense. There were only so many bloodsworn folks to go around in the NYPD, though. They also used police retirees when necessary, most of those being oathsworn, and referred by active duty bloodsworn. Detective Hall and Officer Wendell were both trained in evidence collection, despite it not normally being their job if they were at a human crime scene. Even if it wasn't their usual responsibility, they watched the two Virehnai carefully, ready to stop them.

Michel quietly crouched down beside Elaina.

"Elaina, sweetheart. We're here. You're okay. Everything will be okay." Michel reached out and touched his index and middle finger ever so lightly on her arm. The only reaction was that she blinked.

"Elaina, Reman is here. We have medicine for you. It'll make you calm and sleepy. When you wake up, you'll be fine."

Reman pulled out a bottle and handed it to Michel, and then pulled out what looked like a large, round bandage. He tore open the sterile package it was in and held it in his hand. "Can you put twelve drops of the valtharinex on there?" Michel did as he was asked, and then he and Reman traded the bottle for the loaded bandage. Michel gingerly affixed it to her wrist and then pressed it once. Michel said, "We'll be here for you when you wake up, Elaina." Both men got up quietly and went over to Walt.

"Are you sure that will work?" He asked them.

Michel nodded yes, and Reman said the same, but gave more of an explanation. "It's a sedative, delivered transdermally with a microneedle patch to help absorption. In about five minutes, she'll go to sleep, her muscles will relax, and she'll let go of Amalie. Once she does that, we'll need to get her horizontal, comfortable, and in a silent room until she wakes up on her own."

"Where are you going to take her?" Walt asked quietly, in a similar low tone.

Michel answered. "That's a good question. We can't really move her out of this building; she's in no state to be transported anywhere. It would be too noisy."

Walt had an idea. "Can we move her back to our suite?"

Michel shook his head no, and then added, "Still too noisy." He looked around. "You don't have a spare bed or sofa we could use, do you? We could relocate something to lay her on to an empty room."

"There's a futon in what used to be her old bedroom…"

"That works." Michel looked over at Evan. "Can you get with building maintenance, and make that happen, pronto?"

"Yes, sir. On it."

Twenty minutes later, Michel gently carried Elaina to a room in her old suite that was set up for her. Someone had thoughtfully left a chair there, as well. It would be a long night.

Meanwhile, Detective Hall and the police officer were going over the elevator carefully, missing nothing. Evan from building security returned, and stayed nearby, in case they needed him. "Evan, can you do me a favor? At some point this evening, can you email me the link to the camera feed for this elevator?"

Evan laughed. "I'm ahead of you there, sir. It's already sent."

"Good man. Thanks. That helps."

The detective began bagging and tagging evidence. First was the man's building ID.

That was a surprise, and where little bells first started going off in his head.

The man lying before him was very definitely Virehn, and the cause of death was definitely 'death by Compact.'

The ID? It listed his name as Raul Martinez. It was issued by Scotti Management, Inc, and looked to be genuine. How could such a mismatch be? You don't make a mistake like that. It meant that someone turned him, but who? It would've had to be since they issued him the badge.

Hall fingerprinted the man and then went on to attempt to get a blood sample, as well. The sample was harder to get because he was dead, and the blood was no longer pumping. There was no time like the present to get it; It's not like it was going to get any fresher. The detective pulled out a vial and a sharp needle, and pricked the arm he was slumped over on, counting on the fact that his weight would dam up the blood there, as it pooled. The man's blood flowed out in a slow leak into the vial. He only needed several drops, but took the time to wait for a whole vial. Considering the mismatch he was looking at, it seemed a logical thing to do. He assumed that they may need more of it than usual. He capped the vial, wrote on the side, and once he activated a chemical ice pack, he stowed both into his bag. The bodies were moved to VarenCorp's morgue.

That building in lower Manhattan housed the both the New York HQS for VarenCorp, and the offices of VarenCorp USA. That was also where VarenCorp's morgue was located. Detective Hall made sure the evidence he'd recovered went into a particular VERY secure evidence room nicknamed "The Vault." He had a feeling it would be a long night, and he'd be sleeping there tonight, if he got any sleep at all.

When Elaina woke up the next morning, if she didn't know that alcohol had no effect on her anymore, she'd have sworn she'd been out drinking the night before. Her head felt like she was having what might be the worst hangover of her life…only compounded by the fact when she woke up, she didn't know where she was, either. It was an empty room, with nothing in it, and she was on a…what? A futon? A not especially comfortable one, at that. It made her laugh. In her college days, they used to call it a 'flip n'fuck.'

Even as she was trying to figure out what in the hell she did to have earned this hangover and that she must've drank enough to black out - suddenly the night before came crashing all at once into her memory, leaving her in tears. It didn't answer why her head felt like it did, or how she got where she was, but she knew with a certainty that Amalie was dead.

As Elaina was waking up, Michel, Reman and her father were all nearby; however, it was Reman who'd asked to be the first to interact with Elaina.

Reman came through the door, juggling two mugs and two bags of blood. "Hi Elaina." He sat beside her quietly, poured each of them a bag, and silently handed her one.

"Hi." Elaina took the cup from him. She took a sip, and then stopped, looking down into it. It reminded her of the new life she had...that Amalie no longer had. It broke her.

"It's my fault. I...I didn't even have time to tell her who he was, or why he was attacking me." Reman took the mug from her before she spilled it or dropped it as she cried.

Instead of stopping her tears, or telling her 'Everything will be fine,' he let her cry—at least for a little while.

"Elaina?"

She looked up at him. "How do you feel this morning? We had to give you a sedative last night."

"Is that why I feel like I have a hangover? I have more of a hangover this morning than I did after I went out and got wasted, like you suggested." He chuckled. She made a face.

"We gave you valtharinex; that can happen sometimes. Last night, you were in shock, and that's what's used to treat it." He offered the mug back to her. "Drinking some of this will clear that feeling off."

Elaina took the mug back from him and drank some. After a few moments, he gently asked her, "What happened?"

Elaina took a deep breath and tried to keep her shit together. "Everything was fine, at first. We both got on the elevator. I was on my way to my old apartment to give Evan back my keys, and after that, I was supposed to meet with Papa; Amalie was going straight to the gym. I was supposed to meet her there after the meeting. We...were...still working on honing my reflexes." She stopped, trying not to get stuck right there in her story. It occurred to her then that Amalie didn't even have to come with her to mid-town; she volunteered to. She pulled herself away from that thought and continued.

"The elevator door was nearly closed, and someone put their hand through, and we heard a man ask us to hold the elevator. He got on as I was trying to hit the 'open door' button. He got on. The door was closing; he said 'hi' to Amalie. I looked up, and I recognized him right away; he recognized me, too. That's when he threw himself into me, almost knocked me over, and started hitting me. Everything was happening all at the same time. Amalie had never seen him before; she didn't know he was part of my previous attack, and I didn't have time to tell her. She jumped into the fight to protect me, and both of them dropped about the same time...and there was nothing I could do about it. About any of it."

Elaina started sobbing again. "It's my fault. She died protecting me, and neither of us realized until too late he was a Virehn, too." Her sobbing grew harder, the more she tried to put what was dogging her heart and mind into words. "All I can think...is if I could've protected myself...it would've been self-defense...but...the Compact...read it as a...a...." All Elaina could see was Amalie, laying there while she stood by, helpless to do or change a thing. Reman reached out for the mug, and she handed it back to him, as she furiously wiped at her eyes, trying and failing to get a hold of herself.

"Elaina?"

She looked up at him. "I know you and Amalie were close. Did you love your friend?"

Elaina sniffled, nodded, and said "yes," even as her face was tinged in pink from her tears.

"Amalie loved you, too. She may never have come out and directly said it, but do you know how I know that? It's because the last act of her life was in defense of you. She wouldn't have done that if she didn't love you."

"But...Reman...it's still my fault. How do I get past that? Ever?"

Mentally, he sighed. Different tactic.

"Humor me. How long have you been Virehn?"

"Six days."

And how old was Amalie?

"133." Elaina could see where he was going with his line of questioning.

"So, in Virehnai time, you're a baby. A newborn. Right?" She nodded.

"If you were out on the street and saw someone attacking a baby or a very young child in front of you, wouldn't you step in? Try to stop it?" He paused. "I've not known you very long, but from what I know of you, I think you would." He paused again, to give a moment to let his words sink in...and then slowly, gently told Elaina, "That's...what...Amalie...did. Amalie was young enough herself, especially compared to many of us, including myself...that like you, even after having been alive 133 years, had never fought another Virehn in anger. You said that everything happened quickly. Don't let guilt eat you alive. Amalie wouldn't want that. She did the same thing you would, motivated by love and caring."

107

Elaina was calmer and quieter. After a few minutes, and some more of the blood he'd brought her, she asked, "What now?"

"Your dad and Michel are both eager to see how you're doing; aside from that, the detective from last night will stop by to interview you about what happened a little later. Apparently, he interviewed you after the first attack. I believe his name is Hall." He stood up and looked at her. "Amalie's memorial service will be this evening." Elaina nodded. "Are you ready for company?"

"Yeah." He walked to the door and opened it.

Elaina stood up as they came in. Her dad rushed over to her and hugged her for the longest time. Michel put his hand on her shoulder.

"Are you okay? I was so worried about you..." her dad asked. She'd never seen her father as frazzled as he was now.

"I'm fine. I feel like I have maybe the worst hangover of my life, though. Reman told me the blood would help. It is."

"That's good, good." Her dad looked a little like he might cry, too. Michel told him to get rest shortly after they settled Elaina into her old suite. He tried; sleep wouldn't come, and when it finally did, it was restless. He was tired and was afraid for Elaina. He felt better seeing that she was her normal self this morning.

Elaina turned to Uncle Michel, who gave her a bear hug. Elaina was struggling not to cry again. She looked up at him. "I'm so sorry about Amalie." she told him. "Virehn zuth akret." He hugged her tighter and said the response. Even as he hugged Elaina, he found himself sad not only for what she'd been through, but sad for losing the woman he'd seen for years as a daughter in law. Joining the sadness was worry. In the back of his mind, he questioned the safety of his newest child. She'd been attacked twice now; both times in a building that was SUPPOSED to be secure. Michel couldn't understand it and had no clues who would be behind it, or why. It made him question if someone was targeting his children. The only thing he knew was it smacked of old-fashioned Virehnai treachery, despite the Compact.

Once Elaina was ready, the group of them piled into a limo and headed back to the complex in Lower Manhattan. Uncle Michel and her dad headed for Uncle Michel's office; Reman headed back up to his office, and Elaina went to her suite, to get a shower, change clothes, and rest a bit in her own bed if she wanted to before heading up to Uncle Michel's office to meet with the detective.

Elaina stood in her shower, all ten heads pointed at her, music going…and cried. Cried for the friend who gave so much of her time teaching her. Cried for the shopping trips she wouldn't have any more. Cried for the goofy sense of humor she'd miss. Cried for the life cut short.

An hour and a half later, Elaina sat in Uncle Michel's office; she was okay, if morose. The one thing she could do that cheered her up marginally, she did: She and Amalie purchased the shirt and shoes she was wearing on a lunchtime speed-shopping foray.

Present at the meeting were Detective Hall, whom she recognized, and Uncle Michel. Uncle Howard and her father were also there; all seated around Uncle Michel's conference table.

"Sorry to keep meeting you this way," Detective Hall told her. "Feeling better today?"

"I am, thanks."

"Do any of you object to recording this interview?"

Elaina nodded her head no. "Do anything you need to." Michel said.

"Fine." He had a small digital recorder, which he started, and sat in the middle of the table. "Interview of Elaina Jacoby, regarding the Compact deaths of Amalie Bisset of Clan Robichaux, and Raul Martinez, of Scotti Maintenance, Inc."

"Ms. Jacoby, had you ever seen the man in the elevator before yesterday?"

"Yes, sir. He was one of the three men who attacked me in my apartment before I ascended."

"Which of the three men was he?" He flipped through notes he'd taken when he interviewed her after the first attack. "Was he the man with the gun, the man on the bed, or the man that came up behind you and grabbed you?"

"He was the man that was laying on my bed, looking smug."

"Describe what happened last night, if you please."

Elaina went over her whole evening; that everything was fine until the man wanted to get in the elevator. When she looked up, they were both surprised as they recognized one another. He immediately started attacking her, and Amalie jumped in, trying to stop him. When Amalie did that, he began fighting with her instead. "Everything happened so fast." Elaina told him.

"You're absolutely certain when you encountered him the first time that he was human, and not Virehn?"

"Positive." She shook her head. "Mostly positive. NOW I'm questioning everything. I thought he was human...but by the time either of us realized he wasn't, it was too late..." The last part of her statement came out more like a whine.

"Don't stress yourself, Ms. Jacoby. We're simply trying to determine his status, to the best of your recollection. I can't say more." He paused.

"I think I've got all I need for right now." Detective Hall picked up the digital recorder and shut it off.

"I'm not supposed to say this; and none of you heard me say it - but one thing we're trying to figure out is who the hell Raul Martinez IS." He looked directly at Michel. "There are no records of a Raul Martinez being a Virehn; all the records provided from Scotti list him as human, and oathsworn to Clan Sabin. In his personal file at HQS, he's listed as human. The picture on the ID and in the file matches the body. But the corpse currently taking up space in the morgue at VarenCorp is definitely a Virehn."

Michel nodded. In his mind, it appeared some of his worst fears might be true if someone was making a Virehn off the record.

After Detective Hall left, Elaina looked over at her 'uncles,' hoping for some sort of explanation that would make her feel better. Anything.

"Why? Why did the Compact take her, if she was defending me?"

"We aren't sure; there are things about the situation we don't know that won't be answered definitively until they officially get the Vel'sheth involved. Don't know which it'll be, but whichever Vel'sheth it is, their job will be 'trace, discover and judge.' He'll taste a drop of both of their blood, and that will help determine the answers to some big questions, like who was his sire, and was he working with anyone, and why the Compact took both, and not just him."

She looked at them. "What's next?"

"Why don't you have some down time? Relax, rest, read a book, watch tv... Something to get your mind off of things before the memorial service tonight." He sighed. "There's family in Concarneau I have to notify, and then a succession planning meeting to chair."

The news that Amalie died sent ripples throughout the Robichaux clan, and the humans that were allied with them. The details mostly weren't known–only that their newest sister, Elaina, was there when it occurred.

The Virehnai were stunned at the news; deaths didn't happen very often. To have two happening so close on each other's heels had tongues wagging as to cause.

The humans? That was another story entirely. Tongues were wagging alright–but for all the wrong reasons. It left room for another of them to be made Virehn…and word spread quickly, akin to a feeding frenzy. It disheartened Walt Jacoby when both of his sons came to him and asked him to plead their case to Michel. Maybe Walt wasn't at his best when each of his sons stopped by; he'd been up all night worried about Elaina, and truthfully, had little sleep. What Walt found most telling was that neither of his sons bothered to ask how Elaina was, or how she or Michel were handling the loss of Amalie, though both knew their sister was involved.

It made Walt sad, and wondering where he went wrong. He hadn't remembered being like that when his own father was running things, and his siblings weren't, either. He wasn't sure if it was the culture around the Virehnai that had changed for humans, if it was the world itself, or a maybe an unholy combination of what effect the modern day's focus on wealth and youth has on people in the periphery of the Virehnai. He was glad Elaina was fine, and was worried that someone was targeting her, while his sons were hellbent on getting ahead. It was a question for another day, or a discussion with Michel.

"Ask Michel if he'll consider me, please?" Doug asked earlier. "This is my chance. I'm not too young, and not too old…"

"No."

"What…? What do you mean, 'no?'"

"Exactly how it sounds. I will not go beg Michel on your behalf."

"Why not? I deserve a chance to be a Virehn, too."

"What exactly do you think you deserve, Doug? You live in an executive suite, have women chasing you, more money than most men your age, cars…" He shook his head. "Why can't you be happy with what you have, and actually enjoy it? Or maybe even settle down, get married, and have some kids?"

"Are you fucking kidding me, Pop? I ask you to go to your patron and ask him to consider me, and I get some shitty ass speech about being happy with the life I have?? Why won't you just ask him? Isn't it your duty to look out for us?"

Walt answered back frostily. "Watch your tone. I have looked out for you…your whole life. You want for nothing, apparently, except for what you may never get. Here's a newsflash, Doug: Michel makes up his own mind, along with the Clan elders. I have NO input into that decision. Only the Sethari of Clan Robichaux decides who ascends. Besides, from what I know, after Elaina ascended, there is next to NO chance that someone from the same family would be picked. They try not to do that on purpose."

Doug stood up, angry and annoyed. "I guess Elaina's your favorite now…" As he was walking out the door Walt called out behind him, "Check on your sister and see how she's doing…It could've been her that died last night, that you'd be asking me to succeed." Doug left, waving it off.

When Rob requested a meeting about 45 minutes after Doug did, to ask for the same thing that Doug had - to meet with Michel on his behalf, Walt was getting a little crispy, mentally. As far as

Rob was concerned, his father was totally dismissive, and his father's words tore him up.

"Rob, I love you." His father said and then laughed. He actually laughed. "I tell you this out of love for you: you have thin skin now. If anyone says anything to you that you don't want to hear, you get angry and lash out at whoever you feel wronged you. Those are bad attributes for a Virehn to have. You're a good man, Rob, but first you need to learn to tame your temper and learn how to play nicer with others." His father paused, even as Rob began bristling. "You don't really have the temperament they're looking for to become Virehnai, and even if you did, it's like I told Doug, when he asked me to plead his case with Michel: they will not pick another person from the same family branch so soon…" His father was trying to be both honest and kind, but Rob didn't take criticism or truth well and never did. Like his brother Doug, Rob stormed out, and like his older brother, never once asked if Elaina was okay.

Walt Jacoby sat in his office, contemplating. He was normally proud of all of his children, except for maybe today; he couldn't be prouder of both his daughters. The exchange he had with his eldest daughter stood in stark contrast to the interaction he'd had with his sons. When Janet stopped by, she brought him a cupcake decorated at home by his four-year-old granddaughter, Hayden. She came over to check on him, to see how he was doing. She kissed his cheek before leaving. "I'll see you Friday evening; fair warning. I'll have the crotch goblins in tow…"

His grandchildren were his pride and joy. "You've got to stop calling them that, honey…" He said, laughing. "Are carpet gargoyles better?" She asked him, one eyebrow raised.

"NO!" He said, unwrapping the gooey blue cupcake with a smeary red smiley face on it. Janet making him laugh was the balm that his heart needed. "Just whatever you're doing…please be careful."

"I always am, Papa. I'm headed downtown to check on Elaina. I know Amalie's service will be tonight. I'm going to head down there in advance and be there for her. I know those guys have been good friends since she started interning. Tonight's going to be rough for her."

Walt's heart swelled in pride for his girls. He didn't get it all wrong.

Janet had a kind, caring heart, as did Elaina. Janet had been through so much, including her spouse's death from cancer, leaving her raising those two precious little girls on her own. Walt thought Janet would make an excellent Virehn as well. He would be loath to tell either of his sons, but he'd go to bat for Janet to become a Virehn long before he would either of them. Janet never asked. Janet wanted to live a simpler life. She had a house, separate and apart from the world of the Virehnai, and he was proud of her for knowing her own mind and heart, and going after her own dreams. Had she wanted a job at any of their companies, she could've had one for the asking. She was a teacher because she wanted to be, wanting to make a difference in impressionable, malleable young minds. Walt knew his sons looked down on her for her choice.

Elaina, unlike her older sister, worked for him, and she'd done an exemplary job. She had a good work ethic and never relied on the fact she was the boss' daughter and didn't expect favors. He'd had no clue Elaina would ever ascend, but he was happy the Sethari chose her. Mentally, he knew his sons would never ascend, not that he could tell either of them that. He already had compliments from others about their dealings with his youngest, and while the messages were congratulatory and sincere, he felt an undercurrent of 'what happened with your sons?'

It made Walt sad. Doug was butthurt and jealous of Elaina because he felt like it should've been him, and he felt slighted and passed over. Now, instead of saying that it was Michel 'playing favorites' with their sister, he had been 'accused' of it, too. And then there was Rob. Walt knew Rob felt dismissed; He'd seen all of Rob's emotions play across his face, which was nothing new. Walt wasn't trying to be mean or dismissive. He simply tried to tell him the reasons they would never let him ascend, but unfortunately, it fell on deaf ears. All Rob knew or would ever know was the sting of criticism, which he'd never taken well, and what Walt knew was the abject jealousy of his youngest sister and Doug. The only sibling he didn't feel jealousy of was Janet. The only reason he didn't was he felt superior to her. It left him despairing of the future. These two men were going to take over everything he built someday, and not run it into the ground?

Walt sat there quietly, fiddling with the cupcake wrapper, folding it and unfolding it. There was plenty on Walt's 'to do' list, but as he mangled the wrapper in his hands, he was contemplating going upstairs and taking a nap before going to Amalie's memorial. He was tired, emotionally wrung out, and now wasn't the best time to be contemplating the fitness of his children to take over his businesses someday. He didn't understand what happened with his sons. He and Carrie had raised all their children the same. They loved them all the same. He always championed them when he could and tried best as he could to make sure they had everything they ever needed or wanted. What went wrong?

Janet was a sweetheart and surprised her. Elaina heard a knock at her door, and there she was: She came bearing hand-drawn cards from her nieces, Sophie and Hayden. She and Janet sat on her sofa, and Janet looked at her and asked, "Are you okay?" Elaina shook her head no. Janet opened her arms wide, and she cried in her sister's arms for a while. By the time they were ready to walk upstairs to the Hall to attend Amalie's memorial, Elaina felt better. Janet's presence was like that. She was always the calm in the middle of the storm.

The memorial for Amalie was smaller than the one for Johannes had been.

When Elaina and Janet walked in together, the group in the Hall was mostly Virehnai: clan siblings and friends. The humans that were there were people who worked with her at the law firm or were her friends through it. It surprised Elaina to see Detective Hall there, though she knew he was probably there in an official capacity, scoping out the crowd. Uncle Howard told her he was bloodsworn to Clan Westcott.

Normally, the Hall was off-limits to humans, unless they had a reason to be there, like this evening. She and Janet took their place alongside their father, who hugged both of them and gave each a peck on the cheek; "Hi Papa," they said. Their mother Carrie wasn't there this evening; instead, she was babysitting Sophie and Hayden, and eating cupcakes, which her granddaughters were likely wearing by now.

Her brothers were both there, standing behind their father. Though Doug said hello to her and Janet, Rob ignored her. At least he was nice to Janet. Both of her brothers were acting a little chilly. Elaina noticed there were many of the Lightner family attending, most of whom were bloodsworn to Howard VanEtters. They knew and worked with Amalie as well.

As Reman approached the dais in the center, the room quieted down, and he spoke.

"Zuth' akret. Setha'ra Virehnai."

"This evening, we are here to remember our sister and friend, Amalie Bisset, the beloved of Johannes Robichaux, her sire; both of Clan Robichaux. Her death is tragic; it needn't have happened and shouldn't have. It makes the loss that much more poignant."

"For those of you who are visiting among us, 'Virehn zuth 'akret. Setha'ra Virehnai' is a phrase you'll hear us say and repeat. It means, 'The blood remembers. The flame endures.' Our blood contains our truth. Truly, our blood contains our truth, and at times like this, that knowledge sustains us. Why? Many reasons. First among them, that our love for Amalie, and the Virehn she was, is carried in our blood; for the humans in our midst, that love, friendship and caring lives in your hearts. None of us who knew her will ever forget her, nor the love we had for her. She was a bright light, and so young."

"The other reason we hang onto the fact that our blood contains the truth? Blood will tell us the truth of what transpired, shed light, and give us the details we lack today. The Compact took both Amalie and the man who attacked her, but we will know why. We will have answers, though, as with any truth revealed, we may not like where it leads us."

"Michel, will you please join me here?" Reman asked. Michel had been standing next to Uncle Howard; they'd come in together, in the middle of a discussion with a woman she now recognized as Carolyn Brownell, the NY CEO of VarenCorp, and a tall, sandy-haired man. They were all standing together, still. Michel joined Reman at the dais.

"Amalie's sire, your son Johannes, preceded her in death and isn't here to mourn her end. Michel, the duty falls to you, as head of Clan Robichaux." Michel was somber, standing there. He bowed his head. Both deaths were a lot to endure in such a short time.

"Your son Johannes carried your lineage, and the memory within it. Even as everything Johannes was as a Virehn started with you, so does Amalie carry your lineage and all those memories." Reman handed Michel the knife and then turned to the dais to pick up the bowl that had a flame in its center. The light from it danced wildly, and cast shadows around the dimly lit chamber, particularly as he turned with it, and faced Michel once again. Michel cut his palm with the knife and bled a bit into the bowl.

"Will the Sethari, the elders of Clan Robichaux, along with Elaina Jacoby, and our honored elders of Clan Sabin please come join me around the altar?" They included Elaina because Amalie died protecting her; she'd asked Reman and Michel if it would be appropriate for her to say something. They agreed that considering the situation, and her involvement, it was. Some of those gathered knew what transpired; most didn't and would find out shortly. It might help quell any lingering rumors.

From within the gathered crowd, those called, including Elaina, came forward. She stood alongside Michel. She realized she recognized more of them now than she had for Johannes' memorial. Uncle Howard was among them, as well as Uncle Howard's eldest children and clan members. Elaina recognized Carolyn Brownell this time, who nodded at her somberly; the tall sandy-haired man alongside her, she assumed, was her brother Darren Wheeler.

Reman began speaking again, once everyone stood in a circle around the dais. "Our sister Amalie walked among us, and we knew her in multiple ways: as a Virehn; an ally, as family, as a friend. In death, she returns to the Flame whence she came, her soul now free of its physical bonds. We give her name to memory. Those closest to her carry her story in their blood." The priest handed the stone bowl, flickering wildly, to Michel, who bowed his head for a few moments, and then, turned and passed the bowl to Elaina, who cried as she prayed for Amalie. She handed it off to Uncle Howard, who bowed his head, praying silently. Each elder of Clan Robichaux took the bowl, and prayed likewise, until it circled the dais, and Darrin Wheeler, after praying, handed the bowl back to Reman.

"Like any story, each of us has a beginning and an ending."

The priest held the bowl in one hand, and with his thumb and forefinger, snuffed the flame out. "Amalie Bisset's life ended yesterday. Each of us who knew her carries a bit of her spark within us, all of us; Virehnai or not. Whether Amalie's memory dwells in your blood, or in your heart, say her name often, and remember her. Every time you do, that bit of her she entrusted with each of you is rekindled, and she lives again."

Reman stood there and contemplated the bowl before him for a moment before continuing. He knew the next part, for many, would be a bombshell.

"It is truly tragic how our sister Amalie departed us. A Virehn attacked our newest sister, Elaina Jacoby; Amalie lost her life after attacking him while defending Elaina. Bound by the Compact, both their lives were forfeit." There were light gasps heard around the room, human and Virehn alike.

"Earlier I said that while Amalie's life is at an end, her story is not yet finished. As part of that story, and because she was with Amalie when she left us, it's only fitting that Elaina say something about her friend's last moments."

All eyes turned to Elaina, who spoke.

"The man who attacked us attacked me once previously, after I'd been named, but before I ascended. When he got into the elevator with us? He was going to kill me this time. Amalie didn't flinch, didn't hesitate. She defended me and gave everything—because the love and friendship we had for each other made her brave." Elaina sniffled and tried very hard not to cry.

"The Compact? It didn't care about the motive. It took both Amalie and our attacker. I care very much. I want to know why Amalie died. Virehn zuth akret. My blood will always remember; not only why she died, but that she was truly my friend until the very end."

Scattered throughout the hall, people said "Virehn zuth akret" in reply. Michel reached for her hand and squeezed it.

Reman continued on. "We will hear the end and know what happened. Even from a tragedy such as this, good emerges. As one life ends, another is kindled. One story's end is another's new beginning."

"The Sethari before us, our elders, have chosen Amalie's successor. Michael Eric Ratner, you are named before all gathered. Witnessed by the blood. Witnessed by the oath. Witnessed by the Flame." Michael stood between his uncle, Dave Lightner (the Lightner in Jacoby, VanEtters and Lightner), and his mom, Carla

120

Ratner, Uncle Dave's baby sister. Michael stood taller and took a deep breath when his name was called.

The Vel'sheth asked him, "Michael Eric Ratner, do you come forward freely?"

Michael nodded yes, even as his mom hugged him, and his Uncle Dave shook his hand. Michael answered, "I do."

Reman looked around the room at those gathered and nodded. "Jeff and Howard, will you come beside me here?" Jeff Garvin, Uncle Howard's son, who was on the other side of the dais standing with the elders, changed position to stand on the other side of the Vel'sheth, with Michel on the other. Jeff was to be Michael's sire. She and Uncle Howard switched places, so that he stood beside Michel. Reman handed the knife first to Jeff, and he cut himself even as Michel had earlier, adding his blood into the bowl. They then passed the knife to Howard, who did likewise. After they passed the bowl back to Reman, he bowed his head over it and intoned a low prayer. He looked at Michael. "Come, son. Approach the dais, kneel before me here, and be seen by us."

Elaina had been in Michael's position less than a month earlier. She smiled at him as he approached the dais, and she was leaving it, and went back to stand alongside her family, her part done. She could guess the raging emotions he was feeling. He smiled back at her, and then at Reman and the others as he approached the dais and then knelt before Reman as requested. Reman, still holding the bowl, softly intoned what might've been a blessing over it. He then handed the bowl to Michel, as head of Clan Robichaux. The blood shed by Michel, Howard and Jeff was within it; Amalie's flame was still extinguished. While Michel held the bowl, Reman took a finger, and dipped it into their mixed blood; blood that represented both the Virehn he would succeed, and the family he would become part of.

The priest looked down at him, into his eyes, and with his bloody finger, marked him between his eyebrows. "You may rise."

Michael stood up, and the priest turned and picked up the knife from the altar and handed it to Michael. She couldn't hear Reman's low instructions to him, but she knew Reman asked Michael to shed his own blood into the bowl.

"Very well." Reman said, after he finished, giving him more low instructions on what he should do next in the ceremony. When he was finished with his instructions, Reman continued, so that everyone could hear.

"Michael Eric Ratner, we see you. You stand among us, recognized. You will join us. As I said before, when one life and its flame and story ends, another begins. Endings and beginnings happen together, always: while we have reason to grieve, there is also an opportunity to celebrate, giving us the opportunity to temper our grief. Your story starts here, and now." Reman handed Michael the bowl, and then took one of the taper candles that had been burning on the oval altar all along, and faced Michael. Elaina remembered from her own ceremony how heavy the stone bowl was, and the smaller bowl nestled within that contained a fragrant oil. He used the candle from the altar to set fire to the liquid in the smaller bowl. Once again, the flames caused light to dance around the chamber.

"Michael, this flame is your flame, and we light it today in front of everyone assembled here. I ask you, while yet human, to take the flame; speak the name of the one whose footsteps you follow in, and step into memory." He nodded, prompting him.

Michael looked down at the bowl. "Amalie Bisset, I speak your name, that you might live on in my memory, and my life."

He lifted the bowl up high and said, "Amalie, I carry your fire forward." It remained aloft in his hands for a few moments.

The priest smiled at him, and reaching out for the bowl, which he handed it back. Reman placed it back on the altar. Michael went to stand beside Jeff and then Reman once again addressed those gathered.

"Let Amalie Bisset's name be remembered. Let her flame be honored. May the truth still to be known about her death be told and may the blood that knew her bear her truth into the days to come. Virehn zuth akret."

All the Virehnai present repeated the Val'sheth's words:

"Virehn zuth akret."

The older Virehnai who were attending Amalie's memorial saw her death and the attack on Elaina starkly; it smacked of treachery. It might take time, but they would know the truth of it, wherever it led.

9

BETRAYED

Detective Patrick Hall was at the offices of VarenCorpUSA. Its headquarters were on the top ten floors of the building that housed VarenCorp's NYC headquarters.

He attended the memorial for Amalie Bisset the night before, but learned nothing new. The one thing he accomplished with his attendance was to sit down and have a discussion with Dave Scotti, Bobby Davidov, and Darren Wheeler to figure out the mess that represented Raul Martinez. He needed to know what they knew about him; it surprised them all to discover Mr. Martinez was now on a slab in VarenCorp's morgue and was no longer human.

Along with VarenCorp's files on him, Scotti's own files showed him as oathsworn, human and employed on a call-in basis as elevator maintenance. Dave Scotti was adamant that a background check had taken place. Dave didn't know the man well, but he was the oathsworn grandson of a friend of their family, bloodsworn to Bobby Davidov. There was no mistake. Even if Elaina Jacoby was now questioning what she remembered out of grief and shock, there was now more than enough evidence to show someone turned Raul without knowledge or permission; they simply didn't know how, when, or who. Detective Hall also had the security footage for the elevator car. Raul Martinez definitely started the altercation by attacking Elaina. Once he and Amalie began fighting, he watched them both die by Compact. Everything was exactly the way Elaina had described. He showed the footage to them, and judging by the surprise on their faces, their reactions and information were genuine. He was positive there was no subterfuge or treachery on their parts.

Last night's meeting, while informative, left him anxious. Detective Hall was now searching all the databases for the man's fingerprints and seeing what information that search had turned up. VarenCorp fingerprinted everyone that was issued permanent retention badges as a matter of course. There were also many police databases, and he would be in VCFIS. He would also search IAFIS, NGI, and Interpol's AFIS and Biometric Hub too, simply out of due diligence. Detective Hall stared at the screen in front of him, somewhere between shock and disbelief.

He got a hit. Several, in fact. They boggled his mind. What in the ever-loving hell was he looking at?

When he ran the prints for Raul Martinez…he also got hits under the names 'Marco Albergheri,' 'Carlos Rau,' and 'Gabriel Durand.' When he cross checked all of THOSE names against VCFIS, he discovered that Carlos Rau was an employee of one of David Lambert's privately-owned companies, Equinox Holdings, and was also employed under the name 'Gabriel Durand' in Paris - as an oathsworn remote IT freelancer for a website company, L'Atelier Digital. Both of those companies were privately owned by the CEO's of VarenCorp London and Paris. When he checked all those same aliases against Homeland Security's Passenger Name Records (PNR) database, he discovered that under the name 'Marco Albergheri,' he'd traveled between New York, London, Zurich and the Netherlands five times in six weeks, and fifteen times in three months…and under the name 'Gabriel Durand,' he'd traveled to Rome four times in three months, and Paris twice. Every place he was employed considered him a good and conscientious employee; no one ever had a problem with him, his work, or attitude. The only thing Hall could figure was the man must've panicked when he realized Elaina recognized him. If this man hadn't ended up dead in Robichaux's elevator…how long would 'Raul' have kept this charade up, and what was the ultimate aim?

Detective Hall decided quickly whatever this represented, and the ramifications were well above his pay grade. It made him question who else was involved in whatever 'Raul Martinez' was involved in. It scared him; knowledge of this kind could get you dead, depending on who knew what you knew, and who it threatened. He closed the browser after clearing the history and then cleared out the cache for good measure. He picked up the phone and called his boss' boss, Archie Fuller, directly on his emergency line.

Archie had been a bloodsworn detective in the early 1950's, and was shot on the job, and was in the hospital hovering perilously between life and death. Several clans decided he was too valuable an asset to lose, and he was turned, as part of Clan Westcott. He's currently the Director of Security for VarenCorp USA – and works closely with the Directors of Security for Europe, South America (S.A.) and Asia. All four of them report directly to Ari Cottrell, CEO of VarenCorp International.

Once Director Fuller picked up, he identified himself as the detective who was working the Compact deaths at the Robichaux building–and based on his findings; he was advising him he needed to stand up a Red Team immediately. The operating procedures and protocols that underpinned VarenCorp specified what conditions would prompt such an action–and based on what he saw, it indicated a system breach.

"Are you certain, detective?"

"Yes, sir. We've got a breach."

"Scope?"

"International."

He heard Director Fuller swearing under his breath. "Where are you now?"

"Downstairs in IT."

"Be in my Conference Room in twenty minutes. It's show and tell time. We'll see what you've got."

Director Fuller hung up, then walked to several offices within VarenCorp's NY headquarters. The first people he notified were principals on his security team; all he had to say was "We're standing up a Red Team; conference room at 10:30," and people were scattering. Next, Fuller stopped at Eliška Novak's office; she's head of VarenCorp USA. On his way back downstairs, Fuller stopped at Carolyn Brownell's office to tell her the same. Carolyn's next move was to call Michel; "I can't elaborate, Michel, but I need you to report immediately to the Director of Security's conference room for an emergency meeting. They're starting at 10:30."

"I'll be there as soon as I can, Carolyn."

Michel was already in a meeting; because of recent events and Michel's gut instincts, he had his own security people combing through its logs. Between Amalie's recent demise, and two separate attacks on what was supposed to be a secure property, Michel tasked them to look for inconsistencies in the files of humans that contractually worked in any Robichaux or Clan owned building for the past six months. Surprisingly, they found two. When Carolyn called, his team was briefing him on it. One was a woman employed by Scotti Management in housekeeping, named Patrice Dixon. They also found another man from Scotti Management employed in building maintenance on a call-in basis; When Security showed the photos to Elaina, she didn't recognize the woman, but the man, she did. He was the man who stood by her window, holding a gun on her. His name was Malcolm Harwell. After Elaina identified him, they attempted to go through Scotti to have him called in. He was a no-call, no-show, which was unusual for him…unless he'd heard about Raul's demise.

"Good work, everyone. That call I just took? I've got to head off to a meeting with Carolyn Brownell, and Director Fuller. I have a nasty suspicion it probably has to do with all of this…" Michel gestured. "Keep digging. I'm taking this with me," he said, picking up the document outlining the details of their search from the table. "Thanks."

When Michel arrived at Director Fuller's conference room, the meeting was already in progress; he knew it would be. There was no way he could've gotten there on time. Fuller's secretary let him into the conference room. As he entered, Carolyn said hello, and patted the seat next to her. Her deputy, Matteo Andriotti, was sitting there, along with Detective Hall, and Darren Wheeler. Bobby Davidov sat beside his sire, Darren. Of the others around the table, he only knew two because they were in his own clan. They nodded hello.

Carolyn introduced Director Fuller to Michel. They knew of each other, but their paths hadn't crossed previously.

"Nice to meet you, Michel; sorry it's like this. Detective Hall was briefing us on a security breach he discovered while investigating the Compact deaths at your mid-town facility. Unfortunately for us, it's scope is international."

Michel looked at him in surprise. "International? In what way?"

Fuller turned to Hall. "Detective Hall, do you mind getting Michel up to speed?"

"No, sir." He answered and turned to Michel. "Sir, the man in the elevator that attacked Amalie had a permanent retention badge issued by Scotti Management. In all our records, he's listed as human, and it shows his name as Raul Martinez. Here's where the problem starts: I've discovered that the man downstairs in the morgue…aside from now being Virehnai…has three other aliases. Raul's been busy. With one of those aliases, he's had access to your buildings. Using two other aliases I found, he's simultaneously employed at Equinox Holdings; and at L'Atelier Digital. Equinox Holdings is privately owned by the CEO of the London office, David Lambert; L'Atelier Digital is a private company owned by Violette Fontaine, CEO of the Paris office."

Detective Hall let the information settle. That this man, oathsworn, was working directly for two different VarenCorp CEOs under aliases, was chilling; so was the fact that someone unknown to any of them turned him. It flaunted any semblance of normal protocol. Normally, if he were to become Virehnai...because he was oathsworn to Clan Sabin, they would do the honors. Michel wondered if being turned was in payment for services rendered.

Before Detective Hall could go on, Michel unzipped his folio and pulled out the papers from his own meeting. "When Carolyn called me, I was in a meeting with my security team. They found inconsistencies in our logs I was unaware of until this morning. You'll want this, I think." He slid the paper across the table to Hall and then told everyone what his team found.

"Their search came up with two people. It looked like nothing major; simple inconsistencies in the records we had on them." He looked over at Darren and Bobby. "Both are through Scotti Management. One of my security officers showed the badge photos we have on file to Elaina. She'd never recalled seeing the woman before, but she identified the man. Malcolm Harwell took part in the first attack on her; he was the man that held a gun on her. He's on a call-in basis; we tried calling him this morning. He was a no-call, no show."

"We have...more?" Director Fuller was unhappy, as his day just shit on him some more.

"At least one," Michel answered him. "The woman in housekeeping might simply have a problem in her record. Her name's listed there, along with his, and their badge access records for the past six months. I'll have my people search back farther, along with checking for others."

"Please do, Michel." Director Fuller turned to Detective Hall. "I need you and your folks to quickly and quietly research these people in the same way you did 'Raul.' We've got a live one. If we can find him, we can interrogate him and see whose he is." He then addressed Michel. "Don't approach the woman; let us do checks on her first. We don't want to spook her if she's dirty, but we don't want to target her if she's not. we may have questions for your child, Elaina. Detective Hall was getting to that before you walked in." Fuller looked over at Hall. "Floor's yours."

"Looking at the information we have, and even the information you gave us, we know we have someone targeting VarenCorp CEOs. What we don't understand is how your company or Elaina figures in. We don't know why 'Raul' singled her out; he's been inside so many buildings that it makes it difficult to speculate who his targets are. We hoped that talking to her might give us…something."

"Feel free to talk to her whenever you like. I'm certain you'll find her completely cooperative."

"Thanks." Detective Hall nodded at Michel and then turned expectantly to his boss.

"My next actions will be to teleconference with David and Violette; Detective Hall, would you stick around for that teleconference? If you want to remain off camera and keep your name out of it to protect you, I've got no problem doing that." Fuller turned to the others in the room. "Everything you've learned at this meeting stays within this group; the information divulged here today is sensitive enough that it could either be 'incompatible with life,' or might alert someone that we're on to them. We don't know how far this goes, whose involved. It needs to be treated carefully. We may further task any of you as needed. There'll be another meeting here, at the same time tomorrow for updates, unless something emergent happens in the meantime. Thank you all for attending."

There aren't that many Vel'sheth, truly. Why? Most Virehn wouldn't want to deal with having more than their own ancestral line knocking around in their heads, much less the part of the job where they use magic to call up the egregore, Varet'Sul'Akha. Most won't even say 'Varet'Sul'Akha.' They either say 'the egregore,' or 'the entity,' or 'the Tribunal in the blood.' Most Virehnai don't want to be on a first name basis with it. At any given time, there are only 20-25 of them worldwide. There are three are in the New York Metropolitan area:

Reman, who was offered a position at the Hall with Clan Robichaux, and is now part of the Clan;

Joao Perreira, once hailing from Lisbon, and moved to the Americas, first to Brazil, and then to New York. Clan Westbrook offered him a similar job.

The third works with Clan Sabin. His name is Gottfried Waldman. Of these three, Joao wears a dual hat. Not only does he act as the Vel'sheth for Clan Westbrook, he secured an "as needed" job with VarenCorp security through Director Archie Fuller. If they have a crime (Compact-related, or otherwise, where the truth in the blood is necessary to know,) he's the one that tastes the blood or performs a ceremony calling on Varet'Sul'Akha to determine guilt or innocence. There are similar Vel'sheths that work for VarenCorp Europe, S.A., and Asia.

After Raul Martinez was found dead in the elevator along with Amalie, Detective Hall, as a matter of routine, took a vial of blood from both. The next day, Vel'sheth Joao was called in. He tasted both of their blood from each vial; he didn't look at the names. Initially, the names are inconsequential. Amalie's blood was relatively easy. Her sire and pedigree was known. Raul Martinez was another story, entirely. When Joao tasted him, he saw a man. He didn't know his name; he wouldn't. The same thing could be said for his sire. In a case such as this, he would have to list it out as Sire1, Sire2, Sire3 – and write details for each one. He kept going back until he found a sire he was familiar with…but it's painstaking. and you may still come up empty. Unless you have a famous, well-known or especially prolific sire in your lineage, it requires a great deal and long hours of research, and it isn't always successful.

Normally it's easier; VarenCorp might have its share of both champions and detractors, but they're quite good at keeping tabs on Virehnai, no matter how many times they change their names, relocate, or reinvent themselves to inherit. Thankfully, the times when Virehn are made in secret are rare.

While he could not pinpoint a lineage or pedigree, there were several things Joao could testify to with a certainty. Raul was one of those who took part in Elaina's assault; he saw it through the man's eyes. They did something else to her, too, but didn't know what. He couldn't see it, because Raul didn't from where he was.

He may document his lineage eventually, but either way, Joao was positive that Raul received the 'gift of becoming' as a reward for his participation in the first attack on Michel Robichaux's newest daughter, Elaina Jacoby.

When Joao compared the individual stories their blood told, it became obvious how they died. Raul knocked Elaina over and likely would've continued his attack – except Amalie stopped him from attacking her further. If Amalie ceased her attack entirely, or waited for further provocation from Raul, she would've been fine. Unfortunately, in the heat of the moment, there was just enough of a pause that when she attacked Raul, Varet'Sul'Akha saw it as a separate attack, unprovoked. Amalie died for her actions, and Raul died for his. The egregore never considered that Amalie was still protecting Elaina, because she successfully stopped Raul's initial attack.

Joao looked at the vials sadly. Varet'Sul'Akha was a tribunal in the blood–and mostly got it right–but then, there were times like this. One man, secretly made Virehn as a reward for actions meant to skirt the Compact and get around Varet'Sul'Akha; and a young woman, who thought only to defend her friend, and didn't deserve the fate the egregore doled out to her. It was a sadness. Joao picked up Amalie's vial. Virehn zuth akret.

Now, he had to write up the report and file it.

Mentally, David Lambert was flipping the fuck out.

He'd been having a normal day, with no problems at all–at least until he got a message from Leonie Meier, VarenCorp Europe's Security Director, that he needed to attend a secure teleconference with her, and Director Archie Fuller from VarenCorpUSA. It went downhill from there. David was petrified; certain his malfeasance and treachery had been discovered.

He sat down in the conference room enabled for secure teleconferencing, and joined in. Director Fuller was on one screen, Director Leonie Meier was on another, and it surprised David to see Violette Fontaine of the Paris office on the final one.

Fuller went first.

"Thanks for joining us on such short notice. I know it's getting later in your day. I briefed Leonie ahead of time; now I get to catch you guys up." He paused for a moment, looking down at what was in front of him. "We have an international security breach, and both of your offices are involved. That's why we stood up a Red Team this morning. What I'm about to reveal needs to be kept in the strictest of confidence and goes no further than you. Understood?"

Both David and Violette said yes. Director Fuller continued.

"We had a Compact-related death recently on a Virehnai property here in Manhattan. In investigating it further, we discovered we have a larger problem; so do both of you. We simply don't know how far or deep it runs. The man that was found dead in the elevator was a Virehn, yet his ID badge and records confirm that he started out as an oathsworn human, employed by Scotti Management, who fell under the aegis of Clan Sabin. Someone secretly made him a Virehn."

Both David and Violette looked confused, and Fuller continued. "In attempting to find out who the hell was lying on the slab in our morgue, we investigated him further, only to discover a trail of aliases, extensive travel between the USA and many European countries-only to conclude that this person represented a danger to all of us. He's not the only person we're investigating. We need to see how far the breach goes, and hopefully, who it leads back to."

"What is it you need us to do?" Violette asked.

"Look at a picture of the Virehn who died in an elevator here in Manhattan and tell me if you know him." Fuller put 'Raul's' badge photo on the screen. Seeing the photo on the screen, all David could think was 'I'm screwed,' along with a long, pronounced mental 'fuckfuckfuckfuck....'"

Violette gasped. "That is Gabriel Durand! He's one of my freelance web designers! He's a genius with IT. Sometimes he's here physically, but usually he works remotely." She shook her head, trying to process that her web designer was involved. "I can confirm he was human the last time he was here in the office. It was about six or seven weeks ago." She paused. "Merde. He was fantastic, too. Easy to work with, very attentive to detail; talented."

"That's Carlos Rau. Carlos is....was....working with my property management team. I knew him but didn't see him very often. The last time he was in my office was about six weeks ago, and I can verify he was human. I only ever got good feedback on his performance."

"And there lies the crux of our problems. Whoever the hell this person may be, they never made waves, had good performance reviews, and did nothing to make anyone question him." Fuller paused for dramatic effect. "If it wasn't for him ending up dead as an unknown Virehn in an elevator, we wouldn't know he held multiple international aliases."

David cautiously asked, "What happened, that he ended up dead by Compact?"

"He worked as on call elevator maintenance at Michel Robichaux's building in midtown Manhattan. Robichaux's child, Elaina Jacoby, was attacked a month ago, after her succession ceremony but before ascension. Three men attacked her, but they got away. We couldn't determine who they were or how they got key access to either her floor or her suite. Apparently, the other day when 'Raul' got on the elevator, he and Elaina recognized one another, and he attacked her."

"Oh no. Is she okay? Was she the other Compact-related death? I used to be close to Michel before he headed for the states." Shitshitshitshit......

"Elaina's fine. Her clan sister, Amalie Bisset, was on the elevator with her, and defended her. Amalie's the one the Compact took. Elaina had only been turned; she's less than two weeks old." Fuckfuckfuckfuckfuckityfuckfuckfuck.....

"I don't know either of them, but I'm sorry for Michel's loss." He paused for a minute, hoping that they would take the emotions playing across his face as concern for Michel. "What should we do now?"

"I need you both to go through your building access logs across the board; all clan and personal businesses, and see if you find any mismatches, or anything unusual. If you find something, send it to me and Leonie both, encrypted. Michel found more names when he had his security team scrub through their building access records earlier. I hope I'm wrong, but I suspect you'll find others."

"We're quietly checking at our level, too," Director Meier told them. "If you think you've found someone, please let us take care of it. We don't know how far this goes."

Once the teleconference was over, David Lambert had a small meltdown at his desk. How could he not?

All that kept running through his head, over and over, was, "Did they know? Could they?" He wasn't feeling guilty so much as he was afraid of discovery. How much did they know? They obviously knew Carlos worked for him. What else did they know about his dealings with Carlos?

As he sat there running situations and circumstances through his mind, trying to determine what their logical end would be, he panicked. He was thinking–realizing–someone had set him up.

Carlos Rau had been in his office the day he'd discovered the theft of the property titles. They were still listed as belonging to SanguineHoldings, even now. Carlos and one of his sons were in the room with them when they discovered the theft and were discussing their options. "I know enough that I can look at the metadata for you, to see what's going on…" Carlos tapped away on the computer for about 15 minutes, and said, "Does the name 'Robichaux' mean anything to you? Someone named Robichaux keeps coming up in the metadata…"

David had been so angry. He'd just served on a Council against Michel, and now, here was his name, coming up in information about title theft. Michel had his own holding company and had moved away from being a lawyer toward real estate years before. Once Carlos showed them information he'd found, David and his son were discussing their options, and the possibility of bringing in a forensic accountant. Carlos recommended several. He'd had no reason to believe Carlos was involved in ANY of it...then. In retrospect, now he was questioning everything.

It was after that meeting, when he and his son Liam and Carlos were leaving for the day, that Carlos said "I shouldn't say it, but you know…that's just rubbish that someone who's your mate would treat you that way. If you ever need me to sort him out for you, let me know…It might not be right, but I'm your man if you need me." He claimed to 'have access.'

Carlos' offer did a mambo in his brain as he got angrier and angrier. Several days later, he asked 'Carlos' if he could access John Robichaux's schedule. Carlos sent him a week's worth of John's schedule, which proved invaluable to him. It appeared John would have a meeting that took him to New Jersey. The overarching plan was to orchestrate the death of John Robichaux.

The woman he'd found that caused the accident on I-95 between Newark and Manhattan, he'd found on Reddit, on a thread where the woman, named Millie, was discussing her recent cancer diagnosis with others, and was distraught by what her children would have to endure while she was sick, and feared for where they would end up. Millie divorced her first husband who was now incarcerated at the New Jersey State Prison in Trenton, and her second husband, her children's father, died recently from a heart attack. She had no other family to speak of. He reached out to Millie; flew to meet her, and set up a very generous trust fund for her children. In return, she'd cause an accident. He was, thanks to Carlos, able to give Millie a description and license plate number for the car. Millie would cause the accident. The man David hired from the dark web, Carl, would make sure that John Robichaux died in that accident. Carl Ferguson owed no allegiance to anyone. He wasn't oathsworn. David paid him well. John Robichaux died that day, and he thought that with John's death, the thefts would end.

Later, after more money disappeared from his accounts, David and his sons decided that they might want to take up Carlos on his offer, with some provisions. They decided they wanted an RFID chip in Elaina, but they didn't want her hurt. They wanted her to feel unsafe. Carlos said he would be discreet and would make it happen. That's exactly what he did.

Now…David was wondering with all the aliases 'Carlos' had, if Carlos manipulated him into asking for what he did, and doing what he did. The resentment against Michel had two centuries to build. Did Carlos take advantage of that anger? David didn't know. He only knew what the results were: the death of John Robichaux, an RFID chip implanted in Elaina Jacoby, and now…Carlos, or whoever the hell he was…dead in Manhattan. It left him frightened, wondering who knew what, and if he'd left himself open to being blackmailed.

It seemed upon deliberating on the situation, if he kept a cool head, he might survive this...at least as long as his blood wasn't required. If there was a tribunal, and a Vel'sheth were required to use his blood to determine truth–he'd be dead by egregore before his next breath. If he could keep it from going there and keep suspicion away from himself–he'd be fine.

Upon further reflection, he did the only thing he could think of to protect himself. He gathered all the information he got from the forensic accountant, and all the proofs of theft he could, and compiled it into one document. At some point, he would claim that he'd found all of this and was planning to make charges against Michel; once he attended the briefing with Fuller and Meier, it made him question if someone else had something to do with the thefts. That was his story, and he was sticking to it.

Feeling marginally better about his chances of not being caught, before heading home for the night, he emailed his son Liam. He didn't explain anything; he couldn't. David told him he was responding to a tasker from VarenCorp International; they were looking to tighten up security, and needed the info later that morning, so this should be his priority once he arrived at work. The question that needed to be answered was: Were there any inconsistencies going back for a year? If so, he should put what he finds into an email and send it back to him encrypted.

David got to work the next morning, only to have Liam camped in his office twenty minutes later. "I found someone. You won't like it. It's bad."

"Who?"

"Your secretary, Christiana."

"Whoa. She's Virehn." His brain was now in overdrive, connecting dots he couldn't explain to Liam. Christiana put in two weeks' notice, and left about a month ago, headed for somewhere in Central Europe. If she was involved or implicated, then she would've had access to all the emails and correspondence that went back and forth between him and every other VarenCorp office.

Director Fuller went from having a bad day to now officially having a bad week.

He met with the Red Team to get an update the next day, and what he learned wasn't good; not good at all. Violette asked her people to do a search and found nothing. David, though, had his son run a search, and got a hit: David's former secretary, Christiana Emmorton. It wasn't anything in her personnel file; that had been exemplary. Both men had worked with her, seen her at social events through their companies, for years. She'd decided that she wanted to relocate from outside of Paris to London, and VarenCorp helped her settle in; part of that was helping her find a job, which was at Equinox Holdings. What was odd, and what made Liam bring it to his sire was that Christiana had access she shouldn't have. Not only could she see the emails (encrypted or not) that went between VarenCorp London, and every office they communicated with because of the position of trust she held, but 'someone' gave her access to VarenCorp Europe's servers. Christiana left her position a month ago...and Liam had discovered that not only were her accesses still intact, but someone had recently accessed those servers via her login information. Liam wrote it up, and sent it encrypted to David, who sent it on to Director Fuller as requested. Liam asked David if he wanted Christiana's accesses to end.

"No. Leave them in place for now." David Lambert looked at Director Fuller later that day during their teleconference, and asked him, "Did I tell Liam correctly, sir?"

For a few moments, despite being Virehn, Archie Fuller almost felt like barfing. Christiana wasn't bloodsworn or oathsworn. She was Virehn. Whoever she was, she was doing a very careful tap dance to keep herself out of the reach of the egregore. Christiana was a traitor, providing information only...to someone. What she had seen or accessed on VarenCorp Europe's servers, or why she wanted to peruse them in the first place; who she was informing, or what the endgame was, was anyone's guess. To him, it only implied that there was much, much more going on that anyone had expected. He looked at each of them that was on the teleconference. "Here's what I propose. I'm going to end this teleconference, and have another one that includes all the Security Directors; then, I think we're to where we need to bring Tim in." Fuller paused.

"For safety's sake, I'd like David and Violette here in Manhattan; Leonie, too, if you don't mind. I'll talk with Tomasz momentarily and get him here as well. I'll see you all tomorrow, here, at 3pm."

The teleconference ended.

David, Violette, Leonie, and Tomasz Bernacki, who was head of VarenCorp Europe, one of those known as 'continental heads' all found themselves headed to JFK Airport, in the US. David Lambert ended up sitting in first class beside Leonie Meier after they made a brief stop at Heathrow while he and others boarded. While he had her undivided attention, he showed her what he had. All of it implicated Clan Robichaux via metadata. He told Leonie, if it was truly Michel that was doing this, then he would like to file a complaint. If it turned out that this was 'Carlos's' doing, then the others needed to know about it.

Leonie looked over the packet. "I agree; we need to bring this up at the meeting." It surprised Leonie Meier at what Lambert had in the packet he showed her. From discussions with Director Fuller, she was positive that Robichaux had nothing to do with any of this, and the treachery simply went deeper than anyone knew. This, however, looked damning.

They arrived separately from one another, except for David and Leonie–and found housing via VarenCorp. Because of their level within VarenCorp, there were executive suites waiting for Leonie and Tomasz at VarenCorp headquarters. Violette and David were both told they would be at the Shadowhope New York Hotel, which was a VarenCorp property that served both humans and Virehnai. Once settled, they received word that there would be a meeting the next morning at 10:30 am that they must attend.

That meeting was to be a mostly in-person meeting at the NYC office of VarenCorp. Everyone who'd been part of the Red Team was there, such as Carolyn Brownell, Michel Robichaux, Detective Patrick Hall (the only human in attendance), and Director Fuller. Now added to the room in Manhattan was Security Director Leonie Meier, Tomasz Bernacki, Eliška Novak, David Lambert, Violette Fontaine, and Timothy Warner, the DC CEO whose sire was Ari Cottrell. Finally, at Tim's insistence, the CEO of VarenCorp International, Ari Cotrell, would attend via secure teleconference in Zurich, Switzerland.

The meeting started out okay but took no time whatsoever turning into a free-for-all.

Director Fuller started off first; he welcomed Ari and thanked him for attending; he thanked everyone who traveled to be there and thanked everyone who'd been working as part of the Red Team. Detective Hall wasn't in the room, and neither were the IT/security guys that had been involved in either the investigations or standing up the Red Team. They were observing. Director Fuller understood at this point that Hall or his own security twinks could end up dead for bringing all this forward. The office they were having the teleconference in also had cameras monitoring inside the room. Ever want to be the proverbial 'fly on the wall' during a meeting? That's what Patrick Hall and Fuller's IT and security folks were doing. They were watching everyone and taking notes.

"You say we have a breach? If we're having THIS meeting, I'm assuming it's a serious one?" Ari said.

Director Fuller replied, "Yes, sir. Multiple bad actors, who have physically infiltrated Virehnai properties, along with gaining access to emails and maybe servers; all of them have multiple aliases."

"How did that happen? Who's at fault?"

Leonie spoke up. "I think it's not one thing, or a particular person or group; it's a combination of factors, sir. Complacency: a feeling that we're safe; occasionally employees are not adhering to standard protocols. Whoever is responsible found chinks in our armor."

"Are any of our people directly at fault? Are we harboring traitors?"

"If you mean of the Virehnai sort, we may have one. David informed us yesterday that his former secretary, Christiana, left his employment a month ago, with two weeks' notice. What makes it damning is that in the wake of what we found, we discovered she had accesses she shouldn't have, saw information she had no call to see, and may have accessed the European servers mere days ago – although her last day was over a month ago." Ari's expression darkened, but he let Fuller continue. "As far as the human factor? Well, the people with aliases are mostly oathsworn to Clan Sabin through Scotti in the US, and Clan Koch and Zimmerman Corp in Europe. That those humans could be employed in both places without tripping our security leads me to believe someone also hacked us."

Before anything else was said, Leonie turned to Director Fuller. "Sorry for interrupting, but I have other information shared with me on the flight I should bring forward." Fuller nodded, and Leonie turned to Ari.

"Go ahead," Ari told her.

"David told me that his businesses have been undergoing attacks for several months, to the tune of millions of dollars, and property titles stolen from his holding company. When he brought in a forensic accountant, he learned that all the metadata tracked back to Clan Robichaux."

Michel sat up straighter in his seat, blindsided by what was said.

"Michel, what do you have to say about that?" Ari asked him.

"I did no such thing. What reason would I have to do that?"

David looked at him. "I was leading the council that was trying your case; we judged against you."

Michel looked at David. "Just because I lost doesn't mean I'm going to target your businesses and steal from you."

Leonie chimed in, "David, show him your reports." Leonie looked at Michel. "Read them. You have to admit what's there on paper is pretty damning."

David practically threw them at Michel, and Michel slapped the document to a stop in front of him. He glanced through it as the others watched. "I see what you mean; but I swear to you, neither me nor any of mine had a thing to do with any of this."

"I wish I could believe that" he said sarcastically. "I haven't known how to trust much of what you say for a long time."

Michel looked at him, confused. "I know you don't like that I changed affiliations, and moved, but no matter what lies unsaid between us, I wouldn't do this to you," Michel said, gesturing with the paper, and sliding it back down to him.

"So, you're saying that despite what that paper implies, you had nothing to do with it?" David asked, with lots of attitude.

"I swear and affirm to it. I had nothing to do with that, whatsoever. No one in my employ, human or Virehn, was directed to either." Michel replied, testily.

"That's why I believe we've got a bigger problem than we know of," Director Fuller said. "Call it a gut feeling."

Tim Warner, Ari's biological great nephew, and child, spoke up. "How do we figure out where the threat is coming from? Whether it's within our ranks or coming from outside of them? We need to crack down on people taking shortcuts and fix the issues with complacency." He paused. "I'd like to know why all of this seems like it's taking place on Robichaux property." Tim looked at Michel.

"I don't know why," Michel said. "I'd like to know myself. I've lost two people within six weeks."

Ari, watching the exchange, between Tim and Michel got a look on his face. His eyes narrowed, and he smiled–but it wasn't in a nice way. "That's what comes of mollycoddling your human employees, treating them like family, and letting them get too close to us."

There were many that vehemently disagreed with Michel's view of family, and Tim and his father Ari were chief among them. Both were Draz'kul, and as far as they were concerned, all the problems the Virehnai had–regardless of faction - tracked back to getting too close to humans.

Tim knew the Sulahnai saw matters differently, but saw Sulahnai like Michel taking things too far, and felt it ultimately put them all at risk. 'As always.' Tim thought to himself. 'Sulahnai caused how many wars by getting too friendly with their food?'

Michel bristled at the notion. "Treating the humans we're allied with more kindly allows them to respond better than if you merely treat them like servants. They're our helpers, not our slaves. We don't mollycoddle anyone."

Tim huffed at him. "Come on, Michel. We've all heard that your youngest child was calling you 'Uncle Michel' while still human. If you ask me, that's begging for trouble, if not for being too close, by having others in your orbit accuse you of favoritism."

"I didn't ask you," Michel said, in a frosty tone.

Before Michel and Tim could begin arguing in earnest, which would accomplish nothing save ruffle some feathers, and prompt Ari to anger, Director Fuller stepped in. "Wherever anyone believes the fault to lie, it truthfully doesn't matter right now. Rather than trying to assign blame, we need to focus on fixing the breaches we have; that and trying to determine what direction it's coming from is imperative. We can always circle back and do an after-action report and see where it leads us. Right now, we have more pressing issues. Agreed?"

Tim, Michel, and David all nodded.

Fuller looked at Ari. "I sent you a copy of our Red Team's findings in email, but the summary is this: we have trusted, oathsworn among us with multiple aliases, and we've found some of them; we don't know if we have them all. We don't know what they're trying to accomplish, their end game, or their motives. This worries me most: we wouldn't even know we have a problem right now if it weren't for the dead Virehn that's lying in our morgue here…and he was recently turned; we don't know by whom. Every human we've found so far with multiple IDs has excellent work records. ALL of them. We wouldn't have had any reason to look at them. They would have stayed completely under the radar…except for the Compact-related death."

"As I recall," Ari said, "that was someone from Michel's clan."

Tim made a noise disguised badly as a cough.

Michel ignored it and replied. "Yes sir. My son's mate, Amalie Bisset. Amalie wasn't the man's intended victim, though. The security footage shows clearly that it was Elaina, my youngest, that was the subject of that attack, as well as a prior attack while she was still human. Amalie was merely defending her. Elaina ascended only six days before that."

Ari was shaking his head. "So none of you have any idea at all where…any of this is coming from? "

"No, sir." Director Fuller answered. "What I know, I got from the report Joao sent me earlier today; he's still working on researching the man's lineage, which could take some time. The only things he could determine based on his findings was that the man, Raul, took part in the first attack on Elaina Jacoby after her succession ceremony; he was made Virehn as his reward for that, and Amalie Bisset only died because she attacked Raul after she stopped his second attack on Elaina. The egregore killed her after deciding her continued attack was uncalled for and unprovoked."

"What a fucking mess you've handed me." Ari said.

There was a chiming noise coming somewhere from within Ari's office. "Excuse me." He turned away for a moment, and when he turned back, he said "I'm sorry. I have to cut this short." He shook his head and made a gruff noise out of frustration. "It appears I have another fire to put out; can the Security Directors, and Tomasz, and Eliška please remain? Everyone else is excused. We'll meet again tomorrow."

10

BETRAYED AGAIN

While there was a relatively high-level meeting going on via teleconference at VarenCorp headquarters, Rob Jacoby sat outside of a deli several blocks from the midtown offices of Jacoby, Lightner and VanEtters, grousing about his current situation. He talked to his father the other day, for all the good it did. The laughter that seemed to follow him out the door as he left his office was still rattling around in his brain. He hadn't wanted to go to Amalie's service, knowing that they would name someone–but he knew his father would chastise him if he didn't go. Worse still, once there, it was much like when Elaina was named. Michael Ratner would ascend. They had both his naming and succession ceremonies at the same time–so there wasn't any lobbying to be done past that. It was a done deal. Rob worked with him before; he couldn't figure out what Ratner had that he didn't. So much of his life was like that. He had what he felt were no good options, and took plenty of grief from his father, and from Doug, too. The only thing is, now he knew for sure how they felt about him. He knew Doug saw him as weak, and his father told him point blank he needed to learn to 'play nicer with others.' What the fuck did he think he'd been doing his whole life? Playing nice got him nowhere.

Today, he was waiting for a man. His work calendar showed he had a meeting, but he didn't specify with whom. The man he was meeting with was one of the oathsworn guys that came in and out from Scotti Management. It wasn't the same guy who'd approached him, wanting first John, and then Elaina's schedules. Rob had been worried when John died that he was responsible, but they said for certain that it was an accident; With Elaina, he almost felt bad that she ended up getting attacked. Almost. In her case, he was certain that the information he provided on her schedule, and her suite number was the critical information the man needed to attack her. The man, a fellow named Raul, promised that his sister wouldn't get hurt. Someone wanted to 'teach someone a lesson.' He was on board for that. As promised, they roughed her up. Elaina was scared and geeked out, but no one physically hurt her.

The man he was meeting today contacted him yesterday evening at home, saying "Hi... You don't know me, but I was a friend of Raul's."

"How can I help you?"

"My name's Malcolm; I know you helped Raul access a schedule. Can you help me with that?"

"Yeah. Whose schedule do you need?"

"I'd rather not discuss it on the phone. Can we meet at the Crosstown Deli at noon and discuss it in person?"

"Sure. See you there."

Rob wasn't sure what Malcolm was up to, and truthfully, wasn't sure he even cared... Whoever cared about him?

Knowing that he would meet with Malcolm the next day teased him with possibilities. Rob kept thinking about it, and it kept him awake for quite a while before sleep finally came. His last thought before sleep claimed him that night was, "Do I dare to say it out loud?"

The next morning, when Rob woke up, he realized he'd decided and had come up with a plan of his own. He was done fooling around and hoped to change things for himself. Rob's decision? Elaina and Doug needed to be removed from his picture permanently. Even if he wasn't ever going to be chosen and ascend, at least Rob wouldn't have either of them meddling in his life, and particularly in Doug's case, lording it over him as his boss for the rest of it. He kept thinking of the meme one of his friends had sent him: 'If you aren't the lead dog, the view never changes.' He knew that was fact, first-hand.

Rob knew his plan would come at a cost, but he was willing to pay for it. Providing a schedule and even other information would be a small pricey to have his sister and brother 'un-alived.' He still couldn't say 'killed' to himself, even if he knew that's exactly what he wanted done.

"Rob?" A man wearing a hoodie asked.

He looked up. "Malcolm?" He nodded and sat down in the chair across from Rob.

"You can get a schedule for me, then?"

"Whose?" Rob asked.

"Michel and Howard."

"I can." He paused. "I have a favor of my own to ask, though."

"What would that be?" Malcolm gave Rob a sideways glance.

"I have a problem, and I think you can either help me solve it, or you know people who can."

"What's the problem?"

"It's not a what...it's more a 'who.' I need my brother and sister out of my picture. Permanently."

"That's gonna cost you more than calendar access, I'm sure." He looked at Rob closely. He was a little surprised, actually. "Who are we talking about?"

"My brother Doug, and my sister Elaina."

Malcolm's eyebrows went up, and he whistled. He knew very well who the man he was talking to was, and who those people were, and he even suspected when he said, 'my brother and sister.' Malcolm needed to hear him say it. "A calendar definitely won't do it. She's Virehn." He tapped his fingers for a minute on the table, and said, "I'm thinking," as he stared off into traffic passing by.

He looked back at Rob. "Here's what I can do. It's not my call. I'm going to ask my boss if he wants anything to do with this. If he does, I'll tell you the cost, and you can decide if it's reasonable. If he doesn't, or his terms seem too steep, for a price, I may at least hook you up with someone who can help you. You good with that?"

"I am," Rob said. "When do you need the calendar?"

"As soon as you can get it, but there's a catch: We're looking to have access to Michel and Howard's calendars, but our timing's critical, and any changes to either of them could…cause issues. Can you give me your credentials and password?"

Rob looked surprised and stammered for a minute. Malcolm continued. "Giving us those credentials might go a long way in helping to achieve your…other request. No promises, though. Anything you can give us is better than nothing, but we're hoping for the crown jewels. It needs to look like you're checking their calendars, not someone hacking in from outside that could be denied access, or worse, put someone on to us." Malcolm paused for a moment. "Are you willing to do that?"

Rob thought for a minute. Giving away his login and password came with risk, but he believed the adage 'fortune favors the bold,' and gambled. He took a crumpled receipt out of his pocket, flipped it over to the blank side, and grabbed inside his jacket for a pen. He wrote his login information on the back and slid it over to Malcolm. "Fast enough?"

"That'll work. I'll check with my boss, and I'll let him know you had no hesitation in cooperating with us. No promises, remember? Meet me at the coffee shop up the street at 8 am tomorrow? I'll be able to let you know then whether we can help you."

"Thanks. I'll see you there." Malcolm reached out his hand, and he and Rob shook on it.

When Rob went back to work, he did it with a little spring in his step.

Less than an hour later, Malcolm Harwell was meeting another person; this time in Times Square, within the TSQ Food Court. There were plenty of people coming and going. It was where they usually met up, if they had to. He'd worked with him before, when they attacked Elaina Jacoby. Shame Rob Jacoby wanted his sister whacked. Elaina was a nice piece of ass.

The care they took in setting up the meeting was warranted, particularly now. Raul was toe-up on a slab at VarenCorp, and because of it, VarenCorp was poking around. In the attack on the Jacoby woman, Raul had been the one laying in Elaina's bed; he was the man that trained a gun on her. The man that got to grab her from behind and fight her while naked was Alex Carpenter, the man he was meeting. He was always the lucky one! So far, he was still damnably lucky – and hadn't been discovered. Alex had at least six different identities – maybe more. He knew a few of them - and they were as solid gold as they got. He probably had more accesses still, but most were for 'contingencies.' He was an IT guy, and all the companies that used his services did so because he was oathsworn and whenever they needed quick-turnaround IT installs or emergency help with computer systems or servers, he was called in.

Malcolm wasn't entirely sure what Alex's real name was; it was better that way. Alex was the name he used whenever he was in New

York. In DC, he worked in Tim Wagner's office, as Joe Shackleford. He was currently 'seriously' dating a woman named Diana Favreau that was on loan from Jacoby, Lightner and VanEtters to Wagner's VarenCorp office. Lucky bastard, he got to play Dušan Popov and fuck a pretty girl for info as his job there.

As he sat there nursing his cup of coffee and was occasionally checking his watch (in a train station, that's what everyone's doing), Alex came up and sat down. "Sorry, my train was late. Had a stiff on the tracks coming up into Newark."

"Figures. Damned inconvenient of them." Malcolm pushed the cup in Alex's direction. "Plus, your latte's getting cold, now."

"I'll live." He grinned and took a sip. "Nah, it's the perfect temperature." He got down to business. "Do you have anything for me before I head off to the airport?"

"As a matter of fact, I do." He took the receipt with all of Rob Jacoby's login information and handed it to him.

"Sweet."

"When is your flight?"

"Red eye, from Kennedy via British Airways, with a short layover at Heathrow before heading to Basel."

"I thought we were only supposed to fly in via Zurich and then drive." Malcolm said, eyes raised, questioning.

"It's just this once. The boss told me to, so I'm not arguing... He's even sending the lovely Christiana to pick me up. Yummy."

"God damn, you lucky sonofabitch." Malcolm shook his head in envy as Alex grinned ear to ear before adding insult to injury as he told his friend, "I'm gonna let her feed from me, too....among other things."

"Rub it in."

Malcolm went home then, taking the subway. Once there, he ordered carryout, grabbed a beer, and took out his phone. He used the app 'Threema' to stay in contact with his boss, and others. Aside from being encrypted and secure, they could chat anonymously, which was safer all around. He had several secure contacts on his phone. To be entirely secure, they only added contacts face to face. He added his boss initially while he was visiting Basel, Switzerland, two years earlier.

He brought up his boss' contact and sent him a message via Threema:

"Delivered the information you require to Corsair, who will test access shortly, before passing it on to you, as requested. Odd wrinkle: Troy wants to know if we can help him whack his brother DJ and sister EJ. What do you want to do? Let me know; mtg scheduled for tomorrow 8am EST. Is there anything you need he could provide in exchange?"

The message was sent. Shortly after that, his meatball sub and fries were delivered, and while he was eating, he heard an alert telling him he had a reply.

"Thanks Stormtrooper. Should we change Troy's handle to Death Star? I propose you tell him yes. Gather a team. EJ needs to make sure she doesn't get hungry, but don't let her get hot. DJ should learn to watch where he walks. Sidewalks aren't always the safest places in large cities. In exchange, tell Troy I need a digital master key set for the executive level for the office building in lower Manhattan so I can play Father Christmas and deliver some gifts to old friends."

Once he was out of the meeting, Michel all but ran to the relative safety of his own office. Once there, he called Howard.

"I'm back. Got time for me to update you?"

"The meeting went that bad?"

"More or less."

"On my way."

The meeting left Michel completely frustrated. He knew that many people – but particularly Tim and Ari - didn't agree with how he conducted his businesses or his clan, particularly regarding the humans. His one worry at the moment was that Ari would have the idea for him to either step down or would arbitrarily replace him- even temporarily. They had tolerated one another well enough when they were all Draz'kul. Once Michel changed allegiances to Sulahnai, they had no problem letting him know they didn't like it, and didn't like how he handled....well...anything, as it related to the surrounding humans.

It was contentious enough that before World War I, there was a meeting about Howard Jacoby; Ari and Tim both complained long and loud about him having a human as a best friend. He always did love Howard; called him "HJ" since he already had one good friend named Howard. In fact, HJ had been named after his long-time clan brother. Despite the age difference, the experiential difference, and that one of them was Virehn and the other human – they were sympatico. They thought alike. HJ had a great mind for business. Many people 'in the know' attributed HJ's success to having a Virehnai patron. Truth be told, HJ was an incredibly smart man; ballsy, and willing to take calculated risks that often paid off handsomely. Most never gave HJ the proper credit because Michel bankrolled him. Did the money help? Sure it did. Having a wealthy friend who will take a chance on friendship and brainpower combined never hurts. Truth is...together, he, HJ and Howard made a great team. That's why the firm used to be Robichaux, Jacoby and VanEtters.

Michel offered on numerous occasions to turn him. To his credit, every single time–HJ said no. "I wasn't meant for that, Michel. I understand what you're offering me." When Michel thought about it, he realized that HJ probably didn't want to watch his wife Concetta age and die, so he modified the offer.

"I can turn Concetta, too..." They were married when he was sixteen to her fifteen. They were pushing fifty, then.

"Thank you, Michel, my friend. My answer is still no. We've planned our whole lives to grow old together. We've got a home, more money than I thought I would see in one lifetime, and beautiful children."

"You can live for a long time and watch over your family; not merely your children, but your lineage. Virehn dream of doing that."

HJ sighed. "No, Michel. You and I – we have much in common – but your long life and the need for blood won't be one of them."

Every few years, Michel asked HJ if he would change his mind. Every time, HJ said no. Concetta passed away at 64. HJ's grief was so palpable that Michel was afraid he would die simply of a broken heart. He did everything he could to keep his human friend anchored in this world. Michel had met no one he wished would become Virehn more. "HJ, are you sure I can't change your mind?"

"No, Michel. I've lived a good life, known the love of a good woman, and I have good, respectful children, who will someday inherit from me. I'm looking forward to joining Concetta...somewhere. Heaven? That's what the church says I have to look forward to, but they don't know."

"Our Vel'sheth priests believe in reincarnation - that when Virehnai die, we come back again as humans, our souls free to return. You could still be reunited with Concetta, even if you become Virehn."

HJ looked at Michel over his glasses, and shook his head, slowly, no.

"I don't want you to die. You have options. I can give that to you."

"That's the way of life, though, Michel. I know you're different – outside of the normal way of things, and that you'll be here long after I'm dust, and forgotten." He looked Michel directly in the eyes; many humans wouldn't. "When I'm gone, remember me. That Vel'sheth Reman puts a great deal of focus on the 'blood remembering.' Your blood will remember me, and that will be enough. Your blood will remember me for a thousand years…maybe longer. That's almost like immortality. I don't know many men that can claim that." He patted Michel's arm. "Someday, when I'm long gone from this world – if one of my children or grandchildren would make an especially good Virehn? Offer them the long life you offered me. It's not my destiny, but it might be theirs."

Within the year, Howard was gone, too. It always irked him that if he thought too long or too hard about HJ, that eventually, thoughts of Ari and Tim followed. That they felt it necessary to have a meeting about his friendship with HJ annoyed him to no end.

Before he could indulge his sad state of mind further, his clan brother Howard showed up and saved him from it. He sat down in the leather chair across the desk from Michel.

"So how bad was it?"

Michel shook his head and let out a long sigh. "Where to start…? When I was accused of stealing properties and money from David…? Or maybe when Ari and Tim accused me of mollycoddling and being too close to all the humans we work with…? Or maybe when Tim was questioning why so much of this is happening on our properties, with the implication that I must've provoked it?"

Howard's eyebrows went up. "They were reaching back into the past for some of that, weren't they?"

Michel nodded his head 'yes,' slowly. "Tim even mentioned the fact that Elaina calls me 'Uncle Michel. At least he didn't directly bring up HJ. When he mentioned Elaina, I was thinking he might. Especially since she's HJ's granddaughter."

"He would." Howard shook his head. "HJ was a better and smarter man than either of those...skvernitsi!" Michel chuckled at the Bulgarian epithet. "I'm not sure the pair of them have ever known love in their entire life. Tim particularly, based on how he treats the surrounding people, particularly women. Tim might have a good mind for business, but he's still one of the cruelest people I've ever run across. People don't so much respect him as they do fear him, regardless of WHAT century he's in. Sadder still? That arse doesn't know the difference. Consider the source, Michel."

"I'm trying to, but what if they want to replace me?"

"Tim can suggest it, but it'll never happen. Know why? Nobody will stand for that. You're older than most. If VarenCorp can replace you, they can replace anyone. No one would want to be next. Tim might be blind to the shitstorm that would cause across the board – but Ari certainly isn't."

Before Howard could say anything else, there was a gentle knock at Michel's partly closed door.

"Hi Em. What's up? Need something?"

"Do you care if I come in and snitch a bag of blood?"

Michel rolled his eyes, made a face at her, and then gestured toward the mini fridge. "After all this time, Em, do you REALLY think I mind?"

"No...but I didn't want to interrupt you."

Howard rolled his eyes and laughed. "It's just me, Em. Come on, we're all family here. Interrupt away. It's a welcome detour from the topic at hand, anyway. I'd rather see you than talk about Tim Warner any day."

Emily made a grimacing face at the mention of Tim, and passed by them both to Michel's mini fridge, quickly grabbed out a bag of blood, and closed the fridge back up.

"Thanks Michel; Howard. I'll leave you two to your...discussion. I hope you find something more pleasant to discuss than...Tim." Her expression changed and softened looking at the two men. Emily wagged the bag of blood around. "Thanks."

"You're welcome, Em." Michel laughed again and looked at Howard after Emily closed the door. "Thanks for the reminder, Howard. Tim hates how we do things, and so does Ari. He disliked Dio; I can only imagine what he thinks of me! But what you said is the truth: We're all family here. If they don't like it, they can just fuck right off. You do what you need to for family...human or Virehn alike. If only I could've figured a way to talk HJ into letting me turn him."

Howard looked thoughtful. "I know."

Michel smiled wistfully. Even at the risk of secondary thoughts of Tim and Ari – the thought of HJ would always bring a sad smile to his face. Damn HJ. The bastard was right. His blood would always remember him.

"I always said there was no human I wished would allow me to turn him more than HJ." Howard looked up, quizzically. "I told him the same. Michel looked at him. "I'm so happy that Elaina said yes."

11

TANGLED WEB OF DECEPTION

Emily texted Michel early that there would be a meeting with Ari and several principals, and unlike yesterday's meeting, this would be hours earlier, and attendance was mandatory. Em took the time to point out that in the email, 'mandatory' was in ALL CAPS. "Be forewarned. Hope your day doesn't suck."

Michel's first thought was that it was a continuation of the meeting from the day before, and he had a niggly fear in the back of his head that Tim and Ari would gun for him, particularly since Em pointed out that bit about 'MANDATORY.' It sounded as if it could go down that road the day before. He was grateful that Director Fuller seemed to think there was something bigger going on, too. Maybe that would be some kind of saving grace.

The more Michel thought about the earlier meeting, the more it convinced him of it. He had plenty of time to think about the meeting, in its minutest details, including voice inflection and words chosen. Michel spent the whole night turning everything over and over in his head like a Rubik's cube, looking for a solution that wasn't immediately apparent. He arrived at the same conclusion Director Fuller had. There was something bigger at hand, going on behind the scenes. It left Michel afraid that all they were seeing was the top portion of the iceberg…the bulk of it was beneath the water, and yet to be revealed…and like the doomed ocean liner, they were chugging full steam ahead, straight for it. They weren't seeing the whole picture. Too many things didn't add up.

Michel tasked his IT team after Howard left to go over financial records for all their joint companies and ventures that came under Clan Robichaux's umbrella, searching for the same kinds of inconsistencies that David Lambert had accused HIM of perpetrating. The relative speed that his team got back to him, affirming that there was, in fact, money being siphoned out of Shadow Dance by David, he found startling. Did he dare believe the metadata?

He had more faith in his estranged friend than David had in him...but, like David, Michel also saw clearly what the data implied. That whole 'read it and weep' thing only went so far. Michel knew as well as anyone that anything could be faked with enough time and effort. The people on the receiving end of whatever was faked usually wanted to believe what they saw, playing plainly into bias. David can read that data from yesterday forward and backward and swear to its integrity because that's what it said on the paper in black and white; Michel knew it was patently FALSE. He knew he had done no such thing, nor mandated that any of his clan do it, either. That worried Michel the most: someone wanted them all fighting. Someone must know that they were once good friends and now had ideological differences that could be exploited. But why? What would they gain from it? To what end?

Michel quickly dressed, stopped by his office, and grabbed a bag of blood and his favorite mug and read again through the papers his team had prepped for him yesterday. He wanted all the pertinent details fixed in his mind; he worried that after yesterday's meeting, Tim would use the situation to attack him, or his businesses. He had failed, long ago, in trying to do the same over HJ. Virehnai have a long time to harbor grudges and memories of either failures or perceived slights. Tim was especially prone to that.

Finishing up his breakfast, he went to the sink, rinsed the cup, and then stowed the paperwork in his messenger bag. When he unlocked the office at 5 am, it was well before his early meeting downtown, and it was early enough that Em hadn't arrived yet.

When he was leaving his office to head for the meeting, she was diligently sorting packages at her desk.

"Good morning, Em."

"Good morning, Michel. Headed off to your meeting now?"

"I am. Wish me luck."

"Well, good luck; particularly with Tim and Ari." Em snorted. "And kick Tim for me, if you get the chance."

They both laughed. "Any spot in particular?" he asked her.

Her eyes narrowed, and she smiled like a Cheshire cat. "I'll leave it to your imagination." She winked at him.

"Have a good day, Em. See you when I get back." Michel told her as he walked out of the office.

"You, too."

Mentally, all morning, Michel had been prepping for one meeting; he was positive he knew how it was going to go, the accusations that might be leveled, and assumed he would fight the same old fights with some of these people that he always had. Once he sat down–this time, in a different, much larger conference room lined with large video monitors on the walls and saw the titles of the Virehnai attending from…well, shit! From everywhere…Michel quickly realized something:

This wasn't the meeting he'd prepped for.

The meeting that was held in the main conference room of VarenCorpUSA's office was one for the history books; at least, it will be if it ever gets declassified by VarenCorp International. It appeared they would have a very high-level meeting. All those video walls were showing the who's who of VarenCorp, and there were many sitting in the room here in New York as well. The largest monitor had Ari's title displayed, but he wasn't on screen yet.

David was here already, sitting at the opposite end of the table, and on the other side of him. Carolyn and her brother Darren Wheeler were there seated together, as was Tim Warner, Directors Archie Fuller, and Leonie Meier, and people from their teams, along with several executives from VarenCorp USA. Of the Virehnai attending via teleconference, some were already seated, while others weren't there yet. The titles displayed told a story: the CEO's of VarenCorp Ottawa, Vancouver, Chicago, LA, Paris, Brussels, Rome, Budapest, Moscow, Istanbul, Tabriz, Cairo, Delhi, Rio de Janeiro, Buenos Aires, Sydney and Kyoto were all represented. That's like…everyone.

Suddenly, Michel wondered what was going on, and why was he here, at THIS meeting? He knew personally several of the people that were or would appear soon within those monitors; that happens when you're almost 2500 years old. Michel made a conscious decision a long time ago that his businesses would be personal; he would keep to his Clan and his own and leave the politics and intrigues to others; he'd seen first-hand what that combination could do to people. He wanted none of it. His own sire, Diotimus eventually chased that power, and died as a result; so did Vibia.

The main reason Tim and Ari gave him so much shit about changing allegiances was because of his age, more than anything else. Maybe it frightened them what it might mean to them, personally, if others of a similar age that they counted on changed sides. Maybe they thought he had…sway…over others? He didn't know for sure, and probably never would. The only thing he knew for sure was that there were many who disliked his Sulahnai beliefs– and Michel decided it wasn't worth it for him to fight those fights repeatedly. Some days he wondered if Tim simply liked the satisfaction garnered by lording over someone and making them his bitch. He knew Ari did. It would fit.

The others from the major VarenCorp offices joined one by one, along with Ari. As soon as Ari appeared on camera, it got silent.

Ari looked stressed; something that Michel had seen rarely in the thousand plus years he'd known him.

Ari stared into the camera, at what he knew would be all their faces, wherever they sat in the world.

"Of all the meetings I envisioned having in my long life, this one was never on my list."

Ari looked down and back up, trying to gather his thoughts. "Director Fuller–I believe I owe you an apology. You were right. There's something else going on. I don't know how deep it goes, or how far it reaches–but it's life and death. Every one of us...every Virehn each of us knows and loves may be at risk."

You could see Ari's words registering on people's faces, boredom replaced with concern. Those were strong words to come out of Ari's mouth. He was nothing, if not measured and calculating. Those words were like him throwing caution with wild abandon to the four winds.

"My afternoon and night after yesterday's meeting has been...non-stop. I know of no other way to put it. Yesterday, a lot of shit hit a lot of proverbial fans; be prepared to duck. No matter what you do, it's headed your way."

"My first call was from a bloodsworn security team that traveled to upstate New York. They were called there to a mass murder scene by a local oathsworn officer. The scope of the murders and the media attention it started immediately receiving is what prompted them to call the emergency line directly, per protocols before calling Carolyn. Because of the team's swift action, we...might not be discovered...but it made it quite clear to those of us involved yesterday that we have a major problem." Ari had their undivided attention. Other than Caroline, Tim and the Security Directors–this was the first time any had heard what was happening.

"While I was dealing with that…mess…I got another call, this time from Carolyn; bloodsworn police officers were dealing with a similar murder scene in Fishkill, NY that's also making the news - as if we didn't have enough going on."

He sighed, and all Michel could think of to describe Ari was tired and harried. He looked directly into the camera and said simply, "Friends, we are under attack."

He let his words sink in, then continued. "I know most of us don't watch the human news or involve ourselves in their day-to-day drama unless there's a reason. We now have that reason. This is what we're dealing with:"

One of the video screens flickered, and a newscaster from a station in Albany appeared onscreen.

"We start off tonight's program with breaking news," she said, as the video showed a helicopter view of a sea of flashing police lights, several ambulances, and cars backed up where traffic was stopped and they needed to find another way around. She continued reading as her voice narrated the video. "Police were called earlier in the day to a grisly murder scene in Helderberg, where a family of four was found murdered in their home. There is currently a manhunt underway for the perpetrator. Hackett Blvd. is currently closed to traffic, and police are asking residents to report suspicious persons. At least one eyewitness reported seeing a man covered in blood running alongside the road in the area.

Reportedly, the family friend who discovered the gruesome scene described the victims as 'looking mauled,' as if by an animal. Police have confirmed bloody foot and handprints found throughout the home."

The news anchor's narration continued while pictures of the dead family flashed up on the screen; family photos showing happy times and smiling faces, and then closeups of each of the victims as they mentioned them, along with the activities they were accustomed to.

"The victims were Frank Kimball, aged 51, his wife, Patricia, aged 42, and their two daughters, Beverly, aged 17, and Maria, aged 14. They were all well known to others in the community; Mr. Kimball was a beloved music teacher at Berne-Knox-Westerlo Elementary School; his wife was involved with the PTA at Berne-Knox-Westerlo Secondary School, where both of their daughters attended, and their daughter Beverly was a senior, and a member of the competition cheerleading team."

The video began showing the memorial against the wooden fence, and zooming in on items left in memorial, as she spoke about the tributes.

"The news of the brutal murders has hit this local community hard. There is already a makeshift memorial set up alongside their fence, with teddy bears, cheer poms, flowers and photos. We'll have more on this breaking story as more information is available."

The screen went dark, and Ari continued.

"That's what led the news last night on all the stations in Albany, along with Manhattan AND the national news. To update you, the suspect is in custody. Ari paused for dramatic effect. "Downstairs. In this building."

Exclamations, surprise, and even a few curse words in a variety of languages were heard, all translating roughly to 'shit!'

"A Virehn did that?" The CEO of VarenCorp Ottawa asked, incredulously.

Ari nodded tiredly, "Yes," shaking his head slowly. "Here are the pictures of the scene that DIDN'T make the evening news, courtesy of the lead officer from the security team that called me. He texted these to me from the murder scene last night."

It was a veritable horror show, even for a Virehn.

Blood on the walls sprayed in what looked like random directions. Bloody footprints. Bloody handprints. A white kitchen, drenched in blood. Frank Kimball, lying on his stomach on the white kitchen floor with some of his extremities…detached, and facing the wrong directions. Their daughter Maria was on the other side of the kitchen by the countertop, with her face half eaten away, and blood and chunks of flesh surrounding her. One of her ears was stuck to the oven door. There was blood tracking between the rooms, as if a chase had taken place. What remained of the mother, Patricia, and their daughter Beverly were in the master bedroom. There were pieces of their bodies scattered all across the room, making it hard to determine which parts belonged to which woman; the room drenched in blood. The handmade quilt and the happy family photos on the walls had blood splatter all over them.

The conference room was full of Virehnai who were or had all been hunters of humans. Most of them, besides being Apex predators, familiar with a need for taking blood, were older than most Virehnai; their positions of power attested to that. The people attending this meeting were some of the oldest and most powerful people in their insular world. Even these Virehnai, whether sitting at the table or in the comfort of their home office, were aghast at the carnage splayed on the screen.

"I haven't seen a scene like that since the Fourth War." someone muttered. Another replied, "I've never. Holy shit." The CEO from Budapest exclaimed "Te jó ég!"

Tim spoke up, looking at his sire, as he asked a question within a question that he didn't dare voice aloud. "I don't see how that can even be." He looked directly up at his sire on the monitor with a questioning look. "Are you certain?"

Ari nodded. "The officer that sent the pictures sent me the security footage, too. That's been confiscated by us for the time being. The press is being told the family's security system malfunctioned. Here it is." Ari looked away for a minute and punched a button on his side. The security footage came up next, and it literally showed scenes from different camera angles and rooms of a frightening, ghoulish looking man, ripping frightened people to pieces as he drank their blood and ate their flesh. It repeated from victim to victim, room to room as they tried to get away from the man–but never would. Their lives ended brutally, in the worst manner they could've. Terrified, fighting for their lives, bleeding out and being...literally...eaten alive, until they weren't anymore, and blessedly, were beyond pain and fear. Some watching gasped. The level of violence was stunning, even in a room full of predators.

There was stunned silence after the video ended. All of them sat as they contemplated what they'd viewed.

"Who DID that? And why?" The CEO of Los Angeles asked.

"We don't know the why...yet. But we know who." Ari brought up a picture. It was a man with blotchy red skin that looked like badly distressed leather. There were sores or boil-like swollen patches that oozed blood, faintly reminiscent of the bubonic plague, which some of them had lived through. His eyes were wild and unrecognizing. His hair was mostly gray, and though it was hard to tell, he looked like he was in his 70s or 80s. He was drooling, which was in stark contrast to the dried blood on parts of the rest of his face.

"That...That's a Virehn?" David asked, his face registering the confusion.

Carolyn looked over at David, sighed and sadly nodded yes. "He's raging out of his mind and has broken out of his restraints three times already. We tried giving him Veltharinex." You could tell that Carolyn was having a rough time as well. "It made him worse. He's unrestrained, but locked in a cell, with orders that no one goes in or out." Carolyn paused. "One of my staff died getting him INTO that room." She looked up at the ceiling, shaking her head.

"What a mess," someone said, and the room again grew silent.

Ari replied, "Agreed. Especially once you see the next photo." He tapped a few buttons on his side as he said, "We identified him an hour ago." A picture flashed up on the screen, followed by gasps around the room–and the world, from wherever the CEOs all sat.

The man pictured from his VarenCorp file had dark hair, brown eyes, a friendly smile; a piece of hair that always seemed to be unruly and was about 30 years of age. He was one of Darren Wheeler's sons, Jacob Ralston, who was made Virehn during the Spanish American War. He and his own family had moved two years ago to the Albany area to spread away from Manhattan and form his own small Clan…and several knew him.

"Normally Jacob kept to himself; he was well-thought of. He hunted with care, drawing no undue attention to either himself or his activities. He didn't make waves." The people in the conference room and attending teleconference alike were stunned.

The CEO of LA spoke up. "If you showed me that mug shot without telling me who it was, I would never have connected the man in the picture to the Virehn I knew or remembered."

"Nor would I," Tim said, and then looked around the room and into the camera. "Nor would any of us."

"It gets worse. He didn't merely kill and feed from all of those humans. He killed and ate most of his own clan in a similar manner." Ari told them.

Everyone looked in stunned shock at Darren, who was quiet; sad, staring down at his hands as he fiddled with them. "I'm still coming to terms with the ghoul who killed those humans in such a ghastly way is my son, Jacob. Or that I lost seven people associated with my clan in much the same manner."

"How is Jacob still…alive? The Compact should've taken him for how he murdered the humans because it could've outed us–but…his own…" David asked.

Before David could finish his thought, Ari's voice boomed through the speakers, as he shouted at them. "Every. Last. One of you. In this room. Is sworn. TO SILENCE about THAT particular piece of information. NO exceptions!" He paused briefly, and the rest of what he said wasn't shouted–but it was still forceful. "This is your ONLY warning. Everyone on this call, whether in person or by teleconference, plus the security teams–are the only ones who know the Compact failed. If that gets out, I'll truth test every damn one of you, and the responsible party will spend the rest of their miserable immortal life locked in a cell while they hibernate…for eternity. That's NOT an idle threat. I'm serious as a tomb." Ari let it sink in, as everyone sat in stunned silence…from both the revelation about the Compact, and Ari's manner and threat.

"If you're wondering why the Compact failed…the short answer is, 'we don't know.' That this man did what he did, and the Compact had NO effect on him at all, is the most frightening thing I've heard so far." He paused, struggling for words, which, for Ari, was unusual. "Several of us discussed this earlier; we came to a short list of possibilities: It could be magic borne, though we've had no use for witches since the Fourth War; they aren't unheard of, but are rare now, since no one actively turns them. Aside from that, most witches today don't have the power they used to. Maybe Jacob fed from someone who was sick, but didn't realize it, and it had an unusual effect on him. It could be possible that someone used magic on a person who he then fed from–but again, the lack of Virehnai blood witches kind of prevents that. Maybe he possibly reacted to something in his environment. Once we learned of the similar situation in Fishkill, though–it makes me think it goes back somehow to magic; Jacob and the woman in Fishkill didn't know one another and wouldn't have fed from the same people."

"Who could be responsible for this?" Violette asked. "Why would they DO such a thing?"

Security Director Leonie Meier looked at Violette. "We don't know. Oathsworn humans carried the security breach out, except for one individual. We all know it's possible to use humans as proxies where treachery is concerned. It's difficult, but not unheard of. Archie and I talked about that right before the meeting;" Leonie said, gesturing toward Director Fuller, seated beside her. "We're both worried that this isn't finished. We were afraid there is an endgame. We're thinking the groups that want us outed to humanity at large might be responsible, more than anything, because of the media coverage it's garnering....but we don't know that for sure, and won't until we can test their blood. It could also be a group who wants to see the Compact ended...which is disturbing, considering that Mr. Ralston killed another Virehn and lived to tell the tale." Leonie sighed. "The problem with all of this is that we're only able to react to what happens and aren't at a point where we can predict what they might do."

Ari nodded, and added, "There are many who question why the Compact is still in force, or question those of us old enough to be party to it for signing up generations into the future, compelling them to be party to it. Those are questions to be entertained in a civil discourse, not...this way. We suspect the breach we've been dealing with, somehow, connects to all this–unfortunately, we haven't figured out how yet." Ari sighed and ran his hand through his hair.

"If you didn't all catch the upshot earlier...we have ANOTHER scene that repeats all of this in Fishkill. It was a little late for the national news, but tomorrow will be another bad day for press reports. The Virehn woman in question killed a young mother while her husband was at work, along with her infant, and a three-year-old. The five-year-old survived by being smart enough to hide in the closet. Here's a photo of the woman from the scene, alongside her file photo." Ari punched a button, and as the image filled their screens, there was an audible gasp. Most of them knew the woman, if not personally, by reputation. Her name was Florence "Florrie" Travers. She liked to socialize and frequently made the newspapers' society columns in Manhattan. Some referred to her as the "Queen of spray tan," which she would apply copious amounts of makeup on top of, in her attempts to blend in with human society, hiding her paleness.

Even as they were all letting what they saw sink in, Ari voiced something others may not have dared to. "With Florrie's penchant for getting her face in the humans' society pages…thank heaven for two small favors: that she was at her Fishkill home, and not her Manhattan address, and that the press doesn't have her name–and her file photos - to equate with the murders…."

Carolyn looked at all of them; she'd known about Florrie coming into the meeting. "I saw Florrie last week at a function. I'll be honest with all of you. This is freaking me out." Darren patted his sister's shoulder.

"So…now that I've updated you on all of that, I should probably let you know something else that probably relates to all of this; we just don't know how it does yet. Several of us sitting here attended a meeting held yesterday, both in NY and via teleconference. You need to know that we stood up a Red Team several days ago. This may all go deeper than any of us know. "

Ari let the information sink in a minute. "We're investigating a series of international breaches involving multiple people that were discovered here in Manhattan–involving data, information, and personnel. A Compact-related death on one of Michel Robichaux's properties prompted the discovery of the first breach. That discovery led to us realizing that one of our trusted individuals wasn't who they said they were; in researching that, we discovered multiple individuals with multiple identities…that uncovered other breaches. The worst of them–so far - involved a former executive assistant of David's with accesses she shouldn't have had. Despite leaving his employment a month earlier, he learned she was still accessing European databases as of several days ago. We have no clue what information she may have given to who, why she would betray her own, or what kind of damage and vulnerabilities it might've caused. There were also many properties and large sums of money that were being siphoned out of David's privately owned companies; the metadata involved showed that Clan Robichaux could be involved."

Before Ari could go further, Michel interrupted. "Sir?"

"I'm not going to argue with you Michel." Ari told him, coldly.

"Sir, I wasn't going to argue; I wanted to add information we discovered yesterday afternoon. It's…relevant."

Ari looked at him, still angry that he was interrupted. "Go ahead," he answered, voice terse and clipped.

Michel pulled out the sheaf of papers his team had given him, and slid it across the table up to David, nodding at him, and then turned back to the monitor showing Ari. "To quickly summarize, Ari, I asked my IT team to research the same type of potential thefts that occurred at David's companies at my own companies. There are similar thefts from one of my companies of approximately four million dollars, and the metadata gathered implicates David and Equinox Holdings."

David was quickly flipping through the papers Michel gave him while he was explaining it to Ari. David looked up into the monitor, at Ari. "What he says is correct." David slid the papers down to Tim, who began looking at them.

There was a soft tapping on the door. One of the staff from VarenCorp USA poked their head in after waiting for a moment. "Excuse me, I've got an urgent message for Ms. Brownell." The young woman quickly walked across, and handed it to her, and then left, even as Carolyn was reading the message. She looked up at Ari, and then around the table.

"We've got another one, sir; this one's in Ithaca."

"Of course there is." Ari shook his head and sighed. "We should wrap this up."

Ari addressed Michel and David directly. "I think what you provided us today, Michel, would confirm that you and David were part of a distraction tactic." Director Fuller chimed in, "I agree," as did Director Meier.

Tim spoke up, looking first at David, who sat beside him, and then to Michel, across from him, pointedly. "You are both victims; someone has manipulated data to make it look as if you are being attacked by the other. After seeing this, I don't believe either of you started the recent aggressions between yourselves. Others did, hoping your natures would follow their course." Both men looked thoughtful. Tim had a point.

Ari added to what Tim had said. "That worries me; THAT prompts me to believe it was treachery; it implies whoever was responsible knows you both well enough to know your personal issues and your history. I recommend you make your peace between yourselves and make restitution to one another. Allow it to rest, knowing that someone ELSE wanted you to fight and was responsible. Once we know who the guilty party is, they will pay."

Ari then addressed everyone.

"Take all of this under advisement. They could manipulate any of us as such, if we allow it. Whoever is responsible found a weak spot and took advantage of it. Be vigilant; be wary of who you allow into your spaces, and how. Tighten up your ranks around you. Aside from some of us being victims of manipulation, any of us could be targets." He stopped speaking.

The CEO of Prague spoke up. "Anyone heard any recent rumors about Black Sun? Where are Magnus and Ferdinand?"

Heads shook around the room, along with several half-stifled groans as they all looked at one another to see if there was any news. Magnus Iovanni and Ferdinand DiLallo were problematic during the First and Second World Wars and were part of the reason there was nearly a Fifth Virehnai War. They sought to reinstate an old Virehnai cult that's chief aim was to both dominate and rule over humanity, instead of either hiding in plain sight or coexisting with them, and they too played Virehnai against each other in an attempt to manipulate them, without doing anything that would explicitly cause the egregore to take notice. It was like a centuries' long game of whack-a-mole. Every time the Black Sun showed up, they were swatted back down, and eventually, they popped up somewhere else to cause trouble.

"Not that I know of," Tim said. "Let's fervently hope not. We've got enough problems right now without adding THEM into the mix."

Ari continued. "After living as long as I have, I don't believe in coincidences, and I'm sure neither do you. Any of you. The thought that we would discover those thefts and the breaches so close on each other's heels…and then have both Jacob Ralston and Florrie Travers killing humans and Virehnai alike, with no Compact-related consequences?" He shook his head vehemently. "It's NOT a coincidence."

"Thank you, everyone." Ari continued, wrote something down in front of him, and looked back up at the camera on his side. "Everyone except for Tim, Carolyn, Tomasz, Eliška, David and the Security Directors are excused for now. We'll reconvene later to update you on the situation." He addressed Michel and Darren directly. "If we require either of you, we know where to find you." Michel and Darren both got up to leave. As Darren stood, he heard Ari call his name and looked up. "Darren? Virehn zuth akret. I'm sorry for your clan's losses, truly."

Darren, looked up, and said, "Thank you, sir," even as there were many repetitions of 'Virehn zuth akret,' both via teleconference and in the room. "Setha'ra Virehn ka'anel. Thank you, everyone."

With that, Michel held the conference room door open for Darren and then turned to shut it. The two men walked toward the elevator together. While they waited, Michel turned to Darren. "Virehn Zuth Akret."

Darren nodded, and replied, "Setha'ra Virehn ka'anel."

Rob Jacoby got to the coffee shop to meet with Malcolm early; he was cautiously excited, hoping that Malcolm and his boss would help him with his plan.

Malcolm nodded at Rob as he went in to get a cup of coffee for himself and then sat down across from Rob once he had it.

"Good morning," Rob said to Malcolm, as he sat down.

"Morning." He took a sip and knew the man across from him was anxious. He'd thought as he sat down that Rob looked like he had to take a piss. He decided not to play with him and make him wait. "So; I talked to my boss last night, and he will help, but only in exchange for one thing, which you may or may not be able to get."

"What does he want?" Rob's foot was tapping in anticipation and a little out of fear that it would be something he couldn't get.

"He wants a digital master key set for the executive level suites, like the ones the housekeepers use when they clean in the evenings after everyone leaves. They get assigned nightly. That key set needs to be delivered to a woman named Patrice Dixon, who will quickly clean several executive suites and then return them to you. Wear gloves when handling them, unless you want them to find your prints and ID you later. Then, I recommend you drop the set someplace where they'll be found…like a ladies' room, a lunchroom or an elevator." He paused for a moment, while he was looking at Rob. "Can you do that?"

Rob thought about it and then nodded. "I think I can."

Malcolm said a little sarcastically, "Do you 'think you can' tomorrow evening?"

"Yes, I'll make it happen." Rob nodded. "When would I get help with my problem?"

"We'll start with your sister after you finish your part of the bargain. Does she have any events coming up?"

"Only one. Michael Ratner's ascension party," he said, with a tinge of anger.

"Are you going?"

"Yeah. If I don't, I'll be in trouble with my father."

"Well, now you have a reason to go. Do you know where it will be held?"

"They haven't announced it yet. They usually have it someplace in lower Manhattan. Elaina's party was on South Street, close to Battery Park."

"When you know, let me know." Malcolm paused. "Do you know if she hangs out anywhere?"

"I overheard her at her party discussing with her new boss someplace she and Amalie went called Sanguinarium Obscura. I think it's a club. That's all I know about it."

"Never heard of it; I'll do some digging and see what I come up with. It's something. With your login credentials, I'll look for opportunities on her calendar. We'll find something that'll work."

The next morning, Rob manufactured a reason to be in the downtown office later that evening, and was working at one of the 'floater' desks — courtesy desks set up for days when an employee's work took them out of their regular office. A few people said hi to him, but most ignored him. The later it got, the more people shuffled out–particularly between five and six pm, which was normal. He didn't want to make himself too visible, so he left on the later side, closer to 6. Usually, housekeeping didn't start making rounds until 6:30. He walked up the steps from his floor up to the suite to minimize the chances that someone would see him.

Rob wasn't sure which of the two floors that comprised the executive suites that the woman would start with. He wasn't entirely sure he could get the keys. They were on a ring, but they weren't actual keys; they were digital keys. That's why he needed to steal them from the lady who normally did them. What if she was wearing them, as some did? He tried not to think about that. Rob hesitantly left the relative safety of the stairwell.

It didn't take him too long to find her, as she left one suite to go down to the next. The doors were recessed about a foot back from the hallway itself, so at the moment, she couldn't see him. The woman had a cart with cleaning supplies and a vacuum cleaner; her purse was there, along with a drink. He watched her reach for her keys to open the door. Luckily, she wasn't wearing them! Before she could unlock the door, her phone ringing broke the silence and nearly scared the shit out of him. She pulled her phone from a pocket and cursed, tossing the keys back on top of her purse. If Rob wasn't so tense, it'd be funny. The woman's phone ringing had startled him, but now she was on the phone, occupied.

It sounded like she was arguing with one of her kids about something they wanted to do. He wasn't far from her; her back was to him, and she walked toward a window, even as she started cussing at the daughter as he could hear the daughter yelling back. It was now or never. He moved quietly to the cart, swiped her keys, and while she was still arguing with her teenage daughter about meeting up with her friends, he turned tail and headed down the stairwell.

For his next trick, he was to meet up with Patrice Dixon. Rob had to find her as well. She should be–if Malcolm told him correctly, somewhere around the eighteenth or nineteenth floor. It turns out she was on nineteen. He walked up to her and her cart. "Yes?" She looked up at him suspiciously as he approached her.

"Patrice?" She nodded yes, hesitantly.

"I'm Rob. I'm supposed to give you these." He handed her the keyset he'd stolen minutes before.

The woman looked relieved. "Thank you." As she pocketed the keys, she asked him, "Where will you be? I'm supposed to give these back to you once I'm done cleaning."

"I'll be waiting in the stairwell here on nineteen around the corner there."

"Okay; I'll see you in a little while."

Rob headed back for the stairwell, even as she headed in the opposite direction with her cart toward the elevator.

Patrice Dixon worked in housekeeping through Scotti Management for eleven years. She kept a low profile, was friendly to everyone, and always did her job in an exemplary manner. Unfortunately, she had a gambling problem and owed a lot of money to some not-so-nice men. Malcolm and his boss have been blackmailing her–and for this one favor–they will pay all her debts, and Patrice will have a clean slate.

Patrice had ONE job to do — the one she's doing tonight. It's the first and only time she'd ever been disloyal to the Sabin clan, or any other. Her job tonight? Using the key Rob gave her, she was to go to the top level, to the executive suites, clean the offices up there, and while she was cleaning Michel and Howard's suites, discreetly put a bag of blood into each of their mini fridges. Patrice didn't want to do it, but the man blackmailing her told her if she did this ONE thing, this ONE time, they would forget they ever knew her and would never contact her again. Patrice was careful not to do anything that would draw undue suspicion to herself as she cleaned this evening–particularly since she had the creepy sensation that she was being watched for the last couple of days. This evening as she met Rob, and he gave her the key set, she made sure she was running a little late.

Patrice was of a similar height and build to the woman who normally would clean the penthouse; they both wore the same gray uniform–and that woman was usually late, so she needed to be as well. Patrice assumed she'd be on camera, which is why she purposely kept her head down and stayed focused on doing her job. She went first into Michel's office, and did a thorough job of cleaning, and then into Howard's office, repeating the process. In her cart, she had two bags of blood. While she was cleaning around the mini fridge in each office, she quickly added a bag of blood to each. She didn't know for sure what she'd just done–but she knew it couldn't be good. Patrice was trying to focus on the fact that her own problems would disappear.

She finished cleaning as quickly as she could and went back down to nineteen. Before she went back to cleaning her regular floors, she went looking for Rob in stairwell. He was where he said he'd be, sitting on the steps. Patrice handed him back the keys. "Have a good night," he told her.

Rob quietly went back upstairs and opened the door a crack, watching from the relative safety of the stairwell. The cleaner he'd lifted the keys from was having a bad night, as far as Rob could tell. She was chatting to herself like a magpie the whole time. First, she had an argument with her daughter; then she lost her key set and couldn't find them. The woman was completely distraught. "Oh God, what am I going to do?" You could tell by the level of panic that she didn't want to report her keys missing. She whined to herself through tears. "I'm know I tossed them on top of my purse. I swear to God I'm gonna ground Sherry for calling me to argue."

As Rob watched her, she dumped the contents of her entire purse on the floor. "Dammit. I gotta find them," she whined, as she put everything back in, bit by bit. The woman, still crying, made a noise somewhere between whining and groaning out of sheer frustration. "They've got to BE here…" The woman began searching the cart. "They HAVE to be here...." Rob only saw her do it once, but by the frustration and level of talking to herself, he assumed she'd done it at least once before. "Ohmygod, I'm SO going to get fired..." In tears, she headed toward the ladies' room.

Rob quickly came out from the stairwell and deposited the keys into the top of an open box of purple nitrile gloves and then left. Passing a trash can, he took off the hot, itchy black nitrile gloves and tossed them in.

Mission accomplished. Now it was Malcolm's turn to deliver.

12

REALITY CHECK

Director Fuller emailed everyone a couple of hours later. Michel figured Fuller was busy enough with all the shit going on that he'd accidentally left him on the email distribution; he read it anyway. Inquiring minds want to know.

"Watch the national news," it said, "as homework and prep for tomorrow's meeting. This way, everyone's on the same page when we get here. For those of you outside the states, or who miss it, we'll be downloading them, and links to the broadcasts will be sent out later."

Michel figured he might as well watch it, anyway. Ari was right about one thing: Virehn rarely bothered with human news. Normally, the only time they did is if humans are threatening to annihilate everyone, including the Virehnai along with themselves. He sat down at his desk and turned on his computer. Michel didn't actually own a television. He watched the streaming national broadcast in stunned silence.

It wasn't pretty. It was also clear to him that VarenCorp in particular, and the Virehnai in general now had their hands full.

All the major networks were covering the attacks as a serial killer now. There were too many similarities in the deaths and the three crime scenes to ignore.

The report he was watching started in the studio, with a news anchor doing a voiceover, as the video showed an aerial view of a pretty house in the woods, and the title under it said "Ithaca, NY."

As the camera pulled out to show a wider shot of the area, you could see Lake Cayuga nearby. The video cut to a driveway with some police cars in it as others were just arriving, and there were officers walking around the area, along with officers putting up police tape everywhere, and a detective from a distance talking to a young woman near the front door. The news anchor told the story:

"When young Therese Baker got off of work today and drove out to meet her friends at this rental bungalow by Lake Cayuga, she was thinking she'd be having a fun weekend with friends. Instead, when she got to the front door, she found it ajar, and when she opened it, she made a gruesome discovery. Instead of finding her boyfriend Taylor Carson, her best friend Desiree Connolly and Desiree's boyfriend John Moore waiting for her to go to dinner, she discovered all three of her friends dismembered, and a bloody, disheveled man sitting on the floor in the middle of it."

It cut back to the news anchor at the desk. "The photos and video we've obtained are quite disturbing. If you have young children with you, you may want to send them out of the room or hit pause now. Viewer discretion is advised."

The video cut to the living room of the bungalow; there was blood sprayed everywhere. Officers arriving on the scene tried to cover body parts with sheet-like drapes, but there was so much blood there was no way to hide it. It was on the walls, the fireplace; all over the furniture. The young woman who made the gruesome discovery of her friends told her own tale to a reporter on the scene before the police arrived. The title running over the video of the bungalow said, "Voice of Therese Baker, eyewitness."

"I saw the door, like, not closed all the way, hanging open, and I called out, you know? Since I didn't get an answer, I opened the door, and...all I could do was scream. There was this man, sitting in the middle of the floor. I swear to god, he was a zombie. He was covered in blood, and there was blood everywhere. It smelled weird. It…" she sniffled, and though you couldn't see her, you could hear her crying. "Oh god! He…took them apart. There…were…bitemarks." Therese sniffled.

"It looked like he actually ATE them. There was blood all over his face. I was so scared, because when I came in and started screaming, it's like, he…he…woke up, or something?" She sniffled, and half-gasped, trying to get it out. "I don't know. He had scary eyes, and started screaming, and he had this crazy look on his face…and he started yelling at me, not that I could understand it. The zombie jumped up off the floor and started running towards me, so I ran back outside and ran towards my car. I was afraid he was going to kill me, too. I don't know if he stopped chasing me, or if he ran away when he didn't catch me. I felt like I was in a bad horror movie… The only thing he didn't do was chase me into the basement…"

The news story cut to video of the girl, who had a blanket draped around her shoulders, with the reporter standing next to her, holding a microphone with the station's ID bug on it. She shook her head as she talked to the man interviewing her. "I was so bummed that I had to work today, and that my boss wouldn't give me off." Therese started crying again. "He might've saved my life. If I'd been off like I wanted to be, I'd be in there dead, too."

A detective approached the reporter and Therese while the reporter had her on camera. "That's all for now." The detective put his hand up in front of the camera. The video cut back to the studio even as the detective led Therese away.

The news anchor continued, "I don't know about a zombie, but the man responsible for the deaths of 21-year-old Taylor Carson, 20-year-old John Moore, and 19-year-old Desiree Connolly is still at large. Police are urging residents around Ithaca, particularly around the Lake Cayoga area to keep their doors locked and report any suspicious activity you might see. If you should see the man described, call 9-1-1 immediately."

185

The news anchor looked down and then back up to the camera. "We were told right before we went on the air that the NY State Police and FBI are forming a Joint Task Force, with the cooperation of local police, to investigate these three crime scenes, and to catch the person or persons responsible. Turning to politics...." Michel closed the browser where he'd been streaming the news and began researching the different scenes to see what was being said and reported, aside from what was on the traditional news networks. Social media had already devolved into memes featuring screenshots of horror movies making witty or inappropriate comments about zombies, vicious murders of horny college students near lakes, and 'don't go in the basement.'

Michel's phone buzzed as someone texted him. He picked it up and looked. It was David. "Is it okay if I drop by?"

He texted him back, "yes," and then called down to the doorman. "David Lambert will stop by to visit. Can someone at the desk escort him up, please?"

"Yes, sir."

Half an hour later, he heard voices outside his door and opened it before they buzzed. One of the bloodsworn security officers stood there alongside David Lambert.

"Hello, David. Come on in." Michel turned to the security officer. "Thanks, Todd. Have a good night."

"You too, sir." Michel closed the door and turned to face his once-upon-a-time good friend. "Have a seat, David." gesturing to the sofa.

"Thank you for seeing me, Michel. I wasn't sure if you would let me in or not."

Michel looked at him. "We both got played; against each other, unfortunately. That was a hell of a meeting, wasn't it?"

"We were, and yeah…it was."

"What happened after Darren and I left? Anything you can share?"

David nodded. "Yeah…but you might or might not be too happy with me when you find out. I swear, I had the best of intentions in mind."

Michael's brows knitted together in consternation, but David continued. "To apologize for jumping to conclusions, and to make amends, I convinced Ari that you should be on the task force he's standing up."

"So the email I got from Fuller earlier this evening wasn't misdirected, and he wasn't so busy he forgot to take me off distro?"

David smiled wryly. "Nope, he didn't forget."

"Thanks for the recommendation. Generally speaking, the further away I am from VarenCorp's executive offices, the better off I am, but in a case like this? I think I'd rather be a part of the solution, if I can." Michel pointed toward his computer desk. "I just watched the news. We're up to three now. How many more are we going to find? I'm afraid it's like an iceberg, and we're only seeing the tip. That, and what the hell's causing it?"

"Michel, they don't have a clue. They're chasing their tails. Ari hasn't said it directly, but you can tell he's worried that it's old-fashioned treachery. That the Compact isn't working with those folks is giving him a sincere case of heartburn."

"Of course it is! I thought the same thing when he swore us all to secrecy. He's afraid if THAT little tidbit gets out, he'd be at the top of someone's 'long overdue retribution' list. Think about it. He and Tim both were some of the worst purveyors of treachery before the Compact. Without the Compact being cast, they'd both have been done to death by now." He thought for a minute. "Shit, probably you and me, too."

David nodded in agreement. "Unfortunately, you're right. To live a long life is to make enemies." David paused. "It's preying on his mind, though." He thought for a moment. "The main thing you don't know yet is that they picked up the latest guy from Ithaca tonight. He's in holding two doors down from the others. He was lucid for a while; nobody knows how long that lucidity will last, though. One of Fuller's guys had a smart idea: they looked to see who the closest Virehn was to the murder scene and sent someone there on the off chance it was him. They were right; it was."

"Do you know who it was yet?"

His name is Walker…. Walker Matson. Supposedly, he could answer a few questions before they took him in. Which is a good thing; they said he was in pretty bad shape; they don't know how long he'll live."

"Did they mention what clan he's from, or if he's associated with a clan?" Michel asked.

"He's with Clan Westcott, but Fuller didn't know him or recognize his VarenCorp photo."

Michel shook his head. "Well, there's a tell that a clan needs to calve off and start other groups elsewhere…"

"No joke. Did you know him, by chance?" David asked Michel.

"Nope."

It was quiet for a few minutes, both men lost in thought.

David broached the silence. ""I heard you lost Johannes. I'm sorry about that. Virehn zuth akret."

Michel looked over at him. "Setha'ra Virehn ka'anel. Thanks."

"Look," David said. "I'm sorry. I feel bad that we ganged up on you, and more or less accused you of fucking with my companies. I should've known better than to think you'd do that. I don't get the choices you've made, but I…"

Michel held up a hand. "You don't have to finish that. I get it. I know we've had our issues; I looked at the data you had in that report. If I were a third party looking at it, I would've thought I was guilty, too." Michel shook his head. "I can't help but think someone's gunning for me."

"It's possible. Oh! One thing I didn't get to tell you at the meeting earlier, but wanted to make sure I remembered to tell you; when we were digging through the mess that Christiana left behind, I found something I wanted to pass on to you, that you might want to check out."

"What's that?"

"Your newest child… Elaina, is it?" Michel nodded. This touched on one of the issues he'd been worried about: that someone was trying to do bad things to his niece.

"While we were doing all the looking through the servers and trying to determine the extent of her betrayal – we found something that implied the first attack on Elaina that you mentioned in the meeting wasn't random at all. According to what we saw, the whole thrust of the attack was to put an RFID tracking chip in her. Warn her and tell her to get it removed at some point."

Michel shook his head. "Thank you for letting me know. I'll tell her. I was worried someone might target her to get to me. That's the only logical reason, to me, that someone would. She's new. Elaina hasn't been around long enough to become a problem to someone, like either of us have."

"You might be on to something; it sounded likely to me, also. That's why I was trying to remember to tell you. There's just too much questionable shit going on right now."

Things fell silent between them once more. David looked over at him. "Are we good, in how things stand between us, then? I don't really want to test the issues with the Compact out...." He gave Michel a sideways look, and made a face, and both laughed; it relieved some of the underlying tension between them. "I guess we should do as Ari asked. What do you have in mind for reparations? Have you thought about it yet?"

"I hadn't yet, no. Right off the top of my head, for something practical, I could voluntell my IT guys to help your IT guys do whatever they need to in order to get your property titles back, if you like. Or if you're looking for something more fun, Clan Robichaux can foot the bill for a night at the British Museum for your clan..."

"I should go for the practical one, but the night at the British Museum sounds like fun. The only thing I could think of so far was to rent out a venue in the area and bring in musicians; some Virehnai, some oathsworn - to give Clan Robichaux a few hours of its own private music festival."

Michel nodded, "That sounds like fun, too." Michel chuckled. "You know, there's nothing to say we couldn't do both. Do something fun, and have our teams collaborate to get back everything we both lost to whoever tried to set us up."

"That's a good idea. Think about it. If you'd rather do something else for the fun one, let me know." David got up from where he sat. "See you at the meeting tomorrow."

Michel stood as well. As he walked his old friend to the door, he asked, "How long are you going to be here, anyway? Will you be sticking around a while?"

David chuckled wryly. "Ari asked me to stay for now. Since I'm here, he said I 'might as well make myself useful' to Carolyn and Tim, unless things go tits up back in London."

"I'll see you tomorrow. I sincerely hope things don't go tits up in London. There's enough going on this side of the pond for all of us."

Dir Fuller, after the last meeting with Ari and city heads, had a brainstorming meeting that was "Security only." They hadn't been asked to by Ari but were anticipating 'worst-case scenarios.'

He got several suggestions; some better or more workable given current constraints than others. The best by far had to do with their 911 system. VarenCorp 911 normally doesn't monitor regular emergency channels, but amid the hubbub of everything going wrong, one of their folks thought they should leverage it to help more.

He suggested that their IT department set up a program that has an AI system monitoring all local police channels, looking for terms that could imply 'Virehnai-related.' Terms like 'exsanguination,' 'extreme blood loss,' and 'animal attack,' amid a host of others. Fuller (and the Directors) were impressed. They gave the Virehn who suggested it carte blanche to run with the suggestion, so long as he formed a team that included members from all the other Security teams worldwide. That way, the software could be implemented VarenCorp-wide. They told him as soon as it was complete, operational and functioning, to send a group text to the Security Directors. Leonie Meier stressed to all of them that time was of the essence, and the sooner any suggestions came online…the better and safer for everyone, Virehn and human alike.

Another of the suggestions they found 'do-able' was to travel to the places where there had been murders: Ithaca, Albany, and Fishkill, and have meetings with the police officers that were among the first to respond to each scene. They already saw crime scenes that–according to television reporting–didn't add up. Why not leverage what they already had seen, and bring them on board as oathsworn? There were only so many oath and blood sworn humans to go around, and this was testing the limits of human endurance for those who were already knee-deep in dealing with it. There would need to be more people if they were to handle the crisis and not be outed.

Another suggestion related to getting more officers working with them was to turn any oathsworn officer that was seriously injured while dealing with the crisis. He told the woman that made the suggestion that it was a good idea, and he'd discuss it with Ari, Tim, and the rest of the upper echelons of management. Archie Fuller thought that the meeting went well. The last thing all three Security Directors told them was to 'keep thinking.' Any other ideas would be seriously considered, and any ideas that were implemented would be acknowledged and rewarded, wherever or whoever they came from.

That's how, despite feeling as if he were being pulled in twenty different directions, Director Fuller and his assistant, Noah Shorngetter ended up on a company helicopter, traveling to Fishkill, Albany and Ithaca, to have a meeting with the police officers and detectives that responded to the first scenes in each of their respective briefing rooms. He asked all the groups the same questions: "Having seen what you have seen, who wants to be on a 'special' task force to deal with this problem?"

Most volunteered, to their credit.

"Everyone who opted out, you're dismissed. Thank you for your help on the earlier scene."

Next question: "Who can keep a secret, and will swear an oath to protect that secret?"

They only lost a couple of people, who were dismissed, with thanks. Fuller looked at the rest, in each of those briefing rooms, and went for the final question.

"This is the big ask," He told them. "Of those of you willing to swear an oath to protect a secret, would you still swear it if you knew revealing that secret would mean your life is forfeit?"

One more left. "Are you all certain that you're willing to swear this oath, after what I've shared?" Everyone left in the rooms stayed, now looking at Fuller and Shorngetter curiously, but waiting. "Before you take the oath, I should let you know you can step away from working with us at any time; however, the oath you take, and the information you learn? The commitment to keep those secrets safe is a lifetime commitment. Everyone still good?" When no one said anything, Fuller continued.

"If I can get everyone to repeat after me:

"I swear and affirm that the trust placed in me shall remain unbroken. From this day until my final breath, I bind my word and my life: knowledge gained shall remain sealed, secrets kept inviolate. Should I betray this charge, let my life and blood be forfeit."

Everyone repeated the oath.

"The oath you just took covers what you're about to hear. It goes NO further than your ears, and this room. No discussion of it with anyone. No wives, no girlfriends, no media. Got it?? This is cop to cop; thin blue line territory."

"My name is Archibald J. Fuller. I was with the Manhattan Police for most of my career until I transferred over to work as the Director of Security for VarenCorp." He paused.

"I am not what I seem."

He walked over to one man sitting at a desk in the front. "Touch my arm. Cold, right?"

"Fuck, yeah," the man replied, pulling his hand back quickly, and looking curiously up at Fuller.

"How old do I look?" He asked the folks sitting in front of him.

"Around 50; maybe a little younger…or a little older," the man beside the one who'd touched Fuller's arm answered.

"What about my friend Noah here? How old would you say he is?"

"Not old enough to drink without a fake ID," "Barely old enough to drive," and "Compared to me, a baby," were all answers they heard, and they made them both chuckle.

"That's how old we look – but you'd still be wrong. I had a…we'll call it a major life change…around the time I went to work for VarenCorp." He pointed at Noah. "He had a major life change at a Yankees game." There were some snickers and snide remarks about what a major life change at a ballgame might be for someone Noah's age. Once they got the laughs out of their system, they were looking at them both, trying to read between the lines and not getting it.

"For the record - I was born in 1904." The officers sitting there looked thoroughly confused. "I got shot in the line of duty during a jewelry heist gone wrong on June 11th, 1953. I died the next night, on June 12th, 1953. As far as the world and the memorial wall at the 32nd precinct know, I'm still dead. It's true; I died. I really DID die; the next day, I woke up…as something else." Director Fuller smiled a very toothy, obvious grin for them, baring his fangs. Several of them jumped a bit. Others were simply curious.

Fuller's assistant Noah likewise bared his fangs. "Noah was up here visiting from Lancaster Co, PA during Rumspringa to see a Yankee game at Yankee Stadium…in September 1958. Someone used him as an 8th inning snack and turned him after they nearly drained him because they felt bad. For the record, Noah was born in January 1940, was 18 when he was made Virehnai, and today he's 85 years…young." Noah smiled bigger, and their jaws dropped.

"We are what most of you would call 'vampires.' We prefer the name Virehnai. We're very much like you, despite there being some very obvious critical differences." Fuller smiled again, on purpose, fangs in full view. "The main difference is that our manner of life is not quite the same as yours. We don't eat the way you do; We have very long lives. We're not immortal, but we normally are pretty damned close."

"Now, we had our moment of show and tell here," he gestured between him and Noah, "because you all NEED to know this, simply to understand the problem we, as Virehnai, and now you–as officers of the law, are currently experiencing."

"Recently, one of our Virehn got sick, which is for us, abnormal, and unusual. The murder scene splashed all over the news from Helderberg, near Albany? The ghoul that did that was one of us; a Virehn who got sick. Let me show you what the media didn't see: the security camera footage. I'll admit to you straight up–we confiscated it. We didn't do it to 'cover' for the man or bury it. We simply couldn't risk it being out in the open and revealing us to the public; instead, we used it to figure out who he was and try to suss out what's going on. The Virehn in question, Jacob Ralston, responsible for what happened outside of Albany, died in a cell at VarenCorp headquarters this morning from the illness. THIS is what we're dealing with, folks:"

The video from the security cameras flashed up, and in each briefing room, the looks of horror on the faces of those who saw it was apparent, particularly as the teen and the mom were running for their lives and instead met their bloody end. After the video was over, Fuller continued his briefing.

"Initially, we thought it was a one-off...until later, we had another victim in Fishkill...and then another the next day in Ithaca. We don't know the nature of what's causing this yet. We don't know how they got sick, how it spreads....nothing. We've got nothing. We're trying to figure it out as quickly as we can. That's why we've come to you; why we asked you to all swear an oath. Much as we don't reveal ourselves, we're trying the best we can to keep our own people, and yours, safe. The public in your area could be in danger; you need to know the nature of that danger to understand what you're even responding to."

"Aside from that, we truly DO need your help. While we have oathsworn and bloodsworn human officers who work both with and for us at VarenCorp, right now, we're all spread pretty damned thin. If there are more incidents…if it spreads…I don't want to think about it. As officers of the law, we're trusting you to help us keep our secret during our crisis. We need to protect our population while we're trying to protect the population at large."

"Questions?" Fuller asked them at each place. Director Fuller heard lots of questions, and they repeated many of them in the three sessions.

"How many of you are there worldwide?"

Fuller replied honestly. "About 280,000 of us, to 8 billion humans. We're still in the minority, but we're here."

"How many of you live in my community?"

It was obvious the woman who asked was worried about her family. "There are quite a few that live in Manhattan and the surrounding areas; there's probably around 20,000 give or take, stretched between New York, Connecticut, and New Jersey between those who are permanent residents, and those who are traveling. We try to keep low profiles, and we try not to get too many of us in one spot, for our safety."

"What about reports? How do we write it up? Do you get a copy of the report we write, or do you get one of your own?" Everyone was worried about the paperwork.

"Use your regular report form; the only difference is you're going to do two of them. One of them-the one that has all the details, particularly any details that could be explosive or reveal us as a group–goes to VarenCorp. Submit that file first; The one that will get submitted through your official channels will report everything; it won't lie, but some details will be a little light on specifics, and some details will be fudged over a bit. When you submit the report to us, what you'll get back immediately as a receipt will be a report number to fill in on the official one for your normal files. It links the files. If you ever look through reports for something, and it looks like it's linking to something you can't get to…chances are, it's linking to a secret VarenCorp file.

"Who in our chain of command knows about any of this?"

"Here at your stations? Or in your precincts? No one. You're looking at one another. We have officers and detectives throughout the area that work with us, under the same oath you just took, including some retirees; we have officers, detectives, a couple of folks that work for the Medical Examiner that have taken a different oath, a blood oath."

"What exactly did we see in there?"

"What you saw is NOT normal. That's what makes this all 'crisis mode' for us. Normally, our activities aren't noticed by the surrounding humans. We like it that way. What you saw is what we fear is a sickness that could spread among our kind. We're talking to all of you fine folks trying to get ahead of the situation before it turns into more of a clusterfuck than it already is. As we learn more, we'll keep you in the loop."

"Not to be crass; I know you're dealing with a crisis, but what's in it for us?" Every place Fuller and Shorngetter went, they heard some variation on this. People are people. They all got bills to pay.

There were a few uncomfortable chuckles. "Aside from the satisfaction of knowing that you've protected people that live in your community, we'll have records of whenever you're at a scene, and you get double pay besides what you normally would receive. So, your regular pay for those hours, plus a check from VarenCorp equal to double that."

"What happens if we tell someone?" There were more uncomfortable chuckles.

"Don't. You don't want to find out. It isn't pleasant and ends with a body bag and a toe tag."

"What about evidence we find?"

"Bag it and tag it, same as you normally would, to protect the evidential chain, and log it, the same as you would. The only difference is that WE get it, not your regular evidence room. We have our own evidence room, our own lab, our own people, all secure. There's a code to put in that overrides your system."

"How do we handle it? How do we report it to you if we either come across or someone reports another scene like…that?"

"You call us. At VarenCorp, we have our own 911 system that functions right alongside the national 911 system. There's only one difference: call 9119 instead."

"No more questions?" He waited a moment. "Good. I'm going to ask you all to come up, and sign your full name on the sheet of paper that Noah has over there, followed by your social security number for ID purposes, and your badge number and precinct for our system ID. This does two things for you: If you need to report a scene that looks or feels like what you already experienced, this IDs you in our system, and routes it to us. Call us FIRST, directly; then your local 911. Aside from that, having that info on you guarantees you get paid that double-time we told you about."

"The procedure is this: Dial 9119, identify yourself as "oathsworn officer last name," give your badge number and location to the operator you speak to, and then relay the salient details. When the VarenCorp detectives arrive, identify yourself to them by name and badge; they'll be looking for you, but don't make them look for you, capice? They'll take charge; they're still going to need your help."

"Finally, if any of you would like to work with us regularly after our crisis is over and be a VarenCorp detective or officer while you're off duty, put an asterisk after your social. We're always looking for police willing to moonlight using their current credentials. There are multiple benefits that come along with it. Normally, it's not as demanding as it is right now, but there's always a need for good police in our system."

David Lambert left Michel. As he sat in his hotel suite, he felt marginally better, and less like an ass.

It bothered him he had been so easily manipulated, using his own prejudices and fears to prod him into retribution against Michel.

Should he have done what he did? No. Would there be consequences if someone discovered it? For certain. Truthfully, David felt like he was lucky the egregore that policed the Compact hadn't taken him out yet, based solely on the guilt he felt.

There was nothing he could do to bring back Michel's son Johannes. Dead is dead. Still, he needed to let Michel know that his newest progeny had a tracking dot in her ass. Was it disingenuous that he himself was the person responsible for both the attack and the tracking dot? Certainly. But David made himself feel marginally better, because he found a legit-sounding way to tell him it was there. At least he knew now. Elaina would be safer in the face of everything going on.

That was one thing that had been preying on his mind after finding out about Christiana's actions. Did Christiana know about Carlos helping him with the RFID dot? Did she pass that knowledge along to someone? Did Carlos tell anyone, and if he did, who? There were so many things he didn't know that he felt like he HAD to tell Michel. He never wanted the girl to be hurt; he was simply trying to get back at Michel. The only thing he was certain of was that he felt like a heel for how he acted. David assumed that because he himself was capable and willing to do something treacherous, Michel would be as well. He projected his own thoughts onto Michel, who was innocent of treachery.

David had known better. Somewhere along the line, he forgot. Now it was on him to make up for it…assuming someone didn't come along, that would blackmail him. The thought of everything he'd potentially left himself open to by acting against Clan Robichaux by hiring the oathsworn to act on his behalf was staggering. In all his years of life, it wasn't one of his smartest moments. He allowed mistrust to blind him to the reality of the situation.

While David was sitting there, morose as he contemplated his actions, and worrying that somehow, someway, they would catch up to him and burn his ass, he heard his phone chime, letting him know he got an email. He looked at it and grimaced.

It was from Fuller and Meier. There was another Virehnai crime scene, bringing the total to four. This Virehn, according to the email, at least had the presence of mind to call and let them know she ate her neighbors and needed cleaners. The woman was now locked up at VarenCorp downtown and was answering questions.

Holy shit. He wondered the same thing Michel had. How many of these would there be?

As David was surfing the computer two hours later, trying to find out more, he heard another chime from his phone. He looked to see what it was. It was from Ari.

Emergency meeting in an hour. Well, shit.

The call came into VarenCorp 911.

"Hello. I'm Connie Travers. I need…help."

"What kind of help do you require, ma'am?" The Virehn dispatcher on the other end of the phone asked.

"I… I woke up in my neighbors' home only to find that I…killed them." The woman's sharply indrawn breath as she gave voice to what she'd done showed the level of discomfort she felt. "I…ATE them. Please hurry. I don't feel well; you'll need to bring cleaners. It's a mess. I'm sorry."

The dispatcher immediately notified Directors Fuller and Meier, along with Ari Cottrell; She also dispatched a team of cleaners, including Detective Hall and a couple of oathsworn police who were listed in a call-in basis to the scene of Ms. Travers' impromptu feeding mishap. They were getting quite the workout these days. She also dispatched VarenCorp security to Connie's home to take her into custody.

Both crews were stunned at what they found in each location. The VarenCorp security team that showed up at the Travers home knew Connie, more by sight and reputation than from talking to her. They were stunned by her condition. Normally, Connie appeared to be in her late 20s to early 30s. What they found was in total contrast to the polished, impeccably dressed woman they knew. Connie was dressed in a tasteful pale pink Burberry three-piece suit–that was irredeemably splattered with blood and gore from her impromptu late-night pig-out. Despite all the expensive makeup she had applied, you could see that she had wrinkles where she never used to, and her coppery brown hair was now shot through with gray. She was contrite; apologetic, even.

"Why did you eat your neighbors?" they asked her.

She looked at them blankly, shrugged her shoulders, and replied, "I don't know. I don't remember going to their house. More than anything, I only remember waking up there and seeing my neighbor Stu and his wife Delores dead and in pieces in their bedroom. Oh my, what I did to them. I...ate his leg!" What she'd done horrified Connie. It was out of character.

"Do you remember anything before you went over to feed from them?"

"No. I've been...out of sorts...for about two days. It was strange; my hair was getting gray, and my face was all blotchy, and I've felt achy. But two days ago, I got hungry, and I haven't stopped being hungry yet."

"I have to ask, but ma'am, are you aware that your sister Florrie died recently?"

Her indrawn breath and her expression told them no, she didn't.

"What happened?" She asked them. She was so gore-covered, it was hard to see her blood-tinged tears at hearing the news.

"We're still trying to figure it out, but she experienced something very similar to what you're currently experiencing."

"Oh, no!" Connie exclaimed, "Poor Florrie." Her eyebrows raised and her eyes got wide. "Oh no. Am I going to die, too?"

"We don't know, Ms. Travers. We have to ask, though. When was the last time you saw Florrie?"

"I was staying at her house in Fishkill for the past month. I came home three days ago."

"We're sorry for your loss, Ms. Travers. Virehn zuth akret."

She replied "Setha'ra Virehn ka'anel. Thank you for your kindness."

"How are you feeling now, Ms. Travers?" The VarenCorp security officer looked at Connie, who looked…uncomfortable.

"My stomach is in knots. I'm SO hungry it's a distraction." Her arms wrapped around her midsection as if it hurt. "And it's getting worse." Connie looked up at the detective, a pained expression on her face. "Please don't let me hurt anyone else. If you need to poison me to keep me from killing anyone else, I give you permission." Connie shook her head sadly in disbelief at her situation. First, she kills and eats her neighbors, then finds out that her clan sister and best friend died. What a day.

"I'll make a note of that, Ms. Travers. Hopefully, it doesn't come to that, and everything will be fine."

"I hope so." She sat there blankly for a moment. "It'll never be fine for those poor people. There's no way to make it up to them. I can't believe I did that," Connie told them as they were restraining her hands to transport her. "What a shame. I liked my neighbors. Stu was a nice man. He always kept his yard so nice. And his wife Delores was always giving me such pretty veggies from her garden, not that I could eat them."

Shortly after her interview at her home, which was recorded, Connie Travers was headed to VarenCorp's NY headquarters.

Director Fuller interviewed her again himself once she arrived, and Ari was teleconferenced in, to observe via laptop computer.

"While you were at Florrie's, where did you eat?"

"There's a wooded area close to her house that has a path humans use for jogging, though it's not official. In the other direction, there's a small marina. We hunted in both places. It's…easy pickings."

"Do you know who you ate?

"No. I didn't know them. The ones on the path were jogging and fit. The guy from the boat had been drinking, though." Connie clutched her stomach, trying to stay focused on Fuller's questions.

"Did you share someone, or did you hunt separately?"

"We shared someone. We normally do...when we're together." Connie whined while holding her stomach. "I'm so hungry. I've answered your questions. Please give me something to eat..."

They brought her a mug of blood, which Connie gulped as if it were ice cold water on a hot day, even spilling some of it on her chin, which she wiped her hand over and licked off her fingers. It didn't help her hunger pangs. In fact, it made her more agitated. "More...please." She looked up at Detective Fuller and whined. "Aaaaaaaaaaaaahhhhhh."

Luckily for Fuller, he decided as he was watching her to step away out of the room to figure out what to do next. As he neared the door, Connie screeched at the top of her lungs and broke her bonds. He barely got the door closed and locked as she lunged for him and screamed shrilly, like a wild animal in pain. It was her eyes that would stay with him. They went from attentive and lucid to vacant, and then wild, like a caged animal; quickly. With little warning.

The entire interview was recorded; While Connie grew agitated and wilder, Fuller went back up to his office and called Ari back. He wasn't going back in there soon for his laptop.

"Sir, did you hear that? They're clan siblings. They fed together. Maybe they were unlucky who they ate, but it makes me ask, were they being targeted?"

"Do me a favor. Get one of your security folks to research her; where she's lived, her lineage. Maybe what we already know about her will give us some clues." Ari shook his head, combed his hand through his hair. "In the meantime, let the task force know to gather in an hour. We need to be prepared; pro-active. At least let people know that if they notice anything off, to call us, to notify someone like she did."

Michel along with everyone on the task force, got called in the middle of the night, and attended the emergency update.

"Thank you, everyone, for being here. We've had a busy night tonight. Archie, go ahead. Floor's yours."

Archie Fuller sat up straighter and then looked around the room. "We have Walker Matson in holding downstairs, locked up for his own safety….and ours. When we brought him in, much like Connie Travers, he was lucid for a bit. While he was, we interviewed him. It's recorded. What you're about to see next is Leonie and I interviewing Mr. Matson."

Both Security Director Fuller and Meier sat in chairs across from Mr. Matson. He was bound to the chair at the hands and feet.

"Can you please undo the restraints?" He asked them. Director Leonie Meier smiled at him and shook her head no.

"I'm sorry, Mr. Matson. I'd like to, but from what we've already seen of your condition, it's safer for us to leave you bound while we're in here."

He shrugged his shoulders. "Whatever."

"We need to ask you some questions related to what happened to you today." When Mr. Matson said nothing, Director Meier prompted him. "What happened to you today, Walker? How did you end up in your neighbor's house?"

He looked haunted, with an expression that implied his body had betrayed him. "I don't remember how I got there; I don't remember going there at ALL. I only remember waking up in the middle of the floor."

"What did you experience?" Fuller asked.

"I was covered in blood, and...gods above...chunks of flesh, on my pants. I was surrounded by what felt like a sea of bodies, but I realized that there were probably only three or four people there. It looked like more because I must've literally taken them apart. I was trying to count torsos; I'm relatively certain that I drained them. I kept having to re-count the body parts, though, because I kept losing count. I don't know how long I sat there trying to do that. It could've been a couple of minutes; it could've been an hour, for all I know or remember. I was sitting there, and while I was trying to make sense of it all, including how I got there and why, I heard a woman's voice calling out names. I didn't recognize the names." It was obvious to both Fuller and Meier that he was still having a bit of difficulty maintaining focus.

"What happened next?" Meier asked.

"Oh. I heard a voice, and I looked up toward where it sounded like the voice came from. That's when I realized the front door was open a couple of inches. While I was looking at it, I saw fingers come around the edge of the door and push it open. There was this pixie-looking blond-haired girl who poked her head in and looked at me." It was obvious he was mentally seeing it as he was describing it.

"Her eyes got wide, (his did too, as he recounted his story) and she started screaming. Oh holy hell, the shrill note she hit while she was screaming made it feel like there were ants doing a mambo up and down my spine. Her screaming scared the shit out of me, and all I wanted to do was get away. The last thing I needed was to be discovered, you know? I've always tried to not leave a mess when I hunted; not kill anyone. I wanted...needed...to put distance between myself and the mess I was sitting in."

"When I ran for the door, all I can guess is she thought she was going to be next. She ran out the door and kept running, and I peeled off and headed for my house."

"What did you do when you got home?"

"I meant to clean up and take a shower; change clothes. Instead, I sat down and I kept zoning out. I don't know how you guys found me, but I'm glad you did. I didn't mean or want to kill those people. I...don't know what came over me."

"How were you feeling in the days prior to this?"

"Weird."

"Describe weird. Weird in what way?"

"I woke up achy. Last week I found a gray hair, and this morning, I was mostly gray. My skin felt bumpy at first, and now it's all blotchy; and...there's a place on my leg that's...weepy? Kinda bloody? I don't have any bandages...I ended up using a piece of duct tape to cover it."

"Where do you normally hunt?"

"Those woods. Sometimes humans, sometimes deer. Because of Lake Cayuga, there's usually plenty of people around, at least during tourist season. During the winter, I'm more likely to either have deer, or drive further abroad to find a human meal. Depends on the weather, or sheer laziness on my part."

"Does anything stand out about any of your food recently?"

"No. Nothing out of the ordinary."

"Do you see other Virehnai socially?"

"Occasionally, if I'm traveling into the city for clan-related events."

"When was the last time you did that?"

"About two months ago."

"Shared any meals lately?"

"No. There's nobody that I know well enough nearby that I'd want to share with. I keep to myself, unless I have a reason not to."

"Thank you for your cooperation, Mr. Matson."

The video cut off; the screen went black. Tim added, "Within an hour of that interview, Walker Matson ceased being lucid...and hasn't regained his lucidity again. It's good we got to him when we did."

"How did you know where to find him?" The Ottawa CEO asked.

"That was fortuitous." Fuller continued. "The other day, Leonie and I had a Security All Call; we asked everyone for ideas. This was one of them. Someone suggested that if we know the address of the suspected...uh...'feeding mishap'...that we should look around the area to see who the closest Virehn are and do a health and welfare check on them. This was the first time we used it...and it worked like a charm. There was a house in our records that was Virehn-owned, less than a mile away from the mishap by Lake Cayuga. Bingo. We sent a pro-active crew just in case. Good thing we did; not only were they able to bring him in, but we interviewed him."

"That was a good call on your part, sir." David said.

Fuller nodded. "Thanks." He chuckled. "We're paying all those folks; might as well leverage all their brains, right?"

"What happened with Connie Travers?" Michel asked.

"She's hanging in there," Tim said, looking over at him. "I doubt she'll make it. Her periods of lucidity are shortening in length and frequency; her violent outbursts have increased."

Director Fuller looked over at Tim. "Speaking of Connie, can you bring up Connie's interviews?" Tim punched a key on his laptop, and video once again filled the monitors.

"This was taken at her home," Fuller narrated. "One of our security officers recorded it on his cell phone, since Connie was lucid and feeling chatty."

"Wow is she a mess," Violette, the CEO of the Paris office, said. "That video tells me a lot; I'm not close with her, but I've known the Travers sisters for 50-60 years; she came to some of the earliest haute couture shows in Paris. She comes here…" Violette corrected herself, and sighed, "…she came here…for Fashion Week with Florrie every year. Connie would never consent to being recorded looking like that if she were in her right mind. Look at how disheveled her hair is. And all the blood on that pants suit? Smeared on her face, and hands? Oh my. Those details are SO disturbing to me."

"The video that will come up next is what we recorded here with Connie." Fuller narrated.

Everyone heard the questions, and Connie's responses, but what got the most attention was Connie's actual physical demeanor, and her lucidity as it slipped, and hunger took hold. They watched as the woman clutched her stomach. She was so hungry she was all but crying and whining for food. When a mug containing blood was given to her, they could see her all but chug-a-lug it…and then watched it have no positive effect on her whatsoever.

Normally, if a Virehn is in a state of severe hunger, even several mouthfuls of blood would be enough to make the pain subside, if not go away. That…didn't happen. In fact, shortly after that, everyone could see her expression as she slipped OUT of lucidity, and then the camera hit the floor as Director Fuller ran out of frame, headed for the door. She broke her bonds, and her eyes became like a wild animal's. "She's had periods of lucidity since, but...few." As Fuller said that, the video wrapped up with the camera at floor level, pointed at a wall, as Connie began screaming at Fuller as she pounded on the closed door.

The video stopped.

It was sobering, and they all fell into silence.

Ari's voice broke through it. "Now it's my turn. We'll leverage your expertise on behalf of our kind. What should our next steps be?"

Fuller raised his hand, and Ari acknowledged him. "Archie?"

"Yesterday, I visited with officers that were at all the scenes. One of our suggestions was to piggyback on what they've already seen and see if we can garner some new oathsworn officers to help ease the load some. We only have so many to go around, and many of them still work at their precincts, which is part of what makes them especially useful. The other suggestion, we're implementing even as I speak. We're going to be bringing on-board an AI system that monitors all the police channels for keywords like "bloodbath, exsanguination...and other terms that might imply one of these attacks took place. If we can get to the scene faster, we can be part of controlling the narrative."

Ari nodded. "Good work. Thanks, Archie."

Michel raised his hand; about the same time Carolyn did. "Michel?" Ari said.

"We need to get the word out to people. In the same way Director Fuller had an all call, I think we need to have one at the clan level for everyone." Before Ari could say anything–because everyone knew the 'compact-problems' were uppermost in his mind, and his face was already registering consternation, Michel rushed on. "…not details. Signs and symptoms ONLY. Every one of those people who are dead or locked up and dying woke up one morning feeling 'weird,' as Walker Matson put it. At least we should make everyone aware of the symptoms and give them someplace to report themselves to. It won't help them, but at least we'll know that there will be fewer murder scenes and chances for us to be outed, and fewer humans that die like those did."

Ari nodded. "Okay. We'll consider it." Ari acknowledged Carolyn next. "Carolyn? I saw a hand from you, also."

Carolyn looked at Michel. "I was thinking something similar, but not the same. They might dovetail, though. I was going to say set up a report line. I was thinking of sending out an email and telling people 'if you feel like 'this,' or notice 'that,' call the report line."

Ari nodded. David raised his hand. "David?"

"Both ideas are good. What I like better about the All Call is that people aren't always good at checking their emails. It would make more of an impact also, I think. However we get the word out, whether it's telling people signs and symptoms to watch for, or telling them to show up at a clan All Call? It needs to use every means of notification at our disposal - automatic calls, text messages, and emails. There are too many ways my people ignore me as it is."

Violette tried and failed to smother an ill-timed laugh. David looked at her and stuck out his tongue.

Ari closed his eyes; he didn't need them to act like children. "On topic, please."

Violette chimed in, sheepishly. "Sorry, sir. What about us? We're not at our home offices, or near our clans." His brow wrinkled for a moment, and she continued, "I guess what I mean to say, that David and I have traveled here. Virehnai love traveling; there are people living away from their clans, or who choose purposely to live away from others. How do we reach those people?" Ari nodded.

"Usually, Virehn who travel let VarenCorp know when they're abroad, but they don't always; particularly when they maintain multiple homes in places where they may have lived at on and off for centuries, and they're traveling between them. There would need to be a way to notify everyone."

Ari nodded. "Good point, Vi. Thank you."

Tim looked up at his father. "Where will we put anyone who either reports or we know is sick? There's only so much room here. We can set up a line; we can tell people the dangers…but when they show up here…there's only so many places we can safely lock them into." Ari nodded, but Tim continued. "Right now, it's not so many; we're okay. But what if a significant portion of our population is dealing with…that? We need to look at big pictures, too."

Ari nodded. "I agree."

Leonie Meier raised her hand.

"Leonie?" Ari acknowledged her.

"However we get the word out, we need to have a name to call it. How do we tell people what to watch for, other than to call it 'weird?' We need to take the fear we're going to create, and at the very least, give it a name."

Director Fuller turned to his counterpart, Leonie. "That goes back to the conversation we were having about the symptoms yesterday." She nodded, and he continued. "I was thinking about that, and I did have an idea." Fuller turned toward the monitor with Ari in it and looked up. "I suggest we call it Virehnai Aging Sickness; VAS for short, or maybe Aging Syndrome, or Virehnai dementia. Something along those lines. Humans often encounter these signs and symptoms as they age over decades. Whatever this is seems to cause a similar pattern in us, that isn't normally in our nature and is considerably accelerated."

Ari nodded. "Thank you," he said to Director Fuller. To everyone else, he said, "Of those suggestions, I think I prefer Virehnai Aging Sickness, or VAS. What does everyone think? Show of hands to adopt that as the name?"

One by one, hands were visible in the room, or on the monitors, and they voted the name in. Violette commented after the voting, "In some ways, I think Virehnai dementia is probably closer to truth...but if we called it that, it would scare the hell out of everyone. Calling it a 'sickness' at least implies there might be a cure at some point."

Ari looked at everyone. "Thank you, everyone, for your suggestions. At least what we're facing now has a name: Virehnai Aging Sickness." He wrote something down and then looked back up.

"I'm going to make a command decision here: Every clan will have a mandatory All Call. Those who are abroad and can teleconference in should be allowed to, to hear information firsthand; otherwise, show up to your clan's headquarters, or check in with your clan as soon as possible for information." He paused. "Carolyn?"

She looked up, and said, "Yes, sir?"

"Please set up a way for people who miss their emails, their meetings, or who are traveling to call in, and get the same situation briefing that those who attend the all calls in person will; also, there will need to be a number for anyone—worldwide—to report to. Can you and your IT group take care of that, and interface with the other IT Security offices to make it happen?

"Yes sir. The protocols for doing such a thing are already in place as part of our emergency planning. To run it system wide, we'll need your authorization. As soon as we have it customized to the current situation, we'll need your biometric authorizations. After that, those numbers will be functional to distribute at the All Calls, or any other delivery format we use."

"How long do you think it will it take?"

"Hours, maybe less-unless we run into a problem. I don't expect that. The original protocols set it up for 'unspecified emergency situations' from back in the Cold War era. We've updated as technology improves in case we need to make emergency announcements. Repurposing what we have shouldn't be hard."

"Good." Ari wrote something else down and then looked up. "Here's how I want it to run. Once Carolyn's got the system functional, I'll send all of you, and every registered clan head an Emergency All Call email. I want these to be held within two hours of receipt of email. For all hotels under the VarenCorp umbrella, the Virehnai site director at each property will hold an in-person All Call for every Virehnai currently on site, or ensure they call the number or their respective clans. It'll be short notice for many. Tough shit. Emergencies rarely announce themselves, and they're usually damned inconvenient."

"Tim?"

"Yes, Father?"

"What you said about 'where to put the people who self-report,' is echoing in my brain. You're right. It'll work for a while, but not for long. We need to come up with a better plan for how to deal with our people–but not merely where to put them. That's shortsighted. We need to leverage research people we have in the medical and pharmaceutical fields…and maybe our governments too…to figure out what's causing this, to stop it if we can, and to safeguard the human population. Not just for their safety, but also to protect our food sources, AND keep us from being outed. This could all go sideways in so many ways. I don't want to think about it." He shook his head. "Tim, get together a group of three or four people, and come up with some ideas for 'Plan B.' Use whoever you need to."

"Thank you all for attending. You've got work to do. Be prepared to have clan meetings later today, after receiving my go ahead and an email."

The video screen Ari was in went black, and one by one, the other teleconferencees' monitors did, too. As the people who were in the conference room there in lower Manhattan all began standing to leave, Tim asked, "Can you all stay for another minute?"

Everyone sat back down and waited expectantly for why he needed them to stay.

"Tomorrow, after the update meeting, would all of you mind having a brainstorming session with me for how we can handle Virehnai Aging Sickness down the road?"

David chuckled. "We're you're group of three or four?"

"Why yes," he said. "Yes, you are. Congratulations."

13

FATEFUL MOMENTS

As soon as the meeting was over, Michel headed back to his suite. It seemed too early to head to his office. He changed into a t-shirt and sweatpants and headed for his study.

Michel's study was his inner sanctum; his sanctuary…his safe place, which is why few ever saw the inside. It had memorabilia from places he'd lived; mementos of people–most no longer alive, except for blood memory. He had his sire Dio's gladius, a Roman short sword, hanging on the wall, alongside his own. There were several former weapons on the walls…it could've functioned as an armory. There was a banner that his brother Aleksandr, who usually went by Sasho, used to have hanging on the wall of his great room in Wallachia. It was a golden dragon emblazoned on red, the standard of the House of Basarab, which he'd helped found. Unfortunately, it led to his eventual downfall. There was a green silk ribbon in a little frame behind glass. Once, he'd given it to Aibhilin, who he'd first turned, and then married while living in the Roman British town of Vindolanda. The only living person he had an item from was Howard: There was a Roman Aurius–a gold coin–won in a wager between them from when they were living at and helping to build the town of Vindolanda, close to Hadrian's wall. For years, he used it for 'executive decision making.' Eventually, it ended up behind a frame.

Howard and Johannes were the only people who he'd ever allowed in. Usually, this is where he ended up when he needed to think. Strange as it might sound to other Virehnai, he would sit there, and while staring out at the Manhattan skyline, he would contemplate his problem. That part was normal…it was the fact that he would focus on the flames of his predecessors in his blood and imagine what advice they would give him if they were sitting with him now that others might think strange. He'd once asked Reman about it. The Vel'sheth was a little surprised, but thought it was a nice way to use the memory of those who still had fragments of energy living in his blood.

Michel quieted his mind, and asked the blood that flowed through him, and the flames that were represented in it "We're under attack; we don't know from where. What can we do?"

What Michel saw, he would question as he tried to interpret it, and even years down the road, he'd look back, and question what he saw:

He saw the Virehnai blood witches, Martine, Collette and Agnes — the day they cast the spell that brought the Compact into force, which he always associated with 'magic.'

He saw the battlefield after the battle of Amphipolis, after he awoke as Virehn. There was blood and gore everywhere. It was loud, he was hungry, it was disorienting, and it was downright horrible. He always associated any scenes of Amphipolis with either blood, or war…or 'becoming,' pick any two.

He saw Vibia at Focaria Rubra, the old Scarlet Hearth–which was Ari's stronghold back when he was called Alban Casimir. The clan he founded still had its headquarters in Zurich, and was called Clan Casimir, harking back to those days. What he saw was through the eyes of his sire, Dio. Whenever he saw either of those individuals, he saw 'power.' Seeing Vibia at Ari's stronghold? It was power on top of power. Their power was like night and day: Vibia's power and strength always came with a side of grace and intelligence; Ari's was more like pounding a square peg into a round hole: brute force. He would have his way, no matter what, no matter who, no matter how. He was effective, but until the Compact got signed, he never had the time, inclination or vulnerability to bother being 'nice.' Even now, 'nice,' Michel supposed, was relative, in

Ari's case. He wasn't sure how to interpret that bit at all, other than what they're seeing currently is some sort of power ploy. But from where?

The last bit he saw was also through Dio's eyes. It was Ari–angry, but attempting to control his anger. It reminded Michel of someone playing with an extremely sharp knife, moving it in and out of its sheath, like a nervous tic. Like the previous scene, it was something he'd never seen through his sire's eyes before. He was trying to decide how he should interpret it. He wasn't sure if it meant 'hidden motives,' or something 'dangerous,' 'cloaked' or 'hidden'. Even as he tried to feel Dio's own emotions about the scene, it faded, and the moments were gone. Michel turned from looking either inward, or to the skyline, instead to his desk, and wrote what he had seen–starting with the sharp knife in a sheath analogy that featured an angry Ari. As he'd never seen it before, it would take careful consideration. He heard a chime, showing that he had an email.

Michel pulled his phone from his pocket, and saw there was a message from Ari, and Tim. Apparently, the phone numbers for Virehnai to call were now operative, and the clan All Calls would happen at 8 am Eastern Time, wherever you were. He looked at his watch. It was nearly 5 am now.

Michel headed over to his office and sent out an urgent message to everyone:

"Clan Robichaux:

This is official notification that there will be a MANDATORY Emergency All-Call Clan meeting at 8 am this morning here at the Hall. It is mandatory if you're nearby to attend in person. This is critical: I can't stress enough that it is literally a matter of life and death.

If you don't show, we will track you down; it's that critical. When you come to the Hall, expect to be greeted by Emily, checking off that you're present as you enter. Don't be a

codswaddle; don't make us chase you down. We have enough on our plate at the moment as it is.

For those who are currently abroad, you're the only ones with a valid excuse to not be here. We advise you to please call 212-555-6748. This is an emergency line set up by VarenCorp for the duration of the emergency. I would like to ask if you ARE abroad, please call Emily Hargrove at our main office to let her know in advance where you are, when you plan to return, and we will instruct you further. We WILL have to account for your presence with VarenCorp, as they're tracking this.

"I know this is short notice, but as Ari told us in a meeting very early this morning, "Emergencies rarely announce themselves, and they're usually damned inconvenient." Sorry for that inconvenience. Thank you in advance, and I'll see you in the Hall to fill you in."

Michel Robichaux."

Within moments of hitting send, Howard called him. "What's that about?"

"Where are you? Can I come update you?"

"Please. I'm in my office. I just got here."

Michel wandered down the hall to the opposite end of the uppermost penthouse level to Howard's office. Howard was in before his assistant, Gracie, too.

He knocked gently and then opened the door. There was Howard, getting himself breakfast. "Come on in. Can I get you a mug, also?"

"That would be wonderful, Howard."

Howard opened the mini-fridge and pulled out another bag of blood. Once his bag was finished nuking (it was convenient–it had a sensor on it that only nuked it as long as required), he put the next bag in and grabbed a fresh mug off the shelf. Howard cut open the warmed bag, poured it into the fresh mug and handed it to Michel, who took an appreciative sip. As soon as the microwave dinged to let him know his breakfast was warm, Howard poured it into his favorite mug, took a sip, and sat down.

"What's the emergency? What did you find via the Red Team that warrants all that?"

"It's way beyond the Red Team data breach, Howard. There's something–we don't know what it is, how it spreads–only that there are now four Virehnai that are dead from it, or very sick."

"What? That makes little sense to me. We don't get sick. We used to end up on the wrong side of a vial of poison occasionally, but not sick."

"We do now… We decided earlier that it'll be called 'Virehnai Aging Sickness.' If you want to see what it does, look up 'Helderberg murders,' and click on the local channel for Albany. The report I'm thinking of has a thumbnail that reads, 'Family Massacred.' His brow and nose crinkled up at the title.

Howard tapped for a few. "Here's the one you were talking about." He clicked on it as Michel drank his breakfast, and likewise, picked up his mug and drank.

Howard put the mug back down shortly after, as the report continued, and Michel could see his facial reactions to the carnage.

"What in the hell does that…mess…have to do with Virehnai Aging Sickness?"

"VAS starts with you feeling…off. Maybe achy. You might notice a gray hair, or a wrinkle. You ignore it. Later, there's more gray, more wrinkles. You're hungrier than you used to be, and your mind goes. You get ravenously hungry…lose all your normal inhibitions and learned behaviors that keep you safe and go all medieval on someone. A Virehn named Jacob Ralston got VAS and did that to his neighbors down the street. He's dead."

"That's...horrible."

"Wait, let me send you this. They gave me permission to show it at the All Call as 'show and tell,' both by Ari and Clan Sabin."

A moment later, there was a 'ding' letting Howard know he had an email, and he clicked it. On his monitor, the side-by-side picture of Jacob Ralston's VarenCorp ID photo contrasted with him as he looked when he died came up.

Howard's shocked expression said everything. "Fuck." Howard looked over the monitor at Michel. "He literally, physically aged?"

Michel nodded. "He did. They all have. They thought of calling it Virehnai Dementia, but were afraid to. So far, everyone that gets it dies."

"Holy shit."

As directed by Ari, Michel pointedly left anything out that would lead Howard to connect the dots about the Compact not working on the Virehnai before they died.

"There are other murder scenes here; they're listing it as a serial killer. Are you sure these are all Virehnai, and not human copycats?" Howard asked.

"We're sure. Click on some. They're...gruesome." Howard did as Michel suggested and sat in stunned silence.

"This is treachery of some sort. It HAS to be." he told Michel. "I don't know how, but it is."

"That was the same reaction everyone on the task force had. David apologized, by the way, for jumping to conclusions about the forged data that implicated me in the thefts. To make up for it, he recommended me for the Emergency Task Force."

"That was nice of him," Howard snorted.

"Well, like I told him; I'd rather be part of the solution than not be. It's true."

Howard picked up his mug and drank some more. "It makes me feel better that you're involved, actually."

"Thanks for the vote of confidence, Howard."

"Shall we finish up here and head over to the meeting?"

Both men finished drinking and headed out the door.

"Good morning, Gracie," Michel said, as he passed Gracie's desk. "Morning, Grace." Howard told her

"Good morning, to both of ye." She had a lovely Irish lilt to her voice.

Michel said, "We're headed to the All Call. Walk with us?"

"I will, and call meself lucky to be in the company of such fine gentlemen."

That morning, Elaina went to the All Call, along with everyone else. She said hi to Emily as she signed her in.

Once she was in the hall, she saw Uncle Michel, Uncle Howard and Howard's assistant Gracie Mcanallen walk in together. Uncle Michel didn't see her at first; Elaina thought he looked worried.

Others commented similarly. Once Michel saw her, he waved, and came over to her, hugging her, and then saying, "Do me a favor; hang around after the All Call. I need to talk to you."

Michel went back up to the dais, where he was flanked on one side by Howard, and on the other by Reman. Michel looked at his watch as Emily came in and nodded at him. "Let's get started."

He addressed them all, somberly:

"Clan Robichaux, thank you for attending in person as I asked. While it's always good to see all of you, this isn't the way I wanted to be seeing you this morning. You aren't alone, though. Right now, VarenCorp has mandated that Virehnai worldwide be attending All Calls with their clans, or if abroad, were instructed to contact the VC emergency line."

"When I say there's an emergency–it's an understatement. There is currently an emergency that is ongoing unlike anything we as a people have ever faced. I'm part of the Emergency Task Force that VarenCorp has set up to deal with it. I attended a meeting around 1 am this morning, which is why you're all here this morning."

"As to the emergency? Honestly, we don't know the scope and breadth of it yet. We're afraid this is only the beginning. We–all of us - are currently in danger. The consensus from the meeting I attended is that we believe it to be treachery."

He paused, and there was some murmuring at the word 'treachery.' Most of the people in his clan weren't old enough to remember when it was the number one way a Virehn would die–but all had heard of it. That was the beauty of the Compact; it did away with treachery...mostly.

Michel continued. "Here is what I know and can tell you so far: There are Virehn who have gotten sick and have died." The room was entirely silent. If he didn't have their attention before, he certainly did now. "We don't know the exact cause for their sickness…how they got it, if it can be spread…or how; none of that. That's one of the many things we're seeing right now that worries us. There are too many variables that we either don't know or don't understand. We're thinking they were being targeted; but even at that, we don't know if they were targeted individually, or if we're all being targeted as a group, and they're simply the first."

"The only thing we can say for CERTAIN is this: We're calling the sickness they have 'Virehnai Aging Sickness,' or VAS. The sick Virehnai all seem to have one thing in common that they each ignored. They first noticed that something was 'off.' When I say off, it's only by a little. They saw a gray hair; maybe two. A wrinkle that they didn't have before. Achiness, particularly in the morning. They noticed a change in their skin tone or condition. All of them felt hungry more frequently or required more blood than usual. Because it was weird, but didn't seem like an immediate threat, they ignored it. By the time what they noticed was strange enough, off enough or problematic enough to say something to someone, even in passing– it was too late."

Michel paused, and there was wide-eyed silence filling the hall.

"That is why VarenCorp has mandated the following policy for the duration of the emergency: This is your official notification on behalf of VarenCorp. If you notice anything different from what is good and normal for you, you are being asked to self-report to VarenCorp. Call VarenCorp 911, tell them you would like to self-report, and then go directly to VarenCorp Headquarters."

"Find a gray hair? Notice wrinkles? Realize your bones or joints are achy? No matter how small it seems, call VarenCorp 911. Or if you are afraid, call me, Howard or Emily…but please, call someone. If you want someone to accompany you to VarenCorp Headquarters, someone will. We're family. You don't have to report alone."

"In the meantime, I know we aren't a hunting clan, but I've been asked to tell you not to feed from others during your…" he got an impish grin and wiggled his eyebrows for a moment, "…other…activities for the time being. Stick with the blood provided by our trusted bloodsworn allies. I'll be addressing them later as well; asking them to watch where they go, who they associate with, and to report to us if THEY don't feel well, or if they notice anything strange. If we all work together, human family and Virehnai family alike, we'll get through this."

As he did with Howard, there was no mention of anything that could help them connect the dots. He told his clan even less than he did Howard, focusing only on symptoms, never touching on the fact that the deaths came AFTER a bloodlust that ended with dead humans and Virehnai. He paused, and then asked, "Questions?"

"How long has this been going on?"

"The first two instances were reported four days ago. There were two more yesterday."

"Who's died? Someone asked. Simultaneously, another asked, "Who's sick?"

"Those who have died are Jacob Ralston of Clan Sabin, and Florrie Travers of Clan Rosemont." At the mention of Florrie's name, there were gasps. Everybody in Manhattan knew Florrie. "Those who are currently sick and under the care of VarenCorp are Walker Matson of Clan Westmore, and Connie Travers of Clan Rosemont." More gasps; people knew Connie, too. They came like a matched pair. If you knew one, chances are, you knew both.

"Any more questions?" Michel asked.

"What if I self-report, and it turns out to be nothing? I don't want to waste anyone's time with stupid shit."

Michel looked around at all of them. "If any of you self-report and it turns out to be nothing, I'll celebrate it with you. I'd rather you waste our time with 'stupid shit'" he said, while making air quotes, "than you not say something, and it ends up being too little, too late. I'd rather sit around and shoot the shit with any of you, laughing over nothing than have to preside over even one more remembrance ceremony this year."

"Other questions?" He waited for a moment. "No? Well, then you're all released. If you think of questions later, call or email me."

Michel looked over at Elaina and called her name. She'd been talking to her co-worker Amy. She looked up, and he motioned her to come to where he was. "I'll be down to the office as soon as I'm finished here," Elaina told Amy.

"See you there!"

Michel finished up what he was saying to Reman and Howard and then put his hand briefly on Howard's shoulder. "I'll update you after today's meeting. We're supposed to have another at 1pm, unless they get in touch with us first. Meet me at my office."

"Elaina," Michel said, "Come with me." She followed him into one of the small rooms off of the vestibule. "Sit down; I need to talk to you."

"That sounds kind of ominous after the meeting." Elaina grimaced.

"I'm sorry. The past few days have been so crazy." Michel shook his head. "Let me start again. How are you doing? I'm sorry I haven't been around much to be of any comfort to you."

"I understand; particularly after hearing what you said in the meeting." She paused, "I'm sad; I miss Amalie, but I'm doing okay. Jeff's been working out with me in the gym; he kind of picked up where Amalie left off."

"That's good. I'm glad he's stepped in to do that. How's the new job going? Do you enjoy working with Jeff?"

"So far, so good. I'm enjoying it, and Jeff's cool. We seem like we have a good deal in common. He's a good boss. I enjoy working with Michael, too. Not that what I say matters at all," she chuckled, "but I think you made a good choice in picking Michael to succeed Amalie. I liked him before, but I enjoy working with him."

"I'm glad you approve," he said, with a hint of playful sarcasm. "Really, I'm glad that office seems to be a good fit for you," Michel added, with no sarcasm at all. "I thought you'd do well with Jeff." He paused and then got to the reason he REALLY needed to talk to Elaina.

"Look, here's what I needed to tell you. I found out some more about your original attack because of those meetings I've been in. A person in the Task Force found out something about it and thought to pass it on. Apparently, someone is trying to get to me through you. The attack on you wasn't random; not at all." Elaina's brow furrowed. "The reason they attacked you is someone who has an axe to grind with me decided to put an RFID tracking chip somewhere in you. That was the sole purpose of the attack."

"For real? Somebody's tracking where I go?"

"Maybe. There's a lot going on right now that we don't know, hon. But I'd have to say it's possible; maybe even probable. If someone is tracking you, we don't know who. Be very careful where you go, and what you do until all of this is settled out. Until you get it removed, it's something someone might use to hurt you…and use against me."

Later on, while she was at her desk thinking about everything she'd learned, both at the All Call, and while talking to Michel afterwards…it all felt…scary. The whole meeting was surreal; Virehn weren't supposed to get sick! Usually, anything that made a Virehn feel sick was because of poisoning. She remembered Amalie telling her that. Finding out after the meeting that someone could track her only made it that much worse.

She'd remembered Amalie telling her about past treachery, and the ways Virehnai used to get back at one another. Never did she ever think that she could be part of someone's equation to get back at Uncle Michel.

It was a week since Amalie died. Just a week. It seemed much longer and felt like she was slogging through it. Elaina was missing her bestie. That was one of the hardest things to square with: Amalie taught her everything she needed to know; and now that she's living her life as Virehn, she couldn't shake the guilt that Amalie died because of her.

Elaina knew what Reman told her was true; that Amalie acted out of love, and that she, herself, would've done the same thing. It helped somewhat–but it fixed nothing. Two days ago, Reman emailed her and inquired about how she was doing. She answered him back honestly: "I can't shake the guilt I feel every single time I think of Amalie. How do I get past this?" Elaina asked him.

He told her that "only time would truly fix it; one day you will think of Amalie and not feel like it was your fault. Someday, you'll simply remember something about her or something she told you, and you'll laugh or smile at the thought; maybe wistfully–that she would be here to share whatever was going on in your life. It might seem hard or even impossible to imagine that right now," he told her, "but that day WILL come. Remember Elaina, that you've only been Virehn for two weeks, and Amalie's only been gone a week. Time and distance will heal your sadness. I promise it will." Elaina clung to Reman's promise and chugged on.

Elaina had thrown herself into her work and was quickly learning everything she needed to in Jeff's office. Staying busy was all that she knew to do. That took care of the days; the nights were the hardest. On the bright side, her elder sister Janet stepped in, knowing how guilty Elaina was feeling. She'd taken to calling her nightly, simply checking in to say hello. It was a gift of sweetness, particularly as Amalie herself had admonished her to get closer to her family now, and make good memories, because soon enough, their paths would diverge. Janet and her nieces would age; she would not. That bit of advice from Amalie was a kindness. Elaina sighed. Once again, it was a lesson from Amalie.

The night before the All Call, Elaina took Janet up on her offer to visit her nieces. Sophie 'helped' her mom make cookies as Hayden 'supervised,' and Elaina joined them all in the kitchen. By the time the girls were done, everything was covered in flour, Sophie had icing in multiple colors all over her face and hands, Hayden had icing in her hair and on her shirt, and there was a tray of cookies on the center island to show for their efforts. The cookies were, truthfully–a little frightening looking. The sweet gel icing that Sophie had drawn faces and butterflies and flowers on was a smeary, colorful mess, much like she was. The cookies looked exactly as you would expect a six-year-old with an unsteady hand would create. It didn't matter that they were messy. They were all having fun. At Sophie's urging, Elaina ate two of the cookies and regretted it shortly after. Elaina wasn't sure if she wanted to barf, shit or cry–or more likely–all the above.

Elaina had to laugh at her own misery. Amalie hadn't been kidding. Two cookies with all their inherent sweetness were enough to send her system into what she could only describe as a kind of shock. She'd never been a projectile vomiter before–but she sure was now. Elaina wasn't sure if she wanted to bemoan her state, or cry because Amalie wasn't here to tease her about it or tell her 'I told you so.' She'd promised she would, and she could hear her saying it.

At least Elaina had fun telling Jeff and Michael about her cookie debacle at work the next day after the All Call. Jeff laughed as she related it, and then he turned to Michael, adding, "Do yourself a favor, Michael. Learn from Elaina's lesson. You don't have to go through that if you don't want to…" After Michael walked away, Jeff leaned in a little closer. "Hey–some of us are going to Sanguinarium Obscura tonight. Would you like to go with us? It's open mic night; you never know who or what you'll hear, but it's always good."

"Sure," she replied. When Elaina got back to her desk, there was an invitation through her calendar for tonight; she accepted it. At the moment, it looked like it would be Jeff, herself, Uncle

Michel's executive assistant, Emily, Jeff's sibling Thea Carlsson, and two of her own new siblings, Isabella, and Jake. Elaina had never met Thea; she knew Izzy and Jake–this would be the first time she'd be hanging with them, though. Elaina was looking forward to it. While she was mindful of the fact she still had the tracking dot in her, she wasn't worried; it was a Virehnai venue, and she was with a group of Virehn; she'd be safe enough.

Later that evening, she wore a little red dress with strappy high heels, along with her Sanguinarium Obscura medallion/key. She met up with the group that was going down in the lobby, and they all piled into a black Escalade.

Once they arrived, they sat together between two tables. Unlike when she was with Amalie, there were considerably more Virehnai here this time. Jeff wasn't kidding; Open mic night was popular. There was a quintet that was improv-ing blues; after they left the stage, there were two men that were playing...hell, Elaina didn't know what kind of music it was. They had a woman with them that was singing in what Thea said was Persian. It was hauntingly beautiful, and they played three songs that all seemed to blend one into the other. There was also a man that got up and played classical guitar. As he was playing, another man came up from the crowd, grabbed a guitar off to the side of the stage (for that very reason) and joined him, and began playing a countermelody to the same song. Several Virehnai in the audience began stomping out a rhythm. Apparently, it was something they knew.

There was a short break–not exactly an intermission, and they were all discussing what they'd heard, what they'd liked best and why. Jake was sitting next to Elaina, and she noticed his eyes...narrow. He was looking at Thea when he did it. Elaina looked to see Thea and noticed Thea was looking at Jeff. Jeff was watching a guy across the room near the booths. Elaina leaned over to Jake asking in a low tone, "What's going on?"

Jeff heard what she asked, and turned to her, and answered in a low tone, "Don't look; there's a man who's been staring over here. Anyone that watches you that long and hard is thinking of fighting or fucking." When Elaina's eyes widened, he chuckled. "I promised Michel and Howard both I'd make sure you got home in one piece. If that fellow keeps it up, I'm going over to ask what his intentions are." He chuckled again. "He's nice looking, but I'll hate to break it to him: he's not my type." They all laughed, and it broke the tension.

A few moments later, Jeff got up and approached the man. They talked for a few minutes, shook hands, and the man followed Jeff back to where they all sat. "I'd like to introduce Filip Novotny, of Clan Cervak, visiting from Prague. He wanted an introduction to the ladies at the table." Filip was tall, handsome, with dark hair, and looked to be in his mid-30s. He spoke English with an English accent that had a hint of Slavic. All the women looked up at him. It wouldn't have mattered. Human? Virehn? Filip was eye-candy.

Jeff continued to introduce the women individually to Filip. "The lady with the short blond hair, that's Emily." Emily looked up and smiled. "Hi Filip."

"The lady with the long brown hair is Isabella."

"Hello, Filip" she smiled and did a little wave.

"The blond with curly hair is my sibling Thea," She nodded at Filip said 'hi.'

"Sitting across from Thea is Elaina." She looked up and smiled at him. "Hi Filip."

Filip looked at Jeff. "Thank you." Filip smiled and bowed towards the women. "It is a pleasure to meet such beautiful ladies while I'm visiting here."

"How long have you been abroad?" Thea asked him.

"In the US? About a month so far. I spent a couple of weeks in California, spent a week in Chicago. I've been in Manhattan for a week. I'm going to be in your country for another three weeks, but at the end of next week I'll be traveling to Washington, DC, before working my way back home to Prague."

When the lights flickered, signaling that the music would start again, Filip bowed in their direction again, and said "I should go." They thought he meant 'back to his table.' They were all surprised when Filip, instead of returning to his seat, headed for the stage and picked up a guitar. He sat down on the stool.

"This is a Moravian folk song; it reminds me of home. I hope you enjoy it. It's called 'Mezi Horami.'"

He played it and sang. A lady from the from the crowd that knew the song came up, and stood beside Filip, and sang the harmony to it, ending with applause and foot stomps. The crowd liked it. Jake said to no one in particular, "He's good."

Filip turned to the woman standing beside him. "Do you know 'Ej Lasko, Lasko?'" She said yes, so he began playing it, and thumping the beat with his foot, as the two sang. When he finished that one, he asked her if she knew 'Ach synku, synku.' She said yes to that one, too.

When he finished playing, he thanked the lady who said her name was Anezhka. They hugged, and as someone else made their way up to the stage to take their place under the spotlight, Filip walked back over to them. "That was for all of you to remember me by. I'll be here nights until I leave for DC. I like the atmosphere here." He bowed at them and made his way back to the table he'd been at earlier.

Their group stayed for two more musicians, one playing something Arabic flavored, and the next were four fellows who had a good time playing three Beatles songs. By that time, the crowd was thinning out some, and like many others, they stood and made their way out. Elaina turned and saw the curtained door at the back that led up to the roof and was suddenly flooded with memories and struggling not to cry.

Elaina stood there for a moment, even as the others were walking away; grief swamped her mind. All she could think of was the last time she'd been here with Amalie, breaking into the pool in the building nearby, and the fun they'd had, and how exhilarating it was. Was that only a week and a half ago? It suddenly felt like a lifetime.

It startled Elaina and took her by surprise when Filip Novotny was suddenly close beside her shoulder, and said in a low voice leaning close, "To see such a beautiful woman look so sad breaks my heart."

"You startled me."

"I'm sorry. What makes you so sad?"

"I lost a friend recently."

"I'm sorry for your loss. How sad. It's my job to make you smile again, Elaina." He reached out and grabbed one of Elaina's hands. The others turned around in time to see Elaina and Filip talking, and him holding her hand. "I don't like that," Jeff muttered.

"Jealous?" Thea chuckled.

"I got this," Izzy said, holding up a hand, and turned, walking toward Elaina and Filip.

"Hello again, Filip." Izzy said.

"Isabella." He said, bowing his head in her direction.

"Sorry, Filip. I have to steal my sister from you." Izzy turned to Elaina. "Are you coming, Elaina? The car's waiting for us."

Elaina turned to Filip and smiled. "See? You made me smile. Have a good night, Filip."

He let go of her hand, and she and Izzy joined the others and headed to the Escalade. When Filip grabbed her hand, he'd put his card in it. It made her smile again, much as it would've as a human. What girl doesn't like to be desired? It was a compliment - and he wasn't hard on the eyes, either.

Once they were in the Escalade, Filip was mostly the topic of discussion. "What did he want?" Jeff asked. "Why did he stop you?"

"He didn't stop me; I...I was thinking of Amalie and stopped on my own. The last time I was here was with her..." she said, in explanation. "He came over and asked me why I looked so sad, and said it was his job to make me smile again."

Jake snorted. "I can guess how..." They all laughed. Elaina thought it was sweet, though. "He had odd manners; all that bowing..."

"Uh-huh," Jeff said. "I noticed that, too. Part of it's being European; as Virehnai, they bow to other Virehnai instead of the human response of kissing both cheeks–but...I'd lay money that he's fairly old. Maybe not as old as Howard or Michel, but older than most."

"Really?"

Jeff nodded. "Something in his bearing."

Elaina couldn't say why she didn't, but she didn't tell them about the card he gave her. She merely kept it in her hand, as if it were a souvenir from the evening. When she got home, she tucked it into the frame of the mirror on her dresser in her room.

The next day at work, Jeff razzed her about Filip. It was good natured. As she sat at her desk, her thoughts turned to Filip several times. It was one of those times when Michael Ratner came up and plopped some files on her desk, and she jumped.

"I'm sorry!" He said. "I didn't mean to startle you."

"It's okay." Elaina looked up at him from where he stood. "I was lost in my thoughts, that's all." As Michael turned to leave, she stopped him. "I saw on the schedule that your ritual of becoming is scheduled in a month. Congratulations."

"Thanks, Elaina." Michael looked down, almost embarrassed, and then looked back up at her. "I'm sorry that I'm succeeding Amalie. I know you two were good friends, and she was always so nice to me."

"Thank you. I know exactly how you feel. I succeeded Johannes, and I always tried to remember that my happiness came at a high cost. Don't worry about it. Amalie told me that while she was sad for Johannes, she was happy for me, and he would be happy for me, too." Elaina sighed. "So I tell you the same thing; it comes back down to 'Virehn zuth akret.' I carry Johannes' flame forward, and I'll try to live my life as a Virehn in such a way that it honors his memory. You carry Amalie's flame forward. Remember her and honor her. That's all either of us can do."

Michael nodded. "I hate to ask, but how are your brothers taking me being chosen?"

"I can't imagine they're happy about it, but truthfully, I don't know, Michael. They'd have to talk to me first! Doug's being a little nicer than he was, but I think it's mostly for show, and for my dad's sake; he says as little to me as he can get away with. Rob? Rob ignores me completely."

"That's stupid."

"It is. They used to have my back until I got chosen." Elaina shook her head sadly. "I don't know why they're focusing so much on wanting to be made Virehn; I mean, they're going to inherit everything from Mama and Papa. It's not...insubstantial. Between them, they'll have control of all of Papa's businesses, so it's not like they'll be lacking for power, either." Elaina shook her head. "Doug keeps going on about 'You don't fully comprehend what you've been given,' and it's obvious he thinks I'm squandering opportunities right and left." She looked at Michael. "I don't think I am. I'm aware I have much to learn, but... I guess I didn't realize how different we thought from one another. Is there anyone in your family that's like my brothers?"

"Not in the same way." He thought for a minute. "One of my cousins, maybe; but it didn't stop him from congratulating me after the succession ceremony."

"One other thing Amalie told me I'll pass on to you: she told me that the day I became Virehn, it's like there's a timer counting down on our relationships with our family. The people you love and care about? Get closer to them now and enjoy them as much as you can–because Amalie told me that the further away you get from your ritual of becoming, and ascending–your path and theirs will diverge, no matter how much you still love one another. They age and are dying a little every day; you won't."

He looked thoughtful. "Thanks. Good to know." Michael chuckled. "Amalie was a smart cookie. I've got big shoes to fill."

"You do, but you'll do fine." Elaina paused for a minute. "If you need me for anything…have questions…call me. I don't mind. I'm happy for you; I am. Michel, Howard and the other Sethari made a good choice in picking you to ascend."

"Thanks, Elaina. It means a lot to me to know that. You're coming to my ascension party?"

"I wouldn't miss it."

The 1 pm meeting Michel attended at VarenCorp headquarters was full of more surprises. The first, and biggest, was that the meeting started off without Ari, the Security Directors, or the Continental heads - particularly Eliška and Tomasz – but the heads of South America, Africa and Asia were conspicuously absent from the teleconference as well.

Oddly enough, it seemed like there were more attending via teleconference; maybe that was simply because so many were missing from the physical conference room? Michel didn't have to wait long to find out.

Tim started off the meeting. "You'll notice my father's not here; He asked me to start the meeting without him. He's at a different teleconference that the continental heads, and all the Security Directors are attending. An emergency came up that all are attending to, because of its implications; Father didn't have the time to get me up to speed prior to this meeting, but the one thing he could tell me is…chilling. There's now a case in Europe; from what I understand, it's somewhere in Austria, close to Lichtenstein."

David looked across the table at Tim. "Oh shit."

Tim nodded. "My thoughts exactly." He paused. "As soon as they're finished with that, they'll either be joining us in this meeting, or we'll be having another, and you'll be hanging around a bit, so we can discuss it all together as a group. They felt they needed time to discuss the situation amongst themselves first."

Tim looked at David, and then at Violette. "I know you're wondering about your people. Father said he'd decide today whether he'd be sending one or both of you home. He's taking matters as they stand into account. I suspect if there are widespread outbreaks of Virehnai Aging Sickness, you'll both go home."

David nodded. Violette said, "Thanks, Tim."

Tim turned to those in the room, as well as those attending by teleconference. "While I have you all here, I know we all had clan All Calls this morning, and the call-in numbers are now functional. Did everyone's All Calls go well? Did you have anyone report?"

There were nods, and some muttered 'no one reported,' some thumbs up on the monitors.

"Good." He paused, "I'm going to be working with a team here to have a 'Plan B' in our back pocket, for 'just in case': the plan that addresses what will we do with large numbers of Virehnai if this sickness spreads beyond our capability to house them at our various headquarters. While I'll be working closely with those that are here in the room with me to flesh out those plans and implement whatever we come up with, I'd also like to throw it out to the rest of you for ideas. Think about it. What could we do to mitigate those problems? Any suggestions you have at all will be considered and appreciated. If any of you think of something after the meeting, shoot me an email."

David raised his hand.

"David?"

"The only idea I had, after you mentioned it to us yesterday, might not be a good one exactly, but it may be the easiest."

"Continue."

"Well, we've got properties. I do...you do...Michel does...VarenCorp does. All of us do. What if we take a property we already own, and modify it NOW in case we need it?"

Violette raised her hand, and Tim acknowledged her, nodding.

"To piggyback on what David said, what if we all took stock of our properties, to determine what we have that could be appropriate, and each draw up a short list of them you and Ari could choose from, to move forward with?"

"Thanks, Violette, David. Those are both good ideas."

Michel signaled Tim.

"Yes, Michel?"

"Again, following on David's thought, even if it's a property we don't own…maybe we want to think of buying a decommissioned hospital, jail or some sort of facility that already HAS most of the big modifications we might require. That way, any changes we make are tailoring the property to be more specific to Virehnai, and our current situation."

Before the conversation could continue, there was a light knocking on the door, and when it opened, Carolyn, Directors Fuller and Meier, and Tomasz filed in and found seats, and folks attending the other meeting via teleconference were now populating their screens in the room in Manhattan.

Tomasz spoke. "I suppose Tim told you that there's now a case of Virehnai Aging Sickness in Europe?"

"Yes." Tim and others answered.

Tomasz turned to David, then Violette. "For now, David and Violette, you'll both be staying here, but right after this meeting, Director Meier and I will be headed home."

Ari's monitor came up, and his face appeared on-screen. "Good afternoon everyone. You were told we've now got a case of Virehnai Aging Syndrome here now?"

"I told them," Tim said. "Me, too" Tomasz added.

"Good. We've been running in circles all day. We learned earlier today that a Virehn named Gustaf Meyerhoff, living on the outskirts of Frastanz, Austria, killed the young couple who lived next door to him."

"Does he have all the same symptoms?" Violette asked.

"Unfortunately." Ari continued. "The media following along with the story is…intense. The main reason for the media shitstorm is because the woman killed was six months pregnant, and… Gustaf…ate the baby." There were groans. "At least we can be thankful that no one has connected the issues here to what's happening Stateside. What a fucking mess."

Ari paused for a moment as they took in the information. "If it wasn't bad enough, the local gendarmes tried to apprehend Mr. Meyerhoff and got dead for their efforts." Several of them grimaced. Dead police, no matter what country, were bad.

"I sent security from here in Zurich to find Gustaf and take care of damage control. Whoever came up with the idea of looking to see the nearest Virehn residence to the crime scene gets my thanks. While he wasn't in his home, we found him wandering the hills nearby. Gustaf Meyerhoff is currently staying at our Zurich headquarters. Thankfully, our security team apprehended him before he could eat any more of his neighbors. He wasn't especially communicative; we suspect he won't live much longer."

Ari paused and hit a button. "One thing security could help me with is a comparison of his file photo with the way we found him. Aside from the way they found the scene, the pictures tell the story of his illness, if nothing else does." The picture came up, and like the others, the two pictures would never have thought to be the same individual. "Like those in the US, the man we apprehended here looks vastly different from the man pictured in his photos." He paused and then changed gears.

"How did everyone's clan meetings go? Were there any that didn't happen? Did anyone report? "

Carolyn replied, "I have the lists of everyone briefed this morning. We've accounted for most. There are some that are abroad we've been in contact with. The amount that we'll have to track down and find is low here. So far, none have reported…yet."

Tomasz looked up at Ari. "The same is true with the European clans. We've accounted for most. Carolyn and I were discussing it before we met regarding the Austrian situation. We think most that are unaccounted for are traveling or are staying at a non-primary residence; if the other Corporate heads are okay with it, we think it would be useful to make a primary list of all those who are unaccounted for, and distribute the full list to everyone to locate them."

"Good idea," Ari said. "Any objections?"

Toyo, the head of VarenCorp Asia, and Ana Maria, head of VarenCorp S.A. nodded their heads, and responded 'no."

"Good. Keep me apprised of any who self-reports. Has there been any new scenes reported, Archie?"

Archie Fuller responded, "Not today."

Ari looked relieved. "Good news, for a change. How are Connie and Walker doing today?"

Tim looked up at his father. "Connie's much worse. Walker died early this morning. I…don't expect Connie to last much longer."

"Sir?" Director Fuller spoke up.

"Yes, Archie?"

"When you asked about Connie and Walker, it reminded me. You asked me to get information on Connie's and Florrie's background. I did that."

Director Fuller handed the sheet to Tim, who could put it up on the screen for all to see.

"Are there any names on the list that stand out to anyone?" Director Fuller asked.

No one had any insights based on the women's shared ancestry.

"Oh well. It was worth a try," Director Fuller said. "I suppose we struck out there..."

"Thanks for trying, Archie. Shall we reconvene tomorrow at 10 am and see where we're at then?" Tim asked.

There were nods and thumbs up of agreement, along with a choir of 'yesses.'

"Hope I don't see any of you until tomorrow…."

Michel had a short meeting with Walt at the midtown office building in the multipurpose room, with their bloodsworn humans, much like the clan All Call..

"Thank you for taking the time out of your day to meet with me. We've got a developing situation that is effecting Virehnai. VarenCorp is dealing with it on our end. There's not much that will impact you, as our bloodsworn allies. Here are the two things that will:"

"First, normal procedure regarding blood donation will change. Normally, if you don't feel well, you simply don't provide blood that day and reschedule. For right now, though, if you aren't feeling well, we'd like to ask you to report it to HR, or my office."

"Second, with our developing situation, you'll notice that we will be tightening up our security. If you notice anything odd; if someone approaches you and wants you to do something not ethically correct, asks you to bend the rules 'just this once,' or wants you to 'look the other way,' I'd like to ask you to report it. We're all adults; we're not tattletales, but this is…different. Any reports will be kept in the strictest of confidence. We're in the middle of an emergency, and those actions will help. So to recap – if you're feeling unwell, call our HR callout line, or me. If someone asks you to bend rules, or wants you to do something unethical, or if you see or notice something that doesn't seem right - call my office and talk to Emily or myself. Thanks again. That's all I have for you. You're dismissed."

People got up and were walking out. Walt stood and waited for Michel. "Can we talk in your office for a few minutes?" Michel asked.

"Sure."

They walked to the elevator and took it down a few floors to Walt's office. Both of them went in, and Walt shut the door behind them. Walt's office was full of pictures of his family, college degrees, art projects his kids made for him over the years, along with law books, and a variety of certificates and his degrees on the walls. The huge antique walnut desk and the comfy chairs in front of it were welcoming. Michel took a seat in one of them.

"Earlier, I had an All Call with all the Virehnai; we've got sick Virehnai."

"What? What do you mean by sick?"

"They're aging, and as they age, they turn into…indiscriminate feeding machines, caution thrown to the wind. All the cases so far have the same symptoms and are heading for the same result: death. Because we don't know how it spreads…"

"…You need everyone to report if they're not well."

"Correct. I told you about the breaches; we still don't know if they're connected to this directly, or if it's a distraction. Either way, tightening security won't hurt."

"Well, I'll reiterate all that to everyone. Jack told me you're part of VarenCorp's task force?"

Michel sighed. "Yeah. I hate getting involved in their political bullshit, but with something like the current issues going on? I'd rather be part of the solution than wait to see what they'll do." Michel stood to leave.

"Thanks, Walt. I appreciate it, as always." As he turned to leave, he stopped for a minute. "Before I forget, I learned something else; the night those men broke in and attacked Elaina?"

"Yeah?"

"I found out the sole purpose of the attack was to put an RFID tracking dot in her."

Walt's brow wrinkled in consternation. "Who would do that? Why?"

"It's not entirely clear. The only thing we can guess is that they would consider using her to get to me. I told her about it; she said she'd get it taken out. I wanted to let you know about it, though."

"Thanks, Michel. That's a helluva thing…".

Luckily for Tim and Ari, neither visibly reacted during the meeting as they read over the Travers' sisters' ancestry, along with everyone else. One of their ancestors listed, they were all TOO familiar with….that of Vasilisa of Bucharest -and it wasn't in any good ways. She had been a new Virehn when they were in her acquaintance; they found her difficult. It could've been her age, or her background. They never knew for sure or especially cared.

Back when Focaria Rubra was the main Virehnai Inn, social hub, and place where a Virehn in need from either faction could find help, Vasilisa, while visiting, drained someone on property; accidentally, she claimed. Maybe it was accidental, maybe it wasn't. Focaria Rubra had a policy then that carries on, even today, in their hotels worldwide: No hunting on property. It simply won't work; it's not good for business. As such, hungry Virehnai guests, regardless of faction, can purchase a bloodsworn male or female (whatever your preference) to drink from–but you can't drain them. If you're still hungry, you're to release them, and tell them to notify management to "send another." Should someone accidentally drain their human meal provider to where their body can no longer maintain life - the bloodsworn human is to be turned.

Vasilisa didn't adhere to the 'no drain' policy. As a result, they forced her to turn the man, named Hans Gerber. Vasilisa didn't want to sire a child; she had even less desire to take that unwanted child with her when she traveled back home, so she left him in the care of Clan Casimir with a generous bounty for the Clan. Hans became good friends with Tim, as they weren't so far off in age. Ari's great nephew Tim was only ten years older. He took Hans under his wing until Hans died.

Both men said nothing about their ties to Vasilisa during the meeting or showed surprise as they found she had other children who'd somehow survived. After the meeting, Tim went to his office, which was down the hall from Carolyn, locked the door, and called his father back.

"What do you make of that pedigree?"

"I don't know what to make of it. I wasn't aware any of Vasilisa's children survived."

"Me either," Tim said, pausing. "We thought that VAS was likely to be treachery. Could it have anything to do with what happened, or the Tribunal? Should I be worried?"

"I…don't think so. I hope not." Ari replied.

"Is there anyone left alive that was present for my Tribunal?" Tim asked. The more he thought about it, the more anxious he became; of the many things he'd done before the Compact, one in particular he feared would end up biting him in the ass. Tim had mentally seen the Compact as his 'get out of jail free' card. He was now fearing shadows that were mostly in his own mind, and all it took was the specter of his old friend Hans Gerber.

"No," Ari told Tim. "But I don't believe in coincidences, either."

"Sanity check, Father?"

Through the monitor, Tim could see Ari began counting on his fingers:

"Vibia; she's dead, thanks to the French. Vive la France;"

"Aleksandr Philipou–I took care of him myself; my last official act before the Compact came into force. They'll never find him, and even if they ever do, his brains are scrambled muck by now; it's been far too long."

"Diotimus Artimidorus. Gone also, with my thanks to the French;"

"Vasilisa of Bucharest, gone - courtesy of Vibia, pre-Compact, as she culled the Virehnai from the House of Basarab...or so she thought. She'd be pissed to know she missed some."

"Last but not least, Francois Rochat died during the French Revolution, too. There's no one else I can think of; most of those who were at the Inn and were present for your Tribunal died in the Fourth War, or during the French Revolution. It's probably someone in our own clan. All those we knew of specifically who had an axe to grind are all dead, but I think there's someone among us, who has become a malcontent."

"I think you're right, Father. It's not a coincidence. It can't be." Tim sat, thinking for a moment. "Could it be Michel, or someone in his clan? Aleksandr is his brother; Diotimus was his sire, and he was good friends with Vibia. Through Aleksandr, he had ties to the House of Basarab…so to Vasilisa as well."

"No, I don't believe so. We think that way because we're stronger. If the Compact weren't in force, we would act thus. We were never afraid to do what we must, to achieve our goals. You're thinking that way because you think others are capable of what you're capable of. Michel's…weak. He always has been, and it only got worse once Diotimus and Aleksandr were out of the picture. I think he fancies himself to be 'like Vibia.' Wouldn't he be surprised to know what that pit viper was actually capable of?" He chuckled at the thought of Michel learning his 'she-ro' had feet of clay and a matching black heart. "No, Tim. This is the same man who calls humans family and gets all cuddly with them. His newest called him 'Uncle' while still human, and her grandfather was one of his best friends, and a confidant, no less. Michel has neither the grit nor the brains for that kind of response, and the same goes for his clan."

Corinna Beria was a complicated person on the best of days. Most of her clan siblings seemed to think she lived a charmed life.

Bah! Hog swill!

Some of them were actually jealous of her, never once putting themselves in her place. They all know what Ari is like. Why would they think living this close to him is anything to be jealous of?

What they never once thought of was that Corinna spent her entire life as if she were a prima ballerina, dancing upon a tightrope. Stay aloft, live another day. Fall off, and you become like all the others that are dead or discarded. Corinna does—and has always done

- what she must, to survive. Living close to Ari was no picnic. It never was.

Corinna had a long, sordid, complicated history with Ari Cottrell. When she met him in the city of Urmia in Persia so long ago, she knew him as Arjun Khatri. She was a pretty young thing who'd turned his head. Then, her human name was Nahid, named after the goddess Anahita.

Soon Corinna was a conquest. She lost much to Arjun. Her virginity? That was the least of it. Next, she lost her human life. For a while, all was well. Corinna was smart enough to know that nothing was permanent, whether good or bad. The times you wished would stay golden don't, unfortunately; thankfully, the times that are hard eventually end. Like a river, the tides of time are always moving, and are cyclical. If you stand still like a rock in the middle of a stream, you see it wash around you, and like a pendulum, it moves in a predictable fashion. Her wizened old Mamani told her that when she was just a little girl. With her centuries of life, Corinna had seen the truth of her grandmother's words proved repeatedly. Nothing was permanent. Nothing. Not relationships; not situations; not even immortality.

Corrina knew that her good times with Ari would end. She felt it was inevitable, and unlike so many other women before and after her, Corinna shored up her heart, mind and soul and kept the tender bits sequestered, in a place where Arjun couldn't get to them. They were hers; not his. They were not for the taking.

When he -predictably- ended things, Ari didn't have to do away with her, like he had so many others. Because she prepared for the eventuality by sequestering those fragile pieces of her heart and soul away—Corinna took her new situation in stride and gave Ari no pause or reason to end her. She stayed friendly with him...and so lived to tell the tale. Their relationship, unlike so many others, changed from plaything to eventually becoming a trusted confidant.

Corinna had seen it repeat, ad infinitum. Ari usually killed his playthings, human and Virehn alike. He enjoyed finding and exploiting their vulnerabilities, and once he had basically taken them apart and put them back together all fucked up, he killed them.

She understood why he did it; The last thing a paranoid Virehn afraid of being ended needs hanging in the corners and shadows are the ghosts of jilted lovers' past, waiting impatiently for an opportunity to do away with him. He and Alwin spent lots of time floating rumors that Ari's playthings are, shall we say…well compensated…for services rendered. They make it seem like they eventually become 'kept'–with a wonderful life in the place of their choosing, with money coming out of their asses or some other unlikely orifice, all sealed with a non-disclosure agreement. That's what they put out there; truthfully, they die. If Ari and Alwin didn't obscure what happened to them, he'd have no playthings. Who in their right mind would want to get into a relationship with someone, knowing their life is forfeit? No one. In truth, the line of people who want to end Ari is quite long, even if he's removed his jilted lovers out of the picture.

Corinna sighed. She'd been dancing on that tightrope now for a long time. She remembered fondly when the roof over her head was full of siblings and friends of Clan Casimir. It made her life harder…and easier…simultaneously. She missed the interaction and camaraderie, but those were the exact things that Ari distrusted most. To hear him tell it, all those social interactions were merely cover for malintent. Smiles covered malice. Hugs got you a knife in the back. Friendship was looking for ways to take advantage of, or to discover chinks in the other person's armor. Love came with strings, if it was real. Mostly it wasn't real, and it was just a word, covering ambition or expectations that would go unfulfilled into eternity.

She stopped arguing with him, not long after he banned most of Clan Casimir from the house. Most people never see Ari in person anymore. Corinna always knew what she was dealing with when it came to Ari. One hundred fifty years ago, he permanently banned most of the clan from the property. Corinna tried arguing against it; just because he thought his own family was out to get him didn't mean everyone truly was. His response to her? 'That's reality,

Corinna. Surely, you realize this? Come on, you're not young OR stupid. The strong survive; the weak become dust. You know this.'

That was the exact moment she realized why Ari believed the way he did, and why he was the way…he'd always been. Corinna knew it deep down, of course–but hadn't completely connected all the dots, even after all these centuries.

Ari believed that's how people behaved, because that's how he himself behaved. He believed people would treat him badly, because he wouldn't hesitate to treat another badly. In the back of his calculating mind, Ari was always seeking an advantage over another; always looking for a weakness to exploit. Friendship or love was never truly that; he attached strings to everything, and more often than not, the day you stopped being convenient or useful to him was the day you ended up six feet under. The saddest part: most of their clan didn't resent him until they all had to find other places to be, and he drew apart from them.

Fast forward to today; no one visits. Ever. The last time she saw Tim here, in person, was almost a year ago, and Alwin or Hassan always accompanied Ari. How sad to not even trust your favorite.

Corinna was lonely. She remembered fondly when everyone lived at Focaria Rubra, and all the parties and fun evenings in the Great Hall, where you could sit with another Virehn from anyplace, and enjoy their presence and conversation. Corinna saw it as a simple pleasure.

Likewise, Corinna's life had become interminable. When Ari told her he trusted her, and then asked her to remain with him, taking charge of the house, she had agreed. Corinna contemplated the outcomes of his request and didn't especially like her options.

Corinna had been by Ari's side for a long time. If she left his side to go elsewhere, he would then see her as a threat. The only person who possibly knew more of the misdeeds of Ari Cottrell would be Alwin Hoffman. She was certain if she left, she would meet with an accident that was 'incompatible with life.'

If she stayed, Corinna saw her days stretching on and one day becoming indistinguishable from the next. There was always the off chance that Ari would have done away with her, but as long as she 'stayed in her lane,' this would be a safe option. In fact, she realized belatedly that if she willingly left his side, even if she stayed nearby in house elsewhere in Zurich, whether for love, or friendship, he would see it as a threat and still remove her. He would be positive someone would seek to use her to get to him.

Plainly put, today Corinna saw herself as stuck.

She never expected–though maybe she should've - that Ari would feel as if his safety…his whole life…trumped everything in her own life and her own needs. Her own life, as long as it was, had narrowed to 'Keep my house; ' 'Fetch my food; ' and 'Be at my beck and call.' He texted her when he wanted to tell her something. Mostly, she only saw him when he was hungry or horny.

Cherished daughter?

Hah! More like the maid, with benefits. It sucked, hard.

If Corinna realized that back then, she would've run the opposite direction as far and fast as she could. Particularly when she met a Virehn named Otto. Corinna didn't think she stepped out of line; she met Otto while she was lining up their meal for the night, in a bar. She'd gone back specifically to meet up with him later and invited Otto to her own private apartments only. She enjoyed one glorious evening in his company, and they spent it sharing one another.

The next day, Ari was livid, banning her from not only having male callers in…but from meeting up with other males when she left the house. Otto, for all the fun they had, ended up dead. "Your actions leave me vulnerable. They could use you to get to me. Why don't you understand this?" He all but challenged her to defy him; once again, she could leave, or she could stay. Corinna stayed, biding her time.

It was like her Mamani told her. Nothing good or bad lasts forever. The pendulum swings, the tides come in and out, the seasons change. Sometimes, like watching the hour hand on a clock, it's slow; Slow, not stopped. An observant person realizes that, sees when it is readying to change and prepares.

Corinna had been downstairs in 'Ari's lair' cleaning the conference room. The door to the room was wide open. She saw Alwin come down and join Ari in his office, and he saw her. He ignored her, and she continued cleaning; the only time anyone was ever in there was when she brought in someone to share twice a week. She'd go to a bar with locals and spike her own drink (it had no effect). She could either kiss the guy after drinking it, or she would taste it, and then ask her hapless companion to taste it. Either way, she was bringing home their preference: local and male. That's what irritated the shit out of her. They had her picking up men for them...but she wasn't allowed to enjoy anything from them but their blood? Was she doomed to have sex only with her sire whenever he required her, for the rest of her very long life?

The conference room she was in was directly across from Ari's private office, and she always left the conference room door open while she was in there; Ari would perceive it as a threat if it were closed. Her presence was not a secret, particularly since Alwin saw and ignored her. That they were having a meeting wasn't a secret, either.

It was as she was leaving the conference room that she noticed the door to Ari's office was ajar. Corinna could hear what was being said. It's not like she started out with the thought of eavesdropping, and they weren't trying to be secretive. She could hear Ari and Tim talking, and then heard Alwin and Ari talking afterwards. What she heard, she saw as an opportunity. The pendulum was about to swing.

Ari is paranoid on the best of days. She'd never heard him so worried. Tim either. The names they brought up? Vasilisa? Hans? Diotimus? Aleksandr? Francois? She could hear how anxious they were discussing it, and with good reason: Tim should've been beheaded after the massacre in the Great Room at Focaria Rubra, as the Tribunal decreed. All the fun times gradually ended because of that one event; ultimately, it was a series of bad decisions and egos gone amuck. Someone spiked the humans alcohol with Zar 'Quess. For what purpose? There were many thoughts about that, but she had her own.

Ari tried every way he could to make it all go away. He tried to first pass off the Zar'Quess as being accidental; later, he said that Hans made a dosing error. Bullshit on both accounts. Most of their clan siblings thought Tim and Hans did it on purpose because they thought they could get everybody at the party hot, bothered and naked, having sex and drinking from each other right there in the middle of the Great Room, and until today, Corinna believed that too.

All the humans at the party ended up dead that night. Eight Virehnai did, too…at the hands of Tim, Gabriel and Hans, who supposedly experienced a psychotic break because of the Zar'Quess. How it affected her is that she lost two Clan sisters she was close to that night: Renata Aliberti, and Elise Rochat. Gabriel Rochat, Elise's brother, killed Renata. The other two killed all the rest.

Corinna always thought something else was going on that night. Why? Because Renata was one of Ari's playthings, despite her warnings to the woman. Corrina tried warning her that anyone who was too close to Ari for too long ended up dead. Renata looked at Corinna and laughed. "But you're still here… You worry too much. I'll be fine."

Renata Aliberti was nobility; a distant cousin of Vasilisa of Bucharest, and also of the house of Basarab. Some playthings aren't easily disposed of when they become inconvenient. People notice when nobility disappears.

Elise was flirting with disaster as well; she thought herself to be in love with Tim, not realizing that she, too, was merely a plaything. Elise didn't die with the rest in the Great Room. She met her death naked on a bed in a guest room, her neck broken, supposedly after sex gone awry. Ari tried to distance Tim from it as much as he could.

When Diotimus Artimidorus officially asked her about it as part of the Tribunal, she told him that Tim and Elise had a thing, and she'd seen Tim go off with her before everyone else ended up dead. She didn't know how to tell him more plainly that Elise was simply the first of many deaths that night. Corinna heard one of her clan brothers saying later that Ari wanted Gabriel to kill Renata. That told her something about why the affair got covered up. Power and money for the win.

Corinna heard several things while eavesdropping that she hadn't previously known or heard–and she heard them directly through Ari, from Ari's own mouth:

Everything happening now with VAS that Ari talked about in the all call connected back SOMEHOW to everything that happened that night at Focaria Rubra–and Ari and Tim were keeping it a secret NOW...because it implicated both of them. All the people getting sick, turning into ghoulish creatures and mindlessly killing people before they aged and died, landed squarely at their feet. Huh. Somehow, she wasn't surprised. What would the people on the Task Force say about that if they knew?

Until tonight, Corinna had no clue that Vibia Sabina was systematically having the Virehnai of the House of Basarab killed. Who would've thought it? It made her question if the underlying reason Gabriel killed Renata that night because she was from the House of Basarab...or if Ari was tired of her. It made her wonder if Renata's sisters lived or died. Ari knew about what Vibia did, though. Nearly all the Basarabi Virehnai died by poison. Coincidence? Corinna mentally chuckled to herself, as she could hear Ari saying, "I don't believe in coincidences."

One thing she learned today didn't surprise her in the least–but it DID answer many questions. Aleksandr Philipou's rotting somewhere in extended hibernation. He didn't die on the way to the Compact meeting at Bran Castle, as everyone thought. She never thought that. Corinna wasn't aware Ari had done it, but as soon as she'd heard he disappeared him - she knew why. The day of Tim's Tribunal, Aleksandr saw a man coming out of a room named Tasufin al-Dawashir that was supposed to be dead, sentenced by a Tribunal to death 75 years earlier for the potions and elixirs he created, not that Aleksandr recognized him. Ari had the man living there in Focaria Rubra. That Tash had lived was as much a secret as the room he came out of.

The alchemy room that Tash helped Ari create was the beginnings of the chemical conglomerate VarenCorp owned today. Most of what Ari and Tash manufactured back then was illegal; particularly the vile concoction Tash was working on when Aleksandr saw him. It was a blood-based potion called Naq'thel Veyr, which meant "Obedience of the Void." What made it so vile was that it could make any Virehn Ari gave it to become a blank slate. If you ordered them afterwards to perform a task, that Virehn would carry it out, unquestioningly, no matter what the task. Kill yourself? Kill someone else? Turn someone? Fuck a stranger or anyone else on command? Yes, to all the above. Then, as now, it was illegal to create or possess…or make. Or sell.

Once the potion wore off, and whoever they gave it to was back in their right mind, they had a lot to answer for. Their blood remembered their deeds, even if they couldn't…but their blood didn't remember the potion. After hearing everything she heard tonight…she believed Tim, Gabriel and Hans were all given Naq'thel Veyr that horrible night as a test to see what would happen if they combined it with Zar' Quess. That Ari would do that to his own child, and two other young men from his own clan didn't surprise her one bit.

Corinna listened to Tim and Ari, and then Alwin and Ari for a bit, and all three of them were afraid. In particular, they were afraid of VAS. What frightened them most was the potential failure of the Compact.

Going full circle…the Compact, brainchild of Vibia…had also been Ari, Tim and Alwin's saving grace that kept them all from dying the deaths they deserved…and it was not only failing, but apparently, someone who knew more than they let on wanted some long overdue payback.

Corinna quietly left the bunker, deciding to sit in the garden, with Lake Zurich off in the distance. She needed time to think; to plan. As certainly as spring's promise followed the bleakness of winter, she could see change in her future. She would be ready.

The blood forgets nothing, and neither does the river of time. The Virehnai stand like stones in time's currents, believing themselves unmoved. In the end, even stone must yield to that tide. For centuries, Ari, from sheer hubris, thought himself exempt.

"Virehn zuth akret." Corinna said to herself as she watched light dance on the water.

Ari Cottrell hit the button that disconnected the teleconference call with Tim. Sitting alongside him in his office was his long-time personal security agent, bodyguard, and child, Alwin Hoffman. He had been off camera, observing both conference calls and taking notes.

"What a fucking mess," he told Alwin. He'd said it in the first meeting too, but he meant it with every fiber of his being. He was feeling an emotion he'd rarely felt since the Compact was cast: vulnerability, though he didn't voice that to Alwin. They'd known each other long enough. He probably knew already, anyway.

"Agreed."

"What do you think the end game to all of this is?" Ari asked.

Alwin Hoffman was small, wiry, with blondish brown hair and looked to be about fifty years old. He looked at his sire. Alwin didn't hesitate in his answer.

"I think the endgame is the dissolution of the Compact. The question 'why' is harder. There are many who want to see it fail; either they believe we'll be better off without it, or they want to out us to the humans and the Compact won't let that occur." Alwin looked at his sire – also his boss, and unflinchingly gave him bad news; that's what he paid him for. "There's another subset of Virehnai that wants you dead, including many from within our own clan. Also…" Alwin crinkled his face in distaste, "that connection with Hans Gerber and his sire, Vasilisa of Bucharest. That's troubling to me. Those names coming up now can't be accidental. Not during everything going on right now."

Ari closed his eyes as Alwin ticked down the list, even as he continued listing them. "It worries me greatly that the Virehnai sickening and dying are now in DC and Zurich - closer to you and Tim. Why not Paris? London? Chicago? LA? Rio? Any place ELSE? There's a whole wide world out there, yet the cases are getting closer to both of your doorsteps. It leads me to believe you and he are being actively targeted. It might come down to the Tribunal at Focaria Rubra."

Ari sighed. It meant he would go into strategic planning mode. "I was afraid you'd say that. It was the same conclusion I'd come to. I was hoping I was being 'paranoid.'" He said 'paranoid' with emphasis, mimicking one of his daughters. For a moment, it made Alwin chuckle, but it didn't last long, and it never got as far as his eyes.

"No, you're not being paranoid; not in this case, anyway. I think Clans Sabin and Robichaux are both being targeted as well. Should we warn them?"

"No. They're old enough and paying close enough attention to realize that themselves. If they don't, they…deserve their fate. It is and always has been survival of the fittest. Kill or become dust. Michel and Darren know how to play this game."

"Should we move to our Emergency Continuity Plan?" They developed the ECP during the Cold War days; disaster planning while the humans were threatening to nuke the planet seemed…prudent. It's how his basement became a fortified bunker. As a result, Ari made large donations beginning in the late 1940s to the Swiss Red Cross, and other clans had similar plans or arrangements in their own areas. The ECP wouldn't solve the problems other clans were facing now or might face later, but it would solve some of his own and make him feel safer personally. Knowing the Compact was failing made him once again feel as if he were being targeted. It wasn't pleasant at all.

"I believe that would be wise." Alwin said. "We don't know what this is, or how it's spreading. My first thought is to sequester ourselves here. Hunker down. Nobody goes out, nobody comes in. We get weekly shipments of blood delivered to the gate directly from the Swiss Red Cross instead of Corinna finding us locals." He was writing on a notepad in front of him, then looked back up. "Worst-case scenario, we can hunt the red deer on the property." At Ari's grimace as he contemplated the possibility, Alwin snickered, "It's better than nothing."

"You're right, of course." Ari said, his lip curling up in disgust, and his whole body shaking momentarily at the thought. "But that doesn't mean I have to like it."

"We should meet with Corinna and Hassan to let them know what's going on; Are you planning on having another family meeting aside from the All Call to pass along your suspicions to the rest of Clan Casimir?"

"I probably should, but…I'm not sure I want to. I don't want to give the malcontents lurking in our ranks ammunition against me. If they think I am vulnerable or afraid, that only will embolden them. We've got enough problems without adding to them. It still comes down to survival of the fittest."

"Understood."

"I think I am going to come up with a list of talking points to hand out to all the CEO's to discuss with their clans; safety measures on safeguarding their blood supplies, and changing and implementing versions of their Continuity Plans."

He wrote a note down for himself. "I'm going to talk to Tim first to discuss it with him. I'd like to see what his ideas are after he's done talking with folks–particularly regarding thoughts on his "Plan B" meetings. He was going to have one later today to finalize decisions. Maybe he needs to piggyback discussions about the information we want people to know about our emergency plans."

Alwin nodded and stood to leave. "If you text me when you're ready, I'll be here for it."

"Thanks," Ari told Alwin, who frowned a bit when he saw the door hadn't been closed entirely, and made sure as he left that he securely closed the office door behind him.

For the first time that day, Ari was alone. It had been a strange day, for sure.

Ari lived in the modern-day equivalent of a fortress. Around the 1700's, he finally separated his personal home from his enterprises, like the Velascar Company, which later became VarenCorp. The original hotel in Zurich had grown, changed and was rebuilt multiple times to meet modern standards; it hadn't gone by the name Focaria Rubra for centuries.

He lived in what amounted to a secure underground bunker built beneath a private country estate and grounds dating back to the 1600s near Felsenegg, outside of Zurich, with a wonderful view of Lake Zurich. The bunker was built in the 40's as the Cold War raged. Ari wasn't entirely sure of the last time he'd actually left the grounds of his property. It was at least a century. Maybe two? The homes he once owned in Persia, Egypt, the houses by the sea on the Crimean

Peninsula and Portugal he'd long since passed off to his favorite children. He also owned a home and property on the outskirts of Washington, DC, in the Virginia suburbs–not that he'd ever been there. He bought it solely for the convenience of his children and those of Clan Casimir whenever they traveled. The number of people whom he trusted enough to allow in his presence physically was quite small. Relatively few of his children had access to his Felsenegg estate, but knowing his fear of retribution, even those respected his privacy, stayed away and teleconferenced him instead and unless there was a valid reason to be in the same room. Most of the time, there wasn't. He appreciated that they understood.

Even Tim, whom he trusted, didn't have completely unrestricted access to his physical person. Tim was busy running things in DC, and Ari was trying to make sure he was ready to take over the company and be its face, though admittedly, he kept tabs on him by using oathsworn and bloodsworn spies to ensure to the best of his ability that Tim wasn't plotting against him. It wouldn't be unheard of for a son to do away with his own sire to gain his wealth, power, and position. He did it, so why would he put it past Tim?

The three children he trusted most, aside from Tim, were his daughter Corinna Beria and sons Hassan Khalid and Alwin Hoffman. Hassan was his personal assistant and manservant, and Alwin was his long-time personal security chief. Corinna was not only in charge of the house but also procuring their meals. She and Hassan each had their own suite of rooms. He himself had a suite of rooms upstairs, with a balcony that faced Lake Zurich, although most of his time was spent in the bunker beneath the house, where his office was. Alwin had a separate home on the property: the old carriage house, which was a few steps from the main house through the gardens.

Even though these three, he trusted–Ari was always wary, as was Alwin. It came from multiple centuries of lived experience; Ari learned the hard way that there were always humans (bloodsworn or otherwise) and Virehnai who felt wronged or cheated either in business, or personally. Ari wasn't an angel before the Compact came about; Ari was certain that if not for the Compact and Alwin, someone would've murdered him long ago. He always had people gunning for him–but in the lead up to and during the Fourth war, the number increased exponentially. In fact, he wasn't entirely sure he and Tim would walk alive from Castle Bran until the spell enabling the Compact was cast, even with Alwin present.

Were there still people left who would 'take one for the team' and try to kill him, knowing their own life would be forfeit? Probably. He could only think of a few offhand. Were there any smart enough to engineer something like this? Doubtful. Most of the ones who were ever angry enough to do such a thing had been dust for centuries, or he and/or Alwin removed them forcefully from the picture. He remembered the days of unrestrained treachery–and had taken part in his fair share, before the Compact was cast. Ari had always seen treachery as part of doing business: the strong survived; the weak became dust.

Ari sat in his office, letting everything he'd heard and discussed percolate. He was trying to decide how much of what he'd discussed with Alwin he would keep to himself. Mostly, he thought, he wanted to ask Tim for his take on the situation. At first, Ari believed Robichaux was the target. Then he thought the situation between Robichaux and Lambert was merely a distraction. Now, he's questioning whether it's a multi-pronged attack on himself, Tim, VarenCorp and the Compact.

It figures that the problems were all routed through Clan Robichaux. The children of Artimidorus had been a pain in his arse for centuries; maybe someone knew that and was capitalizing on it, much like he thought they'd capitalized on the problems between Michel and David. Ari wasn't heartbroken in the least when he'd learned that Artimidorus had met with the business end of a guillotine in France.

Between the meeting today, and the calls he kept having to field, he was seriously questioning whether he needed to take draconian precautions. That the Compact wasn't working correctly? That was serious; For him? He saw that as a direct threat to his life and person. If only he could figure out the endgame. Was it the illness and death of Virehnai, or was it disabling the Compact? He was going to assume it was both, plus something they couldn't yet see.. Ari knew no other way to look at the situation. Some of the Virehnai he had known longest poked fun at how 'paranoid' he was–including his daughter Hannah–but Ari saw it as being realistic; being prepared. Strategic in his thinking. Now was the time for him to decide how prepared — or paranoid — he should be.

The one thing Ari knew for certain was that he didn't want to end up like those poor bastards he'd seen so far. It was the reason he'd allowed the test of Mercy's Shadow with sick Virehn who were too far gone to bring in safely. He would happily volunteer to drink a vial of Mercy's Shadow over ice long before he would allow himself to be...like...that. A ghoul that couldn't be satisfied, without two brain cells left functioning to realize what they did. The pictures he'd seen, the videos of the carnage were all but bouncing around in his head doing a nightmarish mambo. What his brain was telling him–shouting at him, in fact–was that someone, somewhere, wanted HIM...Ari Cottrell, head of VarenCorp Int'l, Head of Clan Casimir...to be that ghoul. If he slept–it would give him nightmares. Thankfully, he didn't sleep.

Ari made several personal decisions; mostly around food and people. The best thing he could think of doing was getting blood from his OWN sources. He'd thought to use the Swiss Red Cross, but he had no clue who those donations came from. He had bloodsworn that worked throughout his chemical companies–particularly in the small division, called RKS Pharmaceuticals that made drugs that would work specifically on Virehnai physiology. Most of those drugs required either human or Virehnai blood as a base. Because the blood was being used as a component of a medicine that would be given to others, it was as pure a source as it could be and always had been. Ari decided he would divert blood from there to feed himself and his household from. Red deer??? Bah!! Why would he do that when he could source that for himself?

He needed to update Corinna not to bother hunting for food. He picked up the phone and made a call to RKS.

Delivery it is.

Once the meeting ended, Michel headed for his office.

"Hi Em. Field many calls?"

"Only a couple; one from someone abroad in Germany; another who's in Australia, both apprising us of their whereabouts. Nobody self-reported."

"That's good news; if you get anyone self-reporting, call or text me immediately."

"Will do."

"Can you call Howard and let him know I'm back from the meeting?"

"Certainly."

A little while later, Michel heard a tap-tap at his door, which cracked open.

"Come on in Howard."

"What came out of today's meeting?"

"The big news is that there's now a case of VAS in Austria."

"How? Did it spread there?"

"They looked to see where the man had been. In the past three months, he's been to Marseilles, Zurich, and Bucharest. Nowhere near the U.S."

"They don't know how he got it?"

"Nope. Not a clue. It's getting lots of airtime on their news, though. He killed a young couple; the woman was six months pregnant, and he ate the baby."

Howard grimaced. "That's disgusting."

"On the positive side, we're trying to be proactive and have a plan in place should we have large amounts of people who self-report. That's one thing we're all supposed to do—each clan is to come up with a short list of properties that could potentially house folks should we need it."

They heard a knock at the door.

Moments later, Em poked her head in. "I'm gonna snitch a bag out of your fridge; ignore me." She made a beeline for the mini-fridge and snitched a bag out.

"How could we possibly ignore someone as lovely as yourself?" Howard asked her, and then continued, "…But soft, what light through yonder window breaks? It is the east, and Emily is the sun…" Michel chuckled.

Emily ignored Howard best as she could, threw the bag in the microwave, and hit the button, and then turned and made a smart assed 'curtsy' in Howard's direction.

Not letting his remark go by her, she answered Shakespeare with more Shakespeare, countering his Romeo and Juliet with some well-earned Othello. "Heaven truly knows that thou art false as hell."

Michel burst out laughing–the first good laugh he'd had in days. "Emily, one, Howard, zero." They all laughed, even as the microwave dinged, and she took her bag out.

"I'll leave you two now to your schemes…"

Michel laughed and called out as Em closed the door. "Hey, we're saving the world, here…" Michel exclaimed with mock indignation.

They'd had banter back and forth like this countless times over the years, Michel thought. This time, they might actually save the world. Their Virehnai world, at least.

.

14

SWEET REVENGE

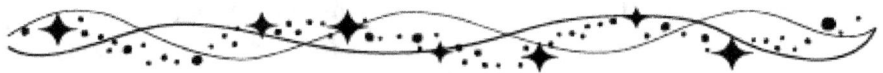

His plan was working like a charm…exactly as he'd intended.

Peter DeBerencourt was at a critical juncture. He had his pieces in play. Robichaux and Lambert were at one another's throats, literally; He knew where Robichaux's newest child was, 24/7, and saw her as a weak spot to potentially get back at Robichaux. Ari and Tim were chasing their tails, trying to keep up. Peter chuckled with a grim glee. Let them sweat a little.

When Raul told him initially what Lambert wanted to do, he realized it gave him an opportunity. It was the same when next, Rob Jacoby asked Malcolm about having his sister and brother whacked. Truthfully, all he needed to do was engineer his 'potion,' called Zuth'kai Morrath, or "The Sweet Reckoning," release it into the wild, and wait for them to tear themselves apart. The lot of them had enough baggage and centuries-buried hostility toward one another that it was merely a matter of waiting for opportunities and then taking advantage of them. Targeting Michel and Howard both got easier once they changed factions. First as a human and now as a Virehn, his 'niece' Elaina would be a good place to screw with Michel. Peter heard he wanted her to still call him 'uncle' after she ascended. How quaint.

Peter waited for such a long time for his opportunity to come along; the timing was fortuitous, and actually, quite gratifying that it was all falling so neatly into place, as if by fate. Finally. The final bit, the final straw, was when he learned Ari was contemplating stepping down and allowing his son Tim to take over VarenCorp, that Peter decided he had to make a move.

He couldn't…no… Wouldn't. He wouldn't allow that to happen. Luckily, fate had decreed that it was 'now or never.'

Actions have consequences, and every effect has its cause—even if the cause isn't clear, and a situation's beginnings are murky. Peter DeBerencourt wanted payback for an event that happened some 800 years ago. Being a Virehn, he had all the time in the world to bring his revenge to pass. He'd hoped that he would see satisfaction when the situation occurred, but Ari Cottrell made sure he wouldn't. Then, the Fourth Virehnai war began, and then came the Compact. Once the Compact came into force, it all but guaranteed that punishment would never come. His heart sunk when he heard that damned witch say that everyone would start with a blank slate. After that, there wasn't much he could do that wouldn't end in his own death, too. Damned Compact. If there would ever be satisfaction, or a reckoning—he himself would be it or engineer it.

Five years before the Fourth Virehnai war, and before they cast the Compact, there was a party at an Inn called "Focaria Rubra," or Crimson Hearth, in the town that would eventually become Zurich, Switzerland. The inn was large, and run by Ari Cottrell—though back then, he went by the name Alban Casimir. The inn had a reputation for hospitality far and wide, and served not only Virehnai, but Knights Templar, pilgrims and travelers of all types…and was a place where Virehnai—any Virehnai, regardless of faction that needed help could receive it. This was based on an accord called "The Concordia Sanguinis"—which was the brainchild of Vibia Sabina Augustus, who was once both wife and cousin to Emperor Hadrian. She had a gift for diplomacy and was trying to stave off future Virehnai wars by breaching the gap between the factions. After the Third Virehnai war ended, the heads of the major clans agreed to the accord Vibia crafted. It helped…until it didn't.

After the Concordia Sanguinis came into being, the Focaria Rubra became a de facto headquarters of sorts, though at the time it wasn't official, like VarenCorp is now. First, it was a Draz'kul stronghold run by Alban and Clan Casimir - but under the Concordia Sanguinis, all Virehnai were welcome, as long as they respected one another, and kept the peace.

The sign in front of the inn showed a flaming hearth with red meat on a spit dripping blood, implying hospitality; the name had a double meaning. Most humans would likely assume the haunch of bloody meat was boar. The Virehnai knew better. Focaria Rubra, because of the adoption of the accord, attracted a very mixed clientele, and it often led to lively parties. The Virehnai, as a precaution, kept their parties private from any other parties that might go on. All humans included in the Virehnai parties were either oathsworn or bloodsworn, and they knew who they were hanging out with. Likely, they were traveling together. Drinking in the Great Room was prohibited, to cut down on faction politics; if you tried it, they banned you. If blood was exchanged a little later in someone's room, no one cared.

It was at one such party, like any other hundred parties occurring there, that the phrase 'actions have consequences' was especially apt, and caused Peter's ire. This party included both humans and Virehnai; not unusual. The humans were bloodsworn, traveling with their patrons, either as their food sources, or as their trusted servants: maybe both, depending on whether you were Sulahnai or Draz'kul–which was standard. The fire was warm on a cold, snowy night, and the alcohol was flowing; not a problem for the humans OR the Virehnai who would feed from them later. Normally, alcohol doesn't metabolize in a Virehn's system. It passes through, unless the human in question's blood alcohol level is extremely high, in which case it's likely to give a Virehn indigestion, or maybe present as 'food poisoning' and make them as sick as if they drank the alcohol themselves. Most of the time, they can tell long before taking a drink that the human in question has had too much alcohol. If they were more inebriated than they looked, the Virehn switched to another source. Much like if a human drinks something slightly spoiled, and it tastes 'off,' they drink something else. Why would someone drink something that doesn't taste right, or might make them sick? They don't, and neither do Virehn.

Normally.

There are many substances that can alter a Virehn's chemistry, and nearly all of them are illegal to possess, or are highly controlled. Most of it goes back to a thorny plant called Ziziphus Spina-Christi or 'thornsap' that grows wild in areas around Israel and down through Mesopotamia, and because there are still Virehn who live in those areas and trade with others, along with the Crusades that were taking place, there were ways to come by it. Even now, there are ways, if someone looks hard enough.

The night of that party, the weather became truly horrible; it was snowing copiously, and everyone was inside. Someone added a substance called 'Zar'Quess' to the alcohol the humans were drinking, which is made with thornsap resin. In a human, drinking alcohol laced with even a bit of thornsap resin speeds up their metabolism, and makes them drunker, faster. If a human unknowingly drinks it, even if they're not drinking to excess, they'll get hammered.

The real reason anyone gives Zar'Quess to a human is because of the effect it has on a Virehn. For a Virehn, Zar'Quess allows the alcohol humans have in their system to take effect on them. A Virehn who has fed from a human who drank thornsap resin-laced alcohol will likely feel a buzz; whether or not they get buzzed, many times it makes them impulsive and aggressive. Some may lose control. Like any compound using thornsap resin, the dosing is critical. A drop or ten– depending on formulation, and what other ingredients are present with the thornsap resin, will either calm the recipient down...give them a good time...or turn them into a raging homicidal maniac. Long ago, an alchemist created the compound that became known as Zar'Quess because some Virehnai missed the ability to get buzzed. It didn't take the average Virehn long to realize you could also use it against an enemy, as an act of treachery. Zar'Quess is one of those thornsap substances that are illegal to possess.

The party in question on that snowy night? All the humans present died, along with eight of the Virehnai. Three of the Draz'kul in attendance killed everyone who died; one of them spiked the humans' alcohol with Zar'Quess. Was it an act of aggression and treachery between factions? Was it simply a dosing error? It could not be determined fully.

Death of humans happens occasionally; it's never supposed to happen within a Virehnai stronghold, regardless of faction, then OR now. This is one of the oldest rules: a version of 'don't shit where you eat.' You don't want dead humans outing a whole stronghold. The party, its mayhem and aftermath, prompted a Tribunal. A Tribunal was a big deal back then, because you needed at least three of the oldest in an area to be judge and jury. There was no Vel'sheth present, so they did without. Luckily, there were two Virehnai at the Inn waiting out the blizzard that were considered Sethari; The Tribunal comprised Diotimus Artimidorus, Aleksandr Philipou, and Alban Casimir himself.

The surviving Virehnai who were present but weren't involved–yet didn't intervene - were fined. That helped with the cleaning bill, which was more than fixing damages to the property. It also included making any humans involved either 'forget' what they saw by paying them off, or 'disappearing' them while paying off the Virehnai who would be 'inconvenienced.' They also made reparations for the families that lost bloodsworn members.

That left the three Draz'kul that caused the deaths of the eight Virehnai. They hotly debated it at the time whether the deaths were 'accidental', particularly once they discovered Zar'Quess was used. The presence of Zar'Quess was the deciding factor, and why there was no leniency for the Virehnai involved. The Tribunal decreed 2 to 1 that all three Virehnai should receive a death sentence. Normally, this would be carried out by their faction, and the clan head would levy their sires a fine. As expected, the one that voted against the death sentence was Alban himself.

Alban Casimir should've waited to hold the Tribunal until the weather cleared; he should've recused himself because of his over-

271

riding interest in the matter. If he wanted it to take less time, he could've requested that Diotimus Artimidorus and Aleksandar Philippou wait at the inn until they could find a third Sethari with no stake in the matter at hand to act as judge. He did none of those things.

Why? It wasn't in his interest to wait. That meant Alban Casimir would be both judging AND carrying out the sentence, as the oldest of the Virehnai present. Focaria Rubra was not only Alban's establishment, but it was Clan Casimir's stronghold, and he himself was head of Clan Casimir. The three Draz'kul sentenced were Gabriel Rochat, Hans Gerber, and Tobias Warrich, all from his clan. More importantly, Alban was Tobias Warrich's sire.

It was determined that Hans Gerber was the one who spiked the alcohol with Zar'Quess. Even his own clan knew that couldn't have happened without Tobias knowing about it; none there were brave enough to dare voice that thought. Even then, Alban was vengeful and brutal; the way others felt they couldn't speak out about it was one more reason he shouldn't have judged his own son's case.

What resulted should never have happened the way it did. While two of the Virehnai charged received their punishment, Alban's own child, Tobias, then around 50 years of age, didn't. Not only were Alban and Tobias sire and child, but they were biologically related. Alban doted on him as he was his only living biological relation; he couldn't, wouldn't, kill someone with familial ties that he cared for. Alban instead delayed Tobias' sentence, promising everyone, including the others who were part of the Tribunal, that he would receive his sentence. He never did. The names change, but that Alban, long accustomed to using his position, age and power to get his own way never did, and likely never will. Today, Alban is better known as Ari, and the child who never received that punishment is now known as Timothy Wagner.

Thinking of it prompted Peter to anger.

At the time of the incident, Peter's name was Francois Rochat...and Ari beheaded his son Gabriel for his part in the bloodshed. It was unfortunate that Gabriel had been involved at all, and Peter always questioned: if he hadn't been friends with Tobias, would it have still happened? Peter hated that his son Gabriel paid a price Alban wasn't willing to dole out to his own child. That hurt; he wanted Tobias' sentence to be carried out, too. It was only fair.

It was worse, however. Peter didn't lose one child the night of that accursed party—he lost two. His daughter Elise was 'collateral damage.' In nearly every way, Elise's death hurt worse. Gabriel died because he took part in the bloodshed...ill-advised, and he paid for his stupidity. It was unfortunate.

His child Elise was not only his clan daughter but was his biological granddaughter. She was simply an attendee at the party, smitten by Tobias' good looks. Gabriel, Hans, Tobias, and Elise had been friends, and Elise looked up to Tobias, even imagining herself in love with him - which contributed to her demise. He'd warned her not to get too close to him, but she chose to ignore him. They were all of a similar age.

His beautiful Elise died at the hands of Tobias that night; she didn't die as the others had, in the Great Hall. They found her much later in an upstairs chamber, mostly nude, choked, drained, and finally impaled. The manner and position in which they found her implied she had been intimate with someone and killed amid that intimacy, either out of anger or passion. Many at the party attested to the fact that they'd seen Elise leave—willingly and smiling—with Tobias. Because no one saw her death, and Alban was protecting his son Tobias, nothing happened in Elise's matter, either. Elise was merely another death at the party.

Peter DeBerencourt lost two of his children that day at a party gone wrong. One, an innocent who was murdered, and the other sentenced for a crime committed. All the while - another Virehn - guilty twice over was absolved by his own father. It was a clear abuse of power even then. After the Fourth War, he'd discussed it with Vibia, hoping to have Tobias' crimes and the fact that Alban covered them up to be addressed the day before the Compact was discussed and potentially cast, while all were gathered on the grounds of Castle Bran in Romania.

Unfortunately, Tobias' crimes went unaddressed, along with Alban ignoring his son's sentence. Whether Vibia buried the matter to help bring the Compact to pass, or Alban pressed others into burying it, he never knew. DeBerencourt was angry, aggrieved, and, more than anything else, very patient. He would have his revenge; he merely had to wait for the right opportunity. Opportunity favored the prepared. He would prepare.

Time passed, names changed, but the truth remained. Virehn zuth akret. Someday, all would come to light, and Tim and Ari, and everyone who abetted the cover-up, at last, would be accountable. All he wanted was justice for Elise, then and now.

Peter bided his time as the years passed. As technology expanded, so did his opportunities. He began making children strategically. Two of his best and brightest were his son, Renee Charcot, and his daughter, Christiana Emmorton. He was proud of both.

Renee worked at RKS Pharmaceuticals, a Swiss company in Basel, where he researched DNA/RNA and their roles in virology, and how the technology can make targeted medicines for humans and Virehnai alike. It was a subsidiary of RKS Chemikalien of Zurich–owned by none other than Ari Cottrell, and under the VarenCorp umbrella of companies.

His daughter Christiana was a programmer and hacker. She managed to get a job working as the personal secretary of David Lambert, CEO of VarenCorp, London. As such, she had access to nearly everything that most of VarenCorp's CEOs and directors did. She did a beautiful job of hacking David Lambert, who never once realized that it was an 'inside job,' and wasn't Michel Robichaux at all. It was almost too easy to manipulate David Lambert. It had been Christiana who intercepted the emails between David Lambert and Carolyn Brownell discussing Ari and his plans for stepping down and letting Tim take over. When Christiana told him that, he told her straightaway to resign and come home. By the time Malcolm pointed out Christiana's handiwork conveniently pointing to Michel Robichaux–she was already home.

His revenge, a 'potion' he first dreamed of and then created, took a very long time to come to fruition, but it would be worth it to see.

While he waited for his opportunity for revenge to come to pass, Peter paid attention to science and medicine, and any scientific breakthroughs that dealt with blood. He used his time, waiting for an opportunity…an opening…and holes in their security. He would need all of that, as well as some good old-fashioned luck. After several centuries, science and technology had leapfrogged into all new territory, which finally made his revenge possible.

He'd heard from Christiana that the upper decks of VarenCorp frantically had meetings and were panicking already; the events he'd set in place hadn't even completely ramped up yet. Peter hoped and suspected they would have their hands so full dealing with the fallout that they would be slow to find the true cause, if they EVER did.

His son Renee initially worked for RKS Pharmaceuticals, which is how they met and became friends. Both attended a pharmaceutical convention in Geneva called The Pharma Tech Summit. They were in several sessions together, and in one of those sessions, Renee had presented a paper on gene editing's role in virology, and the role that CRISPR technology (then in its infancy) might play in medicine in the future. Peter chatted up Renee between sessions, peppering him with questions.

Peter admired Renee's casual brilliance and instincts. It didn't hurt that he worked for a subsidiary of a company owned by Ari

Cottrell, either. He aided Renee however he could, as a strategic move toward achieving his goal. First, he accomplished this by bankrolling Renee's work, which naturally drew the men closer.

It was the fateful day that Renee lamented that his life wouldn't be long enough for all the research he wanted to perform that Renee's career trajectory and life decidedly took a radical turn.

Peter revealed his true nature to Renee, offering to make him Virehn—in effect, giving him the ultimate research tool—the ability to continue his work until he felt finished with it. Once Peter convinced Renee that he hadn't lost his marbles, he immediately accepted without hesitation. Peter continued bankrolling Renee's work, and equipped Renee's home with a state-of-the-art lab, and Renee quit RKS Pharmaceuticals as a day job, staying on only as a consultant.

It was quite an investment of time, money and effort. If it had the intended effect, it would be money well-spent. His son Renee had now sired two children of his own, along with hiring several employees to staff his private lab that were bound by blood oaths. He also had—at Peter's direction—several bloodbound humans that were employed at RKS. Renee saw it as a further way of keeping tabs on what RKS was doing with the knowledge and work he developed. Peter saw it as a failsafe way to have access to RKS should they ever need it and didn't bother Renee with the details of what his research might someday do. Renee never asked; he remained focused on his research. If Renee knew anything at all, it was that somewhere, a couple of bad people would meet the fate they deserved, and right a wrong at last.

Peter's first two targets were obvious: Ari and Tim...especially Tim. His other targets were less obvious, but they were justified. He could no longer make Diotimus Artimidorus, who died during the French Revolution, pay for his part in the resulting cover-up, but his sons Michel Robichaux and Howard VanEtters would do. Diotimus knew and didn't stand up to Ari in the Tribunal; Diotimus, Michel and Howard were all present when the Compact was cast. Diotimus particularly, because he took part in the Tribunal and knew the details of the matter; both the crimes that occurred and that Ari didn't carry Tim's sentence out. He should've spoken out against Ari's hypocrisy and Tim's guilt before everyone's slates were wiped clean. Instead, Diotimus chose only to ask how factions would be represented. Tim stood next to Ari, very much attached to his body, and quite alive - unlike his son Gabriel, or his daughter Elise. It was worse because Tim looked Peter straight in the eyes–and smirked. All Peter could think that day was, "Why aren't you DEAD, you smug prick?"

Peter built his compound outside of Basel on the side of a mountain, as well as built deep into it, and it was not only his home, and his Clan's home base; it was where he worked tirelessly on sequencing Virehnai DNA, to learn what was different about it.

He knew all the legends of how the Virehnai were created, magically. There had to be some way to separate truth from fiction. Somewhere in all the stories, and in the memory in their blood, there were seeds of truth. While he knew magic was involved, he needed to figure out scientifically what portions of the DNA in Virehnai blood physically activated the Compact, and which worked via magics. Peter assumed while there would be a magical component, it still MUST have a biological, DNA-based blood driven component. It wasn't all stories; there was cold, hard science involved. There HAD to be; one Virehn passes both immortality and the Compact on to their child as they are made, and the transfer of blood occurs. You can account for many things in a lab, but quantifying magic and the results of spells upon DNA isn't something scientists try to do or believe can be done–particularly human scientists.

He mentally thanked Messrs. Sanger and Gilbert for their work in sequencing human DNA back in the 1970s. It gave him a guidebook and advice on how to do much the same thing with Virehnai DNA. Peter was putting the human genome side by side against the Virehnai genome, mapping out what changed, or even anything that was odd or different, about it. He certainly wasn't the first to think to do that, or even to actually DO it–but Peter was confident that he was the first to see the promise in manipulating

Virehnai DNA and blood as revenge, along with trying to separate truth from fiction, and magic from biology.

He'd been working on his 'potion' for what seemed like such a short time, compared to how long he'd waited for his opportunity for revenge, but it was oh, so promising. What he'd discovered is that some of the so-called 'junk' DNA in humans was actually not junk in Virehnai; somehow, it was active…and by magic, at that. Granted, it was magic so old and powerful that none today could repeat it. First, you'd have to find a Virehnai blood witch, and then they'd have to be powerful enough. Good luck with that. Luckily, Peter didn't seek to repeat it. He just wanted to target the biological components of what made a Virehn a Virehn. What he came up with, he believed, was horribly brilliant–nearly as brilliant as his son Renee. Peter didn't care that there would be collateral damage, Virehnai OR human. No one cared that his own daughter had once been 'collateral damage.' He hated that phrase. "Fuck them all," he thought to himself. Let them deal with it.

Peter looked tirelessly at many viral illnesses–both in how they presented and how they spread. Many were specific to a particular species…like pigs, birds, cats, rabbits or monkeys. Some viruses jumped between species relatively easily; at least compared to others. His research into rabbit viruses led him to further research and studies on the myxoma and caliciviruses. Both were initially lethal to the rabbit and caused symptoms that were decidedly painful and unpleasant before the infected animal died. What he was looking for specifically was a disease that he could bioengineer to become a human disease that would infect its human host, and then allow the portion that would be fatal to a Virehn to lie dormant within the human's 'junk DNA,' not harming the human. Peter decided that the means of introducing the virus would be a simple, gene-edited cold virus. The human, once infected, would experience some discomfort, similar to norovirus, but then they would feel better, and the portion of the virus that would be fatal to a Virehn would lie in wait, dormant and harmless, unless a Virehn fed from them. It wouldn't matter if they were Draz'kul or Sulahnai; all Virehnai had to feed. He had people who could plant well-placed bags of blood.

The trick with using humans as the carrier was first, giving them a sickness that would present, then lie dormant within them. The next trick was getting it to the right group of humans: meaning ones likely to be food for his targeted Virehnai. The biggest trick of all was to accomplish all his goals without permanently poisoning their food supply. It needed to be something that the humans' immune system would naturally reject in a month or two, junk DNA or not.

Research had shown that particularly with Myxoma, when the Australians and Europeans both used the virus to control their populations of wild rabbits, it didn't take long for the rabbits to build a genetic resistance to it. In as far as he could tell from his testing, humans would do the same. He didn't want to create something that, once turned loose, would end up killing them all, including himself. They already had the Compact. They didn't need something worse.

Those Virehnai who imbibed blood from strategically targeted and infected humans as a meal? Sweet Revenge wouldn't be immediate; oh, no. It would take a couple of days to a week to discover something was…off. Their skin wouldn't look right, but it wouldn't be something they could pin down. At first, they'd probably notice it, but ignore it. By the time they could no longer rationalize the skin problems, or the achy joints? Peter assumed they would know something was wrong but have no clue what to do about it; not that there WAS anything they could do about it. He didn't bother making an antidote. Revenge doesn't offer second chances.

Once a target's skin became blotchy and ruddy-looking, and their hair grayed, the next step in the virus' genesis would be that sudden wrinkles, sags and bags appeared. As their bodies begin inexplicably aging at an exponential rate, his pièce de résistance would occur entirely unnoticed: it wasn't only their bodies aging; those were merely external signs. As they took stock daily on gray hairs and aches, all the while, their brains and cranial blood vessels were aging, as well. Humans call this condition 'dementia.' What made this condition worse in a Virehn is along with the advanced sudden aging of their mind and bodies, they would develop an insatiable hunger. As they began aging, their bodies were no longer taking the nutrients they needed from the blood they consumed...which is why suddenly they became so hungry. They were literally starving to death, despite eating. It was a truly horrific combination.

Beyond the aging, and the hunger, an infected Virehn's brains wouldn't be working correctly, either. As a result, their normal restraints regarding right and wrong, along with hunting habits long ingrained, including...caution!...went right out the window. So desperate were they for sustenance, and not in their right minds - they would even try to physically eat those they would drink from.

It made Peter chuckle a little when he thought about it. If the Virehnai had a problem with Zar'Quess, wait until they experienced what happened when Virehnai have fed from someone infected with Zuth'kai Morrath! Those Virehnai would become insatiable feeding machines without a care in the world. By the time the 'gnawing hunger' phase of the disease hit, they were becoming ghouls. Their bodies were rotting around them, and the blotchy, ruddy patches of skin would not only spread body-wide, but become full-blown tumor-like nodules that first oozed, and then bled copiously, along with their eyes, noses, and other bodily orifices. Once those symptoms occurred, it was usually a matter of a couple of days to a week–a week and a half at the longest–and they would be dead. Pleasant? Oh, no, decidedly not. But then again, long-overdue revenge rarely is.

The first humans and Virehnai Peter DeBerencourt infected with Sweet Revenge were his 'homegrown' test subjects that both became Virehnai...and died...all within his lab, as controlled experiments. The next group would be his testing in the 'wild.' DeBerencourt wasn't about to leave the relative comfort of his home and do something as banal as travel, so he paid his growing group of malcontents that were oathsworn and bloodsworn to him to carry out his testing.

The places Peter targeted first were mostly around New York, New Jersey, Connecticut and Central Europe - to include parts of

France, Germany, Austria and all of Switzerland. Reaching some of his specific targets would be more difficult than others. Ari was reclusive and rarely left his home. Once, having been part of Clan Casimir, Peter was confident he knew how Ari would respond. As Ari started questioning how he fed, and the integrity of his sources, Peter felt he would panic; he hadn't had to be nearly as vigilant with the Compact cast. Ari would turn to the safest, purest blood sources he knew: his own, at RKS, where he controlled the purity of the Virehnai pharma he manufactured.

Tim was reclusive also, though not to the same degree as his sire; his spies told him he regularly brought in women to enjoy. Either he would pick up an infected one where he worked, or an infected one he couldn't resist would be planted in his path.

Michel Robichaux and Howard VanEtters, two of the children sired by Diotimus Artimidorus, were thicker than thieves; their security was good, but not impossible to breach. He was blackmailing someone to get to them.

Florrie and Connie Travers were descendants of Vasilisa of Bucharest. Vasilisa irresponsibly sired Hans Gerber and left him to be raised by the Virehnai equivalent of pit vipers. Hans dosed the humans' alcohol that night, leading to the massacre.

The children would pay for their dead sires' sins. Their sires were at fault for setting all the chess pieces onto the board, and into play; covering up the travesty of what happened to his own son and daughter and ultimately allowed Tim Warner to live and rise to power. The thought that his own children died, but Tim didn't…and that it gave that overprivileged asshole the chance to step forward, take his father's place and be in charge of them all? It was a travesty; a total miscarriage of the justice that was supposed to occur, vs. what actually did. It enraged him that such a thing could happen. His final target was Alwin Hoffman; Ari Cottrell's child, personal security, and VarenCorp's long-time fixer. Alwin helped his sire make all of his sins go away; not just the ones against his family. He saw Alwin as a reprehensible troll with no sense of morality whatsoever. Sweet Revenge meant Alwin would at last finally pay all of his debts to

Virehnai and human society, alike. Heaven only knew what ELSE that man helped Ari cover up. Ari and Alwin's deaths alone would go a long way to righting many wrongs.

Peter had to draw a larger net than he wanted, but for some, he needed to include the places they frequently traveled to or had other residences in. The only reason Virehnai could mostly get away with being as open as they were in large metropolitan cities was they had areas within those cities entirely under their control–like the Robichaux's building complex in midtown Manhattan, where one building had mostly Virehnai employees, and the other building housed them–and they controlled the humans living around them with blood oaths and sworn oaths. Virehnai out in the open tried to be loners, or in small groups, and actively worked to blend into their surroundings. The dynamics of large cities, where most of the humans were so busy they tended not to notice other humans helped the Virehn walking among them stay concealed. Even the Draz'kul had residences in major cities for that reason, along with multiple homes in less congested areas.

DeBerencourt, while wanting to take down specific individuals, felt ambivalent about the others that died. If his targets lost people they loved as he had, he was fine with that, too. There would always be collateral damage in any battle, which is why he was pleased that Rob Jacoby wanted to take out his own sister and brother, much in the same way that David Lambert had been easy to manipulate. Both would be knives to twist in Michel Robichaux's heart–as the knife in his own had been.

A curious side effect? DeBerencourt discovered it accidentally when one of the many Virehnai test subjects he'd made and then infected killed one of his Virehnai lab techs–and the infected subject didn't die from the instant karma attached to their blood by the Compact. How curious. He'd accidentally bypassed the Compact! Since he himself wasn't doing the killing, the Compact let him live when he created the Zar'Quess, not realizing that it was a serious challenge to its existence. Lethal? Certainly. Peter was positive, however, if he could bypass the Compact in ONE way, there were bound to be other ways that weren't lethal to a Virehn. To kill a rival themselves, and live to tell the tale? He was positive that someone would pay vast sums of money for such a thing. He had human lab techs working for him that, for a price, would do exactly as he instructed them, with no questions asked.

Finally. Sweet Revenge, indeed.

15

BAD NEWS

Meanwhile, southeast of Zurich, west of a town in the Glaren Alps called Lerchenweg, a Varen named Albrecht Müller was having a…problem…and so was a family camping by Lake Klöntalersee. His attack started early in the morning, before they were even awake. The family comprised a husband, wife and their eleven-year-old son; the father died first; the son ran into the hills, and the mother died next. Mr. Müller then drank and even ate them both, right there in the tent. Their screams as he killed them woke another family camping nearby, who, fearing for their own safety–quickly left, but dialed 117, which is Swiss emergency services, like 911 and 999 - and let the Glarus Cantonal Police know that something bad had happened at the campground.

When the Glarus police arrived, though it took a bit, they found the tent containing a dismembered man and woman, both dead, and secured the scene. They called it in, asking for additional units, along with some investigators, to collect evidence. It was lucky VarenCorp Int'l had mandated the use of AI police scanners. It allowed them to send a couple of bloodsworn police to the scene. As the police and investigators went over the bloody tent photographing and collecting evidence, they found the couple's IDs. Once they realized they were visiting from Lausanne in Western Switzerland, the detective notified his counterpart in Vaud Canton to visit and notify their next of kin, who was the woman's mother.

After a bit, both Cantons realized they had a bigger problem than they knew–as the first words out of the woman's mouth after "God, no…" were "What about my grandson!?"

The Vaud Canton police called Glarus Canton back and soon, there was a helicopter, searching for the missing child. They found him; hiding, frightened–but unharmed; When they asked him who killed his parents, he told them about a zombie, which most of them didn't believe.

As the manhunt for the killer ramped up, other campers nearby were interviewed, and then asked to leave, as the campground was buttoned down; the roads around the area were crawling with local and national officials, and searches were going on both on foot and by helicopter, which was aided by thermal imaging. They concentrated on several small mountain cottages but saw no heat signatures. The bloodsworn officers quietly notified VC Security of the locations, and Virehnai Security Officers from Zurich traveled to the cottages. The second cottage they searched contained Albrecht Müller.

Getting him out–particularly alive - would prove difficult. This was to be a test case. One of the Security Officers was going to use a tranquilizer dart full of a fast-acting poison called Velthar Morruth, also called "Mercy's Shadow."

Velthar Morruth was an alchemical concoction created long before the Compact. It was a fast-acting poison meant to spare someone the horror of dying a long, torturously slow and painful death from poison meant as retribution–replacing it with a fast-acting, painless death. Mercy's Shadow became useless after the Compact, because the act of giving it to someone would cause two deaths…not one.

One idea that came from the Security 'suggestions meeting' was to brew up some fresh batches of Mercy's Shadow. This day…this place…this cabin was to be its first test; Ari had only recently authorized it.

The security people standing in this alpine cabin knew the Compact was 'stretched thin' in the people who were sick. What was completely unknown was whether THEY themselves would die if they used a tranquilizer dart full of Mercy's Shadow on the sick Virehn. Ari gave them the option to use it if necessary, if the Virehn responsible for the murders in the campground was in a blind rage and couldn't be reasoned with.

Unfortunately, that's exactly what they found. 'Zombie' would've been a fitting description of Albrecht Müller. His eyes were wild and dark; his mind and the ability to put two coherent thoughts together had fled. There was blood coming from the sores on his face and arms, along with his eyes, ears and nose. He ran at the first officer who came through the door, and the second officer standing off to the side took aim and mentally told himself that he wasn't killing him—instead, he was saving Müller from a horrific, painful death as he pulled the trigger. His aim was true. The dart hit Müller in the chest, and the force of it being fired from close range made him stagger backwards, stunned. He grasped for the dart and yanked it out...but the poison did its work. Müller fell over in a bloody heap, dead, and at least out of his misery. The officer was alive to tell the tale—if he could. Instead, he was sworn to secrecy.

If only the officer's day had gotten better from there. That AI emergency monitoring system was getting a workout in the Zurich area today. There was a 117 call that came in for a property east of the campground, but west of the town of Lerchenweg, owned by "Albrecht Müller," by a woman screaming 'she's dead,' and both crying and praying...and basically freaking out over something she'd seen.

What had Frieda Wenger seen that horrified her so?

She came to the Müller farm to check on her daughter, Lina Hess. Lina married into the Hess family. She saw them as strange, insular, and cult-like because they lived away from town and kept to themselves to the point of being antisocial. She'd been trying for days to reach Lina. Frieda Wenger did not know what she would find—but what she found was completely unexpected. She had been in Lina's little bungalow only once, though there were six or seven matching bungalows dotted around, like a weird compound. When she pulled up the long winding drive to her daughter's bungalow—

the door was open, and there was a godawful stench. When she went inside, her daughter was on the floor of the front room, lying face down, dead, and missing an arm. Frieda picked up the phone and dialed 117 immediately, flipping out.

They sent officers; the normal Glarus Canton police, along with a few bloodsworn ones. They went from bungalow to bungalow, and into the main house. The bloodsworn officers called VC Security regarding the sheer volume of carnage. There were easily the remains of twenty people, probably more - in various stages of decay. They learned that Mr. Müller was Sulahnai, and he had both oathsworn and bloodsworn humans that both lived and worked on his property there outside of Lerchenweg. Before the Virehnai Aging Sickness made it to Lerchenweg, the farm must've been a lovely setup. They lived in little houses on his property as caretakers, particularly when he was abroad. It was in a meadow in the mountains; it couldn't be prettier. Unfortunately for his family group, Müller got sick, ran out of humans, and because the property was a little more remote, and on the way to Lake Klöntalersee – it took a while for anyone to realize there was a problem–until Frieda Wenger got anxious because she hadn't heard from Lina.

The next Task Force meeting was a late-night emergency meeting. Ari Cottrell briefed all of them about the bloodbaths near Lerchenweg, which might as well have been sitting on Ari's front doorstep.

Then, it was Tim's turn to brief them all on the numbers of Virehn self-reporting. Today there were twenty reported in the US, mostly in New York.

The thing that was worrying Ari and Tim most–aside from the potential of personal retribution, which was looming larger and ever larger in their minds–was that if things weren't handled correctly, the world would notice their presence, at the worst possible time, in the worst possible manner. It was one thing to be outed as 'your friendly Virehn neighbor' that lives nearby, and is just like everyone you know…only not quite human anymore–and another matter entirely to have the bulk of humanity learning of you via those

Virehn who were randomly turning into zombie-like ghouls and leaving behind them a wake of carnage.

"We don't know what this is," Ari told them. "We don't know the scope–other than it's not simply a US problem anymore; it's affecting us here in Europe, too. We don't know how many are infected, or where they'll turn up. We initially thought Clans Sabin and Robichaux might be targets, but now we're not sure if that's true, or if there are many targets. We can't find any similarities between the scenes other than what symptoms they show and what it causes them to DO. An infected Virehn gets sick rapidly, and from all we can tell, from the onset of symptoms to death is around two weeks, and for most, their brain–their cognitive abilities and reason–become compromised before they near death. Once their brain is compromised, death follows hours to days after. As far as anyone can tell, that depends on the individual Virehn."

"What are you proposing?" Carolyn Brownell asked Ari.

Tim answered. "We're not without resources, but we will need help. This situation is dangerous for all Virehnai, regardless of faction. Humans too, whether they're bound to the Virehnai or not."

He paused. "There are Virehnai in the employ of the CDC, and at Johns Hopkins in Baltimore and other research facilities here in the US; there are others that could be useful, employed in helpful places worldwide that could work with these as well."

"Wouldn't that entail revealing our true natures to others?"

Tim shook his head. "Possibly. We're going to have to go further afield, I'm afraid. I'm going to reach out to my contact at the CDC and see if I can get a meeting with the Director of the CDC, as he recommended, and see what happens from there."

The card tucked into her mirror greeted her every morning.

Elaina wasn't sure what she felt, if anything, for Filip, but she was looking to do something different, and she felt like she needed to live a little. She kept remembering how it felt to be in the pool, and the water dripping down her body, making all the little nerves that she never realized she had sing. Elaina wondered if Filip could have that effect on her. Maybe it was ill-advised, maybe it wasn't - but she decided she would go to Sanguinarium Obscura. She dressed in her favorite little black dress, and made sure she was wearing her medallion/key, and then rang down to the concierge in the vestibule that she needed a car to take her there.

Once inside, she sat down, roughly where she'd sat with Amalie, listening to the blues trio that was playing. It wasn't nearly as busy as it had been on open mic night; still; she sat enjoying it. They were quite good. After a while, she heard a familiar voice: just not the one she expected. It was her clan brother, Jake.

"What are you doing here tonight, all alone?"

"Oh, hi Jake." She looked at him as he sat in the chair beside her. "Listening to music. They're good, aren't they?"

"Should I translate that to mean, looking for Filip?"

Elaina laughed. "Busted, sort of. I know what you said, but he seemed like a nice guy. What are you doing here?"

"You met Brioni, right?" He tapped at his medallion. "She and I are dating. Brioni gets off in about forty-five minutes, then.... Well, the rest is none of your business." They both laughed.

"Understood," Elaina told him.

"Do yourself a favor, though. If you run into Filip, be careful. He might be a nice guy. Hell, he probably is - but he's traveling. If he's half as old as Jeff thinks he might be... My point is, you don't know him. There's no one here to vouch for him, or for him to be accountable to."

Elaina looked at Jake. "It's not the first time I've dated, Jake, but I think your concern's sweet."

Jake shook his head. "No, you're missing something here. Okay. So, for example: when I started dating Brioni, I knew of her - enough to buy a medallion from her. Before the first time I went out with her, Jeff introduced me to her, because I asked him to. That's normal. There are lots of ways that Virehn can...uh...fuck with each other while they're fucking. That's a little crass, I suppose, but it's true."

"Dating, and some...of the activities that more often than not go along with it...makes you vulnerable in ways I'm relatively certain you haven't experienced as a Virehn yet and never contemplated as a human. When Jeff introduced me to Brioni, it was officially. By doing that, he's telling Brioni and her clan that I'm someone who's known to him. In our case, we're from the same clan. It was as if Jeff personally, along with the whole Clan were vouching for me, in case I did anything that took advantage of Brioni's vulnerability.

That's why Filip sought an introduction from Jeff. It's bad form for a Virehn to approach another in a social setting without an introduction if you're not from the same clan. Filip was correct in how he approached all the ladies the other night, even if he was...strange...in how he got Jeff's attention. He told us what his clan affiliation is in Prague...but truthfully, he's unknown to us. He's not got local friends here...or a clan or family that we know of locally that could truly vouch for him. And on top of that, there's his age, too. The older you are, the more ways you know to both sense and exploit your partner's vulnerabilities. It makes for great sex, but like anything else, it can be used against you, as well. For him to want to be with you, as new a Virehn as you are, would be like a 50-year-old human hitting on a 14-year-old... Old enough to know the mechanics, but too young to understand the ramifications."

Jake shook his head and laughed. "I don't know if Michel would thank me or strangle me for telling you all that, but in the spirit of 'brotherly love,' you know....I don't want to see you get hurt."

"Thanks, Jake. I appreciate it."

"Lemme see your phone." Elaina handed it to him, and after a few moments of furious tapping, he handed it back. "You now have my cell number in your contacts. Do me a favor? Let me know when you're headed out of here, and on your way home, please?"

It was sweet and annoying, simultaneously, but Elaina agreed. If nothing else, it was nice to be cared about. "I will."

The blues trio ended their set. The next person who came up ten minutes later was playing folk songs on a violin. While he was on his third song, which seemed sad and wistful, Brioni walked over to where they were, and stood beside where Jake sat. "Hiya Jake."

"Hey, Bri." Brioni looked over at Elaina. "You're…." As Jake was about to prompt her with Elaina's name, she told him, "No. Let me remember."

"From Clan Robichaux. Same as Jake." She paused. "Amalie's friend… Elaina. Hi Elaina." Brioni looked at her. "I was so sorry to hear about Amalie. She was a sweetheart. Virehn zuth akret."

"Setha'ra Virehn ka'anel. Thanks."

"You ready?" Jake looked up at her and asked.

"Born that way, babe."

Jake got up, and he and Brioni turned to leave. He paused and looked back. "Call me when you're leaving."

"I will."

The next guy who got up was playing rock guitar. It was pretty; she was watching him, fascinated. Although it was rock guitar, it was solo, and extremely melodic. Within it, you could hear the influences of many kinds of music shining through, not to mention rhythms and styles that were particular to certain areas of the world.

It felt like it was a beautiful travelogue. She was paying close enough attention to the man playing that she didn't realize Filip had come in and was standing beside her watching the man, as well.

"He's very talented, isn't he?" Filip asked quietly. Elaina looked up, and he bowed to her. "May I join you, Elaina?"

"Hi Filip. Sure." He took the chair beside her that Jake left twenty-five minutes earlier.

They sat there, enjoying the music and making small talk. Sometimes it was louder than others. At one point, Filip leaned in close, his lips perilously close to her ears and neck; his warm breath as it met her neck ignited nerve endings all over her body. Elaina's not even sure what he asked about the music; her response to his proximity completely overtook it. He could read her reactions like a book.

Filip looked deep into her eyes, unblinking, and then reached out for her hand and clasped it. They sat there for a few moments like that. Suddenly, he clasped her hand tighter, all the while, not breaking eye contact as his index finger from the other hand made stroked her wrist–barely touching it. Elaina's eyes widened, and she gasped at the sensation, trying to pull away. Still not breaking eye contact, Filip chuckled to himself as one eyebrow went up. What he whispered had almost as much of an effect on her as his breath on her neck did:

"I told you it was my job to make you smile. If I'm going to truly make you smile, we need to go to a booth." He released her hand for a moment, stood, and then bowed to her, and held out his hand again. "Elaina?" Filip asked.

Elaina had dated as a human. She didn't consider herself a prude; she didn't see herself as naïve. She was used to the dating scene. Elaina had been in at least one serious relationship lasting longer than a year, dated many guys, and slept with several of them - as friends with benefits. She'd had a couple of one-night stands, too; knew how they worked, knew that going into them, with eyes wide open, and simply focused on enjoying herself.

As of this second, that was all ancient history.

Elaina heard what Jake told her but didn't realize even a portion of the truth of it until this very second. Every single nerve in her entire body was screaming for her to take his hand, to follow him, and let him do whatever the hell he pleased with her and to her. The feelings overwhelming all of her nerves simultaneously made what she felt getting out of the pool naked PALE in comparison.

Because she hadn't moved yet, Filip sat back down beside her and took her hand again. Before he could speak, she looked at him. "I've not been a Virehn two weeks yet. This...this is all new territory for me."

Filip smiled. "I thought you were quite young. I didn't realize you were that young. You haven't been with another Virehn yet, have you?"

She nodded her head no, saying nothing. He sighed and looked at her. "What, then, shall we do?"

Elaina shrugged her shoulders, smiling at him. "How old are you, Filip?"

"I'm 1245 years old. I was born outside of Prague, and I've traveled all over the world. The things I've seen...the things I've done...." Filip sighed, and smiled wistfully at her, as he reached out a finger to move a strand of her hair away from her eyes. "You have a marvelous life ahead of you, with new wonders, and you will see the world in a whole new way. Every day will bring you something new. Cherish this time in your evolution, truly. The older you get, the less novelty there is. Life is always a mix of good and bad, light and dark–and you will always have a mix. It's a fact, though: the longer you live, the less novelty and wonder there is. You'll discover the cycles and rhythm of life, and leave the wonder behind you, as if you outgrew it. Embrace it while you have it."

Elaina wasn't sure what to say. Before she could think of anything, Filip smiled at her. "I would give you...a gift. I've been called a rogue, a knave and a blackguard many times–and sadly to say, what I've been called...? Well, it has a ring of truth to it. I won't deny it. However, if you'll let me, I'd like to take your hand and lead you over to a booth and give you your first real kiss. When I leave here and go back to Prague, I will know for certain you'll always remember me–because we'll always have that between us."

Filip again stood, bowed, and held out his hand to her. As her body trembled slightly, she put her hand into his and stood.

Together, they walked to a booth. He went in first, and she followed. The booth had seating all around, with a small table; a pillar candle sat, lit in the middle of the table. He turned and closed the curtain, and suddenly, it was very dark, and the candle's warm glow was cast within the small space, growing brighter and dimmer at the whim of the flame. Elaina looked at him, not knowing what to do next, or what to expect. She realized suddenly how out of her depth she was.

Filip sat down on the padded bench. "Sit on my lap and let me hold you."

Elaina walked hesitantly toward him, and sat, as his strong arms pulled her toward him. "You fit within my arms like you belong there."

Before Elaina could say anything, he simply said, "Look."

She did. She looked at him; into his blue eyes.

"See me." He told her.

Filip touched his fingertip to her lip and traced the outline of them ever so softly. It made Elaina gasp, as she tried to stifle it.

Next, he touched the side of her neck and caressed it gently, and she shivered all over.

"You're like a fine instrument that's never been played. What sweetness." He said, as he drew his lips closer and closer to hers, her breath in, his breath out - until their lips were nearly touching. She could actually feel the crackle of energy in the still small space between their lips, and it was building. When his lips finally met hers, it was like a shock to her system, a cascade of sensations radiating out from her lips that traveled in a wave. As she kissed him in return, the cascade of nerves firing in response escalated. As the kiss became more insistent, he explored her lips and plundered her mouth. As they still kissed, his hand grazed her breast, and at his gentle touch, she trembled all over. His lips released hers, and he began gently kissing her neck. Several of the kisses, she felt the tips of his sharp teeth gently touching but not piercing her neck, leaving her incapable of rational thought. At that moment, it was his teeth, and her neck, and nothing else. Or so Elaina thought.

While his teeth were grazing her neck, he gently and slowly slid his hand between her knees, traveling several inches–but no further. This was not his instrument to play, Filip thought. Elaina gasped at his deliberate touch, and she squirmed with anticipation.

As deliberately as Filip's hand went there, he slowly pulled it back away, and he abandoned kissing her neck in favor of kissing her lips again; this time, it was less insistent, and more playful, and Elaina discovered she was quite ticklish as a Virehn, despite not having been especially ticklish before. He was making her laugh, even as they were still kissing.

Finally, he slowly pulled his lips from hers, and he looked at her, smiling.

"I've both given you your first proper kiss and made you smile. My work here is done."

Filip released her, and she stood, straightening her dress. He stood also, and they looked at one another, no longer strangers.

He held his arms open to Elaina, and they hugged. "Thank you, Filip. I'll definitely remember you."

He pulled back from her and looked at her. "Virehn zuth akret. At the end of any day, we only truly have immortality within our blood through each other's memories, good or bad. This was a good one."

They went back out, and there were relatively few people. In fact, there wasn't music on the stage; just several small groups of people talking at different tables. Several of them looked up when they came out of the curtained booth. One of them raised a hand and waved. "Filip!" He waved back.

"I'll be over, Mark." Filip turned to Elaina. "Are you going to stay for a while, or are you leaving? You can join us if you like. It's the same old rabble rousers after a certain point; I've just met these, but there are plenty of us out there, as we sit and rehash the centuries of poor life choices that led us to this place. I told you I've been called a blackheart. They are, too." He laughed.

"I should be leaving." Elaina told him.

Filip bowed to her, and then grabbed, and kissed her hand.

"Until we meet again, fair Elaina..." he said, laughing.

Elaina bowed back at him in much the same way and said, "Until we meet again, sweet Filip."

Filip saluted her, the men at the table called out 'good night' and she walked to the exit. She picked up her phone, as Jake had asked. Instead of outright calling him, she texted him.

"I'm leaving the club right now. Thanks for the advice. Filip was a gentleman. Talk to you tomorrow." Her next text was to the driver, who replied that he was out front. "I'll be out shortly."

Elaina stepped out of the door into the coolness of the night; standing there on the landing, she turned and began the trek down the steps, crisscrossing back and forth down the metal steps. Her footfalls seemed loud, but it was nearly 3 am. No wonder.

Reaching the bottom, she turned to make her way out front to the street, and to the car waiting for her.

Half an hour later, the driver tried texting Elaina and didn't get an answer. He tried texting and calling her fifteen minutes later. Used to people taking their time coming out of Sanguinarium Obscura, the driver was now becoming concerned that she wasn't answering. An hour later, he called the main number for Sanguinarium Obscura.

Late as it was, it took a few minutes for someone to answer the phone. "Hi. I'm Elaina Jacoby's driver. Can you let her know that I'm still out front waiting for her?"

"Reddish hair? Black dress?"

"That's her."

"She left an hour ago. She probably found a different way home," the person told him, trying to be helpful.

The driver called back to the concierge at the residential building.

"Hi Randy. Did Elaina Jacoby check back in? Come home a different way?"

"No. Nobody's come in or out of the building here for nearly two hours. It's a quiet one tonight."

"Damn. We've got a problem. I'm still here at Sanguinarium Obscura, and she texted me an hour ago that she was going to meet me out front and never showed. I just called up, and they confirmed she left right after she called me. She's not answering her texts or cell."

As Elaina walked out to the front of the building, a homeless man stepped out of a doorway and startled her.

"Hey, lady. Got any spare change?"

"I'm sorry, I don't."

"Pretty necklace. Bet it's worth something."

"I don't recommend you try that." Elaina told him as she tried to move past him.

"Oh, no, you say?" The man reached out to grab his arm. She knew what to do, how to handle this; she went over the moves first with Amalie, and then with Jeff.

Before he could make his move, and while Elaina was focused on him, something she hadn't trained for occurred: Someone wielding a 2x4 stepped out of the doorway, and hit her in the head, like he was swinging for the center field bleacher seats at Yankee Stadium.

Lights out.

After they knocked Elaina out, they tied her up and carried her out to a van parked at a meter one street over from the back end of the club. The door opened. Inside were Malcolm and Rob. Malcolm turned to him. "That's her, right?"

Rob nodded.

Inside the van was a large metal dog crate. Malcolm opened it up, and they stuffed her in it, and then padlocked the door closed.
Elaina woke up. Her head hurt; she heard a couple of people she

didn't know, and her brother Rob, talking. What a weird dream. First she was kissing Filip, then there was a homeless guy, and now she could hear her brother talking.

And then, Elaina remembered the kiss from Filip that sent electricity coursing through her body. She remembered walking down the stairs. The homeless guy wanted money and threatened to take her necklace.

It took every ounce of her determination to keep her eyes closed. Instead, she used her senses to focus on her surroundings. She could smell…gasoline. The grease from fast food someone had eaten earlier–burgers and fries, which smelled disgusting. Even if he wasn't talking anymore, she could smell her brother's cologne. She could hear traffic, and the bumps, speed up and slowdown that was common to driving in Manhattan–until she could tell that they went across a bridge. She wasn't sure which. It sounded different than the road had. When they started talking again, she got angry as the words registered.

A man's voice said, "How does it feel? You'll be the master of your own future soon. You're not losing your nerve, right?"

"Hell no, Malcolm! When do we take care of my brother?"

Mentally, Elaina had alarm bells going off in her head. Much as Doug had been a dick to her recently, she didn't want Rob offing him, either.

"Not until we know this one's safely tucked away. Then, your brother will meet with an accident."

She heard a phone ring. A minute later, she heard the man that was doing most of the talking laugh, turn the ringer off, and reply, "I'm sorry. Elaina's not here right now. She's locked in a dog crate and can't take your call right now. Kindly go fuck yourself."

Her brother laughed. He fucking LAUGHED.

The impact of the words–what the other man said, so casually; what her brother said, and what all of it implied, including his complicity in all of this…? It filled her with an urge to strangle him herself. What in the name of all that was holy had she ever done to him that warranted THIS? As far as she knew, the only thing had been getting picked by Michel and the Sethari to ascend. Elaina continued to pretend she was still out cold. The only thing Elaina was certain of was that her brother would pay. If she could do it herself, that would be much better. Maybe they would continue to talk and dig a hole for themselves. Virehn zuth akret, assholes.

Unfortunately for her, they didn't.

Elaina sat there, cramped and unhappy, pretending to still be out cold. She heard one man say, "Take the next left." The van lurched left. After a bit, he said, "It should be up here on the right. Go further down to the end. It's by the piers."

She heard 'Malcolm' tell Rob, "Here's your sister's phone. When you get out of the van, pitch it off the pier into the East River before we move her."

Moments later, the van lurched to a halt, and the engine stopped. The side door to the van opened up, and you could hear several people jumping out.

Malcolm told them to "…be gentle in moving her. Better not to wake her up."

The other men that had been in the van–she wasn't sure who or how many; she was still pretending to be unconscious–actually did a decent job not jostling the cage too much. There were several of them carrying it. No matter what they would've done, the cage would move awkwardly.

Wherever they took her it smelled old; of dust, mold and mildew. Closed up. For a moment, they sat her and the cage down momentarily.

"Where are we taking her in here?" Rob asked.

"This warehouse belongs to my boss. It's unused; hasn't been for years. It's a firetrap." They all laughed. "There is a security guard; mostly he's here to keep vagrants from trying to squat before my boss torches it for the insurance. The idiot spends most of his time sleeping, if he's here at all. If my boss is lucky, he'll burn in his sleep when it finally gets torched." The word 'torched,' hung in the air, and it hung in Elaina's mind as well. That wasn't good; not good at all.

They picked her up and carried her for a while longer. They set the crate she was in down. Elaina heard keys jingling. Moments later, they picked her up again, carrying her several feet.

"Now what?" Rob asked.

Malcolm answered, "We leave her here. She's locked in the crate; We'll lock this door behind us. By the time she wakes up, we'll be long gone. She won't know how she got here...won't be able to get out, and then the building will go up in flames. No one will know what happened to her. They'll wonder if she's alive and left her clan, especially once they find out she went off into a booth with some guy. There's nothing that ties her to this place; nothing that ties you to this place; nothing that ties you to me." Malcolm laughed. "She'll get hungry...at least until she burns to death."

"Are you sure?" Rob asked. "Can't we poison her? Kill her now while she's out?"

"Well...Not really. We have nothing strong enough on us." Malcolm chuckled. "I think you'll find your sister's actually awake, and has heard all of this, though."

"WHAT??!!" Rob was panicking. "Good," she thought, angrily.

"Hi Elaina. You awake?" Malcolm asked.

"I sure as hell am," Elaina answered, her eyes flipping open, and looking at the assholes responsible for her situation. "Thanks, Malcolm. I've heard everything all of you have said. Rob, you're a twatwaffle. I swear to God Almighty that you are. You don't deserve to be a Jacoby. All you've ever received is love…"

"So you say. All I get to be is Doug's fetch and go get it boy for the rest of my life, and YOU get to have all the glory. Fuck off." Rob spat angrily.

"May the rest of your life be alarmingly short," she told him. She didn't know why she said that. It seemed appropriate. "And fuck you, too. As a big brother, you SUCK. Do you know that? Do you know how disappointed Mama and Papa would be right now if they could see you? You are a worthless little prick that was only ever a disappointment to them, and that's all you'll ever be, even if Doug and I are out of the picture. Someday, Mama and Papa will KNOW you're responsible, no matter how hard you try to hide it. By the way, you aren't and never were worthy of becoming a Virehn. You aren't even worth the air you're breathing NOW as a human being."

Rob screamed, grabbing a discarded crowbar from off the floor, and began swinging it randomly at the cage, spending his anger. It dented the cage somewhat, but it didn't make him feel any better.
Elaina laughed at him. "Asshole."

Malcolm decided it was time to assert control over the situation. He waved at Elaina. "Sorry, toots. You seem like a spitfire. Maybe in another life. This one's gonna end here, though. Soon, this place'll go up in flames. You'll die hungry. Sorry about that. It was nice meeting you."

"Fuck you very much, Malcolm."

He waved at her cheerily, and then they all walked out, and she heard the door lock.

Elaina thankfully, cried then; waiting until after the men left her alone. She didn't want to show them weakness.

"What the actual fuck???" she thought to herself. The thing that was raw on her soul was the fact that she was being put through all this by her own brother. He planned that she would die. He laughed that she would be hungry. He KNEW they were planning to torch the building.

Elaina wanted to keep crying, but she didn't.

There was something that Elaina didn't understand but hoped would count in her favor. The RFID tracker thingy that's in her somewhere? Rob seemed unaware, but she knew Malcolm wouldn't be, as he'd helped get it there. Maybe they thought she didn't know about it? Maybe they weren't aware that Uncle Michel knew about it? Elaina was certain she would be missed; even if the limo driver didn't report it, they'd ask questions when she didn't show up for work tomorrow. She focused on that: she was loved, and they would both miss and look for her.

The only thing that worried Elaina that she tried not to dwell on was that they planned to set the building on fire. She hoped they would find her before the building went up in flames. She remembered Amalie telling her that "fire is incompatible with life."

Anger kept her anchored; focused. Elaina spent her time sitting there cramped in the dog crate, contemplating what she was going to do to her worthless asshole of a brother given the opportunity. On the bright side, Rob didn't have the Compact protecting him. She could strangle him with her bare hands and wouldn't die. Bonus.

When Elaina disappeared after going to Sanguinaria Obscura, and wasn't answering texts or calls, the driver of her limo, realizing that something was wrong, called Michel.

"Hello?" Michel answered.

"Hello sir. I'm sorry to bother you, but there's a problem."

"What's that?"

"Your daughter Elaina?"

"Yes?" Michel groaned inwardly. This couldn't be good. This was the type of scenario he'd feared all along.

"I drove Elaina to Sanguinarium Obscura tonight. She texted me she'd be out in a couple of minutes…and then never showed up at the car. When I called the Club, they told me she left right around the time she called me. I checked with the concierge. She hasn't returned."

"Thank you for calling," he told the man.

Michel tried not to go into panic mode; he'd been worried that Elaina would be targeted to get back at him–and that's exactly what it looked like happened. Fuck.

His first call was to Jeff –more than anything, because he'd tasked him to monitor her. Call it a hunch, or paranoia even. There had already been two attacks. What would stop a third?

"Have you heard anything from Elaina?" He asked Jeff.

"No, sir. I haven't talked to her since yesterday. What's wrong?"

"She went to Sanguinarium Obscura tonight. She was supposed to meet the limo and didn't." Jeff groaned, as Michel continued talking. "The limo driver called me to let me know; no one knows where she is, and she's not answering her phone."

"I'm sure we'll find her, Michel."

He answered sharper than he meant to, "I'm sure we will too; I want it to be alive…"

"I'll be up to your suite momentarily after I call Father to let him know. I'm sure he'll be up, too. We'll find her."

"Thanks, Jeff."

Next, he called Jake. "Hi Father," Jake answered.

"Have you seen or heard anything from Elaina?" he asked.

"Yeah. I saw her earlier. I ran into her at Sanguinarium Obscura tonight when I went to pick up Brioni. She was planning on meeting a man Jeff had introduced her to when we all went, named Filip Novotny. I asked Elaina to text me when she was leaving. She did." It got quiet for a minute. "Hang on, Father." Jake said, and then continued, "I screenshotted her message to me. I'm sending it so you can see."

Moments later, Michel received a text. The screenshot Jake sent him implied nothing wrong: It said, "I'm leaving the club right now. Thanks for the advice. Filip was a gentleman. Talk to you tomorrow."

Michel ran his hands through his hair. "Now what?" His deep sigh wasn't necessary, other than he felt wrung out, suddenly. "This is all my fault."

"Why would it be your fault, Father?"

"Because with everything going on, I knew damn well that someone could use Elaina.…"

He remembered, suddenly, that she had a tracking dot in her.

"I've gotta go. Is Brioni with you?"

"Yes, sir."

"You don't have to come up, but if you do, you can bring Brioni." Michel told him and then hung up.

His next call was to David Lambert.

He didn't even say hello. "What's up, Michel? It won't wait until the meeting?

"Huh? What? Meeting?"

"The emergency one everybody on the task force was called to in an hour?"

"What the fuck? We're having a meeting?" Michel sounded panicked and frazzled. A meeting was the LAST thing he needed at the moment.

"Wait...wait. Hold on. You sound..." He paused. "What's up?"

"Elaina's missing. Her driver called me to let me know. She went to a music club, was coming out...and disappeared. We have no clue who took her, or why."

"Oh God. I'm sorry, Michel."

"I don't know if she got the tracking dot out or not, but do you have any of the information that would be useful for us to track her location, assuming she hasn't yet?"

"I do. I remember seeing the frequencies somewhere. I'll get it for you, Michel. I'll help any way I can."

"Thanks, David." As long as they'd known one another, despite the past couple of centuries where they waffled between love and dislike–here, and now, at the moment that counted the most–David was there.

"I'll send you what you need. Do you want me to let everyone at the meeting know what's going on so you can concentrate on finding Elaina?"

"Please."

Moments later, he got a text from David. "It's a UHF RFID with a real time location system, 433 MHz Military grade. Somebody paid lots of $$$ for it."

Michel got another text a couple of moments later, "Call VarenCorp's 911–they probably have access to people and equipment that could help you." He read David's text; his next call was to VarenCorp 911.

"VarenCorp 911; Mitch Raines. What's your emergency?"

"Hello, I'm Michel Robichaux, head of Clan Robichaux. My newest daughter, Elaina Jacoby, was previously attacked twice. Tonight she went to the club Sanguinarium Obscura, texted both her driver and her brother that she was on her way out…and then disappeared. She's not answering her phone. This isn't like her. We believe she still has a UHF RFID tag equipped with RTLS – real time location - in her body. I need help finding her." As Michel was talking, he could hear the man he was talking to typing.

"Let me pull up her file, sir." There was a brief pause while he was reading it. "I can see–her file was flagged because of Amalie Bisset's Compact death, and again regarding a data breach; Normally, we ask that some time passes to make sure the Virehn in question didn't merely need a change of scenery. However, since your child's file has so many flags on it–I'm going to err on the side of caution and send this up the chain and escalate it." More typing.

"I see Detective Patrick Hall was involved in both of the other events. Would you like me to send him out to you if he's available?"

"Please." Michel responded.

"You said she wasn't answering her cell phone. I have her number as 917-555-4319. Is that correct?"

"Yes." More typing.

"I see Detective Hall is available, and I'm...sending him the details right now. Considering all the flags on her file and that he put them there himself, I've also sent all this information to Director Fuller, as well. Where are you currently located, sir?"

"At Building 39, suite 4700."

"Thank you, Mr. Robichaux. We'll have Detective Hall out for you as soon as possible. Once the request is escalated, he'll be running point." As the emergency services operator was updating him, he could hear a knocking at his door.

"Thank you." Michel told the operator, and then hung up. "Come in," he called out.

It was Jeff and Howard. "I just called VarenCorp 911. They're sending Detective Hall, since he's worked with us previously."

"That's good. They're taking it seriously." Howard said.

Michel ran his hands through his hair out of simple frustration. "I have one more call to make; I've got to call Walt." Howard put his hand on Michel's back. "We'll find her."

"I hope so. I've had too many losses already this year." Michel picked up his phone and tapped out Walt Jacoby's number. It rang quite a few times before he picked up.

"Hello?" Walt answered, groggily,

"Walt, it's Michel."

"Michel. What's wrong?" There had to be something wrong. Why else would anyone be calling before 5 am?

"I have bad news. Elaina's missing at the moment; we're afraid it's foul play."

"Oh, no. What can I do to help?"

"Not much, truly. I wanted to let you know. You're welcome to join us in my suite if you want. Remember when I mentioned the tracker she had in her?

"Yes.."

"Did she tell you whether or not she removed it?"

"I didn't have the chance to bring it up yet, and she didn't mention it." Walt told him.

"That could actually be in our favor." Michel told him, hopefully. "She didn't mention getting it removed to me, either. If it's still in her, we might be able to pick up the signal."

"I'll be along as soon as I can. Hopefully, luck will be on our side."

"Hopefully. See you soon, Walt."

Walt's wife Connie was the first to get updated. Next, he called his children: Her brother Doug hadn't seen her for days; Janet flipped out, having talked to her earlier in the day. Rob's phone went to voicemail. "Call me when you get this, Rob."

David Lambert sent the final texts with the frequency information to Michel.

Damn. If he felt like an asshole before, he was feeling it even more this morning after talking with Michel. David was currently waffling between 'Elaina wouldn't be in this situation if not for me,' and 'they wouldn't have an 'easy' way to find Elaina, if not for me.' How David felt varied by the moment.

Would someone…could someone…use Elaina to get revenge on Michel? Yes….but that kind of thing wasn't as frequent as it used to be. David remembered 'the old days.' But that was what was messing with his head most: guilt. He'd done that. He'd gone there; not once, but twice, with Michel's son, and maybe now with his daughter. Even as a 'frenemy,' Michel had showed him more honor and kindness than he had given Michel. How could he have been so easily manipulated?

David Lambert felt like a chump. A prime asshole. Guilty. Culpable. Ah, hell. At least the egregore hadn't taken him out. Thank goodness it was very literal and didn't look at how guilty a person felt–otherwise, he'd be pushing up daisies by now.

He got his parts together and went to the meeting at Headquarters. When he walked in, he noticed the atmosphere was quite tense; the meeting hadn't even begun yet. Folks were already somber. Haunted looking; maybe frightened.

What the fuck caused THIS meeting, then? 'What didn't he know?' he wondered to himself.

He saw Director Fuller, and walked up to him, planning to let him know Michel wouldn't be there. Before David could say anything, Archie Fuller told him, "I know. Michel's daughter. Thank you for passing on the frequencies you found. I think it'll be helpful in finding her. I've already passed on to Ari that he won't be here, because he's dealing with that–and I also let him know that you two were cooperating, and the information you provided him is helping aid in her rescue." He patted David's shoulder. "Really. Thanks."

David took a seat, and the video monitors were populating with faces. He saw Tomasz's face pop up, as head of VarenCorp Europe. He saw all the other 'heads' and 'principals' pop up, along with some monitors being split into much smaller screens – with a variety of people, some he knew, others he didn't. There were many, many more people on this call than he was expecting.

Tim was quite somber as well. As he was walking in, he didn't sit where he ordinarily did. Instead, he sat next to David.

"Hey, Tim."

"David." he acknowledged him. "Thanks for giving that information to Michel. Hope they find his child."

"Me, too. That's a helluva thing to happen before you're three weeks old."

Tim nodded. "After this meeting, I need to get with some of you, and have another short 'Plan B' meeting to update you. And if you don't mind, would you catch Michel up and give him the cliff notes version of the meetings, and then have him call me, please? In fact, depending on how it goes, we may need to do a conference call; we may have some decisions to make, and I'd like your input before that happens."

"Sure, Tim. Not a problem." David paused, and then asked, "What's going on that's got everybody's knickers in a wad?"

Ari's face popped up on the monitor, and the room instantly quieted. Tim leaned over and whispered, "Shit's about to get real."

"I…." Ari shook his head. "I'm not even fucking sure where to begin today. We're in the middle of a shit show, folks." He looked down and then looked back up. "Yesterday, we had the attacks in Lerchenweg. By mid-afternoon, we were seeing our first self-reports. There were twenty-five throughout the day yesterday. Since then, we've had over forty folks report–this morning, alone."

There were scattered reactions. One whistled, there were several scattered expletives muttered, "Merde," "die Scheiße,""Cazzo!," and a spattering of others. Ari ignored them.

"So far, in terms of totals, there are twenty-seven that self-reported in the NY-NJ-Connecticut metropolitan areas; there are forty-one TODAY in the MD-DC and Virginia area, and there are another thirty-two that have reported in and around Central Europe. Fifteen of those are in the area around Zurich. As a total, we've got one hundred twenty-five people that are dealing with Virehnai Aging Sickness, NOT counting those we already have here. I expect the last of the ones that were apprehended at or around scenes will expire soon. As horrible as it'll sound, we decided against giving them Mercy's Shadow, because we're documenting their conditions to compare with all the others."

Ari let that percolate in folks' minds for a minute.

"Also, one of Michel Robichaux's children was kidnapped early this morning, which is why he's not here. The situation is ongoing." Ari shook his head. "I think Michel's being targeted."

"And" Ari said, tiredly, "...we've had two new scenes reported."

Groans followed. "These are spectacularly bad, each in their own way. One is in the Baltimore metropolitan area, southeast of Baltimore, in a neighborhood called Stoney Beach near Fort Armistead. The other is in Laurel, which is a suburb of DC."

He paused. "Where the hell do I even start? At the scene in Laurel, a woman drained and ate her neighbor–a 22-year-old Air Force sergeant, who was living off post. Because he's military, now we've got feds asking questions. They're going to be like a dog with a bone." He shook his head.

"The attack scene south of Baltimore is its own special gift that will keep giving." He smiled, but it looked more like a pained grimace. "We've got him upstairs; I'll show you clips in a moment from his interview. A Virehn named Mark Rotti that's part of Clan Newberry not only drained and ate his next-door neighbor - but he ate her eight cats. Every last damned one of them." Ari looked pained. "The memes..." He shook his head, slowly. "Holy shit. Those memes will NEVER go away. They've taken on a life of their own already on social media."

"Between the heavy social media activity, the military tie, and that the news outlets in DC and Baltimore are questioning whether the 'serial killer' in New York connects with these murders, there are now questions being asked, publicly, about the similarities. If they connect them to the Central European ones–we get perilously closer to being outed at the worst possible time, in the absolute worst possible way. They will only perceive us as a threat to them if we're outed now."

There was stunned silence as Ari let the depth of the issues hang in the air like a bad odor.

"We have several plans being developed. Some, I'm not at liberty to share at the moment; they're still too fluid to put forth. What I can share, I will. Tim, would you please brief us on your 'Plan B' initiative?"

"Sure." Tim sat up straighter; his demeanor changed slightly. He was very well aware that this demonstrated his leadership ability, and he ran with it.

"Several of us here have been meeting; trying to decide what we would do if this day ever came. Well folks, it's here. We've asked many of you for a list of locations that you own that, should the need arise, could house larger groups of Virehnai. We hoped not to need them; that the cases would be few. We're…getting pretty full upstairs. We don't know how VAS spreads yet; some folks who are aware of the Virehnai being held upstairs that self-reported working in this building are getting nervous that they might 'catch VAS' somehow–particularly if it's airborne. Since there are many unknowns regarding VAS–I can't say I blame them." Tim shrugged his shoulders.

"Me and my team are going to be going over the list of properties later, and we'll be picking several. If the property you offered is selected, we'll be in touch with you later today. Our criteria is that they are in a remote location, and that they were once hospitals, jails, retirement communities or asylums. These properties would require fewer modifications overall to safeguard the Virehnai they would house."

"Our IT folks have searched our databases and located bloodsworn and oathsworn allies on record that are or were employed in health fields. Those with experience in dementia and eldercare were flagged, along with those who are virologists, researchers and whose expertise lends themselves to issues encountered with VAS. Several of these are at Johns Hopkins in Baltimore, the Mayo Clinic and the CDC. Our CDC contact has reached out to the Director of the CDC; a man named Dr. Martin Johanssen. I'll be traveling to Atlanta tomorrow to have a face-to-face meeting with him." He smiled. "A show and tell kind of meeting."

Ari spoke up. "That brings us to the video footage Tim's about to bring up. It's the footage of our interview with Mark Rotti. Tim will show this footage to Director Johanssen, after his own personal show and tell."

"You're going to out yourself to this man?" Eliška asked Tim before he brought up the promised interview.

He looked at her and nodded his head yes. "We're to that point, Eliška. I believe it's selectively control who we make aware of us....or be outed to humanity at large. It's a bad option, vs. a worse option."

Eliška Novak looked at Tim. "Wow."

He replied. "For the record, I agree."

Tim punched a button, and people began seeing the interview conducted only hours earlier. He started by narrating what they would see.

"Like Connie Travers," Tim said, "Mr. Rotti called VarenCorp 911 when he realized what he'd done. The interview was conducted in a conference room at the home base of Clan Richardson, which is further south, in an area called Crofton. The neighborhood in Stoney Beach was swarming with police; The bloodsworn officer from the Anne Arundel County Police had Rotti change into clean clothes, while bagging and tagging the clothes that had blood splatter all over them. He thought fast on his feet and had an ambulance come to the house. They packed Rotti up on a stretcher, and EMTs wheeled him out, making him look like a bloody victim headed for a hospital. Instead, the officer took him to his own affiliated headquarters for the interview. That's how Rotti ended up at Clan Richardson, and why the news channels in Baltimore reported that there was a second victim."

"That was good thinking." Director Fuller said.

The bloodsworn officer had his Clan head, Jeremiah Richardson, sit down with Rotti, to ask him questions as the bloodsworn officer recorded it. Rotti looked unkempt; blood covered his face and visible skin, and he was hugging his arms to his mid-section.

"Hello. I'm Jerry Richardson, head of Clan Richardson. What's your name?" he asked.

Agitated and on edge, he answered, "Mark Rotti."

"What clan are you with, Mark?"

"Newberry, out of Chicago originally. I ascended in Chicago, but I was born here in Maryland. I missed home. I'm not affiliated with a local clan. I keep to myself."

"What happened, Mark? How do you feel?"

"Last week, my skin looked…different. Then, I noticed that I ached. A day…maybe two…later, I had gray hairs and wrinkles. I…didn't know what to do. Every day I looked in the mirror, and it was worse. And yesterday, I was SO hungry. It seemed like no matter how much I ate, I stayed hungry. And then I woke up in Mary Louise's house." He looked shocked and stunned. "What I did... Oh, God! Mary Louise was a nice lady. Such a nice lady. She treated me like I was her son. Mary Louise knew I was...not like her...but she didn't care, and she never once asked. I helped her around her house, and we would talk about the books we were reading." He shook his head as he cried, and then asked, "What's wrong with me?"

"You have Virehnai Aging Sickness. What you've described are all the symptoms."

"I'm so sorry for what I did. Poor Mary Louise." His face was bloody from gore and from crying.

"Where had you been recently? Any place out of this area?"

"I went to a Civil War reenactment in Harper's Ferry. I stopped first near Manassas to walk the Battlefield Park at Bull Run. I fought in the Second Battle of Bull Run. At least my gear's authentic." Mark answered somberly.

Then he laughed; it almost seemed manic. Jerry Richardson looked at him. It was odd to see the man switch emotional gears so fast.

"What's funny, Mark? That your gear's authentic?"

"No! I'm NOT sorry about all of Mary Louise's damned cats! I hated those nasty little bastards. They were always shitting and pissing in my garden and hissing at me for looking at them! Those little gargoyles deserved what they got, they did. I won't miss them for one minute. They didn't even taste good, and all that damned FUR getting stuck in my teeth. Those furry little bastards can rot in hell, or wherever it is cats go to."

Tap-tap-tap-tap.

The next to arrive at Michel's suite was Detective Patrick Hall, and Walt Jacoby; they rode up in the elevator together. Howard answered the door. Michel stood and greeted them.

"Walt; Detective Hall. Come on in."

"I was just telling Walt on our way up. I have a bit of good news for you: I talked to Director Fuller ten minutes ago; He authorized anything you need to find Elaina. I have to clear it through him, but I have that direct line."

Michel nodded. "That's good. I'm glad."

"I understand from the message I received you believe she has an RFID tag in her?"

"We know she did. I only found out about it and told her the other day; Elaina probably still has it in her. David Lambert found that info while he was searching his databases for other signs of malfeasance and told me about it." Michel picked up his phone, and tapped and scrolled momentarily, bringing up David Lambert's texts, and then handing his phone off to Detective Hall.

"Oh, that's good. You've got the type and the frequency information, too." Hall shook his head. "You don't know how helpful that is…" He wrote them down in his little notebook and handed the phone back to Michel. "When was the last time anyone heard from Elaina, and who was it that spoke to her?"

"It was a little after 2am. Her last texts were at 2:21 am, to my son Jake, telling him she was on her way home, and then to her driver, at 2:25 am, telling him she'd be down momentarily. That was the last time anyone had any contact with her. Both took screenshots." Again, Michel pulled up the texts that were sent to him and passed his phone back to the detective.

"Thanks." He read through them. "She mentioned Filip Novotny."

Jeff shook his head. "I can't believe she went back there to meet him, after we warned her against him."

"Jake ran into her at the club; asked her to text him before leaving. She claimed he was a 'perfect gentleman.'" Michel told Detective Hall.

"He's visiting from Prague." Jeff said. "We don't really know him; I facilitated the introduction to all the ladies, because he asked me to–but we warned Elaina that he was old; Not as old as you, Michel, but I'd bet he's at least 800 or 900–at least."

While Jeff was explaining how Elaina had met Filip, Detective Hall's phone rang. He stepped away from the group, and was carrying on a conversation with someone. "All right. Thank you."

They stopped talking and waited for Hall to update them. "Elaina's phone's no longer active; the last ping they got off of a tower was in Brooklyn, by the piers north of the Brooklyn Bridge, in an area called Vinegar Hill. That was at 2:57 am."

"Is there even a way to use that RFID in Elaina to help find her?" Michel looked defeated.

"There is, Michel. I can't tell you too much about it. I only know so much myself." Hall exhaled and shook his head. "I can tell you this: one of our R&D groups that has government contracts created some…interesting technology…that not only can we use to locate people in difficult terrains, but it was promising enough that the military's interested, too. While the Search and Rescue unit based out of Brooklyn has some drone units that can be used–they have nothing like this. Most units would have a hard time finding Elaina's tag through a building...much less from the air. This one at least stands a chance: it not only has that RFID with real time location detection, but it can use the local WIFI to help get a signal, too. If we get even a hint of a ping, it will narrow down the search area. Once we narrow it down to a building, we can use hand scanners. Fuller said he was going to talk to his contacts in the NYPD. If we bring our system, they're willing to install it on one of their helicopters to search. If it works, they're making noises like they want to buy a modified version. It could help them locate trapped firefighters in building collapses."

"What next, Detective?" Michel asked.

"After I call Fuller to pass on the location info, we'll head to the main office. We'll take one of the company choppers off the helipad. Fuller's got contacts–he'll use them to get us permission to land at Floyd Bennett Field, where Search and Rescue takes off from. I don't know how long it'll take their folks to get the antenna installed on their helicopters' hardpoints, but VarenCorp created it for ease of use and installation. It'll depend on the avionics guys that are there; it should take an hour, vs. days....so..." As Hall picked up his phone to call Fuller, he stopped for a minute and looked at everyone gathered.

"Be prepared, though; we will not be allowed up in their search and rescue unit. We're on the ground. And the only ones that get to go are you," he said, pointing at Michel, "and you," he said, pointing at Walt, "...and me. Sorry folks; nothing personal. We'll keep you updated."

Detective Hall, Michel and Walt made their way to VarenCorp's main building that housed not only New York's headquarters, but North America's headquarters as well. Walt had been in the building a few times over the course of his life–but not that many. This was a first; considering the circumstances–he hoped fervently it would be the last.

The helipad was on top of the building. Noah Shorngetter was waiting there for them, standing beside the doors with two equipment cases. Once they came through the doors onto the top of the building, a member of the ground crew asked their names.

"Hall, Robichaux, and Jacoby," Detective Hall answered. The man signaled the pilot, who waved them toward the helicopter, and the man from the ground crew indicated they should walk in a straight line to the door. He waited for them as they all got in, and then after they were all seated, the man from the ground crew stowed the boxes, closed the door to the helicopter, and then ran back away...and moments later, they were in the air.

Once in the air, it didn't take them long; they had clearance to land, which Fuller had arranged via his bloodsworn contacts. Ten minutes after they had taken off, they were already landing as opposed to the hour it likely would've taken by car.

The group got out and were met by a bloodsworn detective from Brooklyn named Ray Garcia; Detective Hall got him up to speed while Noah handed off the box containing the antenna to be installed to the avionics crew.

"The only person from your group that is permitted on board will be whoever runs the laptop doing the tracking," Garcia said. "Will that be you?" He asked Detective Hall.

"No; it'll be Noah Shorngetter; he's the guy over there talking to your avionics guys."

"Okay, I'll pass that along to the crew chief, pilot, and flight crew." He turned back to Walt. "As for family, you're going to sit tight right here. We'll have an ambulance on standby near the search area for Ms. Jacoby. I have a medical 'go bag' with blood, bandages and Virehnai painkillers, should she need them. We'll keep you updated, and as soon as we find her, we'll update you."

It only took them 45 minutes to get the antenna attached. By 7:25 am, the search and rescue helicopter was airborne. The triangulation of her phone showed the area by the piers on the East River. It's a tightly controlled area of airspace; close to LaGuardia and near many flight paths. It was one more complication to find her; once they were cleared to enter the airspace, they flew fairly low and started flying a grid pattern as Noah was watching the display on the laptop in front of him. They started with the line of piers at the water's edge and then turned and swept along the buildings and warehouses dotting beyond the piers. They continued zigzagging back and forth. Noah was watching intently, and gasped a bit, as he saw a blip, and then it went out.

"Did you find something?" Garcia asked.

"I think so," Noah said.

"Point out where it was." Noah pointed out on the map to Garcia where he'd seen the blip. Garcia asked the pilot, "Harve, can you double back and fly that last pass again, slower?"

To Noah, he said, "Sing out if you see it again."

Five minutes later, Noah saw the blip, called it out, and the pilot called out the building with the blip to the ambulance that was on standby, as well as sent police units, and coordinated everything rolling to the scene. The pilot found a lot nearby where they could set down, as debris flew up all around. They had to wait for a moment to get out.

The co-pilot jumped out, and opened the door, and nearby was a dilapidated warehouse. Noah Shorngetter and Ray Garcia jumped out. As they ran to the entrance and waited for the police units to arrive, the helicopter lifted back off once they'd moved far enough away from it.

Standing in front of the warehouse door; there was an emergency number to call, and Garcia called it; it was an alarm company that supposedly had a guard on property. The alarm company tried calling their guard but couldn't reach him.

"Who owns the building?" Garcia asked the operator.

"The building's owner is an Austrian company, Schach Immobilien GmbH, of Innsbruck."

"We have an active search and rescue going on, and police need to access the building. We need you to disable the alarm while we're searching."

While Garcia was talking to the alarm company, Noah got out his high-powered handheld scanner and fired it up. He was only getting a weak signal, but then–it was going through walls. At least he was getting something.

Once the police arrived, they used a battering ram on the door. There was nothing to speak of inside the warehouse, except the detritus of years long past. It smelled mildewy and musty. They tried calling out for Elaina, but heard nothing. With flashlights, and the hand scanner that Noah had, they headed further back into the building and off to the right. "Signal's stronger down this way." Noah said.

They were calling out Elaina's name as they headed in the direction that was indicated. Garcia held up a hand. "Shhhhhhh!"

They heard something, faintly. They sped up, heading toward the stronger signal and the sound they'd heard. They came to a locked door. As they were yelling Elaina's name, and could hear her yelling back, a wiry fellow wearing a security uniform that resembled a rumpled sheet came sauntering out of a small office. "Hey, you're not supposed to be in here!"

That's when he noticed some of them wore actual police uniforms, and all of them had guns. He scurried back into his office, and they could see him pick up the phone — presumably to call the alarm company.

"Excuse me!" An officer followed him back into his office. "Do you have keys for that office?" He pointed to the locked door.

"No. Just the outer doors." The guard replied, phone in hand.

"No keys." He told the others standing before the locked door.

One of them yelled, "Who's got the battering ram?" An officer came forward preparing to use it, even as the rent-a-cop came running back out of his office. "You can't do that! Don't you need a warrant?"

Elaina could hear them outside the door, and began screaming, "Get me out of here!!"

"There's somebody in there? How'd she get in there?" The rent-a-cop said, stupidly. They ignored him and concentrated on Elaina.

"Elaina!" Noah yelled. "Are you okay?"

"Sore, hungry and mad, but yeah, I'll be fine."

"If you're near the door, back away from it."

"I'm locked in a dog crate. I wish I could get to the door!"

"Hold tight, Elaina. We'll be in there in a minute to get you out," he told her. "We're going to need wire cutters."

Garcia radio'd, "We found her. We need a stretcher, and wire cutters, pronto." Noah took out his phone, and texted Director Fuller, Detective Hall and Michel that they found Elaina, alive and sore...but safe.

Once Elaina was out of the crate, they introduced themselves and then assessed her condition. She had bruises and dried blood on her head, which she said still hurt. She looked at the stretcher. "I can walk."

"Protocol. For now, humor us, and go for a ride," Garcia told her.

Once Elaina was in the back of the ambulance, Noah and Ray Garcia squeezed in with the oathsworn EMT in the back and were soon in for a surprise.

"Do you have any idea who did this to you, Elaina?" Noah asked.

"I know who did it." she said angrily.

"Who?" both said, simultaneously.

"My asshole brother Rob."

"Your brother did this?" Garcia asked her. Noah's eyebrows went up, but he said nothing.

"Yeah. Rob and three other guys. One of them was part of the first attack on me."

"Do you think you could ID him from a photo?" Noah asked.

"I already did. Uncle Michel showed me his picture after Amalie died." She paused and almost looked as if she might cry. "Please; you gotta let my older brother Doug know he's in danger. Please tell him! I don't know how they plan on doing it, but before they knew I was awake, I heard them. They're planning on killing Doug, too."

"You know for sure that they were planning to kill you and your brother?"

Elaina nodded her head yes. "They said on the drive here before we crossed the bridge that they wouldn't kill Doug until after they took care of me. The last thing the guy told me was that the people who own the building were planning on burning it down, with me inside."

Once they were back at Floyd Bennett Field, where the VarenCorp helicopter still sat, and Michel and Walt and Detective Hall waited, they finally released Elaina from the stretcher. The last thing Noah told her was more a reminder than anything, as he helped her out of the ambulance. "Say nothing else until we're on the helicopter. Too many ears to hear." Sore, she walked to Michel and her father. There were hugs and tears all around. Noah leaned in and said something to Detective Hall, who's eyebrows raised as his eyes widened. He mouthed "wow."

Before they got on the helicopter...Detective Hall stopped Elaina. "Please wait to tell us about your ordeal. It's going to be too noisy, and I need to videotape it." Elaina nodded. and went with the others to board the helicopter.

Detective Hall had to videotape Elaina's interview–especially if what she told Noah was correct; it implied that Rob Jacoby would have a lot of explaining to do.

"Explaining," Detective Hall thought sadly to himself. "If all that was true; if Rob was working with the people from the data breach...the 'Come to Jesus' meeting they would have with Rob would be more like a "You're about to MEET Jesus meeting." What else," he thought, "would they do with an oathsworn person who betrays not only his clan...but his biological sister...one of the Virehnai he's oathsworn to defend?" He'd never seen such a thing. Most take that oath seriously, even if it's not backed up by blood.

When he asked Noah later what he thought would happen to Rob, he looked at him grimly.

"They might settle for putting him into the human corrections system. Or they may hold a good, old-fashioned tribunal and allow the Sethari of Clan Robichaux to decide. No matter what, Rob Jacoby is fucked."

16

A SEASON IN HELL

Noah Shorngetter and Detective Hall, along with Michel and Walt, went with Elaina into a small conference room in the VarenCorp USA headquarters. Noah chose a room that he didn't have to set up a camera in; this room was wired for video and audio, could record from multiple angles, as well as stream to Ari or others in the company if warranted. The interview was being done 'deposition-style,' mostly because of the information Noah had texted Fuller regarding her brother. Without that critical bit of information, they might've concluded that Rob Jacoby was angry at not being given a chance to ascend. The fact that Elaina heard everything she did, recognized a man involved in her attack and knew that her brother was working with them implied they needed to prepare for future actions – whatever forms they might take. It was a betrayal, and they needed to know how deep it went.

There was a knock at the door, and Director Fuller came in and grabbed a chair, sitting down across from Elaina.

"Hi," he told her. "My name is Archie Fuller, and I'm the Director of Security Services here at Headquarters. So you know, this room can record, even if you don't see the camera; I understand Patrick and Noah both told you we'd be recording this?"

Elaina nodded. "Yes, sir."

"Good, good…" He said. "Let's get started then, shall we? For the record, please state your full name."

"Elaina Maria Jacoby."

"Your sire?"

"Michel Robichaux."

"Please tell us what happened that prompted us to need to rescue you."

"Yesterday, I got home from work and decided I was going to go to Sanguinarium Obscura."

"Why were you going there?"

"The last time I was there, I went with several of my clan brothers and sisters. My brother Jeff introduced all the ladies in the group to a man from Prague named Filip Novotny. He was only going to be in town for three more days before leaving for DC, so I went there hoping to talk to him again. I ran into my clan brother Jake."

"I understand from talking to your sire that both of your clan brothers warned you against getting involved with him?"

"That's true. Jake said he was afraid Filip was older than me and had ulterior motives."

"Was that true?"

"Yes, and no, sir. He's 1200 years old, but he was a perfect gentleman. Jake asked me to text him when I was leaving the club, so he'd know I was okay; I did. Then I texted the driver."

"What happened to you that you didn't meet the driver?"

"I left to meet the driver, but a man who looked homeless asked me for money and acted as if he would attack me for my necklace...the key to get into the club. While I focused on the homeless guy, somebody hit me on the head. I woke up in a stinky van, locked in a dog crate."

"Who was in the van with you?"

"I wasn't sure at first. I was kind of groggy when I woke up, but I pretended to be out still. The first voice I heard, and recognized, was my brother, Rob."

Walt gasped; he looked stricken. He was about to speak; Michel put his hand on his arm. Walt knew his sons were angry for being passed over–but he didn't know one of them was angry enough to harm his sister.

"You're certain?" Fuller asked her.

"Oh, yeah." Elaina looked over at her father. "I'm sorry, Papa. None of what I'm about to say next you're going to like." She turned back to Detective Fuller. "I'm sure none of you will."

"Please. Continue."

"They were discussing their plans. Someone Rob referred to as 'Malcolm' asked him if he was losing his nerve. Rob said, 'Hell no,' and then wanted to know when they could kill my brother Doug." Walt gasped, but Elaina continued. "Malcolm told him not until after they finished taking care of me; that they were going to burn down the building soon, and after that, Doug would meet with an accident."

"Did he say how?"

"No, sir."

"Please continue."

"Right before they got to where they were taking me, someone called me on my phone; Malcolm told Robbie to pitch it off the pier after they stopped and got out. Several people carried the crate in. I was still pretending to be knocked out."

"Once they put the dog crate in that little room, Robbie asked Malcolm if it wouldn't be easier to poison me, and he said they had nothing that would work on a Virehn. He said I'd wake up, be hungry, and then burn alive once someone set the building on fire....and then, he told Robbie that it didn't matter, because I was awake anyway."

Noah spoke up. "Elaina, I'm curious. How did all the dents end up all over the crate? Did they drop you?"

She got a sad look on her face. "Nope. When I told Robbie what a piece of shit he was, told him he'd make a lousy Virehn, and reminded him how disappointed Mama and Papa would be, he took a crowbar and beat the hell out of the cage with me in it."

By now, Elaina's father was silently crying. Michel's hand still rested on his arm; Noah put his hand on his shoulder also. All of this was hard for Walt to hear.

"I'm sorry, Papa..." Elaina looked over at her father and started wiping away her own, pink-tinged tears.

He shook his head. "It's not your fault, honey. It never was." He used a handkerchief to wipe his face. "I don't know what's wrong with your brother that he would do any of this."

Director Fuller picked up a folder off the desk his arm rested on. "Elaina. When you were talking to Noah, you mentioned you believed you'd already ID'd the man your brother called 'Malcolm' before. If I show you some pictures, can you please point him out if you see him?"

She wiped her eyes. "Sure," she told him.

Fuller handed her a printed sheet, with the photos of six men on it. Three of them were people whose names came up as part of the "Red Team" breach, including one known to them as 'Malcolm', and three others were random, similar looking men who worked in

Virehnai buildings in New Jersey.

Without hesitation, she pointed to a man in the first row. "That's Malcolm." Still looking at it, she pointed out the other two. "This one," pointing to a man in the second row, "is the one who pretended to be homeless." Elaina pointed back to the first row. "This is the other man that was in the van with us."

Director Fuller took the sheet back from her and put it back inside the folder.

"Thank you, Elaina, for looking at those." He looked over at Walt and Michel. "I'll leave you in these gentlemen's capable hands." When he looked back over at Elaina, he told her, "Do yourself a favor. Take a couple of days off. Spend time with your human family, as well as your Virehnai one."

"Sir?"

"Yes, Elaina?"

"What's going to happen to Robbie?" She didn't ask out of anger or vitriol. She'd seen her father's reaction to the disclosure that his own son had orchestrated the attack. Michel and Walt were both watching to see what he would say.

Fuller looked at her. "I'm not sure yet. It depends on how well he knows the fellows in that van, I think." He sighed, telling her, "That's all we need for now. If we need anything else, you'll be hearing from Noah or Patrick."

Elaina, Michel, and Walt all got up from where they sat and left the room, making their way out of the building.

Noah, Patrick Hall and Archie Fuller all looked at one another. "She ID'd all three of them; not simply 'Malcolm.'"

By now, it was nearly 11 am. Archie picked up the phone and called his assistant, Tina, leaving it on speakerphone. "Can you do me a favor?"

"Certainly, sir."

"Can you check to see if Rob Jacoby came to work today, and if he's logged into any systems?"

"Yes, sir. Do you want to wait while I look?"

"Yes, please." There was keyboard tapping.

"He called out sick from work this morning, sir."

"Hmmm. Not surprised."

"Let me check door access records to see the last time his IDs or keys were used."

"Thanks, Tina. I appreciate that."

She was doing a computer search while he waited, and he could hear keys rapping in quick succession. "Good news, sir. He was back into the midtown Robichaux building by 6:30 am by the back entrance; I have him going up the elevator to the 21st floor, and it shows that he's currently in his suite."

"Thank you, Tina." Fuller hung up the phone, and called the security office for Jacoby, Lightner and VanEtters' midtown building.

"Security Office, Evan McArthur speaking. How may I help you?"

"Director Fuller of VarenCorp here. We plan to apprehend a suspect in your building shortly; the key system says he's still in his suite. I need you to put the building and the garage on lockdown, on silent mode."

"Yes, sir. Consider it done."

"Thank you Evan. You don't need to notify Walt; he was here moments ago and knows this is coming."

"Yes, sir."

Fuller hung up and turned to look at Noah and Patrick. "Time for Rob to answer some questions." He picked up the radio sitting on the table and asked for several officers to go to Robichaux's midtown building to the 21st floor, Suite 2103, and pick up Rob Jacoby.

"Your point of contact with security is Evan McArthur. I just had the building and garage put on lockdown; Rob won't be going anywhere, but we're not sure what his mental state will be, or how combative, or if he's armed or not."

Howard VanEtters usually spent the evenings either reading or painting. He had a bit of a cottage industry going, as he sold his 'masterpieces' on Etsy. Most of the people he knew had long since grown tired of receiving paintings from him, which is why he resorted to selling them. They collected quickly in his suite.

Howard hadn't expected them to be popular, though! Most of the ones he'd painted and sold on Etsy sold as 'historical recreations.'

Most of them were of things he'd seen and remembered, not that he advertised that. The paintings of medieval Italy, France and England were especially popular. Howard stopped painting pictures of Boudicca; modern day imagery in the mainstream media made her look like a cross between Marilyn Monroe mixed with equal sides of Warrior Goddess and Brittania. Unfortunately for him, he painted her how she looked–which was quite ordinary. What was out of the ordinary was Boudicca's bravery, her resourcefulness, and how intelligent she was. She paid attention to details. Oh, yeah. She had flaming red hair, too. That stood out. He found her engaging, but he couldn't bring himself to paint her other than she was.

After Michel and Walt went with Detective Hall to find Elaina, Howard went back upstairs. He figured he'd paint for a bit and then go off to work.

He was working on three different paintings in varying stages of 'finished.'

The first was Venice, the first time he'd seen it; It was around 1580, and they were coming in by boat. Seeing it from the water was beautiful; the light that day was extraordinary. He never forgot it.

The second was his son, Edward. This painting was personal and would never end up on Etsy. The only thing Edward did better than sword fighting was creating swords. Edward was a fine smithy. Edward crafted the sword hanging on the wall in his office; Howard used it for ages - until it became a mere decoration. The portrait he was doing of his son was from memory; it was while he created a beautiful sword, etched with an ivory handle and an extraordinarily rare two carat red diamond set into the pommel meant for Louie the Sixteenth. The shades of oranges and reds from the forge framing him gave a beautiful warmth and depth to the portrait. Howard missed Edward.

The third was of Versailles, prior to the French Revolution. There were many things going on in an undercurrent of swirling treachery among the humans; it pulled in many Virehnai as well, including Edward. He'd been there with his sire, Dio, along with Michel, Edward and David, and like waters with an undertow, many there found it hard to keep their footing–along with their head. While he was working on the picture of Versailles, Michel texted him they found Elaina.

Howard was glad they found her safe and relatively unharmed. Apparently, she suffered a minor head injury, but she would be okay. He was as shocked as Michel and Walt that it was her brother who had done all this. Sad that as he's painting betrayals past, he was musing on modern betrayals. It made Howard question what it was about humans or Virehnai that made them prone to betray those they loved.

It was a question for another day, perhaps. It was time to get dressed, grab a mug, and head down to the office. Howard stowed away his paints. He loved the light in this room, and the view it had. His studio was probably the living room for most of the people with a suite with this layout; Howard could imagine no better use for it and its light than to have a studio, indulging himself with memories of ages past.

He pulled out a bag of blood from his fridge and threw it into the microwave. Moments later, the microwave dinged, telling him that his meal was ready, and he carefully opened it and poured it into a mug. Howard took the mug with him to his enormous walk-in closet, and pulled out the clothes he'd wear today, and quickly dressed. His shoulders felt a little tight, but he ignored it. He took his mug with him so he could rinse it out in the bathroom sink and then deposit it in the dishwasher as he was leaving.

What Howard couldn't ignore was that after washing the mug, he went to brush his teeth. When he looked in the mirror, he thought he looked tired, and as he fixed the collar of his crisp white button-down shirt, he noticed he had a mole the size of his thumb just under his collar line that was new. New.

"Well, dammit all to hell and back." He said, aloud, annoyed.

Howard would go downstairs to his office, like any other day, and enjoy a bit of quiet time at his desk before the day got going. He would wait a little while before letting Michel know he was going to self-report. His friend had a rough enough day as it is, without adding this to it. He would tell no one else. He needed no maudlin goodbyes.

Unlike most of the others who self-reported yesterday, Howard had no illusions about cures. Ever pragmatic, he added "double check my will and final affairs" to his day's to-do list.

As he was leaving to go to his office, he turned out the light in his suite, and turned, looking inward on the room, as light came streaming in through the windows - wondering idly if he'd ever see it again, and suddenly was mindful of a Shakespeare quote from Macbeth:

Life's but a walking shadow, a poor player that struts and frets his hour upon the stage and then is heard no more.

"Funny," Howard thought to himself as he took one last look, "humans seem to think that 'vampires' are exempt from death's inevitability; truthfully, we are not. The time spent on the stage is longer, by far; yet we start as humans, and like humans, someday return to dust."

Before closing his door that last final time, he bowed to no one in particular, and said, "To magnificent dust."

Michel, Walt, and Elaina took the elevator down. Michel was going to run back home to change clothes, and Elaina was going to go home with her father, where her mother and sister were waiting to be reunited with her. As they parted ways, Michel reminded Walt not to mention anything about Rob's involvement yet; at least not until he got a call telling him that Rob was in custody.

"I'm sorry, Walt. Try not to let it weigh too heavily on your mind. You did nothing wrong."

"It doesn't feel that way, but thanks." Michel turned to Elaina, and opened his arms wide, for a hug, as Walt waited.

"When you come back home later, come on up to my suite. I've got a meeting to go to from here, I'm not sure, but I should be back by the time you are." They all waved goodbye and parted ways.

He got back home and changed clothes into something more business oriented. He'd missed the emergency meeting while he dealt with the ongoing situation with Elaina. He was still stunned Rob had betrayed his sister and planned to kill her and Doug both. He found it hard to believe Rob would do such a thing solely because he didn't get chosen to ascend. There had to be more. He hoped there would be no more heartbreak in Walt's future–but time itself had shown him that when someone was so utterly capable of misdeeds and betrayals–it often came in multiple ways and forms. Michel hoped fervently not–but suspected there was more to learn. Michel grabbed a bag of blood, and while it was heating, he grabbed a mug out of the cabinet. He carefully opened the bag and poured it in.

While he was drinking his meal, he heard a knock at the door, and moments later, heard Howard call out.

"Hi! I'm in the galley," where Howard joined him.

"Howard! You got the news, right? Elaina's safe."

"That's good news."

"You won't believe it, though. Rob's involved. Rob was working with the people involved with the breach, and not only did they target Elaina, they were planning to kill Doug, too."

"No." Howard said in disbelief. "That's a hell of a thing. I'm sure Walt's gutted about now."

"He is."

It grew quiet, and Michel had a realization. Something was wrong. Howard seemed...sad. Restrained. Michel realized, belatedly, that he'd foolishly assumed Howard stopped in to find out about Elaina.

"Here I am, chattering on. Can I get you a mug? What did you need to see me about?" Michel asked.

"No thanks, I don't need anything." Howard paused for a minute before saying it out loud and making it...real. "I wanted to stop by before I self-reported."

Michel's mind went completely blank.

"No," Michel told him. "You look fine. I don't see wrinkles or gray hair. It's been a rough few weeks, that's all. Hell, it feels like it's been a week today alone."

Howard pulled aside the collar of his shirt to show Michel the new mole. Michel's eyes blinked. He took a deep breath in. It was like a gut punch, and he felt like he'd already had one earlier.

Elaina's situation ended well. This...wouldn't. It couldn't. Air didn't really want to move in his lungs. Michel's heart skipped a slow beat. This wasn't a statistic in a meeting.

This was Howard.

Michel's mouth opened and closed; he was stunned. "I'll go with you," he told him, trying to keep his emotions together.

"Thank you." Michel stood up from the table and came to stand in front of him. With tears in his eyes, Michel roughly whispered, "Virehn zuth akret." He paused, trying not to cry. "What am I supposed to do without you, my old friend? We've been through so much together."

"We have. And what will you do? You'll remember me. You'll say my name often. My flame will live on in you, and in my children, and all of you will pass it along to others. As for me, I will finally become dust like I should've the day I got run through with a sword in Amphipolis, before Dio had another plan for me."

He put out his hand to shake Howard's, and they ended up in a man hug. It got silent as they stayed there like that for a few moments and then resumed a normal distance.

Michel's eyes were suspiciously bright. "Who else knows?"

"Nobody." Howard said, shaking his head.

"You've told no one else yet?"

"No. I wasn't planning to."

"Why not?" Michel looked pained, on behalf of everyone who would want to say farewell. Howard was beloved; for his sense of history, his sense of humor, and his good-natured banter and wisdom.

"Michel, how do I say goodbye to my children? I…I don't know how. It's too much drama. I'd rather them remember me as I was when they last saw me, and I'd rather the same for my last thoughts of them before I've not got a brain anymore. I don't want to have memories of them all crying for me as the last thing I remember of them."

Michel kept a brave face as he traveled with Howard to VarenCorp to turn himself in, but mentally, he was both in shock– and gutted. He and Howard had walked a long road together. All roads lead to an end. He knew that, and he wished fervently it was to a different end; not this one. He'd seen all too well what VAS looked like. He didn't want that for his best friend, but for all the money, power and cache Michel might have had–there was nothing to do to negotiate or bargain this ending away. All he kept asking himself mentally was, "Did this happen to Howard because of me?" He hoped not, but with Elaina getting kidnapped earlier, Michel had to ask the question. It wasn't sitting easy on his heart or soul.

While Michel was there with Howard on the floor that was turned into an impromptu holding area as he was being admitted, Michel felt his phone vibrate. He looked at it briefly. It was David.

He was sure it was a meeting update. He'd call him later. This was more important.

The lady at the desk told Howard she would ask him a series of questions to update his information on their system.

"When did you first notice symptoms?" She asked.

"This morning."

"What symptoms did you notice?"

"I now have a mole that wasn't there before." He pulled at his collar and showed it to the woman.

"That's the only symptom you're exhibiting so far?"

"It is."

"I see," she said, typing. "Do you have next of kin you'd like us to notify?"

"He's standing next to me. He'll notify everyone else."

She turned to Michel. "Can I get your name, sir?"

"Michel Robichaux, head of Clan Robichaux."

"Sir, since Mr. VanEtters is at such an early stage, you or anyone from your clan can visit him if they choose; at least until we see any mental instability or violent tendencies."

Howard looked at the woman. "Other than him," pointing to Michel, "or my son Jeff, I'd prefer no visitors."

"I understand, sir." She typed on her keyboard for a moment.

"What's your son Jeff's last name? Is that.." Before she said it, he finished her sentence. "Garvin."

"Thank you, Mr. VanEtters. Let's go get you a room and try to make you comfortable, shall we?"

Howard appreciated her attentiveness, but he sincerely doubted his next couple of weeks would be comfortable. The only thing he could hope for, he felt, was that they use him and others in the same boat to figure out how to fix the rest of the poor bastards that would eventually get sick later.

Michel walked with him. The room he was in looked as if someone had hastily and recently subdivided it. It was small.

The lady told Michel that he could bring Howard things to keep his mind occupied…but left out the part where soon, there wouldn't be much of a brain to worry about.

He looked at her.

"I'm an artist. Might I be allowed paints and a canvas or two? I have a painting I'd like to finish before I…leave here."

She looked at him and smiled sadly. "Yes, you may." The woman turned, and left, leaving Howard and Michel alone.

"What would you like me to bring for you?" Michel asked.

"My paint box and brushes from my studio, along with the portrait of Edward that I was working on, and a blank canvas, if you don't mind."

"Would you like me to bring it by later today and bring Jeff with me?"

He thought for a minute and sighed.

"Yes, I think that'll be good. Thank you, my friend. For everything. Everything."

"I'll see you later, then."

"I'll see you later." Michel turned and left.

Rob went through a drive through with Malcolm and the others after they locked Elaina into the warehouse and left her there, her fate sealed. After they ate, Malcolm said he'd be in touch, and they all went their separate ways.

Rob got on the subway and headed home. He came in through the back entrance and went up to his suite. He looked at his phone.

There were two messages from his father earlier asking him to call. Rob snorted. He could guess what those were about. He'd probably just figured out Elaina was nowhere to be found and was hoping someone knew where she might be. He laughed as he mentally pictured her angry, crammed into a dog crate.

He'd also got messages from Doug, and another from Janet. Whatever.

Right now, the only thing he wanted to do was get a nap for a bit. He peeled off his clothes, down to his boxers, and crawled into bed. As he lay there before he fell asleep, he was trying to imagine what his world would look like in the future.

Buzz…. Buzz… Buzz.

Rob groaned and rolled over, trying to ignore it, and thought better of it. Rob picked up his phone, looking bleary-eyed to see who the hell was messaging him.

What he read instantly woke him up, out of sheer panic. The message?

From his co-worker Harry: "Hey! I thought you were just slacking today; :) I didn't realize your sister was missing. Glad they found her. See you tomorrow."

"What? WHAT? What does he mean by 'they found her?'" They were NEVER supposed to find her...at least alive. What happened to 'She'll burn alive in the warehouse?'

How did they find her?

He got dressed quickly, in panic mode. He grabbed a duffel bag and threw some clothes into it; grabbed his wallet and keys from the dresser–leaving his phone - and left his suite, not bothering to stop to lock it, even as he heard the elevator ding. Rob felt like he was on borrowed time. He made for the stairwell, and began sprinting down them two at a time, heading for the parking garage.

The oathsworn officers that showed up at the mid-town building checked in with Ryan; the security office was close to the main bank of elevators in the lobby.

"Hey, are you Ryan? Director Fuller sent us."

Protocol dictated that Ryan would accompany them to help with residential control, as well as locking/unlocking doors, and taking the elevator they needed out of lockdown. Ryan turned to the other man working with him today. "I'll be back."

Ryan unlocked the elevator they would use and stood back to let the police officers on first. He got in and put his key into the lock on the panel, switching it to manual mode.

"What floor?"

"Twenty-one. Thanks."

They rode silently to the twenty-first floor, with occasional radio chatter breaking the silence.

When they got off the elevator, Ryan locked it back up, and caught up with the officers, who were already following the room number signs.

When they stopped in front of 2103, mentally Ryan was flipping out. This was one of his boss' kids' suites. Holy shit.

They didn't need Ryan to unlock the door–it wasn't locked; in fact, it wasn't entirely closed. The officers announced themselves before walking in, but they realized Rob wasn't there and had left in a hurry.

The officer in charge, a bloodsworn man named Paul, radioed out, "Suspect is no longer in his apartment."

Paul turned to Ryan. "You're going to need to warn people to stay put in their offices and lock their doors. We don't know what he's going to do when he finds out he can't get out."

Ryan radioed down to his assistant downstairs. "Take the system off of silent, please."

Moments later, little red lights started flashing. For now, they left Rob's apartment and started looking for him. In the hallways, those red lights were bigger, flashed brighter, and there was an audible alarm as well.

Paul turned to the three other officers. He pointed at one. "You: stay up here, in case Jacoby tries to come up and barricade himself in his apartment."

He looked at the others. "The rest of us will head back downstairs." Paul turned to Ryan, "Once we're down, please lock down the elevators again."

"Yes, sir."

Paul turned to the other two officers. "You're headed with me to the parking garage," pointing at one, and then turning to the other, "You'll hang with Ryan downstairs, in case you field any calls where he tried to go into an office or someone else's suite, and to let Director Fuller in. Notify us immediately when Director Fuller gets here."

"Will do."

Meanwhile, Rob Jacoby sprinted across the parking garage to his little red Mercedes. He quickly unlocked it and got in; starting it.

It was then that Ryan had the alarm changed from silent to audible. The alarm sounding as it echoed throughout the garage startled him and then sent a wave of adrenaline through his system as he panicked. He screeched through the garage, hoping somehow to make it out before they closed the garage doors.

When he reached the exit, it was only to discover it was closed. "Shit-shit-shit-shit-shit!" Rob yelled to himself as he put his car into reverse and backed up wildly. His only thought was to park his car in a spot that wasn't his, and then hide under random cars, or inside cars he found to be unlocked. With any luck, he'd keep it up long enough to slip out during the brief moments they took things off lockdown to let police in and out and move around. That's what he did. Rob got out and moved away from his car quickly, and tried to stay low, hoping to stay off the cameras; he knew they were there.

From his vantage point in security, the officer left with Ryan sat in front of the bank of cameras and radioed out to his boss. "Ten to fourteen:" (which was Paul's radio ID) "Please be advised the suspect is in the garage and discovered he can't get out. He parked his car, is now on foot on the northwest side by column G15."

"Thanks, ten."

Roughly at the same time, Ryan was letting Director Fuller, Noah Shorngetter, and Detective Hall into the building. The officer watching the monitors saw when they arrived and called it out. "Ten to Fourteen: Kahuna's on property."

Rob didn't realize the extent that none of his escape plans would work until, while hiding in a mini-van belonging to an employee that left their car unlocked, he knew he was no longer alone. He could hear the radio echoing. Rob didn't know who Kahuna was, and he didn't care to find out. He stretched out lower on the floor. Whoever owned it was human and had kids. There were safety seats in the back, and he realized laying there on the floor, that he was laying all over pieces of dropped cereal, and he didn't want to think about what else could be there. He was trying hard not to think or even breathe.

Rob was listening intently to the radio, to determine how close they might be to him; he heard nothing else because the officer turned his radio down after learning that Director Fuller was on property, and heard it echo throughout the garage.

"Ten to Fourteen: Be advised, suspect is in a gray minivan near Column G13."

As Rob lay there on the floor of the van, suddenly he heard footsteps and tried hard to imagine himself invisible.

Moments later, the minivan door slid open.

"Mr. Jacoby. You are under arrest. You have the right to remain silent, and anything you do say can and will be used against you in a court of law."

Rob tried to scramble back away from the door, but he was trapped.

"Come on out, son. You've got nowhere to go." Rob realized right then how fucked he was. As they put the handcuffs on him, he quietly pissed himself as he cried.

"Fortune favors the bold," Rob loved to quote. It was one of his favorites.

He wasn't feeling especially bold at the moment.

Michel's brain was screaming inside. His heart was breaking for the man he'd considered his brother for over two thousand years.

Before Michel could get too tangled up in his own racing, screaming thoughts, he took a deep breath, pulled his phone out of his pocket, and called David Lambert.

David answered. "Michel. I was just thinking about you. I was about to call again."

Michel was quiet for a long moment, prompting David to say, "Michel? You there? How's Elaina?"

Michel paused. "David. I wanted to let you know; Howard self-reported an hour ago. I came here with him. He's upstairs in holding."

David's breath in drew. "No."

Michel paused. "Look, I know you two haven't talked for a long time, but...I... I...thought you'd want to know."

"I'm sorry, Michel. Virehn zuth akret." David sighed heavily. He'd known Howard for...what? Twelve hundred years?

"Thank you for telling me. Can this day get any worse? And for you, today is likely feeling like a day straight out of the pit of hell."

"It is. You said you were about to call me?" Michel asked.

"I was. I told Tim I'd update you on the meetings, and once I've updated you, he wanted you to call him."

David paused and then asked. "Wait. Where are you? Are you still here at headquarters?"

"I am." Michel sighed heavily, as the day weighed on his heart and soul.

"Everything I mentioned about updating you, and needing to call Tim? That was before finding out about Howard. If you want an update, or hell, someone to talk to–come on up. I'm shoehorned into a temp office down the hall from Caroline. It's not much, but you're welcome. Otherwise, call Tim and let him know what's going on."

"If it's okay, I'll come up for the update. If I spend too much time thinking right now…"

"Understood. See you in a few."

David hadn't over or underestimated the office he was in. There was a desk, a computer, and two chairs crammed into a space that might have comfortably fitted the desk and a different chair.

David's door was open; he stood when Michel came in and came from behind the desk.

"Virehn zuth akret, my friend." The two men hugged one another.

They put any residual ugliness that might've remained between the two behind them at that moment.

"Setha'ra Virehn ka'anel," Michel replied, voice gravelly with emotion. After Michel pulled away, David said, "We shall both say his name often, and his flame will sing within our blood."

Michel nodded, and pulled out his handkerchief, dabbing at a stray, pink-tinged tear, escaping. Michel looked at David. "As rough as this day has been, I have to thank you for telling me about the RFID chip and getting me those frequencies. If it wasn't for you, today might've ended differently for Elaina. She's a little banged up, and there's more to tell of her story; I'm sure Director Fuller has updated Tim and Ari by now."

"What happened? I mean, aside from the kidnapping."

"Elaina's brother, Rob Jacoby, was working with the oathsworn folks that were identified in the original data breach." David's mouth dropped open in surprise. "They worked together, with the ultimate aim of trying to kill not only Elaina, but her brother Doug, too. He betrayed them both; the overarching question on all our minds earlier was how far does his betrayal go?"

"Oh, shit. Your day just keeps giving, doesn't it?"

Michel nodded. "Apparently."

David went back around to his side of the desk and gestured to the other chair. "Have a seat, Michel."

"So, yesterday, when they told us twenty-five people had reported?"

Michel nodded.

"It was up to one hundred twenty-five as of 8 am this morning. There were forty in the Maryland, DC, and Virginia area since yesterday."

Michel didn't know what to say. He'd just escorted his best friend and brother to the holding area upstairs. It was already feeling more real to him than simple numbers.

David continued with his update. "There were also two new scenes reported; some bright reporters in Baltimore are questioning why there are crime scenes there and further north with similar attributes and are linking them.”

“Ari’s having fits over that, I’m sure.”

“Oh, he is. It gets worse, though.” Michel’s eyebrows raised at the thought.

“The one scene includes a dead Air Force sergeant. The other? It was an old lady with eight cats…and he not only drained and ate her; he ate all the cats. That hit social media like a bomb. To quote Ari: ‘Those memes will NEVER go away. They’re taking on a life of their own.’” David paused for a moment.

“Luckily for us, journalists haven’t done the mental math yet and linked what’s going on in the US with the two scenes near Zurich. The big message of the meeting is that ‘Plan B’ is a go, because of the volume of people reporting. Ari and Tim talked about it at the meeting–to make everyone feel better, I suppose. Several of us met with Tim afterward to discuss the buildings suggested. We’ve got a short list of buildings that we need to decide ‘go/no go’ on; There are also two retirement facilities that are up for sale outside of DC. One of them is in the Rockville area; the other is in Manassas, VA. We’re planning on buying one of them, and we need to decide tonight–because Tim and I are flying to Atlanta to meet with the Director of the CDC, Dr. Martin Johanssen, tomorrow morning.”

“We’re hoping to push things through at breakneck speed. We’ve been told by Tim’s bloodsworn contact at the CDC to tell the Director upfront that we’re going to need help from the White House, and the President, and seek a meeting with him.”

“Wow. Going straight for the Oval Office.”

“Well, help from the White House could get us past some regulatory hurdles; might make issues easier with the press, and help delay reporters from connecting those dots. No matter what, we need to put in a letter of intent first thing in the morning with the property we choose, and Tim and I will take a copy with us. What's on our side, we won't have to worry about getting financing; Ari has said it'll get paid for upfront. We can take a cashier's check with us for two-thirds of the amount in earnest money, and write up a pre-occupancy agreement, with the cashier's check for the final third delivered at settlement. The sooner we can move people and researchers in, the better."

"How do you plan on convincing the Director of the CDC to help us?"

David chuckled. "Good old-fashioned show and tell," and smiled a rather toothy grin.

"Really? Ari's going to let you out yourselves?"

He nodded his head yes. "And…get this; Ari has given permission to do something I thought for sure he wouldn't: We're going to use the viral nature of the cat memes in our favor. He's going to allow our interview with Mark Rotti, who ate the crazy cat lady and all eight of her cats to be shown to Director Johanssen, and anyone in the White House we deem necessary."

"I never thought I'd see something like that," Michel said.

"Me, either."

"Should we call Tim while I'm here?"

"It wouldn't be a bad idea. Then you can go home and…"

"What?…think?" Michel said, with sarcasm. "I need to go home, though. I still have to tell Jeff and the rest of the Clan that Howard has self-reported; I'm not looking forward to that. My brain's trying not to think of it as it is. Later this evening, I'll be back upstairs to bring Howard paints and a portrait he was working on of his son Edward. Jeff's probably going to be with me."

David looked intently at Michel.

"Do you..." He paused, looking away...almost reconsidering the question, and then looked back, throwing caution to the wind, and asked anyway. "Do you think Howard would mind if I visited him? Knowing the end he's about to meet–I'd like the air cleared between us. I really would."

"I think he'd like that. If you like, I'll ask him." Michel once again dabbed at the corners of his eyes with his handkerchief.

"Please." David thought for a minute, and said, "I know how we can make this call go considerably faster."

"How's that?"

David tapped a few times on his keyboard. "Look at both properties and tell me what your gut reaction is to each, and which one and why you think it would be the best choice."

David spun his monitor around and handed Michel the mouse. Michel scrolled through each, reading the reasons each property was for sale: both companies were in trouble financially; the lack of cash was showing up in the number of regulations being broken, with the residents being put in harm's way.

The Rockville property, Cypress Hill, comprised seven high-rise residential buildings, and came with its own ambulances, staffed with EMTs and paramedics, and a nice medical center. Cypress Hill's residents were leaving in droves because of the issues the facility was having, and occupancy was far below its usual 3200–down to 2300-far less than the 80% occupancy required to break even, contributing to the parent companies' woes. The whole facility sat on 92 acres.

The facility in Manassas, Shady Rest, was quite similar–the main differences were that they had one fewer building, the whole facility was twelve years older, and they rated their occupancy for 2500, with 2100 residents living there. The facility in Manassas also had a medical center, which needed updating desperately, had no ambulance, and it sat on 74 acres.

"Opinion?" David asked.

"The one in Rockville, Cypress Hill. It's newer; there's room for 896 Virehnai. Hopefully, we don't need that many beds. We could actually empty a couple of those buildings out, so that we segregate the Virehnai in one set of buildings and the humans in the rest. There's also more acreage if we need more buildings."

"I thought much the same thing. I think what swayed me most is that we were discussing the need for medical research, and the facility at Cypress Hill is newer and nicer compared to the other. We're agreed? The Rockville property?"

"Definite yes."

With that, David called Tim.

"David. Did you get to talk to Michel?"

"Yes, sir. He's here with me. We just had our own meeting about the Rockville and Manassas properties."

"And? What did you conclude? I know which I picked."

"We both picked the Rockville facility, Cypress Hill. It has more rooms, it's newer, and it has a better, newer medical facility. It also has more acreage."

"I picked Rockville, too. Mostly for the beds, but your other reasons are sound. I'll get someone to draw up the Letter of Intent."

"Michel?" Tim asked.

"Yes, sir?"

"I wanted to let you know I was glad you got your child back home, safe. It's a shame about her brother trying to have her and her human brother killed."

"Yes, sir. Her father's devastated. Before you go..." Michel paused, "I should let you know: Howard self-reported this afternoon. I escorted him. He's in the holding rooms upstairs."

Michel couldn't see Tim's reaction, but David did. Tim closed his eyes and slowly shook his head. Like him or not, he'd known him for a very long time. "I'm sorry Michel. I know you two were very close. Virehn zuth akret."

"Thanks, Tim. Setha'ra Virehn ka'anel."

Tim hung up, and the room got quiet. David looked at Michel.

"Go home, do what you have to, and then get some rest. I'll catch up with you tomorrow after our meeting at the CDC with Johanssen to update you."

Once in his own suite, he collapsed onto his sofa and cried. He had endured so many losses this year. Too many. Today had been too emotionally draining.

When he quieted, he picked up his phone and called Jeff. "Michel. What do you need? How's Elaina?"

"Elaina's fine. She's with her parents. Where are you?"

"In my suite."

"Do you mind if I come down?"

"No, not at all."

Ten minutes later, Michel went to Jeff's suite and broke the news to him that his father had self-reported.

Jeff looked up at Michel, as if he was waiting for the punchline. "Seriously? Father reported?"

"He did."

Jeff held it together, but the anguish showed clearly on his face. "He should've told us. We would've gone with him."

"He was trying to avoid that."

Jeff shook his head. "Damn hardhead. He's always gotta have his own way."

"You know it, Jeff. I need to let the rest of the clan know; but as Howard's oldest son, call a meeting with your siblings and let them know personally first. I don't want any of his children surprised."

"Where exactly is Father?"

"He's in the holding area of the headquarters building. In fact, I'll be visiting him again tonight; he hoped you would come along with me. I'm taking paints and a portrait he wants to finish."

Jeff looked at Michel. "At the risk of sounding weak, would you mind being there when I call our family meeting?"

Michel put his hand on Jeff's shoulder. "It would be my honor. When do you want to do it?"

"I should go talk to him first, so that I can say I've seen him, and..." Jeff hung his head. "I shouldn't have to be doing this."

"No, you shouldn't. I agree. I...never would've picked this end for your father. Being poisoned for cuckholding someone? Maybe. He came close to that in France before the French Revolution– not once, but twice. He was gifted with good looks, charm and quick wit that came perilously close to being his downfall. This? Never." It helped diffuse the tension and sadness a bit.

Michel and Jeff went up to Howard's suite. Anyone who visited him knew that what was everyone else's 'main seating' area or living room was Howard's studio. There, on three easels, were three pictures in progress. Michel looked at them. "I remember that day in Venice. That was a good day."

"Edward." Michel sighed. "That's the portrait he wants to finish. And Versailles. I remember that day, too. That was the day Edward died. It was pretty that day...by the end, though; not such a good day." Michel carefully picked up the smaller canvas with Howard's son Edward on it.

Michel and Jeff looked around for a few minutes, and gathered up the box that had his paints, and the roll he had that contained brushes, and a blank canvas. Jeff looked over at Michel. "We should take a couple of changes of clothes for him. I'll go get them."

Moments later, Jeff came back with a leather duffel bag with items his father might need, and Michel put Howard's paints and brush roll into a large canvas shopping bag. He tested the paint on the canvas gingerly with a finger. It was dry. Michel carefully placed the two 12x12 canvases into the shopping bag, and they went to visit Howard.

Before they transported Rob, someone went up and grabbed a clean pair of trousers for him, and since he wasn't combative, they allowed him to change into them. They didn't want to have their car cleaned after transporting him. Ugh.

They packed Rob into the police car, and instead of taking him to the local precinct (where the officer in charge hailed from), took him to VarenCorp headquarters. When the officer would later write his report, he had specific ways to write it that showed Rob was in custody, but not in the NYPD's custody, much like they would for the Feds. Sgt. Paul Watson didn't fudge the details, but he didn't elaborate, either.

Director Fuller interviewed Rob in the same room Elaina was in earlier.

"You're in a world of trouble, Mr. Jacoby."

Rob said nothing, at first, then told Fuller, "I plead the Fifth."

Fuller smiled.

"Look around you, Rob. Where are you?" Fuller chuckled. "You're at VarenCorp headquarters…not in a police lockup. If you were subject to those laws, you'd be in their lockup. You can plead the 'Fifth' all day long here, but at the end of that day, you're still oathsworn. It's a good thing you aren't bloodsworn. If you were, we'd be feeding your blood to an egregore right now, and the egregore would be your judge and jury. Still, you're in a rather unenviable position, because you've obviously violated the oath you swore to Michel in multiple ways. Hell, probably in ways we don't even know yet." He paused. Rob's face was impassive.

"Let me illustrate what we know about your oathbreaking so far: you sought to have your sister Elaina and your brother Doug murdered. Hmm. One of them is Virehn, whom you're sworn to protect, and the other is a bloodsworn human."

Fuller shook his head. "Tsk, tsk, tsk. You've been around us all your life, Rob. If nothing else, by now, I'm sure you realize we take our oaths seriously, because our blood remembers everything."

He paused. "Those are OUR laws. In human laws, you're still culpable; you were trying to get your siblings whacked." Rob rolled his eyes.

"But wait, there's more," Fuller said sarcastically. "For instance, we know you were collaborating with Malcolm Harwell, Alex Carpenter, and Ross Martell–both to have your brother and sister killed, and we believe, as part of our recent data breaches."

Fuller watched Rob intently for any signs of a tell. Rob blinked multiple times and lost a little of his attitude.

"Gotcha," he thought to himself.

"While we take the breaking of oaths seriously, along with our computer security, we would like to apprehend those men, to discover what ELSE they may have done. We believe not only are they responsible for the data breaches, but they may have knowledge pertaining to Virehnai Aging Sickness. If you will cooperate with us, and tell us how you worked with them, and any information you gave them, there might be some wiggle room with what happens to you, since you're Walt's son."

Rob was aware of VAS only because the bloodsworn at work were talking about it; he hadn't given it much thought, and as he wasn't bloodsworn himself, he wasn't a donor, either. It suddenly occurred to him that if they were linking Malcolm, Alex and Ross to VAS, he might be guilty of the VAS shit as well. He gave them schedules, and then he gave them his login credentials. Mentally, Rob blanched. He hadn't thought about it much why Patrice from housekeeping needed a stolen master key set to go to the executive suites. Since they didn't mention Patrice, he was hoping it meant they didn't know about any of that.

It was quiet for a few minutes while Rob was thinking. Director Fuller broke the silence.

"Why did you do it, Rob? Is becoming a Virehn that important to you?"

"You'd never understand." Rob spat out.

"Try me, Rob. Really. I want to understand." Fuller was trying to sound friendly; less adversarial than he started out... 'good cop' to his own 'bad cop.'

Rob looked at him. "Someday, my brother will inherit everything of consequence from my father and will go from being my 'pain in the ass brother' to my 'pain in the ass boss.' He has plenty to say about me and my attitude now. I don't want to think about him as my boss for the rest of my life. When the opportunity to be something other than my brother's subordinate came up, I wanted it. The first time it came up with Johannes, they picked Elaina, my baby sister. She's only Oth'kaan, for god's sake. The next time an opportunity came up, when Amalie died, I went to my father and begged him to ask Michel on my behalf. He didn't just say no. He LAUGHED at me and told me they would never make me Virehn. Never."

"I'm sorry that situation didn't go the way you wanted it to." Fuller told him.

It was quiet for a few moments.

"So, Rob. Are you going to play ball with me here? Are you going to tell me what you did with or for Malcolm and his friends? We have your phone, and we have someone working with your contacts list now. If you tell us, this goes easier for you. If you don't, you're taking your chances, and potentially at some point, being Walt Jacoby's kid won't save you."

Rob looked thoughtful. He sighed, then answered.

"I gave them schedules. After they chose Elaina and had her naming and succession ceremonies on the same night, Doug and I were talking shit about Michel and Elaina; Doug left, and I was...I was angry. This maintenance guy named Raul stopped and asked me if I was okay. He was nice. I ran into him a few times in the hallways. One of those days, he asked me if I could get him Elaina's schedule and her suite number. He said she wouldn't get hurt; someone wanted to 'teach her a lesson.' So I gave him the information."

"I see. Did he say who that someone was?"

"No. I know that the first attack happened because I gave them Elaina's information. They also kept their word, and they didn't hurt her."

Fuller nodded. "That's true. How did you come to work with these guys to get your sister and brother murdered?"

"Malcolm called me. He said he was a friend of Raul, and they wanted more schedules, if I could get them."

"Whose schedules?"

"Michel and Howard's."

"I see. And did you give him those schedules?"

"Yes."

"What else did they want?"

"That was it."

"Whose idea was it to have your sister and brother killed?"

"Mine; but they went along with it because I helped them." It was true, to a point.

"Very well, Rob. Thank you for cooperating. We'll talk again, soon."

Director Fuller left Rob sitting in the small conference room and closed the door behind him. There was a small office alongside the 'wired' conference room, and Archie Fuller opened the door and stepped in. Sitting at a long table watching the monitors were Detective Hall and Noah Shorngetter.

"What do you think? Is he telling the truth?"

Noah answered. "Some of it. I'm thinking there's more."

Fuller sighed. "I thought that, too."

Detective Hall asked, "How do we want to go about rounding up his friends?"

"We don't want to do anything to tip them off. We got their numbers from Rob's phone. I think we want to go to a data broker with ALL of their aliases and the phone numbers we have, and see what information comes back. Gather as much information as we can, and if we need to, get a warrant to ping their phones based on Elaina's kidnapping case, and possibly seek a court order for their call detail records. I want those men in that room." Fuller pointed in the general direction of the conference room. "I'm going to find out from Ari: considering everything those three men have done, I wonder if he'll grant an exception and allow the egregore to decide their fates?"

Noah spoke up. "Considering what Rob did, and wanted to do, I think we should include him in that, too."

Director Fuller made a face. "I...don't see that happening. He's still Walt's kid. That's not to say he won't be in trouble; but sometimes it's who you are and who you know that does the talking. That's being realistic."

Later that night, when Michel finally arrived back at his suite, he sat there, mentally reeling. The last time he'd had such a consequential week had been as the French Revolution was beginning in earnest. Michel was hoping this season in hell wouldn't be as costly as that one had been...but he wouldn't count on it.

He heard his phone buzz and looked at it.

"Is it okay to come up?" Elaina asked.

"Yes." He replied.

When Elaina got there, she could immediately tell something was wrong. She sat down on the sofa next to him.

"How's your father?" he asked her, before she could ask him how he was doing.

"Papa's coping. He thinks that everything…what Rob did, and that he did it at all, is his fault. I tried telling him that Rob's a grown man and made his own decisions. When you're thirty-seven and terminally stupid, there's not much you can do with that…"

Michel kinda laughed, but he wasn't feeling it.

"Uncle Michel, are you okay? What's wrong?"

He took a deep breath. "Your Uncle Howard self-reported; he's got VAS."

"Oh, no! That's horrible…" Like Michel, Howard had been there her whole life. She looked over at Michel. "Is there a cure yet? Any chance that he'll be okay?"

Michel looked back at her and felt the anguish of the day washing over him. Tears were threatening to spill even as he hesitantly shook his head and pursed his lips. "No," he forced out. "He's…going…to die."

Elaina began crying. Uncle Howard was a sweet, lovable goofball, making odd jokes about history that were funny…after he explained them. And she had three of his paintings that moved into her new suite from her old one. "I'm sorry, I know how much you loved him." Elaina sobbed. "I loved him, too. Virehn zuth akret."

Michel answered back, "Setha'ra Virehn ka'anel." Elaina looked up with a frightened expression on her face, panicked. "You're okay, right?" She was thinking in terms of VAS, but Michel had a larger picture to worry about.

"I think I am." He shrugged his shoulders. "I guess I will be until I'm not." Michel wouldn't sugarcoat it. If someone was targeting him, and got to him? What COULD he do? Not fucking much. "I feel fine. But, like your father, I'm feeling like much of this falls back on me. Someone is trying to get to me…and apparently, they're willing to use any means possible to do it. How can I NOT feel like it's my fault?" Michel was losing control of his emotions, as the wall he'd put up all day crumbled. "Your Uncle Howard just became a casualty, and I think Amalie was, too. You almost were." Michel cried then, as the losses of the past three months caught up with him all at once.

Elaina, still crying herself, reached out to comfort him, and they ended up comforting each other.

17

COMING STORM

Michel normally didn't sleep. It wasn't necessary, but when times were especially stressful, Virehn sometimes rested, and occasionally would sleep. With the day he'd had, after Elaina left and went back to her suite, he decided he'd earned himself some rest. Michel dozed, as he mentally ordered the next day: He had a meeting with the Task Force first thing in the morning; Tim had asked him in an email to be ready to brief everyone about the decision on Cypress Hill while he and David were in Georgia.

There will be a VanEtters family meeting up in the Hall. That meeting would also include Howard's human family. He himself would host a clan meeting immediately afterward. letting the entire clan know Howard had VAS. Later, after Tim and David came back from their meeting with Martin Johanssen, he'd be attending another meeting to get the update. It would be a busy day.

It surprised Michel when he fell asleep. He didn't dream, at least not that he remembered. He got up, got dressed, and headed off to his meeting a couple of blocks away.

When he arrived, there were considerably fewer at the table than there originally were. Tomasz, Leonie and Violette had already gone home. It seemed kind of empty. The only ones sitting in the conference room were him, Carolyn, Eliška and Director Fuller; he nodded and said hello. There was still a full complement attending via teleconference–including Tomasz and Leonie; it seemed strange that they weren't there in person. Michel had gotten used to their presence.

After a few moments, Ari's face appeared as he joined them.

"It's a busy morning so far; There's quite a few things in play today." He paused. "Tim and David are on their way to Atlanta for their meeting with the Director of the CDC, Dr. Martin Johanssen. They're taking copies of a Letter of Intent to show Dr. Johanssen as part of our plan dealing with the crisis. Michel, please brief everyone about the facility VarenCorp is buying."

"Yes, sir. Well, folks, as Ari mentioned, several of us were looking at buildings. Those of you who offered buildings that were chosen know and are likely already working on upgrades to them."

Several folks nodded in agreement, having offered buildings. "VarenCorp found and is in the process of buying a facility to both house and research Virehnai with VAS. It's a retirement community named Cypress Hill, on the outskirts of DC. It can house nearly nine hundred Virehnai, in two of the seven high-rise buildings on ninety-two acres. Aside from the Letter of Intent Ari mentioned, there's also a pre-occupancy agreement that was written up, and a team from VarenCorp DC is," Michel looked at his watch, "sitting in a meeting with the CEO of Cypress Hill's parent company and a gaggle of lawyers for both sides right now."

He smiled and cocked his head. "We're planning to put two-thirds of the asking price down by cashier's check by close of business today, with the final third due at settlement; As soon as the ink on the pre-occupancy agreement is dry, and they have the check, we can move people in."

"It's going to move that fast?" Tomasz asked.

"Unless something unforeseen goes wrong, yes." Michel answered Tomasz.

"Why did you pick that facility? Who decided? Just curious." Tomasz followed up.

"I'll start with 'who.' David, Tim and I researched it as part of our 'Plan B' meetings. We narrowed it down to two properties, and David and I made our recommendations to Tim, who made the final decision after vetting it through Ari." He paused. "As for why? There are two good reasons. The first is that there are significant vacancies at the facility because of mismanagement by the corporation we're purchasing it from. Those vacancies mean we can house more Virehnai. The second and main reason, though, is the on-site medical facility. We plan on adding more equipment and bringing in researchers to figure out what VAS is, and how to cure it. As part of that effort, we asked VarenCorp's records department to identify Virehnai and humans in our sphere with the expertise we need. Someone from VarenCorp will reach out to them between today and tomorrow with either job offers, or directed assignments from their current positions, depending on if they're human or Virehn."

Eliška, head of VarenCorp USA, chimed in. "That 'someone's' me, along with Carolyn," she chuckled. "Ari, I can confirm that the directed assignments have gone out; the job offers will go out later this morning, with the request that our human associates please decide by close of business tomorrow, because time is of the essence."

"Thank you, Eliška."

Tomasz raised his hand from where he sat. "I didn't hear it mentioned, but who will run this facility? Will we establish an associative Cypress Hill Clan to cover all those who are there, while they are there?"

"I'd like to know that as well." Ari said. "Did the 'Plan B' team decide or have recommendations for that?"

Michel looked up at Ari in particular. "Right now, we have recommendations only. David and I, after the meeting with Tim, discussed the criteria for a person running Cypress Hill should meet. We realized we needed to come up with a list of candidates ASAP, as a group. We concluded the criteria for being on that list should be someone who is at least five hundred years of age, has direct experience with corporate management, and has a child or sire with VAS. Hopefully, that criteria gives them the wisdom that comes with age, the ability to manage the facility which will include human and Virehnai subordinates, along with having a personal stake in their assignment. Once we have that short list, you and Tim can decide who goes, and whomever you choose can go down as soon as the ink's dry on the check and the pre-occupancy agreement. We never considered having an associative clan on site, but that's a good idea. It gives an extra layer of structure and support. Oldest Virehn without VAS runs the Clan?"

"I concur with all of that," Ari said. "Make it happen. Did the 'Plan B' team have any other recommendations we should hear?"

"No mincing words," Michel thought to himself. "Yes, sir. We thought the White House or someone else in that sphere of influence may ask what VarenCorp's plans are for the current human employees, along with our plans for Cypress Hill after our emergency is over. They're both valid questions. We're going to need those current human employees; at least at first. It won't look good on us if they all lose their jobs when we come in. We need to know and decide on both topics before we meet with anyone from the White House. If we can say in advance that nobody loses their jobs and we're only adding to the staff and say clearly what we see as the future of Cypress Hill afterwards, it could pave the way for more help right now, or easier approvals."

Ari wrote something down, looking down momentarily, and when he looked back up, said, "You're likely right. I don't like the idea of our Virehnai, sick or not, working so closely with non-oathsworn humans. I'll have to think about that. Did you and David also have a recommendation about how we should proceed with Cypress Hill?"

"Yes. We recommend that ultimately, we keep it as a VarenCorp business; After the crisis is over, as long as we can turn a profit, why not run it? We looked at the numbers. In a retirement community, turning a profit is all about occupancy. We have other human-facing businesses that serve primarily human clientele. We can find the talent we need, and even if Cypress Hill no longer serves Virehnai, we'd do a more effective job running it than the people we're purchasing from. You may want someone else to head it after the crisis is over. Like any of VarenCorp's other businesses, if it seems as if it's a loser, you divest it and sell it. If you decide to divest, as a thank you, you could sell it to the staff and residents to run; they'll have an incentive to run it well. Obviously, all of that's for you and Tim to decide."

"Most of your conclusions make sense. I have to reiterate–I don't like the idea of having non-allied humans alongside us. We've already had difficulties with humans that were oathsworn. You've seen that firsthand recently. I think that makes us extremely vulnerable." Ari said. "I'll discuss all these recommendations with Tim when he gets back later."

Tomasz asked, "Out of curiosity, where are all the folks in the DC area that have self-reported being housed? Is it the same arrangement as in the NY office?"

"It is. Right now, they're being held in the local DC headquarters office." Ari told them. "Tim and I discussed that this morning before he left for his meeting; They're getting tight on space there, same as in New York; There were 106 people who reported from the NY and DC areas; another 37 reported from Central Europe." Carolyn added, "Space is definitely a consideration right now. We can't hold many more."

Ari looked at Carolyn. "Tim told me as soon as we can safely move people to Cypress Hill from there, and DC, the better. Others can be moved to the property closest to them. We are working to address it." He paused. "Michel, as part of Plan B, work up ideas on the best way to move them, please."

"Yes, sir. We'll look into it and come up with recommendations. I have a suggestion, though. At the rates people are reporting, we might try starting with the people who are very early self-reporters. We should be able to transport them without...problems that later reporters have. That would leave those who are too far gone here to be monitored."

"Thanks, Michel." Ari looked around. "Unless anyone has anything else to add, we'll leave this be until after Tim and Dave are back." Hearing nothing, Ari continued.

"As most of you know, one of Michel's children was kidnapped yesterday." He looked over at Michel. "I'm glad she's home and safe."

"Thank you, sir. Me, too."

"What's important to note about this are the details. As you recall, before people started turning up with VAS, we were in the middle of a Red Team data breach. During that breach, we discovered there were oathsworn among us who had multiple identities and were working for multiple corporate heads. We identified a group of them: three we identified in the data breach were also involved in the kidnapping of Elaina Jacoby yesterday. Sadly, there was a fourth individual working with them we would never expect; Walt Jacoby's youngest son Rob was working with them."

Carolyn looked at Michel. "Wait, you mean Elaina's own brother was involved in her kidnapping?" Carolyn asked him.

Ari and Michel both said "yes" at the same time.

"Why would he do such a thing?" Carolyn didn't know Rob, but she knew of and recognized Elaina by sight. Her brow wrinkled up, contemplating it.

"Initially, there were some who thought it might be sour grapes that his sister got picked instead of him to ascend." Carolyn nodded; she remembered hearing through the grapevine that Walt's sons were...unhappy. She didn't realize they were THAT unhappy! Other people's expressions varied; most showed surprise.

Ari shook his head. "It's a bad situation; however you see it.

Director Fuller retrieved Mr. Jacoby's phone, and went through his contacts, and his search histories; they interviewed him yesterday– and if Mr. Jacoby is telling the truth, it's worse, and is damning for him. Archie?"

Director Fuller turned to Michel. "Sorry, Michel. I know this hits close to home."

Michel nodded. "Thanks."

Fuller looked at everyone else, slowly. "While it's likely Michel is being targeted–something similar could happen to any of us. I recommend that wherever you are, for the time being, lock down everything. Take nothing for granted. Take a second look at the humans you have working for and around you, whether it's for your clans, your businesses, or even around you in your offices." He shook his head. "We interviewed Elaina after her rescue; shortly after, we apprehended her brother, Rob, at the midtown offices of Jacoby, Lightner, and VanEtters, and interviewed him as well. What Elaina told us…" Archie Fuller sighed. "The same people identified with the data breach were working with her brother, and locked her into a dog crate, leaving her there in a storage room, with plans to set the building on fire later." There were murmurs and exclamations of surprise. "We learned from Elaina that they were also planning on killing her brother, Doug."

He paused, even as Carolyn's face registered more surprise. "I'm going to put up a portion of the video. It's the first time I've shown it; it's not the whole interview, just the part where he owns up to what he did."

Rob appeared on screen, sitting in the office, and Director Fuller was visible in the shot, too. Rob had an attitude, and it was apparent in how he held himself; the sneer on his face and eye movements.

"Are you going to tell me what you did with or for Malcolm and his friends? We have your phone, and we have someone working with your contacts list now. If you tell us, this goes easier for you. If you don't, you're taking your chances, and potentially at some point, being Walt Jacoby's kid won't save you." Rob exhaled, as he thought before answering his question.

"I gave them schedules. After they chose Elaina and had her naming and succession ceremonies on the same night, Doug and I were talking shit about Michel and Elaina;" Michel sat up straighter at the mention of his name and shook his head. "Doug left, and I was…I was angry. This maintenance guy named Raul stopped and asked me if I was okay. He was nice; I ran into him a few times in the hallways. One of those days, he asked me if I could get him Elaina's schedule and her suite number. He said she wouldn't get hurt; someone wanted to 'teach her a lesson.' So I gave him the information."

Michel was getting angrier the more he heard. His mouth opened and closed a few times until his lips pursed tightly together.

"I see. Did he say who that someone was?"

"No. I know that the first attack happened because I gave them Elaina's information. They also kept their word, and they didn't hurt her."

Fuller nodded.

"How did you come to work with these guys to get your sister and brother murdered?"

"Malcolm called me. He said he was a friend of Raul, and they wanted more schedules, if I could get them."

"Whose schedules?"

"Michel and Howard's." Michel gasped, as did others.

"I see. And did you give him those schedules?"

"Yes." Despite trying to calm himself, Michel's fists were opening and closing. "That treacherous little bastard!" he exclaimed.

The video went on.

"What else did they want?"

"That was it."

"Whose idea was it to have your sister and brother killed?"

"Mine; but they went along with it because I helped them."

After the video cut off, everyone sat in stunned silence. There were always people who were going to use humans to do their dirty work. Treachery still occurred; it simply wasn't as open as it used to be. Seeing proof of such a thing, coming out of the mouth of someone oathsworn, placed so close to the clan he was associated with was sobering.

Director Fuller spoke into the silence, to no one in particular. "Like I said, look to your own interests. Don't merely assume that everything is fine. What worries me is that we don't know how deep…whatever this is…goes, or if it's connected to our current crisis with Virehnai Aging Sickness."

Still angry and upset by not only what he'd viewed but also the events of the day before, Michel spoke. "The schedules bother me, more than I can say. I don't know why they wanted them, or if it's connected…" Michel exhaled, trying to keep all of his emotions in check. "…but yesterday, Howard VanEtters self-reported."

There were gasps. Most knew Howard, much like Florrie and Connie had been known. When you've lived for such a long time, you come into contact with many others; those who didn't know him knew his reputation as a lawyer.

Ari looked at Michel. "Tim mentioned that to me when I talked to him this morning. Virehn zuth akret." People all around the world said likewise, "Virehn zuth akret."

"Setha'ra Virehn ka'anel. Thank you," Michel said.

Ari shook his head. "This is treachery, plain and simple. Watch over yourselves and your people. We'll reconvene later after Tim and David get back.

Emily Hargrove had a bed, not that she slept much. Most Virehnai didn't need sleep or even rest except in cases of extreme stress or shock. Emily was no different. At night, unless she had plans, she'd use her bed as a comfy spot to curl up and read all kinds of things. Fiction...non-fiction...history, she would read it. She was a 'voracious reader.' That morning, when Emily put down her book and moved to get up and get dressed, she realized something. She was feeling...off. She was aware of her bones and her joints. They didn't hurt–but she felt them; was aware of them. That in itself was strange. She hadn't felt a day of illness or malaise since she ascended 382 years ago. She didn't recognize what she was feeling, exactly, except that it was...different.

"Oh, no," she thought. That doesn't bode well. Emily tried to push the thought out of her head. "It can't be Virehnai Aging Sickness. I won't entertain that thought." She got dressed and headed to the bathroom to attend to her hair and the bit of makeup she actually wore. She used little, unless she was going out in public–like most Virehnai. Most had excellent makeup that they were adept at applying; particularly if they had a very public facing job or spent more time in the human world–which many did, even for shopping. Having at least a little more skin color than translucent pale was helpful. It kept people from staring at you or questioning your health status. You blended in better.

Looking in the mirror, Emily made a horrible realization. She had...a gray hair. She plucked it out. Looking at herself and taking quick stock of what she saw, she realized something else. There were faint dark circles under her eyes. As much as she wanted to cover them up, she didn't. Emily knew what it meant; she just didn't want to face it. As she was mentally cursing her fate, and trying hard to stave off tears of resignation, she realized she was feeling hungry.

Before going up to her office and having what would be a hard discussion with Michel, Emily went to her small refrigerator, and pulled out a bag of blood which she heated, and then sat drinking. She didn't know what the day would hold, but she wasn't looking forward to it. She knew people were self-reporting, but she had heard nothing about cures. Was there one? She desperately hoped so. She wanted to make it to 383.

Emily sighed to herself. "One step at a time," her mama used to tell her. 'Good advice for today,' she thought. She finished her mug, and curiously enough, she was still hungry, so she got a second bag– something she'd never remembered doing before. "Oh well," she thought to herself. "If I need it, I need it." Emily looked at the clock. "Time to go." She took her mug with her.

Michel sat in his office after he got back from the early meeting with Ari. He was stunned at the depth of the treachery on Rob's part. He was reeling from the admission out of the man's lips. He'd given out not one but multiple schedules to someone he didn't even know– only knowing that providing them would harm others. Michel found it hard to stomach the depth of the betrayal.

He wrote himself a note: he needed to let Emily know that, for the time being, she shouldn't use his digital calendar; it was compromised. He knew she wouldn't be happy going back to a paper desk calendar.

Thinking of calendars reminded him. After he talked to Em, he needed to talk to Jeff, and then schedule a Clan meeting; he needed to let everyone know Howard had self-reported, and update them as much as he could about what was going on regarding VAS, as well as let them know what had happened with Elaina – and to be especially careful, that there was a possibility their clan was actively being attacked.

When Emily got in, with a mug in hand, she hovered in the doorway.

"Good morning." He told her.

"Your day started early."

Michel nodded. "It did. I'm going to need to schedule a clan meeting for today, and I have a meeting sometime this afternoon with Tim and David and Ari. Come on in, sit down, Em." She did.

"What's up?" she asked.

"Unfortunately, I've nothing but bad news on all fronts. Howard self-reported yesterday."

She gasped, covering her mouth with her hand in surprise. "Oh, no." Emily began crying.

There were two comfy chairs facing Michel's desk. He got up and sat in the chair beside her; offering her a tissue. "I'm still processing it, too. I can't believe he's got VAS. During the meeting I was at this morning, we concluded that there's a better-than-average chance Clan Robichaux is being actively targeted...."

Emily didn't stop crying. In fact, she was crying harder.

"Em?"

Michel asked again, "Em?"

Emily gained control of her emotions enough to speak.

"I'm going to be reporting this morning, too. I didn't know how to tell you."

"Oh Em, no...." He leaned in, and put his arms around his friend, and tried to offer comfort as he could. He cried with her...for her. As he'd said multiple times to multiple people, he'd had too many losses this year, and all of them were hitting too close.

After a while, he asked her, "Do you want me to go with you?"

Emily looked at him through tears. "Would you? Do you mind?"

"Silly goose. I offered, didn't I?"

"I don't know how to process this. Nobody's mentioned cures. Maybe they'll find a cure before it gets too far?"

"Hopefully...," Michel said, non-commitally. He hoped so, but he was fairly sure it wouldn't happen in time for her. At the present, VAS was a death sentence, not that he was going to tell her that. "Before you go report," he said, "go pack a bag with a couple of changes of clothes and grab a book or three so you aren't bored. If you need more, let me know and I'll bring them to you."

Emily stood up. "Thank you, Michel." She looked at him and started crying again. He enfolded her in his arms and let her cry. It had been a long time since he and Emily had been a 'thing.' What had been a relationship in the early 1900s had developed into a long, close friendship. It's why when he decided around 1910 that he needed to find an assistant he trusted implicitly, he could think of no better person than Em. He would need a new assistant. While she ran to her suite to get what she needed, he called Jeff.

"Michel," Jeff said.

"Jeff...a slight wrinkle. Before I can attend your family meeting and set up the clan meeting..." He sighed. "I'm going to be escorting someone as they self-report first."

"Oh, god. Not another. Who? Can you say?"

"Emily."

There was silence on the other end of the phone. Jeff was stunned. They were friends and hung out regularly. They used to be a thing for a while, too, back in the 1950's. Between his own father and now Emily, it hit Jeff close to home. "I'm sorry. I... Virehn zuth akret."

"Virehn zuth akret."

Fifteen minutes later, he and Emily made their way to headquarters, and she checked in. When asked who her emergency contact was, she gave Michel's name, the same as Howard had.

She asked for it to be put on the record that her children could visit were they able. Emily had sired two. Her daughter Ariana, who was living in Chicago with her mate, and her son Stephen, who was working for VarenCorp at Ottawa HQ.

"Can I have my cellphone with me?" Em asked the lady.

"You may."

Em turned to Michel. "I'll call Ariana and Stephen later to tell them where I am and what's up." Em looked sad and a little lost, as she looked back up at Michel. "If... Should.... something bad happen to me, will you please let them know?" Michel promised her. He accompanied her to a small room, like the one Howard was in, and hugged her tightly.

An hour later, he called Jeff.

"I ended up having my own quick family meeting to notify everyone about Father; that's one thing you won't have to worry about."

"Thanks, Jeff. I'm sorry I wasn't there. It's been a morning already. I'm going to plan for the clan meeting at 6 pm tonight. I'm just about to email out. Don't use your calendar for the time being until I can consult with IT for what we should do."

"You've got a lot on your plate. Do you want me to look into that?"

"You don't mind?"

"Not at all."

"Thanks, Jeff. See you tonight."

Michel sat in his chair in his office and composed an email. "There will be a short clan meeting this evening. Please try to attend. I need to update everyone about the current crisis. Sorry that there isn't more notice. See you tonight."

Michel sat there for a few moments and decided he was done with his office for the day. The past couple of days had been hard, and he had a lot to think about and consider. The one place he was longing for at the moment was the sanctuary of his study.

He got comfy; he had a couple of hours to kill before the next meeting. He stood there in the study's doorway, and looked at the items on the walls, as he normally did. Whenever he did this, seeing what was on the walls brought to mind the people each item represented. People whom he'd known and loved–and was grateful for the time he had them in his life. His eyes lingered longest on the gold Roman Aurius in a frame. "Soon," he thought. "…too soon, Howard will be another flame lingering within my blood. A memory. At least they're mostly good memories."

Michel sat at his desk; change was inevitable at the best of times; loss actively cultivated and caused it. Jeff would step into Howard's position. It was the promotion nobody ever wanted to get. Jeff told him something when they were leaving Howard after taking him his clothes, paints, and canvases. They were standing there waiting at the elevator, and Jeff asked, "Would you have a problem if I took Father's last name after he's gone?" Changing your official last name to that of your sire was a mark of respect.

"Not at all. I think it's a fitting tribute." As the elevator dinged and they stepped in, he turned to Jeff and said, "You should tell your father what you plan to do, Jeff. I think it would both honor him and make him proud and happy that you love him enough to do that. Better that he leave this life knowing how much you love him."

Michel's mind was a morass of swirling thoughts. Among all the things that were churning around in his brain, he realized he needed to deal with the immediate issue of finding a new assistant. He was contemplating asking Elaina. He trusted her implicitly. Even if it wasn't a permanent position for her, it might get them through the crisis at hand. During a crisis, it's always good to surround yourself with people you can trust. He trusted Em and would miss her horribly when she was gone. That he could trust her was the tip of the iceberg.

Michel turned, and looked out at the Manhattan skyline, and tried to quiet his mind to seek the wisdom of the flames hiding within his blood. It wasn't working as easily as it normally did. The question that kept screaming out from his heart and mind was, "Why?"

Surprisingly, he saw something, despite the disquieted state of his mind. It was through his sire Dio's eyes. He recognized Ari's old office at Focaria Rubra, but neither Ari nor the location was the focus. Instead, it was what Ari handed Dio. It was a message Dio was taking to deliver for Ari. He knew he was seeing the message and Ari's seal through Dio's eyes. What he saw next, he had NO clue how to interpret. He wasn't likely to forget it, though. The outer parchment, folded into a handmade envelope to thwart prying eyes from reading the correspondence within, was sealed with wax to let the recipient know if someone else had viewed it. If the wax seal was intact, you could reasonably guarantee your correspondence had stayed private. If the wax seal was lifted or broken–it hadn't.

Michel was trying to home in on Dio's emotions, but his own

mind was so full of other things that it was hard. He realized, focusing on the seal, that it represented trust. Ari trusted Dio to deliver the message intact, even if Ari had other, deeper issues with Dio. What happened next while he focused on the scene wasn't anything Dio had seen. It was something HE himself was seeing within Dio's memory. It differed from anything he'd experienced before, and he found it confusing.

The message bearing Ari's seal–as Dio held it in his hand–never lifted off the parchment; never broke. The wax seal seeped blood from around and beneath Ari's sigil. That the seal was in one piece, to him, implied Dio hadn't broken trust with Ari.

Michel knew Ari well enough over centuries to know that Ari...hadn't always played by the rules. Michel had heard rumors that Ari and Tim had founded the Velascar Company with dirty money earned from others' pain. In fact, it was open knowledge that the only reason Ari signed on to the Compact was to guarantee a clean slate for him and Tim going forward. Dio told him that much. Michel knew the current state of things–particularly the Compact not working as it should–would scare the ever-loving shit out of Ari.

He didn't know how to interpret what he was seeing. Did it say something about the message Dio carried? Or did it say something about a breach of trust on Ari's part? Both were distinct possibilities. If Michel interpreted it literally as he saw it, it would be "Trust bleeds." Michel wasn't sure what to make of it. A chime alerting him to an email startled him out of his own thoughts.

He turned to face his desk and wrote the words down before he forgot them.

The chime Michel heard was the alert telling him he had an email; it was letting him know that Tim and David had arrived back at VarenCorp HQS, and that the meeting would begin as soon as everyone was there. Michel quickly jotted down impressions, hoping that it would jog his memory later when he had more time to go over it.

He quickly changed into something more acceptable than sweats and a t-shirt and made his way to VarenCorp.

Michel was afraid he'd be the last one to get there, but Carolyn arrived after he did.

"Now that everyone's here, let's move forward, shall we?" Ari looked annoyed. "Tim; Dave. Welcome back. Floor's yours."

Tim started. "Okay, so we spoke with Martin Johanssen. Nice man. Gotta say he took it better than we thought he would. We explained our nature, and then what VAS is doing to us. He asked us about our numbers: how many of us there were, vs. how many were sick. I shared all of that. We showed him the report numbers and locations. Our report numbers spiked the other day; they're holding as of this morning at the same level, with numbers up in the DC area, and slightly down in New York and the surrounding states. After he saw the numbers and how quickly they've ramped up, he started using the word 'epidemic.'"

Ari looked at Tim. "We figured that; at least he's corroborating it. Did you point out to him it's worldwide?"

"I did. While he's obviously going to be more concerned with what's happening here in the US, we let him know that what is happening in Central Europe is the same thing as here."

"Good."

"When we showed him before and after pictures of Mark Rotti, and then showed him video of the carnage from the neighbor's house, and followed it up with Mark's interview…uh, Dr. Johanssen was…rattled." David said.

"Rattled? That's putting it mildly. I thought he looked like he might puke." Tim told them, adding, "The good news for us is that Johanssen agreed: the President and White House need to be brought in on this before it worsens. He doesn't want the White House to be blindsided by it. He said he'd have his secretary contact us. She already has; We'll be having a meeting with President Colton in three days. He requested we show the President the same information we showed him, along with being able to talk about our current numbers from the previous day. What were today's numbers? Are they up, down, or holding?"

"I checked before coming up; we had twenty-three self-reports in our area, so it's holding at the same rate." Carolyn told Tim. "There were thirty-one in and around DC; slightly down–but there are considerably more Virehnai in Manhattan and the surrounding areas than there are in the DC metro area. The percentage of Virehn living there to Virehn with VAS there is very high." Tim and the others grimaced.

"Over here, numbers are up as well." Tomasz said. "You now have sixteen cases in the UK, David."

"Oh, no," David said, and looked up at Ari questioningly.

"While you now have sixteen cases, all of them, when questioned, recently traveled to Switzerland, Germany or Austria." Ari noted. "Figures." He was silent a minute, but then added, "Go home, and look to your people."

David nodded. "Thank you, sir."

"Does anyone have anything else to add?" Ari asked.

Carolyn nodded. "One of our reports today was Michel's assistant, Emily Hargrave. Some of you may know her."

David turned to Michel. "I'm so sorry, Michel. Others, including Ari and Tim, chimed in also with Virehn zuth akret.

"Setha'ra Virehn ka'anel. Thank you." Michel said.

"I think that's it, folks." Ari said. "Archie, Michel, David...if you could remain, I have a couple of other things I need to discuss with you. Everybody else, thanks. I'll talk to you soon."

Screens went blank, one by one, until the only one left on was the one Ari filled. Everyone else was there in the conference room in Manhattan.

"Tim–I know you'd planned to have David go with you to the White House for the meeting with President Colton, but considering the UK went from no cases to sixteen in the space of less than two days, it's prudent to send him back to deal with it. You can choose who accompanies you, or go alone, if you'd rather."

"After the meeting today with Johanssen, I think I'd prefer someone there with me," Tim told his father, then turned to Michel. "Michel, would you mind going with me? You were involved in both the Red Team issues and the Task Force. There are others I could pick, but I'd prefer someone with your age and knowledge– similar to David's–to be in on this. To me, it only makes sense."

"Certainly, Tim. Anything I can do to help, I'm willing to do."

Tim nodded. "Thanks, Michel."

Archie Fuller nodded to Ari, signaling for attention. "Archie, you have something to bring up?"

"I do. There's something you need to know that didn't get mentioned at the earlier meeting."

"What's that?" Ari asked.

"The percentage of sick Virehnai in DC that work for either VarenCorp or our flagship hotel there is significant."

"What? How so?" Ari replied.

David asked simultaneously, "What do you mean by significant?"

"Nearly sixty percent of the Virehnai that have VAS in the DC area are employees of VarenCorp. Clans Wakefield, Richardson and Lyon have all taken hits. Lyon in Virginia has taken the brunt."

"Who is being targeted?" David asked. "VarenCorp, or Tim?"

"There's no way to be sure." Ari told him. "I hate to say it, but I'd bet that Tim is the target. That's why my clan calls me paranoid. I'm used to that. We've both been assuming — correctly or not — that we're both being targeted, and most of them are collateral damage trying to figure out how to get to us. I hate to say it, but those numbers, to me, confirm our assumptions."

Michel spoke up. "I've concluded I'm being targeted also, although I don't know why. I'm certain they kidnapped Elaina to get to me; she wasn't Virehn long enough to cause someone angst. I wondered if Johannes' death might've been to get to me also, but VarenCorp thoroughly examined it. I went over all the paperwork closely after we got Elaina back safely, and his death looks to be…truly accidental." Michel shook his head. "I can't imagine what I did to who, though I suppose with my age, there's bound to be someone, somewhere."

"There's also the tie-in to the Compact failing." David said.

Ari was listening intently; David had his undivided attention. "All of us were there in person when it was cast. Many of the others that were there died during the French Revolution, or different human conflicts which weren't as well known. Maybe we should look and take mental stock of who was there that's still around and might want to do away with it."

Michel shook his head. "Oh hell, I hope this doesn't come down to Magnus, Ferdinand and Black Sun after all…"

They all grimaced. It wasn't a pleasant thought.

As Michel headed back home, he was a little lost in thought.

He was surprised that Tim had chosen him, but he meant what he said. If Tim wanted him to go, he would. He would do whatever was needed, for as long as was necessary.

A president. "Huh." Michel thought to himself. Michel never met an American president before. He hoped it would go better than meetings with kings usually did. His memories of the French Revolution didn't recommend the experience, and any rulers or monarchs he'd had occasion to meet prior to that hadn't been pleasant either. People in charge, whether they be commoners that rose through the ranks, or were nobility who believed they were ruling by God's will or grace? It didn't matter. They still came with their own agendas, raging egos and, despite being human, would resort to treachery almost as fast as a Virehn would, and messier, at that.

Ari hung up from the call; Alwin was beside him, as usual, just out of sight.

"I'm getting a bag of blood," Ari said, reaching over and pulling a bag of blood from his newly installed mini fridge under his desk, and looking over at Alwin. "Would you like one?"

Alwin's eyebrows bunched up, and he looked at the one in Ari's hand warily. "Source?"

Ari smiled like a cheshire cat. "RKS sequestered blood supply. Got delivered yesterday. You'll be happy to know that I got enough for you, Hassan and Corinna, too. There's a box for each of you in the refrigerator in the galley upstairs."

"Ha! You really didn't want to drink from the red deer, did you?"

Ari grimaced. "Hard pass." He laughed. "If I'm going to pretend to be Sulahnai, I can at least drink from the finest, safest source available. So what if the production of Valtharinex slows down some?"

"In that case," Alwin said, "Yes, please."

Ari reached in and handed him a bag, and they both got up to heat them.

"Shit, man. We don't have any cups to put it in!" Alwin laughed. "The usual packaging doesn't require it." They both laughed, even as Ari produced a mug from a drawer for himself, and another for Alwin.

"I foresaw this need."

"You're good at that," Alwin smirked.

"Why, thank you." Ari chuckled, taking a sip, and Alwin followed suit. Ari looked down into his cup. "So much better than red deer."

Elaina expected there would be a clan meeting, based on when she was in Michel's suite the night before. It was a shock to find that Uncle Howard had VAS. It made her worry for Uncle Michel…and hell, everybody she knew. As Michel promised, there was an email later calling for a clan meeting at six. She noticed there was a second one from Michel, asking her if she would mind meeting with him and Jeff after the meeting. Elaina wanted to talk to Jeff. He hadn't been at work; with his sire's situation, she didn't expect him to be.

She wanted to tell him how sorry she was.

After work, Elaina made her way to the Hall, where others gathered as well. Reman, wearing his traditional red robes, stood by the dais. Michel came in moments later, with Jeff by his side. They walked to the dais where Reman stood and talked with them for several minutes in hushed tones.

The three of them turned, and everyone hushed, waiting.

"Thank you all for being here," Michel said. "I realize it was short notice, and I'm sorry for that. I need to update you on recent events."

"First," he paused, "it's my sad duty to tell you about two of our ranks who reported. Yesterday, I accompanied our friend and brother, Howard VanEtters to self-report." Michel paused, as people were reacting to his words, sadness and surprise clear. "This morning, I accompanied our friend and my assistant, Emily Hargrave, to self-report as well." Michel sighed. "As of this morning, worldwide there are just over 250 sick Virehnai. Most of those have self-reported." At the number, there were gasps.

"Most of you probably aren't aware–but I'm on VarenCorp's Task Force working on figuring out what VAS is, and how it started, along with ways we can deal with the crisis. As part of that effort, VarenCorp bought a property to more comfortably house those who self-reported with VAS. It includes a medical facility that is being upgraded to state-of-the art. That is where VarenCorp will research VAS and continue work on a cure."

"I'd like to reiterate: if any of you need to self-report, and you don't want to go alone, call me. In the meantime, keep Howard and Emily and their families in your thoughts. That's all I have for you, folks."

People gathered into small groups, discussing what they'd heard. Elaina moved away from where she'd been standing with several co-workers to where Michel, Reman and Jeff were talking.

All said hello as she approached.

"Let's go into an antechamber," Michel suggested. Elaina and Jeff followed him out of the Hall and into the vestibule. There were several small rooms, off the vestibule, which were comfortably appointed with chairs.

Michel picked one, and flipped on the lights, as they followed him in. "This'll be quick," Michel said, once seated. "The crisis is causing change, and rapid change, at that. Jeff will take his father's position and office at the firm; there's also the possibility he may move temporarily to run the facility VarenCorp purchased outside of DC, while we try to figure out VAS; He's on a short list for people who may be picked. Howard and Emily will both move there while they're still lucid and able to move safely. After Emily self-reported, I find myself in need of an assistant to replace her." He looked at Elaina. "Would you mind taking that on temporarily?"

"If you need me to, sure."

"I appreciate your willingness to be flexible, Elaina. You need to know that asking you is a compliment. My main criteria is trust; that's why I'd like you to step in. I know I can trust you implicitly. Particularly now, with everything going on."

"No problem. When does this happen? Am I headed to your office tomorrow, or am I wrapping up what I was working on?"

Jeff looked at Elaina, and told her, "Head for Michel's office. I'm sure if anyone has questions, they'll call you. I'm wrapping up my loose ends, too, just in case, and I'm working on figuring out who will take my place."

Michel stood. "Thanks, both of you, for your flexibility."

"No problem, Uncle Michel."

They all went in separate directions; Elaina and Michel to their suites; Jeff had papers for Howard to sign.

Back in his suite, Michel picked up the phone and called Walt.

"Walt; Michel. How are you doing"

"Still processing everything, I think. I sat down with Doug earlier today. It surprised him that Rob wanted him dead. He's still processing everything also, along with a bit of...re-evaluation as well. He was angry with some of what I had to say; at this point, I don't care. He needed to hear it, and I'm beyond sugar coating anything. If he wants sugar, he can go get a donut."

"If you don't mind me asking, what did you tell him?" Michel asked.

"I was going to tell you anyway, so no, I don't mind. First, I told him it was a damned good thing for him that Elaina didn't hold a grudge after how he'd treated her; as soon as she had an opportunity, she asked the officers to warn him he was next. If she held a grudge the way he did, he might be six feet under right now. To me, that's sobering, and I'm thankful that Elaina's got a good heart and a good head on her shoulders. The second thing was about succession. I told him he needs to focus less on trying to ascend, and more on the business. I asked him point-blank if he could do that–because if he can't, I'll leave him money–but he won't be in charge of my interests; he can count the businesses out, and one of the Lightners can step in." Walt paused. "Those two things rattled his world; it really shook him to find out about Rob. Ditto on finding out that I had no qualms about leaving the businesses to one of Dave Lightner's kids instead. It kind of jarred his slats a bit. He didn't expect me to say either."

"I can imagine it didn't make him happy. It's sobering to find someone wants you dead, and he has enough pride to not want to lose the chance to run your businesses."

There was silence until Walt broke it. "I heard about Howard. I'm sorry, Michel. What devastating news. I loved him."

"Thanks, Walt. Since yesterday, Emily self-reported, too."

"Oh, no. As if you didn't have enough going on. I'm sorry to hear that, too. Em was a nice lady. I always enjoyed our discussions about books."

"So you're aware, I asked Elaina if she would mind temporarily taking her place. With everything going on, I want someone that I can trust, and I can trust Elaina."

"I'm glad you can, Michel." Walt's brain went back to the problems of his sons. "I don't understand where I went wrong with the boys, Michel. I never dreamed that Rob was unhappy enough to want his brother and sister dead. I've never heard of someone being willing to kill for the opportunity to ascend."

"It's happened before, but not to us; not here."

"I'm sorry Rob was our first. What do you think will happen to him?"

"I don't know. It'll be out of my hands, Walt. They may ask me for input, or my opinion - but that decision will be at the top-level of VarenCorp." Michel could hear Walt's indrawn breath as he imagined the worst for Rob. Michel saw the video of his interview earlier. Having seen that, he knew he wouldn't be making that decision. "No matter what, it won't happen right away. Director Fuller is focusing on finding two of the men Rob worked with; the third got on a plane, headed to Brussels and disappeared. And being completely honest, Walt, we've got our hands so full with VAS that unless he's directly tied to the outbreak he's not as high a priority."

"That's something at least..."

While Michel was talking with her father, Elaina was in her suite when she received a call.

"Ms. Jacoby? It's Jack, down at the Concierge station. Your brother Doug would like to visit. May I allow him up?"

"Yes, please. Thanks, Jack."

Moments later, there was a knock at the door; Elaina called out, "Come in…" and her brother's familiar face appeared.

"Hi, Elaina."

"Hey, Doug." It was awkward, but only for a minute.

"I'm sorry. I was an asshole to you."

"Apology accepted. Please, sit down." Doug did, in the chair across from her.

"Pop told me you told the cops to warn me, even after Rob and I were shitty to you. You looked out for me, and you…didn't have to."

"You're…family, even when you're acting like an asshole."

Doug snickered, and told her snarkily, "I wasn't acting." They both laughed, and then both became more serious. "I'm sorry Rob helped kidnap you and wanted you dead. Maybe I shouldn't look at things in shades of gray, and I'm trying to excuse my own actions - but as shitty as I was to you, killing you never once entered my mind."

"Imagine my relief." she said, answering snark with more snark. "Really, Doug, it's good to know that. I'm sorry Rob wanted you dead, too."

There was a lull in the conversation, and had both thinking. Doug broke the silence. Pop had me in a come-to-Jesus meeting today. He told me I was damned lucky you don't hold grudges." He looked at his baby sister and cocked his head to the side. "I am lucky in that." He shrugged a little. "Pop reamed me out for wanting to be Virehnai; wanting to ascend. He told me if I don't focus on the firm instead of wanting to be Virehn, he won't leave me his interests in it, and it would be Lightner, Lightner and VanEtters, instead." Doug sighed heavily. Elaina mentally was congratulating Papa on taking Doug to task.

Elaina was careful about what she said to her elder brother next. "This will sound weird, but what was the first thing you ever wanted to do, or be?"

"That's easy. I wanted to be just like Pop."

"Why?"

"Different reasons at different times. He was my hero when I was little. At some point, I admired his strength. Later, I admired him for either his skills as a lawyer or the way he dealt with being in charge."

"You notice that being Virehn or even being wealthy wasn't the first thing you said?"

He chuckled. "True."

"Someday, Papa will want to step down and retire. For what my two cents are worth, focus on the business. If an opportunity comes up where you get the chance to ascend...great. If you don't, it's still great. You'll be in charge of the firm, and be just like Papa, like you wanted to be since you were little."

He sighed. "That's true, but it's also easy for you to say; you've ascended."

"You're right. I can't argue that. You know what, though? I asked Papa if he ever wanted to be a Virehn when we met about my will, before I ascended. You know what he told me? When he was your age or...maybe a little younger, he wanted to be Virehn. But then he met Mama, and you came along, not long after. He decided he didn't want it anymore."

"Why? Love of family?" He said it with more attitude than it deserved, but Elaina let it pass.

"Well, sort of, yes. He told me after having you, he couldn't imagine loving you as much as he did that first day he held you...watching you grow up, and then someday watching you die while he kept living." She paused. He looked stunned. He didn't know that. He never realized that his own presence might've been the reason his father had never ascended. He'd never told him. Somehow, he assumed incorrectly that it was a lack of ambition.

"What Papa told me, and probably told you too, was true: he would've been happy for any of us to be chosen. When you said you wanted to be just like Papa? I think he's looking forward to seeing you marry, and have kids, and watching them grow up. If you question that, look at how happy Papa is playing with Sophie and Hayden!" She paused. "Think of how happy he'd be with a little clone of you playing in the shadow of his desk like you used to, and watching your little Mini-me want to be like you! My position in all this is to watch over all your children and love them. I....won't be having any, other than Virehn children I might sire someday. Still, I harvested my eggs. Did you know that?"

His forehead and brows wrinkled up. "Really? So, are you going to have kids? I thought you just said you couldn't have any."

"I'd have to hire a bloodsworn surrogate to carry it; Could I? Sure. But to what end? To watch my biological child age and die? That's the same dilemma Papa faced." She looked at Doug and shook her head. "My path is different now. It's going to be hard enough watching all of you age and die and then watching generations of all of your offspring do exactly the same thing...age and die, over and over. What the Vel'sheth told me is true. I didn't just die and rise Virehn. I literally died to my old life."

Corinna quietly sat on a lower branch of one of the large chestnut trees in the back of the house. She was barely breathing, making no sound. She was listening. She could hear the heartbeats of a variety of animals nearby. The softer, faster, almost frenetic ones were mice and chipmunks. She was relatively sure there was a cat nearby. The local red deer were easier to spot; their heartbeats were stronger; their hearts were bigger. All she had to do was wait for one to come near, and she would jump down and give it chase.

Ari gave her packages of blood yesterday that came from RKS. There was one for him, which he took down to his office. She placed the packages for her, Hassan and Alwin in the refrigerator in the galley.

Ari was ecstatic that he was getting blood from a pure source. While Corinna understood that, she'd also heard him and Tim, and then Alwin, talking. If they thought they were being targeted–then why would she EVER drink what Ari was drinking? At least until after the crisis was over? Thanks, no thanks. I'll have the deer.

It didn't surprise her he'd done that, though. There were Virehnai all over the world that last week, yesterday or today, found out they were sick. There those plotting rats were, downstairs in Ari's office, all but toasting one another with their 'pure-sourced blood.'

Though neither of them were involved in it, both would surely remember the lessons of the French Revolution. While Marie Antoinette never actually said "Let them eat cake," there were regular people in the streets of Paris who were angry at their plight. The rich and privileged and nobility soon lost their heads, literally. It didn't sit well with Corinna that as fellow Virehnai were receiving what amounted to death sentences, here was Ari, drinking blood others could never pull strings to get…still beating the system.

Corinna let everything she'd heard the other day settle in. The more she contemplated Ari's actions, the more she realized he was simply reaping what he'd sown. That's why she was out here, hunting. It also gave Corinna a curious sense of freedom. She wasn't doing what Ari expected her to do; Instead; she was out hunting deer. Ari would never understand, nor would she expect him to.

It was while she was sitting there, up in the old chestnut tree, that she decided something.

Connecting all the dots was tiring. Everything that was happening to ALL of them ultimately went back to that one night that shouldn't have happened. Was it Ari and Tim and Alwin, doing as they liked, and then running roughshod over everyone else? Yes.

As Corinna turned it over in her mind, she realized she was culpable, too. She'd excused Ari's behavior for years...blaming him, of course, but never once blaming herself. She excused herself, out of fear that he would kill her. Somewhere in there, she realized that as the times changed, she could've left and protected herself; to hide...but didn't.

Corinna would prepare. If the 'pure' blood Ari was drinking made him sick–Corinna would leave and never look back. It would be the Gods and the Universe telling her she'd received 'credit for time served.'

And if he didn't get sick from the blood, she would take matters into her own hands and would smear a bit of Mercy's Shadow into his new mugs.

Before any of that, though–she had a clan sister to tell a story to. If the Universe required her life, she wanted to make sure the truth of that night at Focaria Rubra didn't pass away with her.

"Gotcha!" Noah Shorngetter thought to himself. He was spearheading the effort to find the oathsworn traitors. Unlike their better-known police counterparts, VarenCorp Security used a data broker, feeding it all the aliases they had…and got multiple hits. They immediately worked through their police counterparts to get a warrant for the mobile carriers to use their cell data to locate the closest tower. Using the data broker, they received a treasure trove of known addresses, associates, and telephone numbers associated with them.

Noah looked at the reports from the data broker, and the information he'd just received from the mobile carrier via a warrant. He knew where both were. Noah picked up his phone and called Archie's cell phone directly.

"Fuller."

"Thanks to the warrant, we've got hits. Malcolm's pinging off the cell tower nearest a registered address in Manhattan; Ross Martell's phone is pinging off a cell tower closest to an address the broker lists as his brother's home in Brooklyn."

"Good job. Get folks out to pick them up and bring them here. Any further word on Alex Carpenter?"

"I've contacted INTERPOL and put a Red Notice out on him and all his aliases; that's about all we can do, I think—unless he comes back here. He might; he traveled a good deal. If he doesn't realize he's in trouble, we can pick him up stateside when he returns."

Several of NYPD's finest bloodsworn officers, warrants in hand, apprehended Malcolm Harwell at his apartment in Manhattan; they picked Ross Martell up in his brothers' basement at his home in Brooklyn. They transported both men not to a police precinct, but to VarenCorp.

Director Fuller was angry that Alex Carpenter wasn't able to be apprehended. While they were searching for Elaina, Alex got on a plane at JFK to Amsterdam, and from there, disappeared. Noah was right. He traveled often; Alex Carpenter might return, and if he did, they would be ready.

First, they brought Malcolm into the little room wired for sound and video. Unlike Rob, his hands were chained and so were his feet.

"How well do you know Rob Jacoby?"

Malcolm looked straight ahead at the wall, saying nothing.

"Who are you working for, Malcolm?"

Silence.

"Why did you kidnap Elaina Jacoby?"

Crickets.

"What do you know about Virehnai getting sick?"

Archie Fuller got a reaction to that–his eyes widened a bit, but that was the only tell.

"We picked up Ross this morning, too. If he sings before you do, he'll receive mercy. Are you sure you want that to happen?"

Malcolm said nothing.

Fuller looked at him. "Tsk, tsk. Hard way, it is." He paused for a moment, talking into the air. "Please send in Joao."

Moments later, there was a knock at the door. "Come in."

Joao Perreira, the Vel'sheth who works for VarenCorp on the rare occasions he's needed came in. He was wearing a clerical collar and looked like a priest. He looked at Malcolm, who gave a questioning look, but still said nothing.

"Hello, young man." Joao said. "Do you know what a Vel'sheth priest is?"

For the first time, Malcolm spoke. "If you think I'm going to confess, you're wrong. That won't happen."

Fuller chuckled. "Oh, you'll confess, alright. But your lips won't do it. Your blood will."

Fuller looked back up at nothing. "We're recording, correct?" A voice answered, "Yes, sir." Director Fuller looked over at Joao. "Whenever you're ready, sir."

Joao pulled a small, but very sharp knife and a little plastic communion cup out of a small bag he brought with him, even as Malcolm's eyes widened.

"You can't do that. I've got rights."

Fuller shook his head, and told him, "You're oathsworn, son. Some of those rights stop where your oath to us starts. Like I told Rob yesterday when he was sitting in the chair you're sitting in right now: you see where you are, don't you? You're not in a police lockup. This is VarenCorp. We have the right to learn how and when you broke your oath."

Archie held Malcolm still, and Joao cut his finger and let it bleed into the cup. Malcolm sat stony and defiant.

Joao sat in the chair directly across the table from Malcolm. Taking the little cup, he emptied it into his mouth, and closed his eyes, and let the blood fill his mind with impressions, reading it right there in front of all of them, on camera.

This is one of those times where Vel'sheth training comes into play. Virehnai blood is easy to read, and other Virehnai can do it. There's a clarity brought about by the magic that underpins the Virehnai and their blood. Human blood, too, can be read, but it's more difficult; less clear. What the Vel'sheth sees with human blood is usually murky. It comes in fits and chunks, flashes, feelings and sometimes symbols. Reading Virehnai blood would be like reading a document that was straightforward and easy to understand.

Reading human blood would be like trying to read a redacted document: some places are clear, others are blacked out, and there are ink smudges and smeary fingerprints over other parts. You'll get a story, but it could be difficult to put together. The only times it's especially clear is if there were strong emotions involved, or if they spent a great deal of time thinking about the event before or after. It was a crap shoot, meant not only to reveal what they could from his blood, but to rattle Malcolm into talking using what they could see.

What the Vel'sheth saw within Malcolm's blood was ultimately damning. It gave them leads on where to look. Archie Fuller wasn't watching the Vel'sheth. He was watching Malcolm's face–intently.

"I…see…a house. Flowers in the front yard. Broken glass. A man hitting a woman." Joao's face wrinkled in distaste. "Your father; he was bloodsworn…your mother oathsworn. You blamed the Virehnai for not restraining your father before he killed your mother. Your real name is Eugene Ryan." Malcolm closed his eyes.

"I can't see the man you work for's face – but he's not in this country. I…get a sense he's Virehn. Might have promised to turn some of you that helped him. You are bloodsworn to him, while oathsworn to us. Curious."

"You took part in an attack on Elaina. You particularly enjoyed fondling her, didn't you, Eugene? She wasn't Virehn yet."

Joao paused, trying to get a handle on the disjointed images he was seeing. "I see a woman. Scotti badge. Horses and cleaning supplies. Bloody hands…yours, hers, and Rob's. You promised that woman something." Joao gasped a bit. "You killed her instead."

Joao turned to Director Fuller. "That's all I got, but hopefully, that's enough."

Director Fuller smiled at the man bound in front of him. "Hello, Eugene. You sure you don't want to talk?" The man seated and chained at the table said nothing. Again, Fuller talked to the people in the back that were monitoring the audio and video feeds as they recorded the room for posterity. "Check to see if there were any recent deaths of oathsworn employees of Scotti that are used at Robichaux or other local properties and then investigate them."

When they repeated this with Ross, it was similar. He wouldn't speak; shared nothing willingly. When Joao came in, and he pulled out the small, sharp knife and little cup, his eyes widened in fear. "What will your blood say, son, that your mouth doesn't want to say?"

When Joao tasted Ross, he was stunned. "I see a puppeteer. He...Ross sees himself as one of the puppets. I see flowers, and waterfalls, and...what is that? That's Cornell University, I think. I see mist, and I see flames. You set something on fire." Joao looked over at Archie. "That's all I got, but he has ties to Ithaca and upstate New York."

Archie Fuller looked at Joao. "Thanks, Joao, for your help. We'll take it from here." He then looked over at Ross and thought for a minute. When he spoke, it was to the folks in the back. "Please check on the status of the warehouse we found Elaina in." When he said that, Ross' face showed surprise. Fuller, after seeing his reaction was fairly certain they'd discover the warehouse went up in flames, and Ross thought Elaina had died as planned.

Alex got off the plane in Amsterdam, and Christiana Emmorton was waiting for him to come through the jetway. He had no bags; only a carry on. They moved through customs and left Schiphol Airport, and after renting a car, left the Netherlands behind them, headed for Basel.

Christiana and Alex spent the night at her family home in Dinant, in Belgium. It had gone to her mother in her parents' divorce years ago; it was hers now. She texted Peter to let him know that she and Alex were together.

They made love…and then using her favorite knife, she first cut him, then drained him almost to death…and then she gave him her own blood, killing him. It wasn't a surprise. Alex knew she would; it was part of the plan. For all his aid and cooperation, Peter told Christiana to sire him, and he would be her first child. Christiana told Peter when it was done and then read as she waited for Alex to wake up.

Alex awoke the next day Virehnai, with the world around him screaming for attention as it assaulted his mind. The name he'd rented the car with, Samuel Mozier, was to be his Virehnai name. Alex–now Samuel–spent a day there in Dinant as he acclimated to the smells, the noise, and his new physical acuity - and then they continued on to Basel. Peter hadn't wanted Samuel to be in the US when Elaina or Doug died.

It's official.

VarenCorp is now the proud owners of Cypress Hill Retirement Community, which sits on ninety-two lovely acres conveniently located in the DC suburbs, close to shopping and amenities, and the DC metro and subway lines, and major highways. That would be especially lovely if the Virehnai in question could leave their apartments. They won't be, for everyone's safety.

This morning's update meeting felt more hopeful than some others had, mostly because they were actually doing something; responding to the crisis with something more than a meeting.

"Good morning, everyone. I have good news to report to you. Yesterday, the sale went through. The company that owned it signed all the agreements–including the pre-occupancy agreement. We can move people in tonight if we can get them there."

"Didn't they question why we wanted to be in so quickly?"

Tim laughed and answered the question. "If they had any, they didn't bother asking once they found out it would essentially be a cash transaction. They needed the cash more than they cared to ask anything."

Ari laughed. "Funny how money does that, isn't it? What's next, Tim?"

"They've agreed to a settlement date within 45 days; there are many regulatory hoops we'll have to jump through, and several inspections. One thing that helped was that we agreed to current management and employees staying in place until at least the settlement." At that, Ari frowned, but Tim kept on. "Of the regulatory hurdles, it includes licensing to operate; because the previous owners were frequently out of compliance, we have to prove we addressed and corrected their problems. The plans we have for the medical center will require final approval. Beyond that, Dr. Johanssen thought that there would likely be someone from the CDC that would need to be onsite as oversight, because of the…unusual…nature of our situation."

"If there's so many regulatory hurdles, how can we be moving people in?" Elishka asked.

David started laughing, and they looked at him. "Because everyone we're moving in are older than 55 years of age, and they will be residents. There weren't any rules keeping them out except for their age; legally they're all well over that."

Ari shook his head in disbelief. At least the rules were in their favor. "Did you come up with a plan for moving those that can be?"

"We did, sir," Michel answered. "We plan to rent two 'coach' style buses. Doctors evaluated the condition of the Virehnai who have self-reported, and there are 53 that are here in headquarters that can be moved immediately to Cypress Hill. We'll put half on one bus, half on the other. The coaches will stop at VarenCorpDC briefly to fill up the extra seats with their self-reports, and then the buses will travel to Rockville to drop them off. Despite it not being a standard procedure for Cypress Hill, we'll be traveling at night to minimize the risk travel-wise. Also, late at night, most of the residents of Cypress Hill will be in their apartments, and may not notice, and there are fewer employees on site; that should help, too."

"Do you have the list of names for Tim and me to go over?" Ari asked them.

He looked at David, but it was Tim that answered. "David and Michel gave me the list before the meeting, Father. Want me to read the names to everyone and then email you the full document?"

"Sure."

"The five names put forward for our consideration are Rochelle Fairhope of Clan Westbrook; Jeff Garvin, of Clan Robichaux, both from here; Kennedy Elizabeth Mace of our own Clan that works for Shadowbrook Suites in DC; Matthew deLoache of Clan Wakefield from Baltimore; and finally, Thomas Hellman of Clan Daniels of New Jersey." Some individuals were better known by the group than others. "The document they put together that I'm sending you has a half-page dossier on each, with their specifics."

Carolyn asked, "Who is preparing the briefing for the White House?"

Tim looked at her, and said, "Me, David and Michel. If you want to help us, we don't mind. We're having that meeting right after this one."

"I was curious more than anything else, but I can sit in and help."

Later, they wrote a paper by committee that listed a series of bullet points listing the benefits and expertise VarenCorp brought to the table. Despite never having run an eldercare facility before, they had several things in their favor: one thing was their hotel division. There was their flagship brand, Shadowhope Suites, along with Meridian Inns, and their Lucent and Aurelian boutique brands, and dozens of luxury inns that were once ancient buildings that were converted into premium hotels and resorts. VarenCorp was used to managing properties of different sizes and is completely familiar with catering to all kinds of people – human and Virehnai alike.

Another thing in their favor was there was no shortage of money to throw at either the property or the problem of what's going on with the Virehnai.

Finally, despite the sick Virehnai that would be co-located there, the influx of money combined with their proven expertise at running large-scale properties would make the human residents safer than they were already, and they would get upgrades and ultimately benefit from the changes made for the Virehnai residents. "We plan on continuing operations at Cypress Hill after our crisis abates and aren't looking at the facility there as a short-term answer to our current problem."

18

DEAD MEN, WALKING

Elaina dressed nicely that first morning, not entirely sure what to expect. She was certain she could do whatever Uncle Michel needed her to, but he was at the head or on the board of so many companies, and she knew nothing of most of them. Elaina knew about the structure and workings of Jacoby, Lightner and VanEtters, and was sure there were a million things about his other companies she would have to learn. Elaina saw it as an opportunity to learn more about the broader workings of Clan Robichaux.

When she got there, it made her sad. There was Em's desk, just the way she left it. It would be her desk now, at least for a time. Before sitting down, she went to Michel's door and knocked. She could hear him having a discussion with someone, despite the early hour. She heard Michel say, "Wait a minute," to someone, and then to her, "Come in."

Elaina opened the door and walked in. "I wanted to let you know I'm here." She thought he had someone in with him; apparently he was teleconferencing with someone. "Sorry for the interruption…" she told him. Before she could back out and leave him to his call, he waved her over. "Come on in, Elaina. Come here."

She came in, and then around Uncle Michel's desk and saw someone on his computer monitor she instantly recognized. He had blondish brown hair and a roguish expression on his face. Elaina recognized him from what she saw when she ascended. Michel laughed. "Bend down so he can see your face, hun."

"Oh, sorry." Elaina bent down as the man on the screen

chuckled. He had a nice laugh.

"David, meet my daughter, Elaina Jacoby. She's the one you helped rescue." Michel went on. "Elaina, this is David Lambert, who's head of VarenCorp London."

"Thank you, sir, for helping them find me."

"I'm glad I could help." David told her, with a hint of a British accent.

Michel turned to Elaina. "As soon as I'm finished up talking to David, I need to discuss what I'm going to need for my trip with you. Because David went back to London, I'll be taking his place and heading down to DC to have a meeting at the White House with President Colton." All Elaina could think was, I thought I knew so much about Uncle Michel. He's visiting the President? Of America? Really?

Elaina looked at the monitor again. "Thanks again. It was nice meeting you." She stood and turned to Michel. "Let me know when you need me." Elaina left, shutting the door behind her.

Standing by Em's desk, she sat down in her chair and looked. There were pictures of the children she'd sired; plants; sticky notes of things to remember, and a stack of papers that she would carefully go through later. Elaina sighed. Most of the pictures, she carefully removed from the desk and sat them on the credenza on the other side of the room. The only picture she left on the desk was one with Emily and her daughter. It would both remind her of Em and also remind her she had big shoes to fill. She left her plants as well. Hopefully, she wouldn't kill them outright. No promises, there.

Elaina glanced briefly through the papers. Several of them were bills; they were clipped into neat bundles arranged by company, and there was another that was specifically for Clan Robichaux, which was the largest stack. Actual bills were on top, and then there were dozens of charge notices–similar to when she was at Sanguinarium Obscura and purchased her necklace. Amalie had her charge the clan, and the clan later deducted her purchase out of her next check. These were the slips that told the clan how much to deduct at the end of the month.

As she was sorting through the papers, Uncle Michel's door opened, and he poked his head out. "Come on in, Elaina. Let's chat."

She grabbed a notepad and a pen and followed behind. "Have a seat."

"I don't have lots of rules; I don't expect you to pick up everything instantly. The biggest thing to tell you is don't use the online scheduling right now. Someone from Jeff's office is coordinating with our IT team and VarenCorp's IT departments. They'll let me know when it's safe to use again. He told me once it's done, everyone across all our companies will need to change their passwords for the whole system."

"Everybody?"

"Uh-huh. Not just here, but across VarenCorp, We found out from your brother that he gave your schedule, and mine and Howard's as part of the data breach. Based on what the IT guys found, they're thinking Rob may have given them his login and password, too–so they're locking down EVERYTHING."

Elaina rolled her eyes. "Rob's a piece of work. Sorry."

Michel looked at her. "It's not your fault; it's not your dad's fault, either."

"Guess who visited me yesterday?"

"Doug?"

Her head cocked to the side. "You knew?"

"No, I guessed. I talked to your dad. He…told me he laid down the law to him."

"That's what Papa told me." She chuckled. "Hopefully, it sticks. We'll see."

"My next big thing that I'll be dealing with; I just heard that our meeting with the President was green-lighted. Tim Warner and I will fly to DC for an afternoon meeting in two days. Tim's secretary Daphne will make the arrangements for both of us–but I'll need you to coordinate with her. I will also need you to plan with VarenCorp Hospitality for two nights at Shadowhope Suites by Tim's office. Our meeting will go late enough that it's easier to stay. I may not need both nights, but it's better to arrange for it with the situation at hand. I prefer it if you text me my confirmations and boarding passes, if you don't mind."

"I'll take care of it, and text you the confirmations when I'm done."

"Good, thanks." He looked at her. "Oh; texting. Before I forget, text me whenever you need to. If it's an emergency and you need me to answer back immediately, the code I had set up with Em was NYRN... Need You Right Now. If either of us sends that to the other, we answer it immediately. Got it?"

He paused while she wrote that down. "Got it." Elaina looked back up at him.

"The only other thing I can think of is that I've got a Task Force meeting this afternoon; seems like since I've been on that Task Force, that's all I do anymore is go to meetings. High-level VarenCorp meetings." He sighed and shrugged his shoulders. "Jack's been picking up the day-to-day things I normally do and has been stepping in for me during the crisis. Once this is all past, you and his assistant Corrie should probably sit down and chat."

"Other than that, if you have questions, ask me. If I'm stuck in a meeting and you need advice, call Jack's office to talk to Corrie, or call Howard's office and talk to Gracie. She's by herself in there right now; eventually, Jeff will move in. She told me yesterday she'll work under Jeff as long as he'll have her." He exhaled, willing the sadness of the situation away. "Poor Gracie."

Michel walked out of his office and headed to VarenCorp. If he wasn't careful, someone would suggest he have a satellite office there, like they'd given David–something he didn't want.

When he got there, he was happy to discover he wasn't the last to arrive, though this morning, it wouldn't have drawn Ari's ire. He sat down next to Carolyn. Eliška was on the other side of the table. Director Fuller was there, as was his second, Noah. Most of everyone else was on teleconference. Ari's monitor was blank yet. Tim walked in last and sat down next to Eliška. Moments later, Ari's monitor came to life. They must've been talking.

"Well, let's get this started." Ari looked like he was in a foul mood. Something in his demeanor and attitude, and even tone of voice.

"We've decided who will be the first head of Cypress Hill. It wasn't an easy choice. Each of the Virehnai on that list could do the job and would've had something specific to bring to the table. It came down to deciding what we needed most, not a personality contest. The person we're going to tap to take the position will be Jeff Garvin. He won't go down alone, though."

"We decided our own clan mate Kennedy will go down with him, specifically because of her years with Shadowhope Suites. We'd like them to work together as a team, with Jeff focusing on the Virehnai that will move there, and Kennedy focusing on getting the location up to snuff. The only thing we're still trying to decide is if we'll be offering Matthew deLoache of Clan Wakefield a position somewhere as well. His resume looks like he's a rather accomplished Jack of all trades, and based on that, he would be useful for either Jeff or Kennedy to have around; as he's older than Jeff, it would put him in charge of Clan Cypress Hill." Ari paused, frowning.

"Next, I'd like Archie to expand on the cryptic message he sent earlier."

"Sorry, Ari." Fuller said, looking uncomfortable. "I was trying to be careful. Our teleconferences are secure; some of our other means of communications are still questionable, and I'm getting paranoid about whether the walls have ears."

Ari gestured at him while addressing everyone on the call. "See? Now I'm not the only one paranoid. Welcome to the club. The floor's yours, Archie."

"Yesterday, we apprehended two of the oathsworn who kidnapped Elaina Jacoby; one here in Manhattan, the other in Brooklyn. Both are in the lockup upstairs."

"Good," Ari interjected.

"We had Vel'sheth Joao Perreiera come in and read their blood, as they were being...uncooperative. We learned much from what Joao could read."

"Joao could see Malcolm was involved in the first attack on Elaina Jacoby, as well as her kidnapping. What other things we learned were... I'm getting ahead of myself."

He shuffled through a couple of papers in front of him and then pulled one in particular out. "Let me read to you what Joao saw: "I see a woman. Scotti badge. Horses and cleaning supplies. Bloody hands...yours, hers, and Rob's. You promised that woman something. You killed her instead." Michel sat up straighter at the mention of Rob; several blinked or reacted at the word 'killed,' including Ari. Director Fuller shuffled out another piece of paper.

"We went searching for a woman who worked for Scotti; one

who died since all this started–and we took it back to the dates where David had money funneled out of his accounts. We found four. One died from breast cancer, one died in a car crash on the New York Thruway, another had a stroke. May they rest in peace. The fourth? Bing-bing-bing…We have a winner. The police found her at the bottom of a flight of stairs with a broken neck surrounded by her groceries after a 'concerned person' called it in anonymously. The police wrote it up as 'she missed a step.' The woman's name, some of you might remember seeing before. It's Patrice Dixon."

"Whoa. Wait. That's a name my team found." Michel said "She worked in housekeeping. There were minor inconsistencies in her file between what we had on her, and what Scotti had on her. When we vetted her again, she came out clean."

"It appears Ms. Dixon had accumulated over 100K of gambling debt."

"No. We looked at that in her file. It didn't say that." Michel told him, getting defensive.

"I believe you, Michel. You weren't the only one taking a long look at her. Detective Hall checked her out too, along with the others, for a host of criteria. We don't go down into the weeds, but credit scores are an indicator of blackmailability. VarenCorp has a program that systematically goes through and updates credit scores and other information that might clue us in to when one of our human allies needs help. People who can be blackmailed can be used against us." Director Fuller looked nervous as he considered what he was about to say. "As some of you know, IT is trying to upgrade our security after we learned that calendars and servers were breached. Like Ari, I don't believe in coincidences: knowing of the hacking and seeing Patrice Dixon's name there. Out of an abundance of caution, I asked IT to double check the integrity of the central files, but particularly regarding the auto-updater." He paused.

"Someone hacked it. They said it wasn't anything spectacular. Someone basically got into it and removed a line of code. IT fixed it and notified me, after which I immediately did another search. That's when I discovered Patrice was...compromised." Fuller sighed. "When we sent bloodsworn officers out to talk to her family about her manner of death, and if they were having problems, her eldest daughter showed us stacks of betting slips. Their daughter said she'd been going to Aqueduct Racetrack, convinced that she could fix her debts that way, but it only made things worse. She told the officer that they were about to be evicted. We...believe she was being blackmailed by Malcolm Harwell, and what she did for him earned her a grave plot."

Ari asked, "Now what? What did she do for him?"

"This...is where it goes from bad to worse." Archie Fuller looked at Michel. "I'm sorry, Michel. Because of what Joao read; that Patrice, Malcolm's and Rob's hands had blood on them? This morning we had Joao read Rob's blood."

"What came of it?" Michel asked, a pained expression on his face..

"May I play a video?"

"Please." Ari said.

Tim punched a button, and a moment later, the video came on screen. Rob was in chains in the interview room, and not happy about it. He was belligerent and had an attitude. Vel'sheth Joao came in, and Rob lost a little attitude. Unlike the other two men in custody, Rob knew of the Vel'sheth, and knew some functions a Vel'sheth priest played.

Director Fuller sat across from Rob, and when Joao pulled out his little knife and little plastic communion cup, Rob's eyes widened when he realized he meant to read his blood, and despite being in chains, fought to be free. Two men came in, and held Rob down, as he cried, and screamed, "'No!,' 'No!'"

Rob bled into the little cup, and then Joao took a seat next to

Director Fuller as the two men who held Rob down left. Rob was still crying. Director Fuller spoke before Joao drank from Rob.

"So, Rob. If you wonder why we're doing this... Yesterday, Vel'sheth Joao here drank a sip of Malcolm's blood, and saw blood on Malcolm's hands...blood on your hands...and blood on a woman named Patrice's hands." Fuller, watching Rob intently, saw his head snap up and eyes widen at the mention of Patrice. "What, I wonder, will your blood tell us?" He nodded at Joao, who drank the contents of the little plastic cup.

"Oh. Anger. This one is angry, so angry. Everything I see is on fire." Joao shook off the anger and looked deeper. His eyes squinted and his brows wrinkled, as if he was trying to see something more clearly. "He's hard to read. He has so much anger and hatred it clouds everything in his blood, and in his mind. Let me try something else." Joao reached forward and grasped Rob's wrist, feeling his pulse strongly beneath his hand, and then licked the inside of the cup for the remaining drops of blood. Rob tried pulling away, but Joao's grip was much stronger.

Joao focused on the fear Rob was feeling, using his pulse as an anchor, along with the last drops of his blood from the cup, and found what he sought. "Stolen keys. Housekeeping cart."

As Joao spoke those words, Rob tried to jerk his arm away and began screaming and freaking out. "Executive level."

The video stopped. Everyone was silent, as they were contemplating the implications of what Joao said. Director Fuller spoke. "We checked the security videos for the past month." He paused. "Here are the relevant bits."

There were audible gasps as they watched Rob sneakily following behind and then stealing keys off of a housekeeper's cart. Another shot showed him sprinting in the stairwell. The video showed him approaching Patrice Dixon, giving her the keys. The next shot clearly showed Patrice letting herself into Michel's suite of offices. Her sweatshirt's hood was now up, and her head remained down through most of her cleaning routine. She cleaned the outer office around Em's desk and then went on to Michel's office. Patrice cleaned his office normally, saving the galley area where his mini fridge sat for last. Head still down, she turned and, in a quick, swift move, pulled something out of the cart and put it in the fridge. "Pause the video." Tim did. Everyone started talking at once.

"Everyone, shut up! NOW!" Ari barked at all of them. The room quieted immediately.

Very quietly, Ari asked, "Do you know if Joao is in the building?"

"I'll ask." Director Fuller picked up his cellphone and texted for a few moments. Meanwhile, Ari looked at them, but asked, "Michel. As Sulahnai, you source your blood through your bloodsworn, and are in complete control of the process, correct?"

Michel, sitting there, looked shellshocked. He nodded yes, and slowly replied, "We do. We have a 'health suite' in all our buildings, and our phlebotomists are Virehnai. We get our empty bags for our bloodsworn's contributions from the same group of suppliers as the Red Cross does. They're standard. Our health suite maintains a secure reserve, and they are the ones who make our deliveries."

"I must ask. Did your assistant ever drink from your supplies?"

Michel closed his eyes, exhaled and without looking, answered, "Yes."

Director Fuller signaled for Ari's attention. "Archie?" he asked.

"Joao hasn't left the building yet. He was visiting with some of the sick Virehnai getting ready to move to Cypress Hill. I asked him to come here."

"Good." Ari said forcefully. He looked like he wanted to punch someone. "What else does that video show? You paused it. Why?"

416

"The next shot that comes up shows a clip that our video team worked on. Its enhanced security footage; we zoomed in on it, slowed it down, and sharpened it. I paused so I could take a moment to explain what you would see. Can you hit play, Tim?"

As the video restarted, the scene of Patrice cleaning the area around the mini fridge finished. It switched to a scene that was zoomed in on the cart and her hand, and what she pulled out of her purse filled the screen. What was in her hand was clearly a bag of blood. There were murmurs of surprise. The next scene went back to the unenhanced security footage, and showed her in front of Howard's office, where the same actions were repeated. Patrice cleaned the outer office and his assistant Gracie's desk, and then moved on to Howard's office, and likewise put a bag of blood into his mini fridge. Michel watched her actions stonily; he was angry, and trying to control his rage, which was boiling alongside his grief. That woman was responsible for his assistant's death, and that of Howard. She would not do what she did if Rob hadn't given her the keys and access to accomplish it FIRST. Rob had betrayed him personally, along with Clan Robichaux at every turn. His best friend; his brother and confidante for over 2,000 years was sitting upstairs, along with numerous other Virehnai–all waiting to fucking DIE because Rob Jacoby didn't like his lot in life.

David asked quietly from his desk in London, "Michel, are you okay?"

"No. Someone I trusted betrayed me in multiple ways. If he were here right now, he'd be a crimson stain on the carpet."

Leonie spoke up. "I'm sorry Michel. Virehn zuth akret. We've learned something valuable from that footage, though."

Michel looked up. "Thanks, Leonie."

"Leonie, elaborate please. What did we learn?" Ari asked.

"They went to all that trouble to get blood in. Blood. It's bloodborne–at least for Virehnai."

Before they could discuss it more, there was a knock at the door. Tim called out, "Come in."

Joao Perreira entered. Tim said, "Hello Joao. Please, have a seat."

Once he was seated and comfortable, Ari spoke. "Joao, welcome. Thank you for reading the blood of those who betrayed us. It's appreciated, and it was informative. But now? Now, I need the advice of a Vel'sheth."

"What can I do for you, sir?"

"As you helped us discover, Malcolm, Ross and Rob have betrayed us. It's clear to me that Michel and Howard were both targeted, and those three, along with the woman Patrice, who is dead, all played a part in Howard VanEtters and Emily Hargrave having VAS. Judging by the volume of self-reports in DC and here in Switzerland leads me to believe that Tim and I are being targeted as well." Ari paused. "They were also responsible for the kidnapping of Rob's sister, who's a Virehn, and they planned to burn her alive, and kill her bloodsworn brother. When Rob helped Patrice plant those bags of blood, they meant it to kill Michel. It would be an act of treachery in any case, but Rob is oathsworn to Michel directly; Howard is one of the Sethari of the Clan Robichaux, the very clan he is oathsworn to protect. I know it's…rare; normally not done with oathsworn. Considering the circumstances, could Malcolm, Ross or Rob be sentenced to Khar'Suleth?"

There were several who gasped. That was an old ritual. Rare, indeed. It could be likened to a wildfire. In old Virehnai, it meant "Call of the Bloodbound Flame." A Vel'sheth would invoke the egregore bound to all Virehnai by the Compact with their blood and the flame…by the magic within that blood and ask it to judge those who stand accused. The ritual is said to be terrifying, because being in the presence of the Egregore, called Varet'Sul'Akha can be felt. A Virehn can feel it ring through his blood; a bloodsworn human might feel hopeless or doomed. It wasn't normally performed on oathsworn humans, but based on the acts committed, it would now be up to all the Vel'sheth whether these oathsworn could face the wrath of the 'tribunal in the blood.' The ritual is said to be terrifying. The Egregore is frightening and always answers when called. Once Varet'Sul'Akha is called, and once its judgment begins, those present must see it through to the end. If there are others that are guilty, wherever they stand, they will die as well. This is the reason many likened the ritual to a wildfire: what Varet'Sul'Akha learns, he applies to all, and no one, Virehn or human, leaves unchanged; Those who are present at the ritual are witnesses, forever marked in their blood. It wasn't a 'casual ask.'

Joao's only reaction was to blink. "I will take the matter up with my fellow Vel'sheth, and I'll let you know our decision tomorrow." He looked around at everyone, both there in the room, and by teleconference. "Knowing what I've seen, I believe there is a strong case for its use. So much of what appears to have been done by the oathsworn humans went unnoticed; some because of technology, the rest because of willful obfuscation of facts. Asking Varet'Sul'Akha to judge those oathsworn brings it to his attention. Know this, though. A warning:" He looked up directly at Ari. "Remember that Varet'Sul'Akha will judge those humans, but it won't stop with the humans. Once the egregore is called, it will carry the judgement through to its conclusion, whatever that conclusion may be. If the judgment implicates others, they may find themselves judged as well."

Hearing nothing else, Joao said, "Very well." He looked up at Ari. "Was that all you required of me, sir?"

"It was. Thank you, Joao."

He bowed to them, and said "Virehn zuth akret," before turning and leaving, even as they all replied, "Virehn zuth akret."

419

Ari got off the call with the task force, feeling angry, irritable, and hungry. He went from being in a long meeting with Tim, to going around in circles over who would run Cypress Hill, and then into that hellscape of a meeting with the Task Force. Ari couldn't do anything about the other things, but hungry? That he could fix. He got a bag of blood out of his fridge. "Want one, Alwin?"

"Please."

Ari got out another bag and handed it to Alwin, and they warmed them up, put them into mugs, and sat back down to discuss the meeting.

"What did you think of all that?" Ari asked.

"Holy shit. Sucks to be in Clan Robichaux right now," Alwin said. While he said it jokingly, neither lost sight of the gravity of the meeting they had, nor what happened at Jacoby, Lightner and VanEtters, or to Michel, who was targeted. What happened to him was what they feared most for themselves.

Ari nodded. "And that, Alwin, is why we aren't friends with our food. The only humans we ever have here are those who have been brought in as meals." He snickered. "It pays to be paranoid some days."

"What did you think of the meeting with Tim before the Task Force, about the Virehn directed to move there, and who will be in charge?" Alwin questioned. He had watched Ari and Tim go round and round in circles. First, Tim picked Michel to go with him to the White House in David's stead, and this morning, he fought for one of Michel's children to be in charge. Knowing his sire for as long as he had, he imagined that Ari was wondering about Tim.

"I think some of it makes sense. I'm not sure I buy into the choice of who will be in charge... I don't know what's in Tim's brain right now."

'Bingo,' Alwin thought to himself. "You're referring to Jeff Garvin?"

"Nailed it. I get why. He fit the criteria for being in charge; plus, he's planning to accompany Howard there anyway, so make use of him. I understand Jeff has a vested interest. I get that. I'm not happy because he's Clan Robichaux."

"At least we'll have people included from our own clan, and multiple others, scattered throughout Cypress Hill, across all three shifts. Kennedy will be there; she'll be answering to you, and VarenCorp. Tim's daughter Rosalie will be there. She'll help monitor things, and she'll be working directly with Jeff. If he's doing anything off, she'll report back. We can trust both of them. At least, as far as we can trust anyone, I suppose."

"I believe Kennedy and Rosie will look out for our interests, and I suppose they'll be watchdogging Jeff, too. My other heartburn with Cypress Hill has to do with all the damned humans. All those non-aligned humans near a bunch of sick and dying Virehnai." Ari said, shaking his head in disbelief..

Alwin chuckled. "What could go wrong THERE?" He asked sarcastically.

"I can't state long enough or loud enough how much I don't like that Cypress Hill's current employees are staying." Ari said, finishing up his mug. "I understand, but dislike the rationale; Tim, David and Michel all promised that it would go easier with the feds if we did. 'If we leave the people there that know their jobs, know what they're doing and are better at handling situations for the humans, it makes the humans that know about us now feel better.' I heard it; I got it. I feel as if it leaves us...exposed. Vulnerable."

Alwin nodded in agreement as Ari continued. "I don't like that there are so many humans with no ties and no fealty to us there. There's nothing to keep any of them from sabotaging us, betraying us, finding out about us or outing us... Hell, think about the video we saw earlier. The humans who betrayed Clan Robichaux could do what they did because they're mollycoddled, trusted too much, and mostly do as they please. The chances of all those things happening at Cypress Hill go up exponentially if we leave them in place."

Alwin agreed. "Being too trusting allowed us to be in this mess to start with. You're right. NOW we're supposed to trust random, strange humans, too?" Alwin rolled his eyes and chuckled wryly. "Can I remind you that you pay me to keep VarenCorp out of things like what's about to happen soon at Cypress Hill?"

"I don't like any of it, but I don't think we have much choice." Ari said, quietly.

Alwin stood to leave. "If you need me, give me a shout."

"Thanks, Alwin." he said.

After Alwin closed the door, Ari turned to his computer and brought up a document Tim sent him. Apparently, the meeting he and David had with the Director of the CDC was having benefits already. One epidemiologist at the CDC who was working on dementia research looked at the data they'd gathered, and found a pattern, and contacted Tim to let him know. What the epidemiologist, a fellow named Dr. Charles Wray, told them was this: In an elderly human, they were the most lucid in the morning; gradually as it gets later, they became less lucid until they reach the point where they're confused–called 'sundowning.'

Dr. Wray realized while looking at the data that the Virehnai were doing their own version of sundowning. When they first began losing their lucidity, and snacked on the neighbors, it was most often very late at night…sometimes so late that it seemed especially early. He also learned that while Virehnai normally didn't need sleep, often as VAS raged through them, they slept–most often after trying to feed. From the data he saw, it seemed if a Virehn slept, the effects worsened, and it started the pattern of lucidity/loss of lucidity all over again–and every time that pattern repeated, it shortened exponentially, until they could no longer maintain lucidity at all. It didn't take long.

In the email to Tim, which Ari was reading, Dr. Wray also notified Tim that he had volunteered and would move to Cypress Hill. Not only would he be able to help discover what was attacking the Virehnai–but hoped it would also help him in his research into human dementia. "Win-win," he told Tim. That, and he looked forward to meeting him. Ari chuckled. It sounded like Dr. Wray took the news of their existence better than Dr. Johanssen did. At least Wray saw it as an opportunity. Positive news, for a change.

Corinna stuck to her guns about eating the red deer when she was hungry. Ari and Alwin wouldn't have noticed whether she was using her rations of blood from RKS or not; they would have to pay attention to her first! She could try to make herself feel better and say they were busy with the crisis – but truthfully, since she didn't have to go get them food anymore, her interactions with them had decreased considerably. Hassan noticed. He saw her up in the chestnut tree one day from his suite as she hunted deer and got a laugh out of it. Later, he visited her in her suite.

"Why are you eating deer? You have a fridge full of human blood from RKS."

Her decision made no sense to him, but Corinna didn't want to let on that she'd heard something she shouldn't have.

"After the All Call," she told him, "I don't trust any human blood; not until Father says the crisis is over. No matter how much I hate red deer, at least I know that's safe to eat."

"Suit yourself," he told her. "If you won't use your supply, can I have it?" Corinna happily gave it to him.

Several days later, 'happy' was the operative word. Corinna

was happy that she gave her supply to Hassan. Happy that it did not tempt her before she gave it to him. Happy for red deer.

Corinna was reading a book in a comfy chair, feet curled up under her. She heard an insistent knocking on her door. She called out to say, "Come in.' It was Hassan. Corinna looked up at him when he entered. He seemed upset.

"Is everything okay, Hassan?"

He looked at her and shook his head no. When she looked concerned and confused, he said quietly, "You were right. Right to not drink the blood."

"Huh? What do you mean?" She asked.

Hassan came nearer, and pointed out a brand-new mole near the bend of his elbow, and said, "I have two more; one on my leg, and one on my hip. After I found the one in the bend of my arm, I went looking for others…and found them. It would appear I have VAS."

"Oh, no! Hassan! I'm so sorry!" Corinna jumped up from her chair, as the book fell off her lap, forgotten. She hugged him. He was the only person in the house she felt genuinely cared for her. "Have you told Father yet?"

Hassan shook his head no. "He's going to be angry. Even if he's not angry at me, specifically… Centuries with Father are long enough to know I'd rather not be the bearer of bad tidings. I remember he used to kill the messengers who brought him bad news. Telling him he likely has VAS wasn't on my to do list for today…"

"I know." What else was there to be said? They both knew what their sire could be like. "Father needs to know, though. If he hasn't got VAS yet, he needs to know to stop drinking that blood he got from RKS. If you don't do it for him, at least he needs to let RKS know their blood supply's contaminated. How many other

Virehnai could get medicines they've made with tainted blood?"

Hassan lowered his head in defeat, knowing Corinna was right. "I know VAS is a death sentence…he said quietly. "Still, I'd prefer NOT to tell Father. That way, I'll die in peace. As a ghoul, maybe…but by the time I am one, I won't know or care anymore. Not knowing what you do counts as peace, doesn't it?"

Hassan turned sadly, resigned to his fate, and left. Corinna felt like she dodged a bullet. She felt bad for Hassan but couldn't feel anything other than ecstatic for herself. Free! After centuries of tap dancing around Ari/Alban/Arjun, trying not to die, Corinna finally saw an exit for herself. She pulled her bag out of the closet; this was the moment she'd prepared for. Apparently, the Universe heard her. She didn't have to kill her own sire. Her sire's own distaste for red deer, and his arrogance in believing his longest held company–RKS, was untouchable, did it for her.

Ari sat at his desk, reading the rest of the email exchanges between Dr. Wray and Tim, along with the rest of the emails in his inbox. He so much preferred a parchment or a scroll to digital messages. As far as he was concerned, the only thing they had recommending them was their speed. Their efficiency, to his own mind, was questionable, as people often took things that others said wrong. No one took the same time, care and effort they used to when writing out a message longhand. Instead, they saw emails much in the same way they did those infernal text messages. He hated all of it. He kept his wax seal on his desk, like he'd done for 2,000 years. No, it didn't get used anymore, but it reminded him of the 'good old days' when the care you took in your communications meant something. There was a knock at the door, which interrupted his train of thought.

"Enter." He looked away from the screen to see Hassan at his door.

"Come in, Hassan. What do you need?" It was politer than, "I'm busy, Hassan; Go away," but it meant the same thing. Ari didn't invite Hassan to sit down.

Hassan took a deep breath. "I need to self-report."

"WHAT? What...did...you...say?" Ari's head cocked to one side, and his eyes flashed angrily at his son.

As Hassan began repeating himself, Ari interrupted him, waving his hand. "I know what the fuck you just said. How could that be?" He shook his head in disbelief. "What makes you think you need to self-report?"

"I have three new... Well, they're not exactly moles, they're more like discolored patches...they're new. One is on my leg, the other on my hip...and this one's the one I saw on the inside of my elbow."

Hassan held out his arm for Ari to see for himself, even as Ari cursed like a sailor in countless different languages, some ancient enough that nobody spoke them anymore, his face turning as pink as a Virehn would ever get - from sheer anger.

"Did you go hunting recently?" Ari asked angrily.

"No, sir," he mumbled. "I've only had the blood you gave me."

"GET OUT!" He screamed at Hassan, who turned and quickly scurried out of his office. As Hassan closed the door behind him, Ari started throwing random things from his desk at the door, punctuating his displeasure.

He sat there at his desk, stunned. Angry. Frightened.

Ari was paranoid on the best of days and had been that way for centuries. The crisis itself hadn't bothered him. The thought that

426

Virehnai were getting sick bothered him. Truthfully, what truly bothered Ari most was finding out that the Compact didn't appear to be working correctly for those who had VAS. The thought that the Compact could be dead in the water worried the hell out of him. It left him vulnerable. The one thing Ari Cottrell hated most, whatever name he went by, in whatever century - was that he appear vulnerable. Worse still than appearing vulnerable…actually being vulnerable.

What he'd dreaded for centuries was malcontents in his own ranks; waiting for one of them to use humans against him, or decide to 'take one for the team,' by killing themselves even as he died, as the Compact guaranteed. It never once crossed his mind that tainted blood would come from his OWN lab. His lab was as secure as the so-called 'Swiss Fort Knox,' which was a secure underground data storage facility in the Alps, named for the American 'Fort Knox', where gold was stored. The Swiss version was nearly as paranoid as he was - and that was saying something.

Knowing that and knowing how secure his RKS labs were? That knowledge screamed one incontrovertible fact at him, as he defiantly picked up his new mug, and threw it at the door as it broke, and then broke into smaller pieces when it hit the floor.

Like Michel had been, someone betrayed the great Ari Cottrell. He wanted them to pay.

Ari reluctantly picked up the phone and called Alwin. "Come. Now. It's an emergency."

Minutes later, Ari heard a knock at his door.

"Enter," Ari said. As the door opened, all the shattered bits of thrown, broken objects made a noise and traveled with the door as it opened, and Alwin looked to see what was making the noise. The broken bits on the floor testified to SOMETHING being wrong. He looked over at his sire with concern.

"What's wrong? What's the emergency, Father?"

Ari looked up at him. "We've been betrayed."

"What?" Alwin asked, questioningly, as he sat in his usual seat. "How were we betrayed? When?"

"Hassan informed me moments ago of his need to self-report."

"Wha…" Alwin didn't even finish what he was going to say, as his mind raced through situations and outcomes, and his eyes widened with fear.

"Is Hassan certain? Are you certain?"

Ari looked sadly at him. "Unfortunately. He's got something that's a cross between a mole and a textured patch of skin that's reddish brown in the crux of his elbow, plus a couple more he said he had that he didn't show me."

"Did Hassan go hunting recently after you bade us not to? How is he positive it was the blood we got from RKS?"

"I asked him that, too. He didn't. It doesn't matter," Ari said. "Even if it was the last meal Corinna brought home for us—we all drank from him. I wish it wasn't RKS. Corinna brought us a meal over seven days ago; it only takes 3-4 days for symptoms to appear. I told her not to bring others home right after I arranged for the blood from RKS. If you do the mental math, we were into our first shipments about 3-4 days ago. Either it's the supply itself that's tainted, or someone at RKS betrayed us specifically and shipped us tainted blood. Same result. No matter what, we're betrayed. We might as well be dead men walking."

Alwin's expression sunk. He wasn't happy.

"What now? Look for moles?" Alwin asked sarcastically.

"Well, let's figure out what our options are. Time for a family meeting." Ari picked up the phone and called Hassan. "Hassan? Can you please join Alwin and I down in my office?"

"I'll be right down, sir."

Ari pushed the button on his phone, disconnecting and then called Corinna. Corinna didn't answer.

Moments later, Hassan came down. This time, Ari offered him a seat, which he took. "I don't know where Corinna is." Ari complained. "I tried calling her three times. I wanted to let her know the blood from RKS is tainted, and she has VAS."

Hassan said simply, "I went to her suite after I left here. She left. Corinna was already gone."

"What do you mean, she... she WHAT?" Anger chiseled the features on his face. "That little bitch! So much for trust. Not only have we been betrayed once, but twice, and from within!" Ari was so angry he was literally shaking, and it was making Hassan scared. "All these years I've harbored an inconstant traitor under my roof!" Only after his sire's tirade stopped and he spent his anger over Corinna did Hassan speak up.

"Father. Corinna didn't betray us. She told me days ago after the All Call, and hearing about VAS, that she was too afraid to drink human blood; rather than risk it, she'd eat the red deer until the emergency was over."

Ari still bristled and rolled his eyes at his child's 'sudden' preference for deer. "I saw her from my suite, father. I saw her sitting up in the chestnut tree behind the house, hunting. I laughed at her for it, then, and later on asked her why. When I asked her if I could have the blood you gave her, she gave it to me, without question. Corinna told the truth. The box was sealed. It hadn't been opened."

Even if she hadn't betrayed him, Ari was still angry. "Still, she should've stayed with us," He fumed, silently.

After a moment, Alwin answered him. "What? Stay here? Why? To watch us all die while she's not sick and one of us could kill her?" Alwin shook his head. "Corinna's smart; she's trying to ensure she won't end up dust, like we will."

They all sat silently, each contemplating the shit sandwich that the Fates just handed them.

Ari looked at Alwin and Hassan. "Before anything else, I need to let Tim know what happened, and that VarenCorp's his show now. He needs to take extreme caution to protect his person. He needs to cultivate some extra paranoia." Ari sighed and looked at Alwin. "After I talk to Tim, my next thought is to have two more meetings: one with the security directors and Tim, and then have one with the continental directors. That one, I'm thinking, we should record and have it played at the next task force meeting, with heads of clans tasked to get the word out that Tim will succeed me."

Alwin looked at him, head cocked a little to the side. "Aren't you going to have a clan meeting to tell our siblings personally, as Sethari?"

"No. I think I'm going to task Tim with that. There are too many malcontents in our ranks. If he has the meeting, and he's already assumed control of VarenCorp, and the Directors are aware of the situation–there will be far fewer who could or would challenge him. Tim notifying his siblings will be him asserting control, and they should recognize it as such."

He looked at Alwin. "You don't need to be off screen for this. You either, Hassan." he said, looking to his other son.

He pulled up to his desk, closer to his computer, and called Tim using his secure teleconferencing app, as his sons moved in closer.

A few moments later, Ari's face appeared on Tim's end, in his office. Tim expected to see his father; he wasn't expecting to see Alwin or particularly Hassan.

"What's wrong?"

"We've been betrayed. We have VAS."

Ari's pronouncement was met with stunned silence. "No. You look no different from when I saw you a little while ago," He stuttered. "H..h..how? How can that be possible?"

"There must be another breach. Remember I told you we were going to source our blood from RKS?"

Tim nodded. "Yes. I'm working on setting up a similar delivery for myself. Since they're in Basel, it becomes complicated; we're still working on approvals to transport it; plus, establishing the cold chain to get it here."

"Don't bother. There's a breach at RKS."

Tim's mouth dropped open in surprise; he hastily closed it. "What? That's about as secure as it gets. How could that happen? Are you sure the blood you got from them is their...cause?"

Ari nodded yes. "Our blood came directly from RKS. The outer packaging was intact; the inner packaging with the dry ice was fine, including its tamper-proof seals. Our current situation originates inside the facility. Whether their entire blood supply is tainted, or someone who was vetted and trusted working there betrayed us and sent us tainted blood, targeting us, much like what happened to Michel–that I don't know. After today's meeting and what Archie showed us, personally, I'd go with someone betrayed us, specifically."

"I'll look into it and let them know they need to examine everything...quietly. Hopefully, if it's a personal betrayal, we'll catch the responsible parties before they can disappear into the woodwork." He paused, with a pained look on his face. This wasn't how he wanted to end up in charge of VarenCorp. "Do you want me to come there, Father? To be with you?"

Ari made a face. "No. Why? To watch us die?" It was the same answer Alwin had given him regarding Corinna, and it caused Ari to think of her.

"Oh–Corinna's fine. Hassan tells me she was frightened enough by what we revealed at the All Call that afterward she swore off human blood until the crisis passed. Hassan saw her hunting the red deer instead of eating the blood we brought in. She left a while ago after Hassan told her he had VAS." Ari paused.

"I was angry at Corinna at first; I felt like she abandoned us. When you just asked if you should come here, I realized the truth of what Alwin told me earlier. When I'm gone, please find her, and offer her any of the homes that are Clan-owned, and whichever she picks, transfer the title to her. This house is yours, to do with as you will. Live here, transfer it into clan ownership; whatever you like or choose is fine. I won't be here to care."

"I'm...sorry, Father." It honestly saddened Tim to learn of his sire's impending death sentence, and made him angry, too. He was fighting tears, something that didn't happen often. Ari noticed and smiled at his son. His blood–as both a Virehn and biologically.

"Thank you. If you want to honor me after I depart this life, catch the bastards, please, and make them suffer. In the meantime, watch your own back." Before Tim could say anything else, Ari said, "Shall we invite the Security Directors into our call now?"

Tim looked at his father, and solemnly said, "Yes, sir."

It took a couple of minutes, but soon, Ari saw the faces of his five Security Directors: Archie Fuller, in NY; Leonie Meier in Brussels, Belgium, Prakash Adhikari in Tokyo, Fatma Mahmoud Abasi in Cairo, and Ana Maria Bianchi in Rio.

Most noted Alwin and Hassan's presence, unusual for a security council meeting. Tim was there, which wasn't so odd. What was odd for Tim was how somber and grim he looked. Fuller and Meier both looked shook before Ari said a word.

"Sorry for the short notice for the Security Council meeting, but I had an announcement I needed to make. Effective immediately, Tim is now fully in charge of VarenCorp."

Archie Fuller shook his head in disbelief. "What happened?" He didn't bother asking why. Leonie and others were taking notes.

Before Ari could say anything, Alwin quipped, "We're self-reporting. Couldn't you tell?" Ari turned to Alwin and rolled his eyes, but he turned back to answer Director Fuller. "He's right. We have VAS."

There was a chorus of "Oh no's," and "I'm sorry's" followed by a few "Virehn zuth akret's".

Leonie looked up. "To parrot what Archie said, what happened, Ari? How? What do we need to address?"

Archie guessed, "It had to be betrayal." Leonie and Ana Maria appeared to agree, based on their angry expressions.

Ari confirmed what they already knew. "It was. We're not entirely sure whether all the supplies of human blood at RKS are tainted, or if someone wanting revenge used RKS to betray us to send us tainted blood on purpose. That question needs to be addressed immediately. Medicines currently on the production line could be tainted; any blood they send in response to a request from other blood banks could be as well. Or…we might have one more breach, right under our noses."

Leonie shook her head in disbelief. "You were sourcing your food during the crisis from RKS, and they got to you that way?" She addressed Tim, now her boss. "Tim, do you want me to spearhead this? RKS is in our territory."

"Please do, Leonie. I think I'll have my hands full. If any of you feel like working together on it, that's fine by me. That's what we pay you all the bucks for." Tim told them.

"As I told Tim, if you want to honor me, figure it out, and if it's something someone has done to us by tainting the supply, or by betraying me;" he looked to Hassan and Alwin–"by betraying US - and sending tainted blood? Catch the bastards responsible, make them pay…make them an example. It reminds me too much of what happened to Michel, and Clan Robichaux. This should never happen again."

"Agreed."

Prakash spoke up. "What are you going to do next, sir?"

Tim looked at them. "Going to Disneyworld is NOT the answer."

Ari looked at Tim and acted as if he was suggesting it. "At a theme park? With VAS? Oh god, if you thought the cat memes were bad, that would take it to a whole new level."

When a few of the Directors seemed taken aback by the grim banter, Hassan spoke up. "If we don't laugh, we'll be crying. Or we'll be angry. Our clocks are ticking, and it's a countdown. Why spend our last moments harboring those emotions?" He looked to Ari and Alwin, and back to the monitors, catching his brother Tim's eyes. "I don't know about you, but I've been alive 1741 years. If the sickness gives me less than two weeks, and of that, only a few more good days where I have my full faculties? That's going to go by like a flash" He snapped his fingers. "It'll feel like seconds against a life as long as any of ours."

"Well said, Hassan. And true." Ari said. "Shall we go out hunting tonight, gentlemen?" He turned to Hassan and Alwin. "Just because we're Draz'kul, and we can? What harm would it do now?

What will they do? *Kill me faster?*" He laughed, but it was sharp, and angry. He looked back to the Directors, into their stunned faces. "VarenCorp's well cared for, between my son, and all of you; us? We're already dead men walking."

After the call ended, all three of them got dressed. The agenda for the evening? There were only two things, and they both started with the letter 'F.'

If he was a 'dead man walking,' Ari thought, "I'll go out with a bang. Literally."

Michel got two texts between 4 and 5 am, while he sat in his study, reading Sun Tzu's "The Art of War." His choice seemed fitting, given the day he'd had, and the revelations that came out. The first text came from the continental heads of VarenCorp-announcing an All Call. The meeting this morning was basically a VarenCorp "All call" that said something like 'if you've received this, you MUST attend, whether in person or teleconferenced in. The second message was from David: "Something big's going down. Hang on to your ass cheeks."

Not knowing what was happening, Michel went to the All Call early. Good thing. The room was getting full. Luckily, some folks had second thoughts about sitting around the main table. Michel sat next to Carolyn. She looked worried. She leaned over and told him, "I don't know what's going on, but it's not good. Things have been crazy this morning. It's like everyone's lost their damn minds."

Michel leaned in toward her, "David texted me early, and told me more or less the same thing."

Eliška came in and took the empty chair next to Michel. Like many others, Eliška was somber.

As the room filled, it surprised them that Tim wasn't sitting among them. The monitor they would usually see Ari in was dark as well. Tim's face popped up in it. He looked grim. Tired.

"Thank you for joining us. I have a message from my father that he asked me to share with you." Michel noted what he was seeing, because Tim looked as emotional as he'd ever seen.

Ari's face replaced Tim's on the monitor. Beside him sat Alwin and Hassan, which was unusual.

"Hello, everyone. Thank you for being here. For those of you who don't know them, I'd like to introduce my sons, Alwin Hoffman, and Hassan Khalid. Recent times have been unusual. The challenges that we've been facing are every bit as unusual." Ari rolled his eyes. "Oh….for fuck's sake, I could keep to the script I'm reading, or I could get to the point." He exhaled, annoyed, and looked straight at the camera. "We've been betrayed. Me, Alwin and Hassan have VAS."

There were gasps all over the place, both in the room there in Manhattan, and countless conference rooms around the world.

"Effective immediately, Tim is now the CEO of VarenCorp. I expect you will show him the same level of support you've shown me."

"Any of you who know me also know that it'll be a cold day in hell before I allow myself to become some raging ghoul without a brain that's rotting and bleeding everywhere. For those of you who actually care, you'll be happy to know that the three of us went out and about in Zurich earlier. We fed until we were full and fucked until we were satisfied."

"I've lived a long, long time. I've often wondered what my eventual end would be. Getting sick wasn't anything I saw. Neither was turning into a ghoul. Someone thought to betray me, and to control how I would meet my maker, along with my ultimate demise. To them? To those people? I say, "Fuck you." I've controlled every bit of my life for as long as I can remember. What the hell makes them think they can take control now? They can't. They won't. I told Alwin last week in passing that I'd drink a glass of Mercy's Shadow on the rocks before I'd become a ghoul like those we've seen." Ari held up a glass, and moments later, so did Alwin and Hassan. To the fuckers who thought they would control my death, I say, "Cheers." He looked away from the camera, and down into the glass in his hand. Looking back up at the camera, he raised his glass in a toast, with Alwin and Hassan following suit. "Cheers…and I'll see them in hell." Ari and his sons all drank the milky liquid in their glasses, and died instantly, falling out of their seats and out of the video frame. The Virehnai who were watching worldwide were stunned, dismayed, and even horrified by what they saw. They all just watched the oldest living Virehn take his own life instead of suffering through VAS. None could blame him.

The video cut off, and went back to Tim, who looked…bereft. He had seen the video as it was being recorded and was watching it again. If anyone wondered if he actually cared for his father, they weren't questioning it now.

Tim addressed them. "As the new head of VarenCorp, I tell you this: The betrayals went system-wide and went deep. We have already captured some of them. Others we're checking into. Anyone who was involved and contributed to the loss of the man who was my sire, my father, and the only living member of my biological family I know of…we'll be coming for you. One of my father's last official acts was to call for the ritual of Khar'Suleth for those we know committed treachery and betrayal. I can only pray Varet'Sul'Akha will see those we haven't apprehended and deal with them as well." Tim was choking back emotions. "I received word back before coming on to address all of you that, after consideration, the ritual of Khar'Suleth was approved."

"Please let your people know my father has died and has appointed me to carry on in his place as head of VarenCorp. Go back to your clans and tend to your people." Tim paused. "Those of you who are part of the Task Force, please remain, or remain in teleconference, please."

Monitors winked out, one by one as those who weren't part of the Task Force disconnected from the teleconference. For several moments, Tim's monitor also disappeared.

When it reappeared, he had pink tracks down his face. He had wanted no one to see him weeping for his father. Michel, looking at him, thought it made him more...human. It made him see Tim in a better light.

Many people assigned what they saw as 'weaker emotions' to whatever was left of a Virehn's humanity, remaining in their soul and blood. Michel, like others that were Sulahnai and had humans around them all the time, didn't see that as a bad thing. They saw it as a proof of how all Virehnai started out, and a reminder that the Virehnai took humanity to a place the surrounding humans only ever dreamed of. Not...evolution. Not exactly. They walked alongside their human counterparts on a parallel track. Separate, different...but leading back to that moment when their First Flames worked magic, and they forever diverged from the path their human cohorts remained on. They were tied to one another in multiple ways, whether through the blood that one of them had, and the other required, or the oaths they swore to one another, whether it was simply their word, or by the blood that flowed through their veins.

Tim looked at all of them, clearly heartbroken. "This will be short, folks. Aside from letting you know that my...father...has...passed;" he said, emotionally, "please ensure that there are All Calls to let everyone know that I've assumed the leadership of VarenCorp in Father's stead."

Silent tears began making pink-tinged tracks down his face.

"I also wanted to let you know more about the decision regarding the rite of Khar'Suleth. I was contacted this morning not by Joao Perriera, which I expected, but instead by Leonid Dmitriev, the head of the Vareth'Kai – the Vel'sheth Council of Shadowed Flame. Because of the current crisis, they decided that invoking Varet'Sul'Akha is not only warranted–but necessary. He specifically said that there were too many unknowns that remain invisible to Varet'Sul'Akha, and the only way to truly come to a conclusion about our situation will be to conduct this rite. All the current Vel'sheth worldwide will be in attendance." Tim shook his head. "We are making history, whether or not we wish to." Tim paused. "We have yet to learn which Hall it will be in; Clan Westmore or Robichaux will likely be hosting them."

"Go back to your Clans and tell them what has transpired. To those who are working on getting Virehnai to Cypress Hill tonight, continue that. We'll regroup tomorrow. If I have need of you, for whatever reason, I'll be in touch. I'm going to be attending a remembrance service for my sire this evening. I'd be grateful if you remembered him at your clan meetings."

It was rather late. Elaina had spent her time earlier with her sister and her nieces, Sophia and Hayden. Earlier, she went to FAO Schwarz, and got them both dolls they wanted, along with clothes for them. Their happy shrieks did a mambo straight up her spine, but seeing how happy they were made her happy.

After they left, she started out her evening surfing the web, eventually shutting her computer down and reading instead.

A text from Uncle Michel interrupted Elaina. She looked at it and frowned. Something bad must be up, to have a mandatory All Call at nearly midnight. After finding out about Emily and Uncle Howard, it made her worry for Uncle Michel. She didn't bother getting dressed up, staying in the jeans and t-shirt she was wearing, donning sneakers.

Elaina made her way to the Hall, where others were gathering. Michel looked somber. It surprised her to discover that it wasn't Virehnai only. She noticed a large contingent of the Lightner family there, and saw Mama, Papa, and Doug walk in a little later. She went over to stand with them after they exchanged hugs.

"What's going on?" Elaina asked her father.

He shrugged his shoulders. "Hell if I know. We're here because we got a text telling us it was mandatory. I guess we'll find out shortly."

The Hall was getting rather full. Reman, the Vel'sheth stood by the dais. There were candles lit upon it. Elaina always loved the way candles bounced flickers of light through the Hall. It always highlighted and underscored the magic of the Virehnai, and the essence of the space.

Michel came in not long after and was somber. After a few moments, he looked over at Reman, who nodded.

"Let's get started here, folks." Michel said, and the surrounding conversations silenced, as people waited to hear why they'd been called here, now.

"I'm sorry to be taking you away from whatever you were doing, particularly our human families; I know it's late. There have been changes you need to know about, and it's important enough that it can't wait. The first effects everyone." He paused.

"Ari Cottrell, the head of VarenCorp, and the oldest known Virehn alive, has died."

Michel paused, as people took that in. Ari was a lightning rod. Of those who actually knew him, they either loved him or hated him. Other than that, thoughts of him were based purely on reputation, and what people heard, or believed him capable of. They believed him to be capable of much.

Someone called out, "What did he die of? Who killed him?"

Michel nodded slowly. "He found out that he had Virehnai Aging Sickness. He was betrayed and was quite adamant that he didn't want to let the individuals that betrayed him win. He and his sons Alwin Hoffman and Hassan Khalid died this evening–on video–while drinking glasses of Mercy's Shadow over ice. It was a calculated act of defiance against those who betrayed him, captured for posterity on video."

The balls it took to drink your own death registered on the faces of most of those present. "What they have instructed me to tell you is this: Timothy Warner, Ari's Virehn child and biological relative, is now the head of VarenCorp. We're in...new territory. As Ari - whatever name he went by- was first the head of Focaria Rubra, then The Velascar Company, and now, VarenCorp - for well over a thousand years, we can't be sure what ultimately the change of leadership will mean for all of us; I know Tim has our best interests at heart, and will do his best to guide us through the times we find ourselves in." People were talking, imagining that the end of the news Michel had for them. They were wrong.

"Before I release you, I need to let you know something else. It won't be pleasant to hear. Earlier in a Task Force meeting, I saw it played out on video; it was...difficult...to watch. Friends, one of our own betrayed us." Michel shook his head. "If you wonder why we're having this meeting with our human family among us, I'll illuminate you. Whatever you do, however you take the information I'm about to impart, remember it's only on the individual I'm about to name; not the rest of his family."

Walt reached out, suddenly having a sinking feeling, and maybe a premonition, and with one hand, held his wife Connie's hand, and the other, Elaina's. Elaina felt much the same. Whatever Michel was about to say wasn't good.

"We were betrayed by one sworn to us. Vel'sheth Joao Perreira read Rob Jacoby's blood this morning, and it showed clearly that he stole keys from one of our housekeeping staff…and then provided them to another compromised human. That woman used those keys to place tainted blood into my refrigerator, and Howard VanEtters' refrigerator." The revelation caused a stir among those in the Hall. "Those actions directly led to Howard and Emily contracting VAS." As people began reacting to what he'd said, he held up a hand, and they quickly quieted, even as Walt's head dropped, and he hung on to his wife and Elaina for all he was worth.

All Walt could see was the sweet, rosy-cheeked child that had once hugged Michel's neck. How could Rob have fallen so far? Walt wanted to cry and did his best to bottle it until later. He suspected that once he got back to his home, there was a glass of whiskey, tears, and some reflection in his future. He could apologize to Michel and would; but there was nothing he could ever say that would make his friend feel better. His son had helped to kill someone his family's patron had known and loved for….God? Over two thousand years? There's no way to make up for that.

There was certainly nothing he could do. It made him despair as he stood there amongst the Lightners, and the Virehnai that he'd sworn an oath to, and his son had casually betrayed. His wife's and daughter's hands gripped his tighter. Doug reached out and placed his hand on his father's shoulder. If nothing else, Walt had his family standing with and behind him, even as tears fell, silently.

"In a meeting earlier today with Ari, he called for Rob and the other two oathsworn humans involved to face the ritual of Khar'Suleth." Like the other things Michel had revealed, there was a reaction to the fact that they were going to leave Rob's fate up to Varet'Sul'Akha. Elaina didn't know what it meant; her father didn't know what the ritual was, but he knew who Varet'Sul'Akha was and could do. It made him cry harder. His family didn't understand yet; neither did most of the humans attending. The Virehnai? The older ones understood. Rob would die alongside those he conspired with. The rosy-cheeked little boy Walt remembered would die for what he did. Walt thought he raised him to be good and honest, even if he had a quick temper, and took everything personally. Apparently, not.

"Because a similar betrayal of trust occurred with Ari, I'm positive that the ritual will happen sooner than later. I wish I had better news to tell all of you, but…I don't. The one thing I want to say, I need to say…is to Walt. To his wife, Connie. My friends, this is not your fault. I know you did your best. The fault lies solely on the shoulders of your son. I hold you blameless."

Michel left where he was standing by Reman and walked over to Walt. Walt wasn't expecting it. Michel looked into his friend's eyes, and then hugged him, followed by hugs with Connie, Elaina and Doug.

"Some of you might not be aware, but Rob's betrayal goes deeper than you know. He not only did what he did in betrayal of us, but to his own family. He attempted to murder Elaina and his brother Doug. Luckily, that wasn't successful."

"That's all I have for you, folks. At some point when all of this…." Michel's hands gestured,"…craziness ends, we'll be having remembrance ceremonies." He shook his head and was only barely keeping a reign on his emotions. "There have been too many this year." Michel turned and walked out, heading to the relative sanctuary of his study. Today had asked much of him, and it weighed on his shoulders.

Elaina talked for a few moments with Mama and Papa, trying to make them feel marginally better. When Elaina turned to leave, Mama and Papa both gave her a bear hug. Doug looked at her. He'd already made his apologies. He gave his baby sister a bear hug. "I'm glad Rob didn't get to kill either of us," he whispered in her ear. Elaina was crying pink tears for her family. "Me, too."

She was standing by the elevator to go downstairs to her suite when Michael Ratner tapped her on the shoulder. Elaina looked at him, and he hugged her. "I'm sorry your family is dealing with this. It could've been mine, just as easily." He looked at her and said sadly. "Did you hear the other news?" Elaina's brow wrinkled. "What news?"

"My ascension has been rescheduled until after things have settled down."

"I'm so sorry, Michael. Hopefully, things will get back to some kind of normal soon."

"Hopefully."

Elaina went back to her apartment. She wandered back to her bedroom. She still found it funny that she had one; it's not like she needed to sleep anymore. Her bedroom basically looked exactly the same as it had when she lived in the mid-town building. Same furnishings, same decorations. Elaina even removed her shower heads and shower stereo system and moved them with her to this suite.

As she glanced around her apartment, it looked much the same. It was bigger and had a better view. Aside from that, it could be the same. If she put on a blindfold and spun around, she'd be hard-pressed to say which suite she was in.

Same clothes, and sense of style. Same haircut. Generally speaking, Elaina looked the same, too.

Well, mostly.

Elaina always had a nice figure; always had the same dark chestnut hair. But now, as a Virehn…there was something different about her. Something…intrinsically different…that anyone outside of the insular little world she was part of who met her wouldn't be able to pin down, or codify, but they would sure as hell feel. Some would be drawn to her. Others would be wary, yet never know why.

Elaina Jacoby was different. She felt different. She acted different. She ate different. The day she ascended, she truly died to her old life. Her new one was full of so much promise. The only thing about her old life that remained were the memories; events that informed her of who she was: human kisses from her mom and dad.

444

Boyfriends and best friends. The time spent in school and college. Parties and alcohol. Laughter and tears shared. Those things gave her the humanity that allowed her to walk among humans and not be questioned.

She wasn't quite human anymore, though. Elaina Jacoby was 'human enough.'

DEDICATIONS

To my husband Schoen: this one's been a while coming out… Thank you for reading and re-reading chapters and pointing out typos and inconsistencies when you found them. You've helped me in so many ways; this one wouldn't be what it is without your love and support.

To my sisters, Missy and Amelia: You've both been sounding boards on this one and had so many good ideas. If there's a super snarky line in here, chances are it came from one of you! I look forward to all the fun coming up, between plans for a podcast, and recording audiobooks with Seth!

To Cyndy Collins: It's hard to believe we've known each other for longer than 40 years. When you've known someone for that long, they qualify as family! This has been a hard year for you; We'll get to visit together soon, I hope! That and I'm looking forward to a road trip with you, destination TBD – hopefully, with no traffic circles.

To Jimmy Swierczewski: I wish you were here for this. I'm positive you'd have had input on this one, for sure. I miss you; hell, we all do. You should be here. I can't believe you've been gone for nearly ten years. As David said to Michel, ""We shall say his name often, and his flame will sing within our blood."

To my awesome editor, Annemarie Holmwood, and my beta readers: Shelly Wolf, Kayla Corter, Cathy Beasley, Kimberly

Vacek, and Seth Hench. Seth is doing double duty – he and my sister Missy will be doing the narration for the series!

To the gang at Papertown….Terry, Missy, Kayla, Wendy, Rachel and Lisa! Thank you for all the coffee!!

And finally, to you, dear reader…for taking the time to read what I write!

Dear Reader:

The original premise for Not Quite Human came from a dream from Fall of 2019; the book resulted from telling my husband and my sisters about my dream while sitting around a campfire, drinking wine and enjoying a relaxing evening. The ideas were from all of us; I tied them together and wrote them up. Credit where credit's due, right? All along, I've bounced ideas off of all of them. The book in your hand wouldn't be without their input.

In the vein of 'credit where credit's due,' the Virehnai language used throughout is called "Proto-Virehnai" and it was created with the aid of ChatGPT 5.0. I could've created it myself, but it would've taken considerably longer for this book to come out if I had.

P.S. If you enjoyed <u>Not Quite Human</u>, please consider leaving a review or recommending it to a friend. Something as simple as THAT makes a HUGE difference for those of us who are self-published!

Got questions/comments? I'm easy to find:

http://www.homehearthmagic.com

Facebook: https://www.facebook.com/ElianoraEstelleWarren

Instagram: https://www.instagram.com/elianora_warren/

Pinterest: https://www.pinterest.com/elliewarren63/

Patreon: patreon.com/MagicAbounds

Reddit: u/WitchyHeretic444

OTHER BOOKS BY E.E. WARREN:

Magic Abounds Series:

The Magic Within Us, Book 1
The Magic Around Us, Book 2
The Power Within Us, Book 3
The In-Between (An Interdimensional Fairy Tale) (novella)
(the series isn't finished yet…!)

Ellora (Sci Fi):

Song of the Ancients, Book 1
(this series isn't finished yet…!)

Blood and Eternity Series:

Tales of Blood and Eternity (novella)
Not Quite Human, Book 1
The Night Shift (book 2, early 2026)
Blood Witch (book 3, late 2026)

Non-Fiction:

TechnoWitch: Ancient Wisdom, Modern Tools

ABOUT THE AUTHOR

E.E. 'Ellie' Warren is a daughter, a wife, a mom, a sister, a cat mom, a niece, an aunt, a writer, and a witch. She drinks coffee like a fiend, and retired in 2022 from a job in television to write full-time.

Originally from Maryland, Ellie lives in Seven Valleys, PA on a ridge surrounded by horse pastures and corn fields. Her house is built on top of huge slabs of crystal, with the unusual vibe you would imagine that would go along with it. Her husband is a photographer and a musician, and quite often finds herself writing at his rehearsals and shows. One of her sisters lives directly next door; The other does as she pleases, whenever she pleases. Her daughter, Sam, has taken on the challenge of getting her organized.

This is the first book in the Blood and Eternity vampire series. The next book will be called "The Night Shift," and there are at least three more planned! For more information on the next releases, go to homehearthmagic.com. See ya there!

www.ingramcontent.com/pod-product-compliance
Lightning Source LLC
Chambersburg PA
CBHW070830260626
47170CB00007B/2327